A

BOLT

FROM THE

BLUE

A Leonardo da Vinci Mystery

A
BOLT
FROM THE
BLUE

Diane A. S. Stuckart

BERKLEY PRIME CRIME, NEW YORK

THE BERKLEY PUBLISHING GROUP
Published by the Penguin Group
Penguin Group (USA) Inc.
375 Hudson Street, New York, New York 10014, USA
Penguin Group (Canada), 90 Eglinton Avenue East, Suite 700, Toronto, Ontario M4P 2Y3, Canada
(a division of Pearson Penguin Canada Inc.)
Penguin Books Ltd., 80 Strand, London WC2R 0RL, England
Penguin Group Ireland, 25 St. Stephen's Green, Dublin 2, Ireland (a division of Penguin Books Ltd.)
Penguin Group (Australia), 250 Camberwell Road, Camberwell, Victoria 3124, Australia
(a division of Pearson Australia Group Pty. Ltd.)
Penguin Books India Pvt. Ltd., 11 Community Centre, Panchsheel Park, New Delhi—110 017, India
Penguin Group (NZ), 67 Apollo Drive, Rosedale, North Shore 0632, New Zealand
(a division of Pearson New Zealand Ltd.)
Penguin Books (South Africa) (Pty.) Ltd., 24 Sturdee Avenue, Rosebank, Johannesburg 2196,
South Africa

Penguin Books Ltd., Registered Offices: 80 Strand, London WC2R 0RL, England

This book is an original publication of The Berkley Publishing Group.

FIRST EDITION: January 2010

Library of Congress Cataloging-in-Publication Data

Stuckart, Diane A. S.
  Bolt from the blue : a Leonardo da Vinci mystery / Diane A.S. Stuckart. — 1st ed.
    p. cm.
  ISBN 978-0-425-23217-0
  1. Leonardo, da Vinci, 1452–1519—Fiction. 2. Inventions—Fiction. 3. Apprentices—
Fiction. 4. Murder—Investigation—Fiction. 5. Milan (Italy)—History—To 1535—
Fiction. 6. Italy—History—1492–1559—Fiction. I. Title.
  PS3619.T839B65 2010
  813'.6—dc22
                                                                        2009033716

PRINTED IN THE UNITED STATES OF AMERICA

10 9 8 7 6 5 4 3 2 1

This book is in loving memory of Gene Smart.
I still miss you, Dad.

ACKNOWLEDGMENTS

Special thanks to the many readers who have written to tell me that they have enjoyed Delfina and Leonardo's adventures. Your kind words are cherished!

Warm thanks also goes to my family and friends, who have always cheered on my work. I dearly appreciate your support over the years.

Thanks to my editors, Natalee Rosenstein and Michelle Vega, who have added so much to these books.

And, as always, hugs and kisses to Gerry, who regularly suffers through missed weekends and holidays without complaint while his wife pounds away at the keyboard trying to meet her deadline. Sorry about that, Chief!

A
BOLT
FROM THE
BLUE

1

Wrongfully do men lament the flight of time . . .

—Leonardo da Vinci, *Codex Atlanticus*

DUCHY OF MILAN, SPRING 1484

Bright brown eyes peered over the edge of my notebook, the unexpected sight distracting me from the portrait in which I had been engrossed. I had not anticipated company; indeed, I had chosen a secluded spot in which to work so that I might pass the day undisturbed. And thus I was settled in a sunny patch of grass in a far corner of the great fortress that was home to the iron-fisted Ludovico Sforza, Duke of Milan. Away from the bustling parade grounds and paved court-yards, and far from the main castle itself, I'd thought myself quite alone here beside this low stone wall.

But apparently I was not.

Attempting to discourage further interruption, I frowned at the interloper. Undeterred, he widened his gentle cinnamon orbs in soulful appeal. My next tactic was to ignore his presence, but that reaction merely drew a small snuffle from him.

In the end—as he had doubtless foreseen—I found myself unable to resist such blatant supplication. And so I allowed my stern expression to soften as I tucked my piece of black chalk into the book as a marker before addressing him.

"Hello, Pio. How ever did you find me here, and why are you intent on disturbing my work this fine morning?"

The small black-and-white hound cocked his narrow head, his rose petal–like ears unfurling as if considering the question. Then, with a happy bark, he leaped into my lap and dislodged the notebook so that it tumbled to the ground.

"Fear not, Dino. Pio is not trying to disturb you," a reproachful voice spoke as I attempted to fend off the small beast's enthusiastic licking of my face. "He just wants to know why you are angry at us. He wonders why you have been avoiding us for the past few days."

I glanced up to see my friend and fellow apprentice Vittorio standing before me. Like me, he was dressed in the simple brown tunic over green trunk hose that designated him an apprentice painter in the workshop of the duke's court artist. To enliven that simple garb, he had braided narrow leather strips into an elaborate belt from which he'd hung his purse. He reached into that small bag now and pulled forth a crumb of pungent cheese.

"I've not avoided you," I protested while he waved the treat in Pio's direction. "Did we not spend all of yesterday plastering a wall for fresco together? And the day before, I showed you how to tie the small weasel-hair brushes that the Master prefers for his oils."

"But that is different," the boy countered as Pio bounded from my lap and began an eager dance upon his hind legs. "All of the apprentices helped with the plastering, and you showed Philippe and Bernardo how to tie those brushes, too. But when I tried to seek you out after supper each of those days, you were nowhere to be found. And I am certain that this morning, before you ran off alone with your notebook, you pretended not to hear me calling you."

The offended set to his mouth was a stark contrast to his habitual expression of mischievous glee and made him look older than his sixteen years. Even Pio's clownish behavior for once did not bring a smile to his face. Instead, his glum expression as he laid forth his list of my perceived transgressions quite reflected my own unsettled mood.

Strange that we both should be downtrodden, I told myself, given the special circumstances of this particular day. Being that it was Sunday, we would have enjoyed a few hours of freedom after our obligatory appearance at Mass before returning to our usual duties in the afternoon. But the Master found himself with pressing business outside the castle and had announced an entire day's holiday for his apprentices.

Still, our freedom would not be absolute. In return for this unexpected bounty, he had decreed that we were to use our time honing our craft in one way or another. This meant a day spent sketching or painting or else making detailed notes on any of the various techniques we had learned under his tutelage. But while we were on our honor to follow his wishes, none of us considered secretly sleeping or gambling away our day instead.

After all, any number of aspiring young painters was waiting in line for the opportunity to be apprenticed to the Duke of Milan's master engineer and court artist, Leonardo the Florentine . . . the multitalented man of genius also known as Leonardo da Vinci.

Vittorio tossed Pio the cheese and, not waiting to be invited, dropped to the grass beside me. The hound placed insistent front paws on Vittorio's knee and gave a polite bark to express his hope that additional food was to come. But even the enthusiastic wagging of his whiplike tail was not enough to return a smile to the young apprentice's face. Instead, his frown deepened, and he sighed with great drama.

Retrieving my notebook, I brushed a bit of dried grass from its cover and suppressed a sigh of my own. I knew the boy would not be content to leave without hearing words of reassurance.

"I'm not mad at you, Vittorio, or at Pio," I explained. "And I have not been avoiding you; at least, not purposely. It's just that I—"

I hesitated, a dozen explanations rising to my lips, but none I could speak aloud. I could not tell the boy that my desire for solitude sprang from the tragedy of several months ago. Neither did I dare recount my memories of the events that, like some ghastly and unending feast day pageant, continued to play in my thoughts. For none of the apprentices knew of my prominent role in that heartrending event that had stunned even the most hardened of men at Castle Sforza.

Indeed, only two people were aware of my involvement.

Leonardo was one. It had been at his behest that I had left my identity as the apprentice Dino and boldly disguised myself as a servant girl to a young contessa. Thus smuggled into the noble household, I had served as the Master's eyes and ears in an attempt to learn the identity of a murderer who preyed upon baseborn women.

It had started as a righteous enough undertaking. Soon, however, our clever plan unraveled, while our attempts to bring justice instead had ushered in tragedy. Leonardo had joined me as horrified witness to that final terrible night when two lives had been most grievously lost. The Master and I narrowly escaped death ourselves . . . though for some time after, I'd cursed the fact that I had lived while the others had not.

The second person who'd been privy to my daring masquerade was Luigi the tailor. Once an enemy and now my dear friend, Signor Luigi was my sole confidant in Milan. He was the only one who knew my other, more closely held secret, the secret I thus far had kept hidden even from Leonardo. And for that reason, no one but the tailor understood the true reason for my grief over what had transpired.

I shut my eyes against the soul-searing memories that swept me. Again, I saw the fire blazing through the darkened tower, burning with unimaginable ferocity around a beautiful young woman. Her features twisted in fearful agony as the flames would not be tamed but leaped upon her like blistering serpents. More swiftly than I could imagine, they consumed her glittering white gown and began searing her flesh.

Her screams were echoed by the harsh cry of a dark-haired man dressed in black who was quite as beautiful as she. He ran toward her, his face a mask of horror as he realized he was far too late, that he could not save her. But grim purpose sent him rushing into the fire to join her, determined that he would spare her, nonetheless.

I could not hold back the terrifying vision of the pair wrapped in a fiery embrace from which there could be no escape, save into the cold night. He knew that was the only hope left to them, and so he had made his terrible choice. Intertwined for all eternity, the two had blazed like twin shooting stars as they tumbled from the burning tower to meet their deaths in the darkness below.

Shoving those memories back into a far corner of my mind, I opened my eyes again to meet Vittorio's concerned gaze. He still awaited my answer, and so I seized upon a defense that he would have no cause to question.

"It's just that I have been missing my family, of late," I

replied. "I felt the need to be by myself for a time, lest I be poor company to the rest of you."

As I'd hoped, Vittorio's condemning expression yielded, and he gave a sympathetic nod. And there was some small truth to that particular explanation. Most of us apprentices had come from towns other than Milan, so that visits with our family were few, if any at all. I had not seen my parents and brothers for more than a year now, though twice my father and I had managed to exchange missives when someone from our town happened to be traveling in either direction.

A master cabinetmaker, Angelo della Fazia's skill in wood rivaled Leonardo's brilliance with paints. He had understood the artistic fervor that had driven me to steal away one night, leaving behind home and family in order to study my craft. And he also understood that, given my circumstances, I could not return home so long as I remained apprenticed to Leonardo.

Teasing the hound now with a long bit of grass, Vittorio confided, "I miss my father and sisters, too. But I am much relieved to know I have done naught to offend you. And I know you could never truly be cross with Pio, no matter what mischief he caused, for you love him as much as I do. So, if all is truly well, I shall leave you be."

Contrary to his words, however, he remained seated next to me. Knowing there must be some other reason that the youth had sought me out, I prodded, "The day is already half gone. Why are you still here at the castle, rather than wandering about town with Constantin and Paolo, and the other apprentices?"

"The Master asked me to take charge of Pio for the day. I could not refuse, for Pio loves me best . . . after the Master, of course," he finished with a smug lift of his chin.

I gave him an answering solemn nod.

"Of course," I agreed, though my inner amusement at his self-important air was tempered by my recollection of how the small hound had ended up in the Master's care.

The clownish Pio had once been the beloved pet of the same young contessa who was one of the victims that I mourned. Under her care, the little beast had spent his days sleeping upon soft cushions, eating rich treats, and wearing elaborate embroidered collars as befitted his noble position. More privileged than many at court, he'd even had his portrait painted by the great master Leonardo!

It was during those painting sessions that the Master had developed a particular fondness for the small hound. And when no one else stepped forward to claim Pio after the contessa's death, the Master had adopted him. Now Pio spent his days snoozing in a sunny spot in Leonardo's personal quarters or else wandering the workshop making a friendly nuisance of himself with the apprentices.

"Look, Dino," Vittorio exclaimed, interrupting my momentary musings. "I made a present for Pio. Is it not fine?"

He indicated the wide braided collar that the hound wore around his slim neck. More elaborate than Vittorio's own belt, the collar was nothing short of a leather tapestry made of intricate knots and weaves.

"And see how I've made a matching rope to lead him with," he went on, reaching beneath his tunic and pulling out a long length of braided leather.

He tied that narrow rope to the collar and looped the other end around his belt, so that the hound could wander a few feet from him but not run free. "I think with his new collar, Pio looks every bit as elegant as he ever did when he lived in the main castle."

"He does," I agreed, well impressed with the youth's skill. "Your creations are wonderful, Vittorio. Why, from a distance, the leather looks like beaten metal. Have you shown this work to the Master?"

"I did not wish to bother him with such trifles," the boy replied with a careless shrug, though the color rising in his cheeks told me he was pleased with my compliments. "But that is why I have been looking for you. You see, I made something else, and I wanted your opinion."

Reaching into his tunic this time, he withdrew a ring of leather similar to Pio's collar. He handed it to me, and I realized that it was the perfect size for a lady's bracelet. Unthinkingly, I slipped the leather bauble over my wrist to better admire it.

As with Pio's clever adornment, Vittorio had braided and knotted bits of leather to create a seamless circle. This piece, however, had been crafted with far greater skill. The leather threads were almost as delicate as wire, and he had twisted them into an open filigree pattern to which he'd added bits of colored minerals. Those tiny beads were similar to the large specimens we ground to make the various bright-hued pigments for frescoes, and I guessed that the youth had shaped them from scraps he had swept up from the workshop floor. It was a beautiful example that I was certain had taken many hours of work.

"Any woman would be glad to wear such a fine bracelet," I declared with an admiring nod.

Vittorio's blush deepened. "I am glad you like it. I made it especially for a certain girl. She—she doesn't know that I like her, and I've been afraid to say anything to her. I hope that giving her this bracelet will let her know how I feel."

He smiled at me shyly, his expression hopeful and brimming with a secret knowledge at odds with his usual boyish openness.

Meeting his gaze, I was momentarily puzzled. In the next instant, I was swept by the fearful certainty that Vittorio had discovered the truth about me that even Leonardo did not know. Why else would he have sought me out away from the others, if not to clandestinely confront me with what he had learned? And yet, how could it be? How had he unraveled the secret that had allowed me to remain as apprentice these many months?

How had Vittorio contrived to learn that I was not the boy Dino, as I claimed to be . . . but was instead Delfina della Fazia, a young woman who had disguised herself as a male in order to study painting with the greatest master in Milan and all the surrounding provinces!

I snatched off the bracelet and thrust it toward him.

"Pray tell me you have said naught of this to anyone else, especially not the Master," I cried, leaping to my feet with a swiftness that sent Pio scrambling out of my way. "You must know that your affection is sorely misplaced. Let us pretend you never spoke such foolish thoughts."

"What can you mean, Dino?"

The youth's smile faded into uncertainty. He stared up at me with wide eyes, his blush fading and his expression one of dismay. "Are you saying I should forget that I love Novella?"

"Novella?" Now it was my turn to stare. "Who is she?"

"Why, she is Rebecca the washerwoman's daughter," he replied, his gaze dropping in misery to the bracelet he was turning about in his hands. "She has always been friendly to me, and I thought . . . That is, I hoped . . ."

He trailed off with a shake of his head. Pio, sensing trouble, put a cold nose to the boy's pale cheek in sympathy. As for me, my fear of discovery was washed away by a hot wave of embarrassment. So wrapped up had I been in my own concerns that I had let myself believe that mine was the sole small drama being played out among my fellow apprentices. And now, my thoughtless words had caused Vittorio pain.

Eager to make amends, I seized an excuse to help mend those emotions that I had frayed.

"Pay no heed to my words," I urged, dropping back down beside him and giving his shoulder an encouraging shake. "I—I thought you spoke of someone far older than you. I do know Rebecca's daughter, and I am certain I have seen her give you favorable smiles when you were not watching."

"You have?" A flicker of his earlier grin reappeared. "Do you think she will like my bracelet?"

"I'm sure she will think it a fine gift. Perhaps she will offer to launder your tunic in return . . . That is, if she can manage to chisel it off your back first."

With this small jest—Vittorio was known for his overly enthusiastic approach to plastering a wall—I managed a brief grin back at him. I fervently hoped that I spoke the truth about the girl whose name I had never known until now. Still, I had encountered her several times before, trailing in shy silence after her mother and usually burdened by a basket of linens almost as large as she.

She was a lovely child of Vittorio's same age, possessing the airy grace reminiscent of mythology's nymphs. Her delicate features could have graced one of Leonardo's frescoes, while her pale curls beneath a sober white cap were almost as unruly as Vittorio's tangle of blond locks. In appearance, at least, the pair seemed well suited. Whether she had ever taken notice of the boy, I did not know. But a handsome young painter would be a fine catch for a girl burdened by her mother's lowly station.

I frowned a little as I considered this last.

While washerwomen ranked little better than prostitutes among society's more downtrodden, I had never understood why they were dismissed as scandalous creatures. Did washerwomen not work long and hard and for meager pay? I could think of far more disreputable ways to earn good coin than scrubbing and carting about baskets of wet clothing that were heavy enough to stagger many a man.

Perhaps their seductive reputation stemmed from the fact that they dealt so intimately with male garments, routinely touching the same fabric that had had contact with a man's most private areas. Or perhaps there was another, crueler reason for such universal condemnation. For such women were dependent upon no man for their livelihoods but made their own way in the world. How better to put them in their place again than by besmirching their reputations and reminding them that they were subordinate to the male species?

Then my frown faded. I was certain that Rebecca did not consider herself any man's inferior. A large, black-browed woman of middle years with a brash grin and the familiar red-chapped hands and arms of her profession, she wore her starched white wimple proudly as if it were a crown. She'd first come to my notice several months earlier, when she had elbowed me out of the way to get a better look at a dead woman. She had later played a brief role during the Master's investigation of that same suspicious death.

As often happened when Leonardo was involved, the unlikely pair struck up a friendship of sorts. Rebecca eventually had taken over the laundering of his clothes, while the Master had used her as a model for a series of sketches of the common folk. It had been in this capacity that I had made her acquaintance.

As for the fact that she had a daughter but no husband, I found the situation rather less scandalous than amazing. I also knew I was not the only one who secretly marveled that a woman possessed of as few physical charms as she could have found a willing bedmate, let alone produce from that coupling so lovely and graceful a child as the ethereal

Novella. The man who had lain with her must have been handsome beyond belief and doubtless blinded by love. That or his sole encounters with her had been in the dark!

While I had busied myself with such thoughts, Vittorio appeared to regain his usual carefree air in the wake of my assurances. Tucking the bracelet back in his tunic, he stood. Pio, who had been distracted during the course of our conversation by a lark that had lit upon the wall, now looked eagerly at the boy.

"Come, Pio. We shall leave Dino and his gloomy face to mope here in the shadows while we pay a visit to someone much prettier," he told the small hound, who gave an agreeable bark. To me, he added, "Unless, of course, you wish to walk part of the way with us?"

His tone and expression were hopeful, so that I knew he would be disappointed should I turn him down. I reminded myself that I had been ensconced in my spot since early morning. Perhaps it would do me well to shake off the worrisome cloak of the past for a time and enjoy a bit of amusement.

"I'm sure the Master would not expect me to spend the entire day hunched over my notebook," I agreed and rose once more. The volume in question I took care to tuck under my arm lest it spur his curiosity. I was certain that Vittorio would not ask to see my work unless I first offered; still, I had to be on my guard, as this day's sketches were ones that I was loath to share.

"I'll go with you as far as the workshop," I offered instead, "else I know I will never hear the end of your complaints. But I wonder, Vittorio, if your feet are as swift as your tongue?"

He gave me a quizzical look. Before he had time to question my meaning aloud, however, I flashed him a grin and took off at a run.

2

The earth is moved from its position by the weight of a tiny bird resting upon it.

—Leonardo da Vinci, *Codex Arundel*

An instant later, I heard a shout and a bark behind me; then Vittorio and Pio came rushing past, their long legs readily putting distance between them and me as we headed toward the workshop. I grinned more broadly and slowed my pace, letting them take the lead. The corset I secretly wore beneath my tunic, tightly tied to flatten my female attributes, also held my lungs in check and made running for more than a short distance difficult.

Thus, I found myself the subject of Vittorio's good-natured taunting when I finally caught up with him and the panting hound not far from Leonardo's quarters.

"Ha, you run slow as a girl," the youth declared as I joined him. He strutted about in triumph while Pio was content to flop on his side in the grass, pink tongue lolling. "All your moping has made you grow weak. Look at you, Dino. Once you were taller than me, but I have outstripped you in height as well as speed!"

Standing there beside him, I realized he spoke the truth. He was a good head taller than me and might soon be as tall as the Master. And how had I not realized before now that his once-smooth chin was covered in blond stubble grown in a fair imitation of Leonardo's neat dark beard? Even his voice had lost its childish timbre and had deepened.

For Vittorio was no longer a boy but was almost a man, I realized in chagrin. And surely such was the case with most of the other apprentices with whom I had begun my studies more than a year ago. So caught up had I been in my own sorrows these past months that I had paid scant attention to my fellows, had missed the way they were rapidly taking on adult bearings. And as more time passed, they must notice that I, alone of their number, remained small and smooth-cheeked, voice never growing deeper and form never broadening.

But even if they remained oblivious to such differences, surely the Master, with his keen eye for the human body, would become suspicious when one of his boys never grew to be a man.

To cover my dismay, I assumed an offended air. "You may be faster and taller, Vittorio, but I am still your senior in age. You should show respect to me."

"I respect the fact that you are far slower than me," he replied with a grin, his humor dimmed not at all by my censure.

Giving a light tug to the small hound's lead, he went on. "Pio and I are off to find more pleasant company. But I overheard Constantin and Tito making plans to wander the marketplace and look for likely subjects to depict the apostles in the Master's next fresco. Why don't you go along with them?"

"Perhaps I will, when I finish this last sketch," I agreed

with a careless shrug, though I knew full well I would do no such thing. "Now go, and be sure to tell me later how you fared with Novella."

I gave Pio a final scratch behind the ears and waved away the pair of them. Boy—or, rather, young man—and hound trotted eagerly in the direction of the castle gates. I waited until Vittorio and his charge were halfway across the grassy quadrangle that stretched between the main castle and its battlement-topped walls. Then, after making certain I was alone, I settled upon the rough bench outside the workshop and let my notebook slip to the seat beside me.

My small moment of pleasure had already faded, replaced by the familiar cloak of sorrow. Certainly, the day itself could not be blamed for my unsettled humor. The cloudless sky above provided a cheery blue backdrop for small flocks of birds making their annual return to their native fields. The castle's neatly regimented trees and gardens were in the midst of their own resurgence, tender leaves and blossoms budding with grand enthusiasm from every branch and stem. Even the air around me was ripe with promise, with just enough nip lingering from the previous chill night that the coming warmth of the afternoon would be that much more welcome. Indeed, all of nature seemed to be marching with unbridled eagerness into this new season.

I, however, felt as if I were caught in a perpetual winter.

Once, the prospect of wandering the grand city of Milan would have been most inviting. What better escapade could there be than losing myself in its flamboyant tangle of canals and market squares and narrow cobbled ways? But since that terrible night of several months past, I had sworn off adventure of even the mildest sort.

I sighed, realizing that some small part of me still missed that excitement. It seemed a lifetime ago when I would eagerly wait for the Master to summon me in the middle of the night, so that I might help him solve whatever puzzle was foremost in his thoughts. And as for my elegant page's outfit, it gathered dust lying in the bottom of the trunk where I kept my belongings.

The garb had sprung from Luigi's clever needle, specially commissioned by the Master for me. Disguised as his boy servant, I had accompanied the Master in his dealings with dukes and ambassadors and contes, being paid scant notice by such nobles because of my humble role. Such clothes also allowed me to mingle with the castle's servants, so that I might be privy to secrets that Leonardo could never learn in his position. But now those handsome silks lay unworn these many months, hidden away in much the same manner that I, for all practical purposes, had hidden myself.

"Dino!"

The sound of my name being called shook me from my thoughts. It was not one of my fellows who summoned me but instead was the Master himself. His business in the city must have taken less time than he had imagined . . . That, or some more urgent matter had caused him to return early. Obediently, I jumped to my feet, while hoping that he did not seek me out, in particular.

But, of course, he did.

"It is well that you are here and easily found, my dear boy. You have saved me the trouble of searching you out," Leonardo said in satisfaction, striding toward me.

Despite my dismay, I watched his approach with my usual admiration. While often the Master wore the same humble tunic and trunk hose as we apprentices, other times he dressed with the fastidious elegance of a noble. Today was such a day, though this particular tunic was of more sober cut than the bright colors he usually favored.

Tailored in dark blue trimmed in brown, the garment's sleeves were slashed to reveal the cream-colored blouse he wore beneath. The tunic's short length showed to advantage his long legs encased in parti-colored dark blue and cream trunk hose. A matching puffed cap in blue and cream perched rakishly atop his mane of dark russet hair, which streamed to his shoulders and glinted beneath the midday sun. Given the splendid figure he cut, it was no wonder that Leonardo was accounted one of the most handsome men at Castle Sforza.

A small blade of sorrow abruptly pierced me. For a time after I'd first arrived at his workshop, I'd harbored a thrilling if quite secret admiration for Leonardo, though his behavior toward me—or, rather, toward Dino—had been nothing but paternal. I had even allowed myself to daydream of what might happen between us should he ever learn the truth as to my true sex. But all that had changed when, in the space of a few days, I had found and lost my first great love, the Duke of Milan's dashing captain of the guard.

In my grief, I had blamed Leonardo for that horrific accident that had claimed both my captain and the young contessa. I had finally come to understand that the Master had been but an instrument in setting in motion the tragedy, but the damage to my heart had been done. Perhaps the only good to come of the situation was the fact that, in the aftermath, I had sorted out my feelings toward Leonardo. My regard for him was no longer that of a maid for a man but simply that of a student for his master.

He halted before me, his expression unreadable as he towered above me. "While I am pleased to have discovered you so readily, this day was to be yours," he reminded me. "I had hopes that you might leave the castle grounds along with the other apprentices."

"I was doing as you instructed, Master, and spent the

day sketching," I protested. "I felt I could apply myself with greater attention here at the castle, rather than being distracted by the sights and noise of the city."

"My dear boy, sometimes it does one good to seek out distraction," he countered with a smile. "But since you have applied yourself with such great diligence, let us see what you have accomplished."

Too late, I realized his intent. I opened my mouth to protest, but before I could stop him, the Master caught up my notebook and flipped open its soft leather cover.

The small volume fell open to the page where I'd tucked the bit of chalk, revealing the sketch I had been working upon when Pio disturbed me. I swallowed back a sound of dismay as I watched Leonardo's smile fade, his gaze fixed upon the page. What he would say when he finally spoke, I could not guess. All I knew was that this particular portrait was one I had not wished to share with anyone, especially not with him.

A long moment passed while he surveyed the work . . . a likeness of the archangel Michael, his wings unfurled and blazing sword drawn. It was a common enough theme that I had chosen, the subject as familiar as any of the saints or mythological figures that peopled the Master's frescoes. At first glance, my warrior angel would have warranted no greater interest than any other artist's rendering of that subject.

But I knew that Leonardo would look more closely.

In my mind's eye, I saw what he saw, handsome features rendered in black chalk and set into implacable lines reflecting an archangel's vengeful nature. The figure's pose was traditional, his gaze firmly fixed beyond the viewer. But while dressed in the expected white robes and shiny battle raiment, this Michael's muscular form transcended the usual depiction. Indeed, he resembled not so much a godly messenger as a sensual and quite human male, so that the drawing might be seen as less a study of religion and more a lesson in anatomy.

But what made it more than a simple portrait were the eyes.

I had thought to reflect that same potent male energy in his gaze. What had appeared upon the page was instead something darker, starker. These eyes held no boastful, righteous fury; rather, they silently spoke of the inner pain of a simple soldier who had wearied of the fight, no longer caring that his battles were divinely ordained.

And, of course, I had needed no model for my portrait. The face I had given my archangel was the same handsome dark face that I saw in my dreams each night . . . the same face that I would never again see in my waking hours.

Even as those thoughts flashed through my mind, Leonardo looked up to meet my gaze again. For an instant, his eyes seemed to mirror the anguish of those eyes upon the page before him, seemed to recognize the pain in my heart. My breath stilled for an instant. Could it be that he, too, relived the events of that terrible night, as I did?

Just as swiftly, he regained his usual expression of mild good humor. He closed the notebook and handed it back to me.

"Very well-done, my boy. I believe it is time to put you to work painting frescoes instead of merely plastering walls."

I had no time to ponder that unexpected move upward in my apprenticeship, however, for he added, "We shall speak of your new role later. For the moment, I need you to follow me, as I require your presence in my quarters to discuss this new project I have begun for Il Moro."

He referred, of course, to the Duke of Milan, popularly dubbed "the Moor" because of his swarthy coloring. Had I chosen to sketch Ludovico, I would have paid the greatest attention to the coarseness of his features, which, belonging to a more cheerful man, could have passed for handsome rather than cruel. And, of course, I would emphasize the heavy cap of jet-black hair in which he took great pride, never mind that it had begun to thin in the back.

A coldly ambitious ruler, he had come to his position a few years earlier following the assassination of the previous duke, his brother. While the court advisers were busy pointing fingers of blame for that murder, Ludovico had taken advantage of the distraction to wrest control of the province from his widowed sister-in-law and infant nephew, the rightful heir.

Though he had claimed his assumption of the dukedom had been but a temporary measure until the boy was old enough to take on that role, no one had believed that Ludovico would ever release the reins of rule, save by force. Popular opinion had soon proved right, with even Ludovico abandoning that fiction to petition the pope to grant him the title that he had spuriously claimed. Recognition had yet to be bestowed, so that Ludovico felt compelled to justify his ill-gotten title by waging war upon Milan's neighboring provinces.

And in these modern times, war was being waged less by men and horses and more by machines . . . hence, the true reason for Leonardo's presence in the duke's court. For, despite his title of court artist, it had not been his brilliance at portraiture or frescoes that had brought the Master to his post here in Milan.

Rather, it was his engineering genius—which he had immodestly detailed in a series of dramatic missives to Ludovico—that had first piqued the duke's interest in hiring a man whom others dismissed as an eccentric Florentine.

But surely Ludovico and Leonardo had been destined for

each other. For how could a man of battle like Il Moro resist the chance to employ a master engineer who claimed he could build underwater boats and portable bridges, let alone machines that could discharge a dozen deadly bolts in the time it would take a man to fire but a single shot? And where else would Leonardo have found a patron willing to invest in fantastical designs that, to my mind, might never see light save upon paper?

I suspected that the project the Master had commenced upon was more of this fanciful military equipment. Maybe this time it was the armored wagon propelled by pulleys and cables, rather than by horses. Or maybe it was the folding boat, small enough when collapsed to fit into a cart, but when opened could carry half a dozen men across all but the most rugged of streams.

Once, I would have eagerly embraced such an opportunity to work by his side but—despite my earlier moment of weakness—no more. And he'd understood without it being said that I was finished with acting as his extra set of hands, save in the workshop. Of course, any of my fellow apprentices would eagerly serve in my stead, so that I knew my presence had not been missed these past months.

Why, then, I wondered in some resentment as I obediently followed after him, had he sought me out this time?

Aloud, I merely replied, "I am happy to accompany you, Master, but it appears we are headed in the wrong direction for your workshop."

"You are quite observant, Dino," he said with a smile, "and so I confess that first we must go to the castle gates to meet someone. Did I tell you that I have found an artisan of some skill to assist in the woodworking portion of this design for Il Moro? I fear I had little choice in this, as my competency in that area is somewhat limited."

I doubted that was the case—Leonardo conquered every challenge he put his hand to—but I gave a polite nod. Still, the project must require some great precision, I told myself, else he would have contented himself with Tito's assistance. The son of a boat builder, Tito was one of the older apprentices though newer to the workshop than was I. Despite his tendency toward boastfulness, he was a pleasant enough companion and quite capable with both brush and chisel.

I held my opinion on the matter to myself, however, as we moved at a brisk pace across the broad quadrangle toward the clock tower. The structure, oddly slim and graceful compared with the rest of the castle's architecture, stood as an elegant sentinel visible for some distance. Its clever brickwork bore the Sforza family's rather sinister coat of arms which, quite fittingly, was emblazoned with a wily grass snake.

As always, the main gate was manned by members of Il Moro's paid army. Dressed in scandalously short dark tunics over parti-colored trunk hose, with swords dangling from their hips, they kept swaggering guard over the traffic to and from the castle. Most of the mercenaries were foreign born, some gray-haired veterans and some little more than boys, and ranging from brutishly effective to ruthlessly efficient in their skills at arms. Thanks to the Master, I'd had more dealings with Ludovico's soldiers than I would have liked . . . save, of course, for my time spent with one certain captain.

Depending upon Ludovico's current relationship with his various neighbors, the immense wood and iron gateway at the tower's base might be closed. At such time, visitors had to pass through a small portal cut into that gate in order to breach the broad walls that ran the perimeter of the castle's extensive grounds. With its immense watchtowers—two square, and two cylindrical—hunkering at each of its four corners, it was this forbidding stone barrier that served as the castle's main line of defense against intruders. Of course, since Castle Sforza had been built as a fortress and not simply as a noble dwelling, its complex of buildings and courtyards was enclosed by still more walls. The duke's own quarters were located in an innermost wing of the castle and were protected from outside entry by heavy iron gates.

Today, however, the gate was thrown wide-open, allowing a broad view of the town beyond.

"And I do believe you will find this particular project to be of great interest," Leonardo was saying with some pride as our steps took us closer to the tower. "Unfortunately, we have but a short time in which to finish building the prototype, as the duke is anxious to put my design to test. But should it prove a success, I do not hesitate to predict that my invention will change the very course of man's history."

I was used to such dramatic declarations from the Master; still, my curiosity was piqued. Perhaps he had in mind something more than another elaborate war wagon, after all. And I wondered, as well, why he would need my assistance in building it, when my creative skills were limited to the brush. Whatever it was could not be overly large, or he would have enlisted another of the apprentices with a far more muscular frame than mine as his assistant.

"Ah, here we are," he declared as we reached the gate and took up station along the well-worn gravel path that led from the castle grounds to the clearing beyond the walls.

He pretended not to notice my unease while we stood for several long minutes waiting for whoever was due to meet us. It was a kind gesture, and gratitude momentarily tempered the feeling of disquiet that had filled my breast. For here beneath the clock tower we were well within sight of the two rough-hewn cylindrical towers that served as its flanking counterpoints . . . the two towers that symbolized the pain that filled my soul. Rather than gaze upon them, I kept my attention fixed upon the tips of my shoes.

"—well-known beyond his own town," came Leonardo's voice from beside me.

I realized with a guilty start that he had been speaking for some moments, with the subject apparently this craftsman who had yet to appear. Dutifully, I sharpened my attention.

"It was during my visit to Florence at Christmastide," he continued, "that I saw an example of a door he had made for a noble's private chapel there. The grapevines he had carved upon it were so real that I had to touch them with my own fingers before I was convinced they were not living plants. And so when I determined I needed a master woodworker to assist me, he was the man who came to mind.

"Of course," he added with a shrug, "I first had to learn his name and next discover his home. Then came the task of convincing him to leave his family behind for the opportunity to toil under Ludovico's patronage for a few months."

"I'm certain he was honored by the offer," I responded as I fondly thought how my father had always dreamed of receiving such a commission . . . and my mother, more so!

To be sure, the artisan with a noble patron ofttimes found that a duke's purse strings were tied more tightly than those of the middle class. This I had learned from listening to Leonardo's laments regarding Ludovico, whose disinclination to make good his debts was well-known. But the prestige of having had a patron of rank served to bring other clients more inclined to pay their bills.

The Master, meanwhile, was nodding at my words.

"He seemed pleased with the offer, particularly when he learned the commission would bring him to Milan. It happens that he has family here whom he has not seen for some time."

He gave me a conspiratorial grin and added, "His sole obstacle was his wife, who objected to the possibility of his prolonged absence. But he finally wrote to assure me that he had gained her permission and so would be here to meet me at noon of this day."

He paused to glance at his right wrist. Strapped to it with twin bands of leather was a flat metal box perhaps the size of my palm. This was one of his inventions, which he called a wrist clock. A miniature version of the tower clock above us, it was designed in much the same way to track the day's hours. Though I'd scoffed when I first saw it, I had quickly come to admire the clever device and secretly wished for one myself.

The wrist clock began chiming the hour at the same moment its far larger brother above sounded its own call. Leonardo peered through the open gateway, his expression expectant as he flicked his elegant fingers in the reflexive gesture of his that always indicated impatience.

"Let us hope that our new craftsman views punctuality as a virtue and not as a vice," he remarked, "for I am anxious to begin work this very day."

And I was anxious to return to the workshop, I thought a bit resentfully. I still could not fathom why the Master required my presence. After all, there was no mystery to be solved, no cruelly murdered corpse to identify.

Aware that such thoughts were unworthy—as Leonardo's apprentice I was bound to obey him—I dutifully strove for a moderate demeanor. Meanwhile, his expression brightened.

"See, I had no cause for concern," he exclaimed, "for our good cabinetmaker approaches."

Curious, I followed Leonardo's gaze, squinting against

the glare of the midday sun to discover the subject of his scrutiny.

A knot of milling tradesmen and servants had parted to reveal a tall man of middle years striding toward the gate. His moderate garb—a brown cloth hat and belted, knee-length brown tunic over yellow trunk hose—marked him a craftsman, as did the patched leather sack that doubtless held the tools of his trade. In the opposite hand, he carried a tall, carved stick such as many pilgrims carried while trudging the rocky roads that led to and from the city. Designed to ease one's way over uneven paths, the sturdy stick served equally well as a means of defense should the traveler be set upon by bandits . . . not an unheard-of event in this province.

I frowned, for something about this man seemed familiar. Indeed, with his mane of wavy dark hair and neat beard, he looked rather like the Master from a distance. But it was not this vague resemblance that held me; rather, it was the way he moved humbly if confidently among his fellows, pausing once to assist an elderly man in a tattered leather jerkin struggling with the bundle of twigs balanced upon his skinny back.

By now, the newcomer was close enough for me to make out his features, and my eyes opened wide in surprise. I knew this man, I realized with a gasp, knew him as well as I knew myself!

It was at that moment that the man turned to meet my gaze. He halted again, his leather sack slipping from his shoulder as he stared at me. Then a warm grin split his pleasant features, and he caught up his bag again.

The few moments it took for the guards to wave him and several others through the gates seemed to stretch into hours. I was aware of Leonardo's hand upon my shoulder in a gesture of gentle restraint, doubtless to keep me from making a spectacle of myself before the soldiers. I allowed him to stay my movements, but only until the man was safely past the gate.

Then, unable to wait an instant longer, I shrugged off the Master's grasp and rushed toward the newcomer, flinging myself into his open arms with a joyful shout of, "Father!"

3

Feathers shall raise men towards heaven even as they do birds . . .

—Leonardo da Vinci, *Manuscript I*

"Ah, child, I have missed you!" Angelo della Fazia exclaimed, lifting me from my feet with his hug just as he had done when I was but a small girl.

Then, as if realizing his gesture might appear a far too exuberant greeting to bestow upon a male child, he abruptly set me back down. His gaze flicking in Leonardo's direction, he gave me an awkward pat upon the shoulder and amended, "Rather, it is good to see you again."

"It is good to see you," was my warm response. Not caring what the Master might think, I grabbed my father's hands in mine. "Though I confess I did not recognize you at first. You have cut your beard differently, and your hair is longer."

"That last is not by design," he said with a small laugh. "I am so busy these days with my commissions that I scarce

have time to stop for a meal, let alone sit still long enough for
the barber to shear me."

Frowning, he took an equally close look at me. "I was
hard-pressed to recognize you, as well. Your clothes and your
hair . . . they are—"

"Pray, Father, do not tell me I have changed so much since
you last saw me," I interrupted him, fearful lest he make
a misstep and reveal my disguise. "Despite my apprentice's
tunic, I am still your well-loved son Dino."

"Ah, yes, that you are, my well-loved son," he agreed with
great vigor. "So tell me . . . er, Dino . . . are you well?"

"Quite well now," I responded, certain that my wide grin
should have been proof enough for him.

And I realized that, at least for the moment, my melancholy had indeed slipped from my shoulders like a discarded
cloak. Perhaps the excuse I had given to Vittorio earlier had
been the truth, after all. Until that momentous night when
I had made my decision to leave home in male guise, I had
never in my brief life been away from my family even for a
day. Looking back over the recent months, I could see how I
had instinctively made Leonardo and my fellow apprentices
stand in for the father and brothers I had left behind.

But, here in the presence of my true parent, I realized with
a pang that even the most beloved friends could never take
their place.

Blinking rapidly so that no tears might mar my carefully
boyish facade, I instead asked, "But how can this be, that you
are here in Milan? Surely you are not the craftsman that the
Master has said is to join him?"

"He is, indeed," Leonardo spoke up, satisfaction evident in
his tone. Then his smile took on a mischievous quirk.

"You do not know how pleased I was to discover that the
man whose genius in wood I admired was also the sire of a

favored young apprentice," he told me. "I noted right away that our Signor Angelo had the same family name as you. That was when I recalled you had once told me that your father was an accomplished cabinetmaker from that same part of the province. And as there was some familial resemblance, it was easy to deduce that the two of you were related by blood."

His grin broadened.

"When I first put the question to Signor Angelo, however, he was reluctant to admit any such connection. Perhaps he feared that your work might reflect poorly upon his name. But once I explained that young Dino was one of my more promising students, he was more than willing to claim you. And he agreed to allow me to make his arrival a fine surprise for you."

"Please, Signor Leonardo," my father mildly protested, "my reluctance came from a fear lest some favoritism be shown. I have never doubted young Del—that is, Dino's—talent with a brush."

I held my breath, praying the Master had not taken heed of my father's momentary slip in calling my name. To my relief, he appeared not to have noticed, for he merely nodded. "A talented family, indeed. But let us be off to my workshop. You shall share my quarters for the duration of your stay, Signor Angelo, if that is acceptable to you."

"I am honored, Signor Leonardo."

With that, we started back across the quadrangle. Although I had many questions for my father, most could not be asked in the Master's presence . . . most specifically, those concerning my mother. Instead, I contented myself with eager inquiries after my brothers' welfare.

"Both are well," my father replied with a proud smile. "Georgio has taken on most of the daily tasks for our workshop, and he is bringing in work of his own."

I listened, well impressed, as he named some of our town's

more prominent gentlemen who had commissioned Georgio's services. Then his smile broadened. "As for Carlo, he has found himself a young woman and will be married this summer."

"Carlo is taking a wife?"

I stared at my father in amazement and burst out laughing. "I must admit I am surprised, for he was always one to duck his head and mumble whenever a likely young woman looked his way. You must tell him how happy I am for him."

"Ah, but you will be able to do that yourself," Leonardo interjected, "for I am certain we can spare you from the workshop for a few days to attend that happy occasion."

"That's very good of you, Master," I managed, though I wondered what excuse I could give him for rejecting his kindness when that time came. I met my father's gaze and saw the same doubt in his eyes. Later, when we had the chance for private conversation, I would hear from his lips whether or not my mother would allow me to return home again.

We reached Leonardo's private quarters a few moments later. I gazed about with familiar pleasure for, unlike most of the apprentices, I had been privileged to set foot there numerous times in the past. The single main room served as his bedchamber, as well as the place where he took his meals and entertained his guests. The furnishings were modest if practical: a narrow cot and wardrobe, a larger rectangular table flanked by two benches, and a smaller table and two chairs.

Setting this room apart from most, however, were the wooden shelves lining the far wall . . . or, rather, the objects displayed upon those rows of rough boards. Mixed among the expected crockery were animal bones and clay models of human feet, along with baskets of fur and feathers, and several rock specimens chosen for their intriguing shapes. On the topmost shelf lay what appeared to be the hand of

a gigantic frog but was actually a webbed swimming glove
that was one of the Master's newer inventions. His substantial
personal library—perhaps two dozen different books—filled
any remaining gaps and overflowed onto a stack on the floor
beneath.

Gesturing toward the bed, he grandly pronounced it as
Signor Angelo's for as long as he stayed there. "Do not worry,"
he added as my father attempted to protest this hospitality.
"I have a pallet made up in my private workshop, where I can
sleep in equal comfort."

The workshop in question lay directly off his quarters,
with entrance gained by the single narrow door set into the
far wall. Perhaps twice as large as his personal chamber, it
was the place where Leonardo conducted many of his experiments and built most of his scale models. His larger projects,
I knew, were to be found in one of the locked sheds at the far
side of the quadrangle.

Unlike the main workshop where we apprentices toiled, the
Master's private workshop normally was kept locked whenever
the Master was not within. Once and almost by accident, however, I'd managed a glance inside that secret chamber.

With most of its space taken up with an immense wooden
table, which would take four or five men to move, the place
had been an exercise in ordered chaos. Sketches and notes
covered fully half of that tabletop, with the remaining space
taken up by pens and knives and brushes and paints. From the
walls and ceiling hung both wood and paper models of various
inventions, some appearing to be weapons, and others far more
fanciful devices that I could not identify. I'd spent but a few
moments there, but I knew that—had I been given leave—I
could have spent hours studying what was in a sense the outer
expression of the workings of Leonardo's brilliant mind.

My father made short work of settling in . . . fortunately

for him, as the Master's eagerness to begin their collaboration was obvious. Still, with a gracious nod, he restrained himself and instead played the thoughtful host for a while longer.

"Since you had a bit of a journey this morning, Signor Angelo, perhaps you and Dino would care to stop by the kitchen. I am certain they will accommodate you even this late. I know you two will have much to discuss, and there may be little time for private conversation with him once you and I are well into our project."

"An excellent plan, signore," my father agreed with a small smile. "As you say, we have much news to share."

Turning to me, the Master went on. "Afterward, bring your father back to the main workshop. We will let him make his acquaintance with our other apprentices, and then I shall show him what has brought him here to Milan."

Bowls and spoons in hand, my father and I took our leave of Leonardo and began the short walk across the quadrangle.

"An impressive fortress," he declared as he looked about the series of interconnected buildings that made up the main castle. Glancing up at the battlemented walls of the immense outer walls, he added, "It appears secure against any intruders, and yet the design is pleasing to the eye. The red stone and the white symbolize both strength and vision. And the towers rise with grace, despite their great size."

"I think it the finest palace in all the world," I replied with no little pride, as if I were Il Moro himself hearing his compliments.

My father smiled. "Ah, and how many palaces have you seen in your time, my child? Now, let us hope that the quality of the duke's kitchen reflects the same majesty."

Though the kitchen boy grumbled a bit at serving us this late, we still enjoyed a fine stew and dark bread that appeared to satisfy my father's appetite. And as we ate, I broached the subject that had niggled at the back of my mind ever since I arrived in Milan.

"And how does Mother fare?"

"Quite well. Her health is good, her beauty is undiminished, and her tongue is as tart as ever."

"And does she ever speak of me?" I asked, though without much hope.

My father hesitated before shaking his head.

"I fear she has not forgiven you for leaving as you did, in the dark of night and with no word but a terse note. And, of course, she suspects that I have some idea of your whereabouts. Though she is angered at the notion that I know something that she does not, I think it also brings her some comfort to know that you are alive and presumably well."

I sighed, a painful knot that had nothing to do with the stew forming in my stomach. From my girlhood, my mother and I had managed but an uneasy truce at the best of times. As I grew older, her exasperation with me had grown in equal measure. What decent man, Carmela della Fazia had argued more than once, wanted a wife more interested in drawing pictures than in having babies? If I did not give up my painting, then I surely would never be married.

She had felt herself vindicated when, by sheer dint of effort, she finally had arranged a marriage for me with a well-to-do merchant willing to overlook my reputation as an eccentric young woman. For myself, I'd been horrified at the prospect of wedding a man more than twice my age who was known for his tight purse strings and his fondness for pretty young servants. And so, with my father's help, I had conceived the plan that brought me here to Milan.

"What was said to Signor Niccolo, when he came to make his offer of marriage?" I asked with another sigh, referring to the man who would have been my husband.

My father's lips twitched just a little as he replied, "Your mother told him that you suffered a conversion in the middle of the night and decided to take yourself off to a nunnery where you might devote the remainder of your life to good works."

"Well, at least that would explain my shorn hair," I replied with a flicker of a rueful smile. "I wonder if she will ever forgive me for disappointing her so."

"It is hard to say, my child. Your mother is a woman of stern mind, and she is not prone to changing it. You will need to give her more time, I fear."

I refrained from pointing out that she'd had more than a year to resolve her harsh feelings. Instead, I deliberately turned the conversation to cheerier topics.

"I am so happy that you are here in Milan with me," I said in a warm rush. "I always envied Georgio and Carlo for being able to spend their days with you. If you can but convince the Master that I would make you a fine assistant, perhaps we can work together just as you and my brothers do."

"Do not worry, my child," he replied with a fond smile. "I have already informed your master that a condition of my employment is having you at my side."

We went on to speak of other things. The subjects mattered little to me, for I was happy simply to bask in my father's attention again. But finally, he said, "I know that Signor Leonardo must be growing impatient with us. We must return to the workshop and continue our conversations later. Besides, I am anxious to see where you live and work. Your master has, what, two or three other apprentices besides yourself?"

"There are almost twenty of us, Father," I proudly told him. "I have made many fine friends. There is Constantin, our senior apprentice, and Paolo and Davide and Tommaso and—"

"You share quarters with that many young men?" he choked out, looking aghast. "I had no idea! Surely, that is highly improper, no matter that they think you a boy. I cannot allow that. I shall speak to your master, and——"

"Father, please!"

I glanced about, hoping his cries had not attracted any attention. Fortunately, the only one about was the kitchen boy, who seemed more concerned with stealing a few choice morsels from the plates he was scraping into the garbage pile than listening to our conversation.

"I swear to you, Father, there is nothing unseemly in this arrangement. We each have our own cot, tucked away into an alcove, so it is like being in our own chamber. And I have always been careful to preserve my modesty . . . and theirs, as well. No one has ever questioned whether or not I am a boy. But if you say anything to the Master, suggest any changes to him, he may have cause to suspect the truth about me."

I finished my plea and watched in dismay the struggle that played across my father's pleasant, open features. The artist in him understood my dream of one day becoming a master like Leonardo. The parent, however, was aghast at the thought of his daughter living among so many males with no other female around to safeguard her virtue. And while my father always claimed my mother to be the more stubborn of the two, I knew that he could be equally firm in holding to a notion, should he believe it was the right thing to do.

Finally, and to my great relief, he gave a small nod. "Very well, Delfina . . . or, I suppose I must get used to calling you Dino. No matter, I shall reserve my judgment for a time. If I can assure myself that your fellows do indeed treat you as a boy, I will rest easier allowing your masquerade to continue a bit longer."

"Then let us go and meet them," I urged with a smile. "The Master will be looking for us there, anyhow."

And we did, indeed, find Leonardo awaiting us in the main workshop. As for the other apprentices, they had begun returning from their day's outing and were gathered around him sharing their tales of where they had gone and what they had done. Vittorio had returned, as well—the mischievous Pio still at his side—and looked quite pleased with himself, so that I guessed his assignation with Novella had proved a success. While the youths laughed and chatted, Leonardo listened with his usual air of kind interest, occasionally urging the shyest among them to offer their thoughts.

My father and I observed the scene for some moments before the Master finally noticed our presence.

"Ah, Master Angelo," he exclaimed, giving my father that more formal title now that we were among others. "Let me introduce my assistants to you."

I felt a rush of pride as my friends made their bows and then listened respectfully while my father, in turn, gave them a brief account of his accomplishments. A few of the boys—Tito and Paolo, I knew for certain—had some knowledge of woodworking and appeared suitably impressed by the commissions my father described. For my part, I stood to one side and contented myself with my good fortune at having been born to a father of such kindness and talent.

When my father returned the floor to the Master, Leonardo said, "If you will recall, draftsmen, I gave you a holiday today. A few more hours yet remain, so again I task you with spending them in some enjoyable manner until it is time for the evening meal."

A small cheer rose at this, and under the Master's indulgent smile the youths swiftly scattered. Then he turned to my father and me. "And now, it is time for me to reveal to you the nature of my latest invention, which requires a master cabinetmaker's skilled touch."

We returned to his quarters and waited while, with a show of great secrecy, he left us alone and stepped into his private workshop. He reappeared a few moments later, carrying a cloth-covered object perhaps as wide and broad as my arm. Setting it upon the table, he gestured us closer and said, "You must excuse my caution, but I must first make certain that we are not being observed."

While my father and I exchanged puzzled glances, he checked the door to make certain it was latched and then pulled the shutters closed across the window. What could be beneath this cloth that required such precautions against its being seen? I had been prepared for something substantial, similar to his expandable bridge or his river dredger . . . perhaps a catapult that tossed flames. Whatever lay hidden beneath that length of oiled linen, however, could hardly be of that scale.

I frowned. It mattered little to me what this invention was, for as Leonardo's apprentice I was here at his whim. If not here, I would be toiling in the main workshop or smoothing plaster upon yet another wall in the duke's chambers.

My father, however, was a different matter. He had left behind his own workshop and his own commissions—not to mention my mother and brothers—solely on Leonardo's word. What promises the Master had made to entice him into the duke's service, I could not guess, though I knew full well the Master's persuasive ways. As clever with words as he was with his brush, Leonardo could talk a rabbit into a wolf's jaws. Still, I could not think that he would bring my father to Milan on a fool's mission. But from the expression on his face, Angelo della Fazia certainly had traveled all this way in the expectation of seeing something . . . larger.

"First, I must swear you both to secrecy," the Master reminded us, seeming unaware of our doubt. "Other than Ludovico himself, no one else has been privy to what I am about to reveal. The fate of Milan—indeed, of the entire world—might rest with this invention. And so, I must have your vows that you will not speak of what I am about to show you with anyone other than ourselves."

I must point out that Leonardo had been appointed Il Moro's master of pageantry for a good reason, given that he knew how to add drama to the most mundane moments. He demonstrated that talent now as he paused, his hand upon the cloth, while a look of almost mystic fervor settled upon his handsome features. Despite my earlier doubt, my curiosity was piqued. Perhaps I had been too hasty in my rush to judgment, I told myself as I eagerly gave him my promise of silence.

Nodding, his gaze flicked from me to my father as he awaited a second response. My father was frowning, but I guessed from the inquisitive tilt of his head that he had decided Leonardo would not have brought him all the way to Milan for a trifle.

"Very well, Signor Leonardo, you have my vow, as well. I swear I shall reveal nothing of this matter to anyone else."

Leonardo gave a satisfied smile. "Then I shall hold you in suspense no longer. But prepare yourselves, for I am about to show you the future," he declared and snatched away the cloth.

4

A bird is an instrument working according to mathematical law, which instrument it is within the capacity of man to reproduce with all its movements.

—Leonardo da Vinci, *Codex Atlanticus*

My father and I stared at what appeared at first glance to be a linen and wood crucifix; however, the requisite Christ figure was posed unlike any I had ever seen. Rather than resting supine with arms stretched wide, he was stretched at length upon his belly, hands and elbows to his sides. As for the crucifix's crosspiece, it was constructed of cloth laid over delicate ribbed frame that seemed to resemble wings. Not so much those of a bird, perhaps, but more like the scalloped leathery appendages belonging to a bat.

Certainly, this was no religious carving, after all. Then realization struck with a serpent's swiftness, and I gazed up at Leonardo in wide-eyed disbelief.

It should be said that the Master's doings were of great

interest here at Castle Sforza. From his glorious frescoes, which added color and gaiety to the fortress's gloomy halls, to the elaborate pageants and parades, which provided feast day entertainment, all were subject to scrutiny by various and sundry of the castle's inhabitants. Indeed, he was watched and discussed almost as closely as was Il Moro himself.

During the past few weeks, the rumor passed among the castle servants—and always accompanied by a snicker or roll of the eyes—concerned a new machine that they called "Signor Leonardo's folly." I'd also overheard the occasional whisper from one apprentice or another who had claimed to have seen a drawing of this marvel. But while I had no doubt that the invention might exist upon paper as part of the Master's copious output of sketches both whimsical and sublime, I had never believed he would attempt to build it.

And yet, here it lay before my eyes.

Properly awed, I asked in a respectful tone, "Tell me, Master, is this what I think it is?"

"If you think that it is a flying machine," he replied with a small smile, "then yes, it is.

"A scale model, of course," he was quick to clarify as my eyes grew wider, "although I have also commenced work on the frame of the man-sized version. Still, there are several modifications that must be made to the design before either craft is deemed flight-worthy. Weight distribution is one issue that I—"

"A flying machine?"

The abrupt question came from my father, his tone incredulous. Worse, his usually placid expression reflected more than a hint of anger. Staring at the Master as if the younger man had taken leave of his senses, my father shook his head.

"Can it be, Signor Leonardo, that you summoned me to Milan on a fool's errand?" he sputtered. "I thought to be serving the duke on a project of great importance, but you appear to be having a joke at my expense. I think it best that I forget this matter and return home to my own workshop."

He paused to give me a concerned look and added, "And perhaps I should take my, er, son with me."

"Father, no," I cried before the Master could make a reply.

Clutching his tunic sleeve, I persisted, "I cannot leave, and you must stay as well. Signor Leonardo would not jest about such a matter. I have seen with my own eyes many of his wonderful inventions. If he says he can build a machine that flies, I am certain it can be done."

"Your loyalty to your master is commendable," my father replied in a stiff tone, "but I would be remiss in my duty to let you be led astray. Had God meant us to fly like birds, he would have given Adam feathers, rather than creating him naked and in need of a fig leaf. Surely you must see this is folly."

"Folly to those who are not bold enough to dream."

With those words, Leonardo carefully lifted the miniature flying machine from the table. Holding it in both hands at arm's length, he assumed his familiar tone of lecture that I knew well from the workshop.

"Consider this, Signor Angelo," he went on. "Had you never before seen a bird in flight, you would call me mad or worse if I were to describe such a creature to you. For, without any knowledge that such a feat was possible, you would claim that no creature could leave the confines of the earth for the sky."

He paused to raise and lower the model a few times, causing its cloth wings to flap in a quite birdlike fashion.

"And yet we all know that the falcon can soar with the clouds and that the lark flits from tree to tree with but the beat of a wing. Why should man, with his mighty intellect, not be able to devise a craft to mimic a bird's form, thus allowing him to sever his bond with the earth and join his feathered brethren?"

With those words, he handed the model to my father, who took it with apparent reluctance. I saw a new spark of interest in his eyes, however, as he deigned to study the design.

"Hmmm . . . interesting," he muttered, carefully turning the small machine about. Indicating the supporting portion of the wing framework, he added, "This piece appears overly heavy and rigid for its purpose. Replacing it with two narrow rods would lighten the weight and add flexibility while still maintaining stability. And certainly the choice of wood is a factor. You will require something with strength yet suppleness—perhaps ash—with special care taken for the quality of the grain."

"And that is why I require your help, Signor Angelo," the Master replied with a small smile. "While I am certain that my craft is soundly engineered, building it will require the expertise of a man who understands every nuance of the wood that will form it."

My father merely snorted. Then, with a grudging nod, he conceded, "With the right materials, a large-scale version of this machine should prove but moderately difficult to build. Whether or not it can be made to fly is another issue. What manner of propulsion do you propose?"

"Ah, that is the easy part."

Leonardo strode over to the shelves and held out a hand. My gaze followed, and I saw that he was reaching for a tiny hawk inexplicably perched there between two stacks of manuscripts.

After an instant of surprise—how had such a bird made its way into the Master's workshop?—I realized that the feathered creature was long since dead. But so skillfully had the small raptor been mounted, with its wings spread wide

and its head proudly tilted, that I almost expected it to take
flight at his approach. Of course, it did not, and he carried it
back to where my father and I stood.

"We know that a bird's greatest strength lies in its breast,"
he explained, holding the hawk in one hand and pointing
to that portion of its anatomy with the other. "Those sturdy
muscles allow its wings to beat with swiftness enough to send
it aloft. In comparison, a bird's legs are fragile limbs designed
primarily for clutching at a branch for support or for hopping
about short distances between flights."

He set the stuffed bird upon the table and retrieved the
model from my father. Returning the invention to its original spot on the table alongside its feathered counterpart, he
detached the carved male figure fixed atop it.

"Here is our source of power," he declared, "but what
remains is the question of how it should best be used."

Deftly, he manipulated the figure's jointed limbs. Now
the wooden arms were extended to either side and the legs
were bent, so that its stance mimicked the hawk's flight-ready
form.

"One might be inclined to try to duplicate the bird's
method of locomotion, with tucked legs and flapping arms,"
he went on, "but such an experiment would prove faulty. No
matter how strong the man, such a motion could be kept up
for but a short time. For, unlike a bird, a typical human does
not hold his greatest strength in his chest; rather his legs are
the most powerful portion of his anatomy."

He paused to reconfigure the wooden man so that its arms
were bent and positioned close to its sides, while its nether
limbs were extended to full length.

"To take advantage of that strength," he explained, "I
designed a pedal system that allows the greater might of the
legs to exert the needed force to flap the wings."

"So it will be almost like running in place," I ventured as I tried to picture how this would work.

"Exactly," he said with a nod. "The sky pilot—that is what I have dubbed the man who will operate those controls—will recline atop the flying machine and pedal vigorously to make the wings move up and down, giving the craft sufficient lift. Simultaneously, he will use his hands to control horizontal and vertical movement by manipulating cords that adjust the angle of both the wings and the rudder."

His explanation complete, he returned the figure to its previous position atop the model.

"There are many other principles at work here, of course, but you now know the fundamental theory behind my design. Given that, Signor Angelo, do you still see only folly in this plan?"

My father frowned, holding the Master's calm gaze with a troubled look of his own. I waited uneasily for his reply, knowing that my fate might well be affected by his decision. I could not deny that my first obedience must be to my father; still, Leonardo had become a parent of sorts to me, as well. Were I to be forced to choose between them, it would be a heart-wrenching decision, to be sure!

After a long moment, my father slowly shook his head. "I fear, Signor Leonardo, that I do not believe this machine of yours will ever fly," he declared, the blunt words sending my heart plummeting toward my boots with the speed of an eagle diving for its prey.

But before I could give way to despair, his next words halted that figurative flight as he added, "Still, I have no doubt that you yourself are convinced that you can accomplish this fantastical feat. Under such circumstances, my own feelings matter naught. And so I will be honored to work alongside you on this project on behalf of the Duke of Milan."

It was all I could do not to cheer this great news, but I contented myself with a broad grin. Leonardo looked pleased, as well, and grasped my father's hands in his.

"We shall make fine partners . . . and Dino shall prove a worthy assistant, as well," he added, including me in his smile. Reaching for the discarded length of oiled cloth, he quickly wrapped it about the model so that the small craft was well hidden and its lines blurred beneath the folds of fabric.

"But, for the moment, I think that Dino should rejoin his fellows," he told my father. "For I wish now to show you my progress on the full-scale model, and I must make a rule that only you and I shall have access to the shed where it is kept."

"Do not worry, Master. I understand," I was quick to assure him. "I shall find Constantin, for he told me he will be spending the remainder of the afternoon taking measurements in the chapel for the new fresco. I am certain he can use another set of hands."

"Very good. And fear not—you shall join your father and me in the morning to help finish testing our model."

I left the pair and headed off to the small chapel in the duke's private wing. Safely ensconced behind high walls and an iron gate, and with its own tower, that portion of the castle served as an ultimate stronghold against any outside army's attempt at conquest. There, the duke could make a final stand should the fortress ever be overrun by one of his enemies. For now, however, the soldiers who guarded that entry gave me but a cursory look as I explained my errand and then let me pass.

The chapel was perhaps large enough to hold two dozen worshippers, though the peeling plaster and dust-covered pews indicated it had been some time since Mass had been celebrated there. I made my genuflection toward the small altar and then chided myself for my lapse into blasphemy as I saw, not the martyred Lord, but the design of the Master's flying machine in the crucifix hanging above it.

Constantin put aside his sheaf of notes and welcomed me with a smile. He was sketching the dimensions of the chapel's walls, making notes of heights and lengths as he calculated the needed size of the scaffolding we would soon be assembling there. I grasped one end of the cord he had been using to take his measures and began calling out numbers to him as we made our way about the room.

When we'd finished, we settled in one of the dusty pews. While Constantin filled in the rest of his sketch, we talked about my father's arrival in Milan.

"I am not surprised that the Master kept your father's arrival a secret from you," Constantin assured me with a grin. "He enjoys a clever trick as much as any boy. I am sure he will laugh to himself for many days each time he recalls the look that must have been upon your face. The one thing I do not understand is how he could have known beforehand that Master Angelo was your father."

I recounted the Master's explanation, and the senior apprentice nodded. "Your father must be a talented master, indeed, for Leonardo to have requested his services."

With his next words, however, his amusement sobered into a sigh, and his reedy voice took on a somber note.

"Ah, Dino, you do not know how fortunate you are to have your father here with you. My father is long dead, and yet I still miss him as if he were just now gone. I know I would gladly give ten years of my life to have him back long enough to share one last meal with him."

Then he brightened. "But let us not speak of sad things. We are finished here, and we still have some time before the evening meal. Why don't we go watch the soldiers practicing with their horses in the quadrangle?"

I readily agreed. It was a favored pastime of us apprentices, observing Il Moro's mounted men and their immense steeds as they conducted their warlike maneuvers upon the parade ground. Though they used wooden weapons and practiced prescribed drills, the sight of the armored men and colorfully blanketed horses dashing about still was exciting, no matter that it happened almost daily.

We found a spot a safe distance from the action, though still close enough that we had to duck the occasional clod of dirt sent flying by a shod hoof. Constantin and I were not the only observers, for two of the stableboys and a handful of pages were already gathered where we sat. We youths clapped and cheered each skillful move, all of us secretly picturing ourselves performing such dramatic feats.

I had leaned closer to Constantin to praise one soldier's particularly adroit use of his sword, when I noticed the group of serving women milling not far from where we sat. Some juggled baskets and bundles, others stood empty-handed, but all seemed as enthralled as we by the soldiers' performance.

All, that was, save for one robed figure.

Male or female, I could not tell, for the simple brown cloak muffled the person's form sufficiently that I could distinguish neither broad shoulders nor womanly curves. But what sent a sudden shiver through me was not simply the way that that hood of the figure's cloak was pulled over his head so that the sturdy fabric partially concealed his face. Rather, it was the fact that this decidedly ominous presence appeared to be focused not upon the soldiers, but directly on me.

Shaken, I turned to Constantin and gave him a swift nudge. "Look," I whispered, though I could not have been overheard for the sound of the mock combat, even had I shouted. "Do you see that person watching me?"

"Watching you? Where?" Constantin obediently glanced about, and then grinned a little. "Do you mean those serving women? I fear you think too highly of yourself, Dino, for they are reserving their admiration for the soldiers, and not you."

"No, I mean the one in the robe . . ."

I trailed off as I realized that, in the few seconds I'd been distracted by talking with Constantin, the object of my uneasiness had vanished. Or perhaps the person still stood there but had shrugged off the robe and was merely one of the ogling females, so that I had been mistaken in attributing anything sinister to the incident.

I heard a few shouted commands from one of the soldiers, signaling the end of the demonstration. I rose and brushed the grass from my tunic, deliberately ridding myself, as well, of the uneasy feeling that had gripped me. Obviously, it had been far too long since I'd last joined the Master in a dramatic adventure, I thought with a wry shake of my head. Why else would I be seeing menacing figures where there was none, and attributing sinister motives to innocent passersby? Perhaps it was fortunate that I now had this new assignment working as my father's assistant to keep my imagination in check.

But for the rest of the day, I found myself glancing over my shoulder, lest I discover a robed figure standing behind me and inexplicably watching my every move.

5

Death comes upon wings, as a bolt from above.

—Leonardo da Vinci, *The Notebooks of Delfina della Fazia*

By the next morning, my eagerness to begin work with my father and the Master had banished all memory of the previous day's odd incident in the quadrangle. While the other apprentices had gone off to begin assembling the scaffolding in the duke's private chapel, I had hurried to Leonardo's private quarters to learn my assignment. Now I was too busy juggling the cloth-draped model of the flying machine and fearing at any moment I might drop it or break it, to be concerned about an unknown person wearing a long cloak.

"Let us make haste," the Master urged, shouldering a leather sack that he'd pulled from beneath his table. "There is much work ahead of us, for Il Moro wishes a demonstration of the flying machine as quickly as possible."

"Shall we return to the shed to start modifying the wings?" my father asked, grabbing up his own bag of tools.

Leonardo shook his head. "The duke has arranged for a secluded spot here on the castle grounds where we may finish proving my design away from spies and other curious eyes. It has the advantage of being open to the sky, while being a pleasant place in which to spend a day at labor. We shall give the model that young Dino carries a full battery of tests today and then decide if we are ready to apply what we've learned to the full-sized model."

My father and I followed the Master out the workshop door, the flying machine balanced carefully in my arms. Even swaddled in cloth, the scale craft was as light as Leonardo's tiny mounted hawk. I carried it with the same care I might have used to handle that small creature, arms stiffly extended before me as if in a gesture of offering. Given the secrecy of our work, I was relieved that the three of us drew no unwarranted attention as we marched across the quadrangle in the direction of the duke's familial quarters.

As it turned out, our destination lay not far from the Master's workshop. Halting before its wooden gate, I realized in some dismay that this place was all too familiar to me. It was secluded, as Leonardo had said, surrounded by rough stone walls twice as high as me and accessible only by that single gate. He unlocked the narrow entry and, ushering us in, carefully fastened it shut behind us.

Leonardo would have been familiar with the place, too; thus, it was with some surprise that I saw his expression was untroubled as he strode along the informal stone path that wended its way through the soft, clipped grass. I made my way most reluctantly, unable to forget what had happened the last time I set foot here in this spot. Indeed, how could I not remember the garden where, soon after my arrival at the castle, I twice had looked upon the frightening countenance of Death?

My first encounter had taken place while the rest of the

court was being entertained by a living chess match that Leonardo had arranged at the duke's command. I had been on an errand for the Master, bidden to search out Il Moro's cousin, who was inconveniently absent from the festivities on the playing field. I had all but stumbled across that missing man's body sprawled on the lawn not far from where I now stood, a bloody knife protruding from his back.

Though the greater misfortune obviously had been the conte's, that had not stopped me from cursing my own bad luck in finding him . . . That was, until later. Unsettling as the discovery had been, in the long run it had proved oddly fortuitous for me. Had someone else of the court discovered the dead man, I would never have become the Master's confidante while we investigated together in an attempt to expose a brutal killer and prevent another murder.

Still, I suppressed a small shiver at the memory. In trying to stop that assassination, I had almost become a victim myself. One dark night soon after, I had confronted another knife-wielding assailant in this same garden in hopes of preserving an old man's life.

Foiled in one attempt, that would-be killer had decided I should instead be the one to join the luckless conte in death. I had escaped that most dire fate because of the Master's timely intervention. With such a history, I told myself, the garden should surely seem to me a place of dread and horror.

Instead, the place wrapped me in an embrace of unexpected tranquillity. The breath I had been holding as I followed after the Master slipped from me in a relieved sigh. Truly, there was nothing frightening at all about the garden, I told myself as I gazed about.

Above me and clinging to the rough stone walls were the same twisted olive trees in whose limbs Tommaso and I had hidden that memorable night, watching for the assassin. No longer draped in shadows, they bent quite benignly over the garden, gaps in their branches allowing a cheerful dappling of sunlight to brighten the ground beneath. Nearby was the familiar pair of turf seats, cleverly formed from packed dirt and covered by a velvety layer of grass to create a bench where people could take their ease. Spreading palms swayed in all four corners, while a series of informal flower beds made for bright isles of blooms amid the lush green sea of grass.

I paused at the tiny reflecting pool, a low stone trough filled with pink and yellow water lilies into which trickled a steady stream from a hidden pipe. Not far from it in the lawn protruded the flat boulder where a mysterious figure had rested that same dark night that Tommaso and I had stood guard. Now, however, Leonardo had opened his leather sack upon the granite's smooth surface and was neatly arranging what appeared to be a dozen or so wood dowels as long as my arm.

He gestured me to join him. "Come, Dino; set the craft here while I arrange our test area."

In a matter of moments, he had fastened the dowels together to form two poles a little taller than he. With my father's assistance, they settled both into the ground so that they stood half the width of the garden apart from each other. Between them he strung a tight wire. Then, retrieving the model from its wrappings, he tied one end of a long leather cord to that small craft and looped the other end around the wire. The result was that the flying machine dangled at about chest height from the line.

"Come; we shall begin our tests."

With those words, Leonardo took up another dowel almost as thick as my finger. Using it as a crank, he manipulated the wooden figure atop the model so that its legs moved in a pumping motion, causing the craft's wings to move up and down. Even that small demonstration left me impressed, so that I was eager to see more.

For the next hour, he and my father took turns with the model. One would run alongside it while cranking away at the wooden man, so that the craft made wobbly progress along its prescribed path; the other would call out observations. While the resulting motion appeared more like that of a startled bat abandoned to the daylight than an eagle's smooth glide, after a few adjustments the model did undeniably fly!

Of course, they were not content with this performance. Each time the machine moved back and forth along the line, the men continued to tweak its angles and pitch. Sometimes, the Master would pause to grab up his notebook and make a note or a sketch. For my part, I stood to one side, handing either man the tools they needed and generally staying out of the way. But, watching their progress, my certainty increased that a functional, man-sized version of the craft was possible.

Half of the morning had passed before the garden—again and perhaps inexorably—became a scene of a new tragedy. The disturbance began outside its crumbling walls, however. So intent were all of us on our work that it took a moment for the cries to register upon our ears.

"Master, Master!" a frantic voice was calling, the words faint yet growing louder with every repetition.

My heart gave a lurch at the sound. Surely it must be one of my fellow apprentices crying for help, I told myself, or the shout would have been a summons for Signor Leonardo, instead.

Leonardo dropped his notebook and, my father and I on his heels, rushed to the barred gate. He unfastened the catch with haste and threw it open. No one stood outside it, however. Frantically, we abandoned that tack and scanned the garden, looking for the source of that frightened sound.

"There!" I cried, my attention caught by a movement atop the wall.

It was at the very spot where Tommaso and I had scaled the stone barrier to hide within the olive trees' twisted branches. The climb had been slow and more than a bit painful, the rough stones scraping bare flesh and tearing at trunk hose and tunic. Still, anyone agile enough—certainly, any of the apprentices—could make the ascent.

I glimpsed a familiar brown tunic over green trunk hose as a youth scaled the wall and balanced atop it. I could not make out his face for the tangle of branches blocking my view, but it was certainly one of my fellows. He stood unmoving for an instant; then, with a sharp cry of pain, his body jerked.

I gave an answering cry as I watched him sway there for what seemed a lifetime, though it would have been but the space of a few heartbeats. Finally, with an uncertain flapping of his arms that uncannily resembled the motion of the flying machine, the youth tumbled from the wall to land in a heap at the foot of the olive tree.

As one, we rushed toward him.

Leonardo reached him first, carefully gathering him into his arms. As he did so, I saw that a bloody stain was rapidly spreading down the back of the youth's tunic. And, to my horror, I glimpsed something that resembled a small arrow lodged between his shoulder blades. The youth stirred restlessly in Leonardo's arms, and I heard a final breathless gasp.

"Master," he managed once more, and sagged into stillness.

His head lolled toward me, so that I had my first glimpse of his face. At the sight, I dropped to my knees as if struck, frantically wishing I could scrub the image from my mind but unable to tear my gaze from the waxen features of my friend.

Vaguely, I was aware of my father kneeling beside me and placing one hand protectively upon my shoulder. Softly, he asked, "Do you know this boy?"

"Y-yes," I choked out, the word rough with tears that I did not bother to hide. "He is our senior apprentice, Constantin."

I stared down at Constantin's white face, his half-open eyes staring sightlessly over my shoulder, and did not need to ask if he was dead. Still, disbelief filled my heart. How could he be alive one moment and his life cruelly snuffed in the next? Surely it was not possible!

Leonardo was the first to stir from the momentary paralysis that gripped us.

"Quickly, we must run the assailant to ground. The murder weapon was a crossbow, which means the killer likely was near the garden wall when he shot Constantin. There is still a chance we may catch him fleeing his crime!"

Barely had the words left Leonardo's lips than my father was sprinting toward the open gate with a speed I never knew he possessed. I scrambled to my feet and rushed after him, my own feet hardly touching the ground in my haste.

It occurred to me as I ran that perhaps I should be fearful. Constantin's murderer would have had time to span his crossbow with a new bolt and could easily fire upon me or my father once he saw us in pursuit. But any fright I might have felt at my own potential danger was consumed by the righteous fury that seemed to roar through my veins.

I burst past the garden's gate to see that the quadrangle before me bustled with court activity, as usual. Panting while my ribs struggled against my confining undergarment, I halted for a sweeping glance across the expanse of green lawn, looking for a man in flight. The only one moving at a rapid pace, however, was my father. He was headed toward the main gate but in pursuit of no one in particular, though several people had stopped in their tracks to stare after him. I gave a despairing little groan. Had the killer already escaped us?

Or was he instead strolling about in plain sight among the servants and nobles, his deadly crossbow hidden beneath a cape or tucked into a sack?

I allowed myself a swift, grim nod. He could not have fled so quickly, not without drawing attention to himself, as my father unwittingly had proved. Thus, he had either slipped into an outbuilding or else was masquerading as one going about his everyday business.

"He must still be upon the grounds," Leonardo echoed my thoughts, appearing at my side. His gaze swept the grounds with its intersecting graveled paths, just as mine had.

"We will leave your father to question the guards at the gate," came his swift decree, "while you and I keep our search to the quadrangle and the outbuildings."

"B-but what of Constantin?" I choked out, for I'd not thought the Master would abandon the dead youth. "We cannot leave him unattended in the garden."

"I have settled him there decently, and the gate is locked so that no one other than I may enter again."

I nodded and poised myself to begin the hunt. Before I could take another step, however, the Master put a stilling hand upon my shoulder. The movement mirrored my father's earlier comforting gesture, but Leonardo's expression was filled with cold purpose.

"I shall not let you go, Dino, until I have your promise that you will attempt no heroics. If you see someone who appears suspicious, do not draw attention to yourself. Follow him at a distance and see where he takes refuge."

He paused, and his grip on me tightened.

"But under no circumstances are you to confront any man, no matter that you see a spent crossbow dangling from his hand and guilt written upon his face. I have already lost one apprentice this day, and I will not lose another."

My gaze dropped to the splash of fresh blood—Constantin's blood—across the Master's tunic, and I felt my features harden into the same cold mask of determination that he wore.

"I promise, Master, that I shall confront no one . . . but I vow that I shall find who struck down my friend and bring him to justice."

"Then, quickly, to work."

We parted on those words, each taking a different direction across the quadrangle. Despite my urgency, I kept a restrained pace, aware that I had the advantage in this search. Being both young and humbly garbed, I was likely to be overlooked by almost everyone I encountered. Leonardo, on the other hand, garnered attention simply because of his handsome features and confident air. The fact that he was well-known here at the castle made it more difficult for him to wander about unnoticed.

But while I might have drawn little scrutiny, no one escaped my gaze as I walked past him . . . or her. I dared not assume that a woman could not have been Constantin's assassin. After all, I had already encountered more than one murderous female in my time here at Castle Sforza, so that I knew full well how deadly the fairer sex could be. And a crossbow was a light enough weapon that most women could capably handle one.

Still, what could have driven anyone, male or female, to murder someone whose kindness to his fellows was surpassed only by his talent with a brush?

I gave a furtive swipe at my damp eyes, willing away the

tears. Later there would be time enough to grieve him. For the moment, I must set aside my sorrow and search out the one responsible for this tragedy.

But after many minutes of fruitless searching, I feared that the killer had slipped through our grasp. I had stared into the faces of both servants and nobles, some of whom I saw daily and others who were unknown to me. I'd peered into privies and stables, startling more than a few men and beasts but finding no likely suspects.

Once, I thought I glimpsed the same robed figure that I'd suspected of watching me at the parade grounds, and my heart began to beat faster. Barely had I begun my pursuit, however, when the swaddled form vanished behind a columned portico. But even as I cursed my bad luck, the figure reappeared a moment later at the public fountain.

Aha, I have you, I thought in triumph and rushed in that direction. But by then the concealing hood had slipped back to reveal an old woman's crinkled face, and a fragile, bony hand reached to cup a bit of water for drink. Shaking my head in mingled dismay and relief—for, in truth, what would I have done if the figure had proved to be a burly man with a crossbow wrapped in disguise?—I decided further searching was fruitless.

Leonardo and my father must have had the same thought, for I found them waiting for me at the garden gate. "How did you fare, my boy?" Leonardo asked at my approach.

"I was quite diligent, Master, but I fear I bring no news. I discovered no one out of place, nor anyone who hinted by his actions that he was guilty of murder." With an anxious look at my father, I asked, "Did the guards notice anyone trying to flee the castle grounds with undue haste?"

"It would seem I was the sole one the guards observed behaving oddly," he replied with no little chagrin. "So intent was I in trying to discover that poor boy's assassin that I did not realize my own actions might be looked at with suspicion. The captain of the guard questioned me thoroughly himself."

My father gave a wry snort at the memory.

"An unpleasant fellow, he was . . . foreign, and quite large, with blond mustaches," he proclaimed, describing the man I knew as the new captain of Il Moro's guard. "At any second, I expected the point of his sword to appear at my throat and for him to lead me away. I had to invoke Signor Leonardo's name several times before he was content to leave me be."

With a sidelong look at the Master, he added, "I fear that I misled him with my reasons for my haste. Since I am but a visitor here in Milan, I hesitated to speak the word *murder* aloud when I did not have you there to bear witness in my behalf. Instead, I told him that one of your apprentices had been sent on a fool's errand, and that I was trying find the boy before he wasted a day wandering about the city looking for a merchant who did not exist."

The Master gave a brisk nod of approval.

"I can see where our young Dino has learned his clever ways. It is well that you kept your peace, Signor Angelo. But we should not tarry in sight of all where we might draw suspicion," he added and pulled open the gate. "Let us return to the garden so that we may discuss what must happen next."

Once inside, he closed the gate behind us again and stood before it as if barring our escape. I was glad to focus on him rather than gaze toward the spot near the boulder where I knew Constantin lay. But for the moment, the Master's attention was for my father.

"As I said, Signor Angelo, you spoke prudently when you suggested we would do well not to fling about words such as *murder.* Until we know the reason that my apprentice met so cruel a fate, we must keep such speculation to ourselves.

"And that is why we must make haste to remove Constantin's body from the garden and carry him far from the castle grounds."

6

. . . for us wretched mortals, there avails not any flight . . .

—Leonardo da Vinci, *Codex Atlanticus*

My gasp was audible, even as my tongue momentarily failed me. As for my father, his mild features darkened in outrage.

"I cannot permit such a travesty, signore," he decreed, his tone defiant. "The boy is dead, and by another man's hand. We cannot pretend this did not happen. We must discover the villain responsible and bring him to justice."

"Master, surely you cannot mean to abandon Constantin's body," I cried before he could answer, having finally regained my voice. "He is—was—my friend and your loyal apprentice. He deserves better than to be left for a carrion eater's feast! Why can you not go to Il Moro's guard and tell them of this crime so that they might attempt to find his killer?"

Leonardo raised a hand in protest, his expression as stern as my father's. "Temper your outrage, and I shall explain further . . .

but first, I must show you what I discovered tucked into Constantin's purse as I was settling him beneath a cloth."

He reached into his tunic and withdrew a thin sheaf of folded papers. Smoothing their creases, he wordlessly proffered them for my father's examination. He began to peruse them, while I shamelessly gazed over his shoulder to see what secrets they held.

I needed but a glimpse to realize that the papers belonged to Leonardo. The tightly scribed writing in the familiar mirrored hand that ran from right to left could belong to no one else. As for the sketches that illustrated that text, they showed sections of the very flying machine that we had spent the afternoon testing. I noticed, as well, that one edge of each page was uneven, and I guessed that they must have been cut with haste from one of the Master's many notebooks.

I ventured as much aloud, earning his approving nod.

"The volume that once held these pages is even now sitting on the table in my private workshop."

He paused and shrugged.

"When they were removed from their binding, I cannot say, though these particular sketches were completed perhaps a month ago. And I am not in the habit of reviewing my work once it has been committed to paper. Thus, if not for this day's tragic incident, another few weeks might have passed before I ever discovered the theft."

"And you believe that these drawings of your flying machine are the reason for the young man's murder?" my father asked, his frown deepening.

Leonardo nodded. "As I told you on your arrival, the duke is most anxious for a demonstration of the flying craft. He has fears regarding his treaty with France, which is in jeopardy."

He paused to lower his voice, though there was no one about save my father and me to hear him.

"It is not commonly known, but as we speak Il Moro and a contingent of his men are on their way to a secret rendezvous with the French king's representatives," he went on. "But his greater concern is his alliances within the province . . . particularly the treaty with his newest ally, the Duke of Pontalba. Ludovico's military might on the ground, while adequate, is insufficient to give him free rein in this region."

He raised a cautioning finger skyward. "Should Il Moro prove to these nobles that he holds domination in the sky—a feat that no one in history has ever before accomplished!—his problem is solved. They will have no choice but to submit to him. But if someone else manages to conquer the clouds before he does, both he and Milan will find themselves subject to another man's rule."

While we considered that state of affairs, Leonardo managed what was, for him, a humble expression.

"Certainly, we must allow for the possibility that another man in the region has the intellect to conceive of a similar design on his own," he conceded. "But word of such a genius would surely have come to my ears by now, just as my own reputation spread beyond Florence. And as I have heard tell of no comparable man, I deem it unlikely. But should a person gain access to my design, my notes . . ."

The Master trailed off with a shrug. Returning the pages to him, my father stroked his beard thoughtfully.

"Your drawings that I have seen thus far are detailed. With them, a man with an apt hand and sharp mind might manage to build his own flying machine," he agreed. "But if that had been the intent, who of the duke's allies—or enemies—would be bold enough to set a spy out to steal your design? And why was your apprentice murdered, and yet these pages left behind?"

"Those are the questions that plague me, and the reason

I am loath to let word of Constantin's murder spread until I have a chance to speak with Il Moro."

As he spoke, Leonardo started toward the spot where Constantin lay. Reluctantly, I followed after him, my father at my side with his hand again resting upon my shoulder.

I was reassured to see that the apprentice's face and upper body were covered by the same cloth in which the small flying machine had earlier been wrapped. But barely had I registered that relief when Leonardo knelt beside the still figure and drew back the fabric, exposing the youth's pale, still features.

"Now, we must connect these stolen drawings to Constantin," he coolly declared, his gaze unyielding as he looked down upon his senior apprentice.

"As I see it, two possibilities exist," he went on. "The first is that Constantin accidentally discovered that someone had stolen the pages—perhaps caught him in the very act—and attempted to recover them. But, tragically, his bold attempt was met with violence. The thief dared not let his identity be revealed and so stooped to cruel murder lest Constantin reveal his treachery to all."

He paused and drew the cloth lower, revealing the bloody bolt, which he must have pulled from Constantin's back. The short arrow lay upon the youth's thin chest like a spent bird, its metal tip and sleek wood shaft stained in dried blood, the fletched feathers tipped in gore. I shuddered at the sight, knowing this was one image I would never scrub from my memory.

"The second possibility," he continued, "is that Constantin himself stole the sketches . . . perhaps at someone else's behest, or else with the idea that he might find a person willing to pay him good coin for the information. But something went wrong—treachery among thieves, perhaps—and he was killed for his efforts."

"No, Master," I choked out, shaking my head. "Constantin

would never betray you in such a fashion! Of that, I am certain. Remember, too, that he called for your help with his last breath. Pray, do not let him go to his grave with such a stain upon his reputation!"

Leonardo surveyed the youth's face a moment longer before once more drawing the cloth over his slack features. Then, with a sigh, he rose and led us a decent distance from the body.

"Believe me, my dear boy," he answered my plea, "I do not wish to consider such evil of so fine a youth. But until we discover his assailant, we must prepare ourselves for any explanation."

Straightening his tunic with its rust-colored slash of dried blood across his breast, he addressed my father.

"The manner of Constantin's murder is our greatest clue. You will agree that a crossbow is not the weapon of a common man but that of a noble or a soldier. Did you perhaps take note of the bolt that struck him down?"

"It appeared finely crafted of some hard wood, perhaps English yew, and the fletching is expertly tied," Angelo replied. "But the bolt is short. It must have come from a weapon small enough to be spanned using a simple lever . . . a weapon that could be fired with one hand."

I promptly thought of the crossbows that Il Moro's soldiers used. Most of their weapons were of the sort that required not so much skill as brute force to handle. With a broad bow mounted upon a long stock, these weapons were far more powerful at a short distance than a traditional bow, if perhaps less accurate. But while an archer of but moderate strength could readily nock an arrow onto a long bow, I had seen for myself that spanning a crossbow took far greater force.

The older style of these weapons was still carried by some of the gray-haired mercenaries who filled the ranks of Il Moro's army. This crossbow required the assistance of a large hook that dangled from the soldier's belt and that was designed to catch the slack bowstring. Pointing the crossbow toward the ground, the man would place one raised foot into the metal stirrup mounted at the end of the crossbow's wooden stock, almost as if he were climbing into a saddle. But rather than making a graceful leap upward, he'd instead straighten his leg. The strength of that limb pressing downward would effectively pull the hooked bowstring upward along the crossbow's stock, holding it taut until the string caught upon the stock's locking nut so that the bolt could be properly set.

Such a complicated ritual took time, however, with the result being that a traditional archer could shoot a dozen or more arrows to every bolt fired from a crossbow. Even those more modern weapons, which used a cranking device, could not be fired as swiftly as the long bow. Still, they could more readily pierce armor or shields, making them fearsome weapons.

I knew, of course, that a far smaller crossbow would be used by men on horseback. Efficient if less powerful, such a weapon was light enough to be carried about. But there was no mistaking its deadly force, as we had learned to our fresh grief. For surely this had been the sort of weapon employed by Constantin's murderer.

Leonardo, meanwhile, was nodding his agreement with my father's words.

"As you said, a finely crafted bolt . . . one designed to kill with the greatest efficiency. Such a weapon may bespeak a professional assassin in our midst. That is why I wish to keep the circumstances of the attack upon Constantin confidential until I consult with the duke, and it is the reason for the pretense I have proposed.

"Fear not, Dino," he added with a glance at me. "I shall

not have you take part in this grim deceit, nor your father, save that I shall need him to bring me the wagon with which I shall take the unfortunate Constantin from this place. With a bit of misdirection, everyone who sees us depart will believe that the boy merely slumbers beside me. Moreover, you and Signor Angelo will be able to speak truthfully that you saw us leave the castle and plead ignorance of what might have happened beyond its walls."

I bleakly considered this proposed scenario, picturing Constantin's limp form propped upon the wagon seat next to the Master. It would be a bold bluff, his passing through the gates beneath the guards' scrutiny with a dead youth as his companion. Still, I knew that Leonardo was accomplished at creating illusion and could readily pull off such a ruse, such skill at stagecraft yet another reason that Il Moro charged him with conducting the court's regular pageants.

"I shall remain gone as long as necessary," he went on, "and I will return with Constantin wrapped in a blanket and the story that he was killed by bandits on the road from Milan. Such attacks are a common enough occurrence these days that no one will question my claim. With his death formally established, we will be able to begin preparations for laying him to rest."

My father seemingly had doubts about this audacious plan, however, for he shook his head.

"Such a tale may serve for everyone else, but what of this assassin? He will know that the boy was killed here in the garden and not upon the road. Besides, surely the man responsible is long gone from here and would care not what happens next."

"It is possible," the Master conceded, "but I am not certain that your theory is correct."

Leonardo's expression was considering as he went on. "If

Constantin was killed because of my flying machine, the assassin did not achieve his primary goal of obtaining the information to build the craft. He or his confederates may still be among us. Thus, we must gird ourselves against a possible second attempt at theft . . . perhaps a second try at murder."

As he spoke, I abruptly recalled the mysterious hooded figure I had seen the day before, seemingly spying upon me. Though I had not determined why I, of all people, had warranted such strange scrutiny, it occurred to me that perhaps I had glimpsed Constantin's assassin.

And why not? The flowing robes could easily conceal a small crossbow within their folds, I reasoned in some concern. Moreover, such a disguise could be shrugged off in moments, allowing its wearer to blend into a group of servants or of nobles, depending upon what he wore beneath it.

Not wishing to alarm my father—for surely he would be distressed to learn that I might have drawn the assassin's notice—I waited while the two men conferred a moment longer. Finally convinced of the wisdom of Leonardo's plan, my father gave me an encouraging nod and strode with grim purpose from the garden in search of a wagon. Only when the gate had closed behind him did I confide in the Master my fears about this puzzling stranger.

He listened with keen interest to my story, but his response took me aback. "Odd, how this unknown person made his initial appearance at the same time that Signor Angelo first arrived here in Milan," he coolly observed.

I instinctively bristled at this seeming accusation against my father. Surely he could not think that so fine a man as Angelo della Fazia would have anything to do with murder!

Seeing my reaction, Leonardo was swift to assume a placating tone.

"Do not worry, my dear boy. I do not mean to imply that your sire has any involvement in this matter. But it would seem that someone deduced the reason for my bringing him into the duke's service and decided the time was ripe to strike."

"Do you truly believe what you said earlier, then, that someone else might fall victim to this assassin?" I asked with no little trepidation, picturing my father or another of the apprentices—or Leonardo himself!—lying sprawled upon the ground, a bloody bolt protruding from his cold flesh.

The Master stroked his neat beard, his expression grim. "I am loath to play prophet under such circumstances, but I would venture to say that we have not seen the end of this matter."

"Perhaps since we all dress in identical tunics and trunk hose, he mistook me for Constantin," I weakly offered, now picturing myself as the one lying in a heap with an arrow in my back and my lifeblood spilling into the dirt.

I had no time to dwell on this unsettling scene, however, for I heard the staccato knock upon the gate that was the prearranged signal for my father's return. The Master swiftly unlatched the gate, and the pair maneuvered the small cart and sturdy little horse into the garden. Then my father turned to Leonardo, his manner firm.

"I would not have Dino witness what we must do next to carry out your plan. Let him rejoin his fellows."

"I am of the same mind," Leonardo said with a swift nod, much to my relief.

To me, he added, "The other apprentices should still be in the small chapel preparing the walls for our next fresco. Make your way there, and if they question you, simply say that I bade you lend them assistance for the day. As for Constantin, you may say that you last saw him leaving the castle grounds with me. Give them no hint that anything is amiss."

"As you will, Master," I agreed, sending my father a look of silent gratitude. No matter that I understood Leonardo's intent, I did not think I could bear to stand by and watch my friend being lashed to the wagon like a bundle.

I took my leave of the garden with more haste than dignity. But even with the gate shut behind me again, I could picture in my mind's eye what must happen next . . . the two men lifting Constantin into the wagon and carefully arranging his dead limbs into a cruel mockery of repose. Tied to the seat and wrapped in a cloak, his lifeless form would doubtless pass unnoticed by the guards as Leonardo drove through the castle gates.

I shuddered. I suspected that familiar handling of the dead—no matter that the victim was well-known to him—would not cause the Master much distress. He had examined many a corpse in the time that I had known him; indeed, he was rumored to have secretly cut open dead criminals in the same way that a tanner flayed a beast, simply to further his anatomical knowledge. But as for my father . . .

Despite my distress, I felt a surge of affection that momentarily warmed my chilled flesh. Though willing to risk confrontation when his principles were put to test, my father's veins ran with mild humors. I knew that Constantin's death had touched him greatly, though he barely knew the apprentice. Likely he pictured one of my brothers, or me, when he looked upon the murdered youth. I knew that, while he took part in this charade out of grim duty, his heart was surely wounded by the task.

I left with no backward glance toward the garden, though I did spare several uneasy looks about me as I made my swift way across the broad quadrangle. Surely no one would attempt to strike me down in so public an arena, I reassured myself, taking comfort in the usual bustle of servants and tradesmen making their own way about the grounds. Still, my shoulders twitched in uneasy anticipation of a well-placed bolt between them, and I kept a keen watch for the mysterious robed stranger who might have played a cruel role in this day's tragic events.

Reaching the main castle unscathed, I headed toward the duke's private quarters, where the family chapel lay. For the moment, the apprentices were busy setting up the scaffolding within the narrow chamber and preparing the walls with new plaster. No painting had yet begun, for Leonardo had been distracted by his work on the flying machine and had managed but a few sketches for this particular fresco.

At the duke's direction, the work was to depict scenes from the missing years of Christ's young adulthood. I had seen some of the Master's preliminary drawings on the subject and had found them surprising, to say the least. One, in particular, portrayed the Son of God in a strange land populated by elephants and tigers, and with the surrounding temples oddly domed and decorated in bright colors. As for the Christ figure, he was depicted seated with his legs crossed, and seemingly floating high above the ground before an approving crowd of brown-skinned men. I wondered if Ludovico had seen the sketches and if he had approved them.

I rather suspected that he had not!

Cursorily inspected and ushered past by the familiar pair of bored guards who kept watch at the inner gate, I entered the chapel. Within, the apprentices were hard at work with brooms and rags, removing all traces of dirt from the walls in preparation for the layers of fresh plaster to be troweled on during the next few days. Some balanced upon the newly erected wooden scaffolding as they cleaned cobwebs and soot from the eaves; the rest labored at sweeping the lower walls and corner crannies. Though they chatted as they worked, their tone was respectfully subdued as befitted the sanctified setting.

The sleek hound, Pio, was there, as well. Irreverently perched upon one carved wooden pew, he lay on his haunches with long legs stretched before him and paws neatly crossed in the prayerful attitude that had earned him his name. Unlike Il Moro's men, he appeared quite interested in the apprentices' work, his bright brown eyes taking in every move, though he obediently kept to his place.

Vittorio was the first to notice my entrance.

"Dino," he cheerily called, waving his broom in my direction and hopping down from the scaffolding. Remembering that he was in a house of worship, he lowered his voice and went on. "What are you doing here? I thought you were helping the Master and your father."

Swiping off my cap, I made a quick genuflection in the direction of the altar and then turned to him. "The Master said he did not need my assistance this afternoon and instructed me to help the rest of you, instead."

"But what of Constantin?"

This question came from Tito, who was perched on the scaffold above us, near where Vittorio had been working.

"We've not seen him in some time, not since we returned from the midday meal," he went on, earning the nods of Bernardo and a few other youths working alongside him. "Do you know where he is?"

"I saw him leave through the castle's main gate with the Master," I obediently repeated the explanation that Leonardo had given me. "What their destination was, I cannot say, other than that they left."

Tito's pockmarked face took on a look of confusion. "Are you certain it was he that you saw with the Master?" At my nod, he complained, "Why would Constantin leave without a word to us, and without putting one of the other apprentices in charge?"

"Perhaps he felt we are well trained enough that we can perform our tasks without his watching over us constantly," I replied, making my best attempt at an unconcerned shrug. Then, with a gesture toward Pio, I lightly added, "Besides, he has left a spy in our midst. Pio will surely report our bad behavior should we do anything amiss."

The hound chose this moment to yawn broadly, his pink tongue unfurling like a bright ribbon. He gave an audible groan and flopped most gracelessly onto his side for a nap. Vittorio and the others snickered at the sight, and even Tito allowed himself a grin. I managed a smile of my own, realizing this might well be the last moment of shared amusement among us apprentices for some time, once news of Constantin's murder became known.

Shaking off that thought, I grabbed up Vittorio's broom and vigorously attacked a cobweb. "Come; we must get back to work, lest Pio speak ill of us later. Does anyone know how much plaster we will need to mix tomorrow?"

With my words, the others resumed their earlier tasks. I applied myself to my work, as well, concentrating on the youths' quiet chatter lest my thoughts drift back to Constantin and the unknown assassin who might still be lurking within our midst. Maintaining my air of unconcern took no little effort, though I was relieved that no one seemed to notice my subdued air and false smiles.

No one, that was, save Pio. After a few moments, he roused himself from the pew and padded over to where I stood. He stared at me with liquid brown eyes and touched an inquiring paw to my leg in an innocent show of canine concern.

I bit my lip hard lest it tremble and bent low to give the hound a fond pat, taking that opportunity to discreetly brush the sudden dampness from my eyes. For a moment, at least, my grief lightened.

I sighed. Though welcome, the sweet innocence of Pio would not suffice to assuage the mourning that would ensue in our workshop once the Master brought word of Constantin's senseless murder. I could only hope that his would be both the first and the last killing . . . could only pray that no other apprentice would fall victim to yet another bolt from the blue before the duke's flying machine was completed and his victory ensured.

The Master waited until we apprentices had finished our evening meal and were gathered back at the workshop to break the grim news of Constantin's murder to us. His handsome features drawn into hard lines, he gave the terse explanation that he'd settled upon that afternoon. It was a sadly familiar tale of brutal bandits and swift death on the road leading from Milan.

"But you may rest easy on one score," came his solemn assurance as cries of disbelief met his words. "Know that your fellow apprentice died most bravely in defense of his master. And know, too, that I am both humbled and grieved by his sacrifice . . . and that I would have taken the arrow in his stead, were it possible."

"Master, we must avenge him!" came a shrill cry from behind me, rising over the muttered curses and muffled sobs that had begun to fill the room.

The speaker was Bernardo. The youngest of the apprentices, he could have modeled for the cherubs in any of the Master's frescoes, with his round, pink face and halo of curly brown hair. Now, however, the soft curls trembled in rage, while the plump cheeks were dark with anger and dampened by tears.

"We must find the bandit who murdered Constantin and kill him ourselves," he cried, shaking his fist. "Master, give me leave to go, and I shall search him out."

"I'll go with you," Tommaso exclaimed, his beefy features tight with grief. "What of you, Paolo, and you, Tito . . . and the rest of you? Will you not join us?"

Bold calls of agreement promptly rose from the others. Swept by that tide of emotion, I found myself clenching my own fist and vowing vengeance along with the rest. But as the clamor grew, Leonardo lifted a quelling hand.

"Your loyalty to the good Constantin is admirable," he said, his stern gaze moving across the room until the cries settled to a few mutters, "but such a dangerous mission is a matter for Il Moro's guard. A group of them left the castle soon after my return and now are scouring the countryside for the men that set upon us."

His passing glance halted on me for a few seconds, and I caught the faintest of nods from him.

The gesture reassured me that the duke's men were indeed combing the hills and tree-dotted plains around Milan. And while the brigands they sought were fictional, Constantin's murderer was not and might be lurking somewhere beyond the castle walls. The soldiers would surely be on the alert for any suspicious person, no matter if he were dressed in a bandit's rags or showed himself as my mysterious robed stranger.

To my surprise, Leonardo added, "But though the duke's men are beyond the gates searching out this villain, that does not mean there might not be danger lurking here at the castle. Until this man is caught, I urge all of you to remain vigilant. Do not wander about the grounds alone, and keep a keen eye out for strangers."

Had I not known the true circumstances of the day's events, I might have been puzzled. And, indeed, a few apprentices glanced uncertainly at one another at these last instructions. The only question asked, however, was regarding the fate of our fallen friend.

"Master, what becomes of Constantin . . . That is, shall he be buried here?"

This question came from Davide, one of the older apprentices. Blond and of wiry build and measured temperament, he was known as the workshop's peacemaker, the one who stepped in to settle squabbles and mend torn friendships. He and Constantin had been close friends, I knew. And thus Davide's words echoed with gravity far beyond his years, while his stricken expression reflected all of our grief.

Leonardo nodded. "Most of his family is either dead or living far away in the Greek isles," he replied, "so there is no one to claim him other than us. He shall have a fine funeral and be laid in our churchyard tomorrow afternoon."

He fell silent, and I saw reflected in his face the same grief that I had seen as he held the dying Constantin in his arms. Surely few masters cared for their apprentices as he did, I told myself, swiping fresh tears from my own eyes. Constantin had been equally devoted to him, which was why I knew that his last act could never have been one of betrayal. He had been running to Leonardo, and not simply fleeing someone else.

By now, several apprentices were gathered around the Master, listening to further words of comfort. The rest stood huddled together, exchanging words of praise for their dead friend. As I moved to join that second group, I noticed that, like I, Tito stood slightly apart from the others.

He chose that same moment to glance in my direction. Under the circumstances, I did not expect to see the usual casual smile he normally wore; still, something in his expression took me aback. For his pockmarked face reflected not so much grief as impatience, while his black eyes held anger rather than unshed tears. And though he and Constantin had not been the closest of friends, in recent days I had seen the pair together on numerous occasions.

Noting my scrutiny, Tito's expression darkened, and for a moment he appeared to struggle with some inner emotion. Just as swiftly, he tossed his unruly black hair off his forehead and made his way toward where the Master stood.

I frowned as I joined the other huddled group of apprentices. Surely Tito must grieve Constantin's loss as the rest of us did, I told myself as I linked arms with Vittorio and Paolo. Perhaps he simply was one of those people who embraced anger rather than sorrow under trying circumstances.

Soon after, the Master took his leave of us, with the admonition to finish our usual evening's tasks before we settled in for the night. Under the circumstances, such a demand might have seemed unduly harsh. We all realized, however, that he sought to keep both our hands and our heads occupied while we attempted to reconcile ourselves to the tragedy that had happened in our midst.

Once the last paint pot was cleaned and the final broom tucked away, we gathered a bit uncertainly near the hearth, where the fire lay dying. It was usually Constantin who lit the night's ration of candle stubs so that we might spend an hour of amusement before taking to our cots. No one appeared inclined to take on his role, just as none of us was disposed to indulge in merriment. Thus, it was with unspoken if mutual agreement that we put aside our usual ritual and retired early to bed.

Or, rather, the others did. I slipped out of the workshop and, shivering in the cool night air, made my way to Leonardo's quarters in search of my father.

7

*. . . such an instrument constructed by man is lacking in noth-
ing except the life of the bird . . .*

—Leonardo da Vinci, *Codex Atlanticus*

For once, I was relieved to find that the Master was not
within when I knocked upon his door. Where he would
have gone, I could not guess, though I suspected his absence
had something to do with the day's events.

Instead, it was my father who ushered me inside. He'd
been working at the Master's table, for several candle stubs
burned bright upon it. The model of the flying machine sat
amid scattered papers where my father had recorded notes
and measurements from the test flights he and the Master
had carried out. Glancing at the pages, I noted in some surprise that his sheets bore a striking similarity to those in
Leonardo's notebooks . . . save, of course, for the mirrored
handwriting that was the Master's alone.

My father gestured me toward the bench and took a seat

beside me. I leaned against his shoulder, recalling Constantin's mention of his father, and how he would have given ten years of his life to sit with his parent one more time.

Your wish has been granted, I thought, smiling mistily as I pictured the pair seated at some heavenly table and eagerly speaking of all that had happened since they last had seen each other in life.

My father must have heard my reflexive sigh, for he put a comforting arm around me.

"Your friend Constantin was a fine young man," he remarked, "and a talented painter, as well. I am sorry that I did not have a chance to know him better, but I can tell you that your master spoke highly of him."

He hesitated and then shifted about so that he held my gaze. "And I can also assure you that this cruel charade of carrying the boy's dead body about pained Signor Leonardo greatly. Do not worry, Delfina. I see now that he did what he thought must be done."

"But does he believe that Constantin betrayed him?"

"Your master is a man of the world. He is not naive enough to dismiss the possibility that even the best of us can be tempted. For some, that temptation may be coin; for others, perhaps the prospect of a more prestigious post."

When I made a sound of protest, he added, "But, no, I do not think he suspects the boy of any wrongdoing."

He stood abruptly and paced the small room, stroking his neat beard. Again, I was struck by the resemblance between him and Leonardo. Perhaps had I allowed myself a more critical eye, I might have conceded that my father's features were more pleasant than handsome, and his bearing rather more sturdy than graceful. Side by side, they could not be confused with each other; still, the two men might have passed for older and younger brother, with the Master the fairer of the pair.

As those idle thoughts flittered through my mind, my father halted in his pacing, as if he'd come to a decision. He proved me right, when he began to speak.

"I have given this matter much thought since this afternoon," he began in a tone befitting the day's solemn mood. "I fear that Signor Leonardo has inadvertently opened the gates to evil with this invention of his. It is an unnatural thing, the prospect of a man soaring above the treetops like a bird. No good can come of it, I am certain. I fear that if your duke is given this power, he will use it most cruelly against both enemy and friend."

He paused and shot me a keen look. "I will, of course, keep my agreement with your master and continue work upon the flying machine. But once my part is done, I shall gather my tools and leave Milan so that I do not have to witness what will come next. And I think it best that I take you with me."

I leaped to my feet and stared at him in dismay.

"Father, surely you would not make me abandon my apprenticeship! What happened to Constantin was a terrible thing, but the Master shall learn who killed him. There's no need for me to leave."

"You don't understand, my child," he countered, his expression sterner than I recalled ever seeing. "This has nothing to do with your unfortunate friend's murder. Signor Leonardo has already said that the duke intends to use this flying machine—should it prove successful—to go to war with his neighbors. One province or two falling victim to Il Moro's newfound supremacy would not mean much. Such is the way it has always been, for the dukedoms cannot help but bicker like children. But I fear this time it will be different."

"I don't understand, Father. What difference can it make?"

"If Ludovico grows too powerful," he replied, "he will eventually bring the wrath of Rome upon Milan. The Medicis of Florence will surely support the pope, as will any other dukes not under Ludovico's control. The ensuing war will be bloody, and I shall not leave my daughter here to face such carnage!"

His tone had an air of finality about it that struck me silent. And, truth be told, I suspected he could be right about what might happen should the callous Ludovico gain control of the very skies. But how could I abandon Leonardo and my fellows to such danger?

Not willing to debate the subject with him, I merely nodded my assent; then, to change the subject, I began telling him about the new fresco that we'd begun preparation for in the chapel. I did, however, purposely neglect to mention the scenes depicting Christ's travels in strange Eastern lands . . . most particularly the sketch that showed him levitating above a crowd. I knew my pious father would find it heretical, so much so that he might forget his promise to the Master and hurry me away from Milan this very night!

A short time later, I kissed my father on the cheek and took my leave. Leonardo had not yet returned, and I wondered if he would wander the night until dawn, as was often his wont. For myself, I preferred the comfort of my bed. Thus, I slipped back into the workshop, dark save for the final flickers of the dying fire tucked deep within the hearth.

I negotiated the shadows with care, making my way through the maze of worktables and benches until I reached the converted storeroom that served as the apprentices' sleeping quarters. Running the length of the workshop and accessed by but a single entry, it was little more than a long hallway flanked on either side by a dozen shallow alcoves. While once those hollows would have held boxes and barrels, now each contained a narrow cot and a small wooden chest for storing personal items.

While it might have seemed odd to house a score of young men as if they were but the aforementioned boxes and barrels, it had proved a fine arrangement. In truth, we enjoyed far more luxurious accommodations here than did most of the castle's inhabitants. There were sufficient numbers of both alcoves and cots that we each had a bed to ourselves, while most of the castle's other apprentices and servants slept two or three to a single bed . . . That was, assuming they had a bed and not merely a pallet of straw and blankets laid upon the stone floor.

Of course, the foot of each of our beds protruded from the alcove, leaving but a narrow aisle between the two rows, so it was easy to stub one's toe or bruise one's shin when wandering in the dark. Still, we had the illusion of personal chambers, a grand extravagance for youths of our station.

Moreover, it had been the relative privacy of our sleeping quarters that had allowed me to maintain my male disguise for these many months. Each morning before the sun rose, I used the shadowed alcove to my advantage, secretly donning the corset that flattened my female curves before putting my tunic over it. And, every night, I performed the same ritual in reverse, removing the rough garment again under cover of darkness. I dared not guess how I might have managed such a deception had several of us been tumbled together into a single bed like a litter of pups.

Climbing beneath my thin wool blanket, I reached beneath my tunic and swiftly untied the corset lacings; then, shrugging out of the offending garment, I tucked it beneath my pillow and breathed a sigh of relief. But, not surprisingly, sleep proved elusive this night.

I was not the only one to lie restlessly upon my cot. I could hear around me the muffled sounds of shifting bedcovers, along with the occasional sigh or sob, quickly suppressed. Under cover of darkness, I allowed myself my own silent flurry of hot tears in memory of my friend. Tears finally spent, I found myself staring up at the narrow windows set high along the storeroom's outer wall.

I watched as the dozen slim fingers of moonlight that had thrust their way into the room retreated once more with the passing minutes. I dared not shut my eyes, lest I see Constantin's pale face before me. Neither did I wish to sleep, for I feared I would see his death played out before me again in my dreams. And so I fought slumber for what felt like hours.

I must have been defeated in that battle, however, for sometime later I jerked awake from dreamless slumber to realize someone stood in the darkness beside my cot.

My first thought was that it must be the Master. In times past, when we'd had other murders to solve, he'd often awakened me in the middle of the night to accompany him on some secret errand or another. But the shadow looming beside me was not his . . . was not one that I recognized.

Abruptly, I recalled the mysterious robed figure. Was he the murderer of Constantin? Had he found me here, among my sleeping fellows, and even now was prepared to butcher me in the same way?

But before panic took full hold, the figure softly called, "Dino, are you awake?"

"Tito?" I replied in an uncertain whisper, recognizing the speaker's voice though he still stood cloaked in shadow. "It's late. What do you want?"

"I must talk to you."

His tone held a note of urgency, and as he leaned toward me, I caught a glimpse of his pockmarked features in the ribbon of moonlight that lay over my cot. His mouth turned downward in grim lines rather than rising in the usual casual smile he always affected. I was reminded of his reaction earlier this night, when the Master had announced the news of Constantin's murder. Tito's reaction then had struck me as odd, but now his manner was far stranger.

Abruptly, I sat up in bed. Tito occasionally served the same role as I had once with Leonardo, assisting him with secret projects and confidential errands. Perhaps he knew something about recent events that I was not yet privy to. Perhaps the Master's absence earlier this night had signaled something far more ominous than I had been willing to believe!

"What's wrong? Did something else happen?" I demanded in a soft, urgent voice, trying to tamp down the sudden alarm that swept me.

Tito shook his head. "Nothing else has happened . . . That is, not yet."

His soft tone dropped lower still, so that I strained to hear his last words. "Please, come outside with me for a bit. I—I must confess to you about Constantin's murder."

"Constantin's murder!"

Wrapping my blanket about my shoulders—I dared not take time to don my corset beneath my tunic—I hurried after Tito through the darkened workshop. I judged from the cold hearth and the angle of the moonlight seeping through the windows that it was well after midnight. None of the other apprentices stirred; nor, when we slipped out of the workshop door and into the chill night air, did I see a light burning anywhere near.

My heart pounded like a smith's hammer in my chest as I followed Tito across the shadowed quadrangle. What reason he might have had for killing our friend, I could not fathom. Nor could I guess where he might have found the crossbow to do the deed, save that he stole it from the armory.

I bit back a groan. Saints' blood, why was I the one he

had chosen to unburden himself to, rather than the Master? And what would happen once he made his act of contrition? Would he walk meekly to the guard post and give himself up to justice? Or, his conscience relieved on that account, would he murder me, as well, to keep his secret safe?

I glanced up at the parapets that ran along the tops of the walls enclosing the castle grounds. I knew that Il Moro's men patrolled there both day and night, keeping watch for intruders. Given the current political climate, those patrols had recently been redoubled. If I cried out for help, surely the sound of my fearful appeal would carry across the silent grounds and reach the soldiers.

The question was, would they be able to respond to my summons in time to preserve my life?

Tito halted at a spot near the kitchens, not far from where we took our daily meals. The cool night breeze brought with it the sharp, sour odor of rotting garbage from the nearby pile where the kitchen's leavings were routinely discarded. As the sharp odor wafted over me, my already queasy stomach lurched.

With an effort, I suppressed the sick feeling and faced my fellow apprentice, blanket wrapped about me as much for security as for warmth. Perhaps I'd been a fool to follow Tito like this, but my need to know the truth of Constantin's murder had outweighed my good sense. Besides, he carried no weapons that I could tell—surely a crossbow could not fit unnoticed beneath his tunic!—and I was swift enough of foot that I could outrun him, if need be. And so I would hear him out, and then decide what to do next.

Tito, meanwhile, leaned against the wall of the outbuilding, not noticing—or else not caring—that the stone was damp and the night chill. His arms were crossed over his chest, while his head dropped in resignation. I waited for him to speak; then, when he remained disinclined to say his piece, I forgot my earlier uneasiness and succumbed to annoyance.

"Tito, it is late, and I am cold. Quickly, confess your crime and be done with it," I snapped, my patience at an end.

He looked up, startled.

"Crime? I did not murder Constantin, if that is what you are thinking!" came his sharp protest.

Now it was my turn to look surprised.

"I do not understand. What is it that you have come to confess, if it is not that you cruelly murdered our friend?"

He did not answer at once but spared a glance around us. Seemingly assured that no one would step from the kitchen at this untoward hour to scrape out the cooking pots, he answered, "I did not wish to tell anyone, not even the Master, but my conscience would not let me rest. I thought perhaps if I talked to you . . ."

He paused to take a deep breath, and then went on. "Yesterday, I spoke with Constantin after our morning meal. He appeared upset over something—nay, almost frightened—and I was concerned, for he'd been in that state for several days. But he refused to say what ailed him, no matter that I prodded him for answers. Finally, I grew angry."

His tone grew more somber. "My words were harsh as I parted company with him, but I did not care. I watched him walk toward the garden where you and your father labored with the Master, while I started back to the chapel where the rest of us were working. That was the last time I saw Constantin alive."

I sighed.

"If that is all that weighs upon your conscience, then you have no cause for guilt," I replied with a sympathetic shake of my head. "No matter that your last words with him were spoken in anger, Constantin would have known that you did not mean your unkindness, that you were truly his friend."

"But if I had been his friend, Dino, I would not have let him go alone to his death."

His gaze was level with mine now, and his tone was thick with condemnation . . . but whether that emotion was for me or for himself, I was not certain as he spoke again.

"I know it was not bandits who killed Constantin, as the Master claimed. No, do not try to persuade me otherwise," he added when I opened my mouth to protest. "You see, I regretted my words almost as soon as they were spoken, and so I went after him to beg his pardon. I had just reached the garden, when I heard his cry for help."

"Tito, do you mean that you witnessed what happened?"

He shook his head, dashing my fledgling hopes that this crime might now be solved.

"I heard him call out; then, when I saw no one nearby, I decided I must have imagined it and thought simply to wait for him. A few minutes later, I saw you and the Master and your father rush from the garden. But when Constantin did not follow after, I grew alarmed. The gate to the garden was locked, and so I climbed the wall for a look."

He paused again, and then his voice broke. "I—I saw Constantin lying on the ground, dead, and I knew it was my fault. I knew he had been frightened of . . . someone. If I had put aside my anger and insisted on coming with him, perhaps none of this would have happened. Or, at the very least, perhaps I would have glimpsed the villain responsible."

He fell silent at that last, and for a long moment no words passed between us. Now I understood his odd reaction when the Master had told us what had happened. Like me, he had felt grief . . . but, like me, he had not been surprised at Leonardo's words, for he already knew that Constantin was dead. His anger had reflected his struggle with his own feelings of guilt at what he had—and had not—done.

"Tito, listen to me. You could not have known what would happen," I assured him. "The fault lies only with the foul murderer, and no one else. You should not take on blame, any more than should I."

"I—I cannot help it," he shot back, swiping the back of his hand across his eyes. "And I don't understand why the Master pretends that Constantin was killed by bandits, rather than there in the garden."

I hesitated, tempted to explain the Master's reasoning as best I could, given that Tito already knew the truth of much of what had happened. But recalling the vow of secrecy that my father and I had taken, I stubbornly shook my head.

"Tito, you know I cannot speak of things that the Master has told me in confidence."

"Bah, it does not matter," he softly cried, "for I know what this is about. All of us apprentices know that he and your father are secretly building a flying machine. What else can be happening but that someone is trying to steal Leonardo's plans for it and sell them to Il Moro's enemies? I'm right, am I not? And, somehow, Constantin was caught in the middle of it."

His chin jutted toward me, his manner now at once fearful and aggressive. Unwilling to engage him while he was caught in the throes of such emotions, I wrapped my blanket more tightly about me and turned on my heel.

"I can say no more, Tito," I called back to him. "Now, let us return to the workshop, and tomorrow you can ask whatever you wish of the Master."

I did not look to see if he followed after me. Indeed, I hoped he did not, for I needed time to consider what he'd revealed. The fact that Tito claimed that Constantin had been distraught for several days was telling. Certainly, it was something that the Master must know.

As I approached the darkened workshop again, I glanced

at the windows of Leonardo's private quarters. As when Tito and I had first stepped out into the night, no light burned there. I pictured my father fast asleep within and wondered if the Master had ever returned from whatever errand had taken him from us. He had said he was to arrange for Constantin's burial, but surely that had taken only a brief conversation with the priest.

Despite myself, I could not help a niggling sense of worry. While I knew that Leonardo could hold his own in a fight—to be sure, I had seen firsthand his surprising competence with a blade—that did not mean he could not be taken unawares. As I climbed back into my own bed once again, I could only pray that he was ensconced safely somewhere and not in the grip of the mysterious robed figure who might well be Constantin's killer.

The next day passed soberly as we spent the morning putting the first layers of plaster upon the chapel walls. To my relief, Leonardo had appeared in the main workshop as we were climbing from our cots. I was glad to see his midnight excursions had not brought him any harm, for he looked hale and hearty; still, the solemn set to his features reflected the grief we all were feeling. He himself took on Constantin's role of assigning tasks and directing our progress, wisely leaving us no leisure to dwell upon our loss.

We applied ourselves to the work with great diligence, and not just because the Master was supervising our labors. Instead, it seemed an unspoken agreement that we should do our very best work upon this particular fresco. In that way, Constantin would be proud should he gaze down on us from the heavens in between plastering and painting his very own portion of eternity.

We halted our work earlier than usual, pulling on clean tunics to make the sad journey by foot along the rocky path to the churchyard outside town. It was a familiar trek to a spot that held far too many grievous memories for me. How many more times, I bitterly wondered, would I be forced to make this journey while I lived here in Milan?

Paolo, Davide, Tommaso, and Vittorio shouldered the bier upon which Constantin, wearing his apprentice's tunic, lay wrapped in a simple shroud. The rest of us, along with Leonardo and my father and those castle servants who'd also been Constantin's friends, followed after. I smiled a little through my tears, however, when I glanced back and saw that a final mourner had joined our sad procession.

The small hound, Pio, had roused himself from his usual afternoon nap and now trailed a short distance behind us. He seemed to understand both the solemnity and the purpose of the occasion, for he did not indulge in his usual antics. Instead, he marched with the high-stepping grace characteristic of his breed, keeping dignified pace with us as we headed in the direction of the burial grounds.

As Constantin had no family in Milan to witness this final stop in his earthly journey, we apprentices and Leonardo stood in for his siblings and parent. It was a short service, little more than the bored muttering of the priest who had been pressed into service at the cost of a few coins. Even so, I was swept by melancholy as I listened to the familiar Latin prayers and unashamedly clutched my father's hand. I had come to regard Constantin as a dear friend during these past many months, and I would sincerely mourn his absence in my life.

But it wasn't until we returned to the workshop that the finality of Constantin's death was made clear. Calling us together, Leonardo announced that he had chosen a new senior apprentice to take Constantin's place.

"I have decided upon Davide," he said, giving that youth an encouraging nod.

Davide squared his shoulders and stepped forward. "Master, I am humbled by your trust in me," he replied as the rest of us murmured our approval, "and I shall endeavor to be as fair and diligent in my duties as our fallen friend."

"I have every confidence in your abilities," Leonardo answered with a small smile. "And now, your first job shall be to lead your fellows to the evening meal, after which there are many tasks here in the workshop to finish before you take to your beds this night."

We obediently gathered up our bowls and spoons and, led by Davide, trudged from the workshop toward the kitchen. By then, the pall that had hung over our emotions had begun to lift, so that we managed a bit of conversation over our stew. Then Paolo shared a humorous anecdote about Constantin, which ended with the latter getting the better of Paolo by the end of the tale.

Paolo's self-deprecating account broke the stern wall of silence we'd unconsciously erected around our friend's memory. One by one the rest of us spoke up with an amusing story or quip about him, with our tears now ones of hilarity as much as sorrow. Thus, by the time our meal was done, our spirits were far lighter than they'd been at the day's start.

But I'd not forgotten my conversation with Tito the night before. Seemingly, neither had he, for he'd managed to keep his distance from me all of this day, avoiding my gaze every time I looked his way. And when I would have spoken to him now as we were gathering our empty bowls for the return to the workshop, I realized he was no longer among our number.

"Tito left some time ago, while Bernardo was telling the story about Constantin stepping into a bucket of plaster," Vittorio said when I questioned him about the other youth's absence. "He told me he did not feel well and that he was going to return to the workshop."

I frowned as I licked my spoon clean and set it into my bowl. I did not wish to doubt Tito, for I knew he had been greatly affected by Constantin's death. Perhaps our return to merriment had happened too quickly for him. And so I kept my suspicions to myself, even when Tito proved not to be in his cot or anywhere about the workshop. It was not until Davide was snuffing the evening's ration of candles that Tito rejoined us, slipping past the door unannounced as if he'd merely been gone to take a piss.

And it was not until morning that I learned just where Tito had been and what he had done while he was gone.

8

The movement of the bird ought always to be above the clouds.

—Leonardo da Vinci, *Manuscript Sul Volo*

"You want Tito to assist you in building the flying machine, instead of me?"

My words incredulous, I stared at the Master. That must have been why Tito had been gone for so long the night before. While the rest of us were mourning and praising our fallen friend, Tito had been busy convincing Leonardo that he should take on what had been my role.

"Have I failed you in some way, Master?" I persisted, trying to keep my feelings of betrayal from coloring my tone. "I have worked diligently and kept my counsel.

"And, besides," I added a bit peevishly, "Signor Angelo is my father and not Tito's. That should count for something."

We were in Leonardo's private chambers, where I had come at his summons first thing upon awakening. I had found him and my father seated at his worktable, the pair of them bent over a sheaf of drawings and notes. The model of the flying machine sat nearby, rakishly draped in green silk.

Leonardo leaned back in his seat and gestured me to take the spot on the bench beside my father.

"My dear boy, pray do not take this as an affront," he said as I settled myself. "I have given the matter due consideration and believe it the best solution for us all."

He paused to make another note on the page before him before continuing. "Tito came to me last night, telling me the same tale that he said he shared with you. His distress was genuine and his arguments persuasive. It is imperative that we complete the flying machine before another such incident happens. Tito is a diligent worker with experience building boats, and he has assisted me in the past with my designs."

Glancing over at my father, he went on. "Signor Angelo and I agree that our model has served its purpose, and that it is time to complete work on the full-sized model. One cannot overlook the fact that Tito is far larger and stronger than you, meaning he is better able to provide the brute force needed. And while I do not question your valor, should another assault occur, he would be better able to defend against it."

I bit my lip lest I blurt out a reminder of the times that I *had* been forced to defend myself against an assailant or even leap to the Master's aid when he himself was under attack. How could he forget that I'd survived being stabbed and left for dead inside a locked burial vault, had stood unarmed against sword-wielding assailants, and had escaped a deadly fire unscathed? Yet I dared not speak of these dramatic events before my father, lest he whisk me from Milan faster than a hawk could swoop upon a helpless rabbit.

Instead, I glanced at my parent in silent supplication, hoping he would see the injustice of this arrangement, but he merely shook his head.

"I fear I must concur with Signor Leonardo on this matter. Work on the full-sized model will require strength that a young, er, boy such as you may not possess."

Unspoken was what I knew must be foremost on his mind: his fear that this project held dangers far greater than a dropped plank upon one's toe or a hammer connecting with an unsuspecting thumb. And while I understood his concern, that did not lessen the sting I felt at his words.

My dismay at this dual perfidy must have been apparent, for Leonardo gave me a kind smile.

"All is not lost, my dear Dino," he pronounced with a grand sweep of his hand. "You see, I have not forgotten my words to you from several days earlier. Once the plastering for the new fresco is complete and the outlines of the stencils pounced, you will pick up a brush and work with Paolo and Davide in painting the background."

Once, such an announcement from the Master would have brought me to my knees all but weeping in gratitude. Now I managed little more than a grudging, "I shall be glad to assist them," before making my bows and rushing out the door.

My unsettled humors were further stirred when I almost stumbled over Tito as he was leaving the main workshop. I halted and favored him with a sour look.

"I am surprised you do not fare better when playing dice," I told him, "given your skill in tossing words so that they readily tumble your way."

He did not pretend not to understand my words. Indeed, he had the good grace to look ashamed, if his tone when he replied held a note of defiance.

"I did not mean to replace you, Dino, only to join you in helping the Master with the flying machine. And I will not deny that I would like to gain some of the fame for my part in building it. But you must believe me that my motives go far beyond any glory I might earn."

He paused and gave the familiar glance about him, as if fearing eavesdroppers. "As I told you, I cannot help but worry that the Master may be in danger, after what happened to Constantin. I may have failed our friend, but I vow I shall not fail Leonardo in the same way. He does not know it, but my true plan is to serve as his personal man-at-guard."

At that, he reached beneath his tunic and whipped out a knife that I had never before seen him carry. The straight, sharp blade appeared finely crafted and was one such as gentlemen wore about town for protection . . . hardly a weapon that an apprentice might own, let alone be able to wield.

It was my turn to gaze about lest anyone be within sight or hearing of us. Eying the weapon with mingled admiration and alarm, I asked in a low tone, "Tito, where ever did you find such a knife?"

"My uncle gave it to me. He was a soldier, and he told me every man should have a weapon lest he be taken unawares when danger threatens."

Tossing his unruly black hair from his eyes, he sliced the blade through the air before him as if dispatching an imaginary attacker. Then, to my relief, he hid the knife beneath his tunic once more.

"Don't worry. I can use it," he said with a shrug. "But the Master would forbid me to carry such a weapon, and so I shall keep it hidden. You will not tell him, will you?"

For a single unworthy moment, I considered doing just that. By exposing Tito's secret, I might gain back my role as assistant in this project. Despite the fact that he had been hired by Il Moro to build weapons of war, Leonardo loathed violence and disapproved of carrying arms.

On the other hand, I had seen him wield a sword when

danger threatened and knew he was not foolish enough to let his scruples override the safety of those around him . . . including himself. And, in truth, I would feel better knowing that both the Master and my father had someone with them as they worked who could serve as protector.

Thus, I shook my head.

"I shall say nothing, so long as you swear you will tell me everything that happens each day as you work," I agreed. "And you must tell me if you see anyone acting suspiciously near the Master or my father, so that I may help you to keep an eye on that person."

I thought again of the mysterious robed figure that had spied upon me at the parade grounds and perhaps later as I'd searched for Constantin's killer in the quadrangle. If that person still lurked about Castle Sforza, I had not seen him again. Perhaps those strange sightings had been but a coincidence, merely a visitor who had gone about his true business and was long departed from the castle grounds.

Tito and I parted with a polite enough clasp of our hands, though I admit with some shame that I still struggled with my resentment. And I was further mollified later in the day when, quite unexpectedly, my father appeared in the chapel and summoned me to one side.

"Your master took young Tito with him to purchase more fabric for the wings," he whispered, so that none of the others could hear. "While they are away, perhaps you would care to come see this grand machine of his."

The shed where the flying machine was stored lay not far from the stables. Pulling a large key from his pouch, my father unfastened the heavy lock that barred the pair of large doors. He opened one just wide enough for us to slip inside and then pulled the doors shut behind us. I barely noticed his actions, for I was staring in awe at the full-sized craft in the center of the shed's dirt floor.

More correctly, it was the body of the flying machine that sat propped up on a trio of wooden supports. The skeletal framework of wings lay to one side, one already covered in linen and the other still bare. The body was longer than I'd expected it to be, perhaps twice my length with the blunt little tail included. Though it was of deceptively simple design, my artist's eye could see now that much thought had gone into creating a craft of graceful yet practical lines. Once the finished wings were attached, it would be a magnificent sight, indeed! And if it could truly be made to fly—

"Oh, Father, would it not be wonderful to be the one who piloted this craft about the clouds," I cried, envying the Master the opportunity he would have.

My father shrugged. "I prefer to keep my feet firmly on the ground," he replied, though I sensed he, too, had begun to see the possibilities of Leonardo's invention.

And so I returned to my labors in far better humor than when I'd started the day. My feelings toward Tito were again amicable when he joined the rest of us outside the kitchen for the evening meal.

Once we finished our usual stew and started back toward the workshop, he contrived to fall several paces behind the others. With an almost imperceptible twitch of his head, he gestured me to join him.

"We made quite good progress," he confided, leaning close enough so that I could smell the garlic from the evening's meal upon his breath. His pockmarked features reflected far greater cheer than they had in many days as he went on. "We have almost completed the machine's body, though Master Leonardo declared that the pedal mechanism needs adjustment."

He described their progress in a bit more detail and finished, "And I saw nothing amiss . . . No one spied upon us or appeared unduly interested in our work."

He paused to assume a swaggering manner, putting a hand to the breast of his tunic, under which I was certain was hidden his knife. "Of course, I was ready for any trouble."

"Of course," I echoed, torn between relief and dismay at this show of bravado. Had he ever actually faced someone intent on robbing him of his life, I wondered, or was his only experience that of slashing at imaginary foes?

Something of my doubt must have shown upon my face, for he frowned and added, "Fear not, Dino. I swear that should anyone attempt to harm the Master or your father, I will gladly lay down my life to protect them."

By then, we had reached the workshop, so I had time for but a grateful nod before we rejoined the others. While an air of solemnity still hung over our small band, the mood was lighter than the evening before. Once our usual nighttime tasks were complete—new brushes from boar bristles and weasel hair carefully tied, charred sticks ground to black powder for pouncing stencils, new wood panels sanded for later use by the Master in his painting—Davide called a halt to our labors.

"Tommaso, perhaps you will play your lute for us tonight," he suggested.

Tommaso obliged by fetching the battered instrument and strumming a few chords. This was Paolo's cue to pull out his dice. Within a few moments, an affable game of chance had commenced near the glowing hearth, with the youths eagerly wagering bits of broken pottery in place of the coins that we, as mere apprentices, lacked.

I could not help but be cheered by these signs that our collective heart, while still sorely wounded, had begun to mend. The humble Constantin would not have wanted us to mourn him unduly, I was sure. And so I joined Tommaso in a song about a page who cleverly bested every noble he encountered. Once I was certain the others were engrossed in their amusement, however, I pretended a need for the privy and slipped out of the workshop.

My knock at Leonardo's private quarters was tentative as I recalled my graceless leave-taking from them that morning; still, I knew that my embarrassment was mine alone. My father would already have forgiven my sulky manner, and I suspected that the Master had long since forgotten our exchange. I had no chance to confirm that last, however, for it was the former and not Leonardo who answered my summons.

"It's good you have come," my father declared as he thrust his head out into the night. His quick glance in either direction reminded me of Tito's similar gesture.

Apparently satisfied that no spies lurked about, he motioned me inside and with a firm hand closed the door behind me. His expression was one of worry as he took a seat at Leonardo's worktable. A few pages of notes lay scattered there. He moved them aside along with the now-empty bowl that had held his stew, and I noticed that but a single evening's repast had been eaten. The Master's usual spot was conspicuously empty.

The bed was unoccupied, as well, the blankets stretched neatly across it and Pio lying curled upon the Master's pillow. He opened a sleepy eye; then, apparently deciding that slumber was preferable to greeting a late visitor, he yawned and settled back to sleep again.

Gesturing me to sit, my father began, "I wondered how to send word to you without drawing the notice of your fellows. Does anyone else know you are here? Good," he replied when I shook my head. "You must keep what I tell you a secret from all of them, including your friend Tito."

It was my turn to frown as I saw that no candlelight glowed from beneath the closed door that led to Leonardo's private workshop. If the Master was neither here in his quarters nor toiling in his workshop, perhaps he was still locked away in the storehouse with his flying machine. That, or he'd set off on yet another nocturnal adventure. But why should his absence this particular night seemingly have caused my father dismay?

My own uneasiness growing, I demanded, "What is going on, Father? Has something happened to the Master?"

"Fear not. Signor Leonardo is well," he was quick to assure me. "But his concern over the murder of young Constantin was such that he has set off on a mission this very night. While he did not divulge his destination, he confided that his plan is to ride to the spot where the duke and the French king's representatives are meeting. Leonardo intends to inform his patron what has happened here at the castle in his absence."

My eyes widened. Still, the news was not surprising, though it was somewhat disconcerting. The Master had always been a man to take matters into his own hands. If he feared Constantin's murder was but the beginning of some larger violence to come, surely he felt duty-bound to stop it if he could. And if that meant bringing Il Moro back to Milan, he would somehow contrive to do so.

But what if he encountered Constantin's assassin while traveling along the road to this rendezvous?

I'd not forgotten the possibility the Master had raised that the bolt that had struck down Constantin was of foreign make. The Master—and perhaps even the duke himself— might be risking assassination by consorting with the French! As my worry would serve no good purpose, however, I contented myself with a swift, silent prayer for Leonardo's safety and addressed my father.

"What is to happen with the flying machine in the Master's absence? Shall you and Tito continue to work on it?"

"Our work will progress, yes, for it is in everyone's interest that we complete this cursed project sooner than later," he said with unaccustomed heat. "And if we are all quite fortunate, the design will prove flawed, and that will put an end to Leonardo's folly."

Tempering with a hint of a smile that irate reference to the popular name for the Master's rumored invention, he added, "Before he left, I asked Signor Leonardo that you be allowed to put aside your work on the fresco and return to assist Tito and me. He saw the wisdom of another set of hands and agreed you should rejoin us."

Rather than being pleased, however, I frowned at his words. "Father, this makes little sense. A day ago, both you and the Master insisted that I was too weak for such labors, and that the work was far too dangerous. How can you have changed your mind in so short a time?"

"Ah, you have been around these boys for far too long that you speak with such disrespect," he replied, though his rebuke held more amusement than outrage. "Each day you remind me more and more of your mother."

His tone grew serious again as he went on. "And you are right. Perhaps it is safer for you to remain among your fellows, with a crowd offering more protection than two or three. But with your master gone for the time being, I feel better knowing you are nearby. Besides which"—the twinkle reappeared in his eyes—"working as my assistant will give you the opportunity to learn if your brothers' laments all these years were justified or but an excuse for their laziness."

I could not help but smile a little at that last. "I promise I shall tell you truthfully. But what shall we say to Tito when he sees me instead of Leonardo with you?"

"Young Tito is but the apprentice and I the master," my father reminded me in a firm tone. "He shall be satisfied with whatever I tell him. Now, give your father a kiss good night, and be off with you."

I did as instructed, my embrace rather longer than usual as I gave silent thanks that it was Leonardo and not he riding the dark roads in search of Il Moro.

"Return here first thing when you awaken, and we will walk together to the shed where the machine is stored," he called after me as I started out the door. "We shall begin work with the lark and end with the owl."

Nodding, I made my pensive way the few steps' journey back to the main workshop and rejoined the other apprentices. Tommaso's lute continued to lend a cheery accompaniment to the dice game, which still progressed with great enthusiasm. Tito was among the players, appearing engrossed in the game. I wondered if he had noted my absence and guessed where I had gone. If so, he gave no indication as I leaned closer to see whose fortune was proving better this night.

Too soon, as always, the evening's ration of candles began to gutter. With that, Davide decreed, "To bed, everyone."

Tommaso played a few final notes and then put away his lute. Paolo, meanwhile, had pocketed his dice as his fellow gamblers tucked away their night's winnings of jewel-toned shards. While Davide snuffed the remaining wax stubs, I spared a moment to advise him of the Master's change of plans for me. The senior apprentice added his agreement; then, our way lit by the faint red glow from the hearth, he herded us toward the sleeping alcove.

As I passed by Tito, he gave me a friendly nod but made no comment, for which I was grateful. I was in no mood for idle conversation; neither would I sleep easy this night . . . not while the Master likely lay wrapped in a cold blanket somewhere in the dark hills of the duchy while we apprentices rested comfortably in our beds.

But despite my vow of restless slumber, I fell asleep quickly and awakened as daylight began to seep over the horizon. The other apprentices would not stir for several minutes more; thus, I moved with silence as I donned my confining corset and pulled on a clean tunic. After making my swift ablutions, I laced up my jerkin against the morning's chill and hurried the short distance to the Master's quarters to meet my father.

I was reaching out to knock upon that door when I realized it hung uncharacteristically ajar.

"Father?" I called, disquiet sweeping me.

I gave the door a cautious push inward and looked inside. The chamber was unchanged from the night before, the same empty bowl and stack of notes spread upon the table. Pio continued his peaceful slumber upon the bed, stretched at full length with his thin legs stuck out well past the pillow's edges. But the covers beneath the small hound were still neatly laid, so that it appeared Pio alone had claimed the cot for the entire night.

Of my father, there was no sign.

My heart began a frantic rhythm in my chest as I tried to assure myself that his absence meant nothing. Perhaps he had fallen asleep over his notes and never made it to bed. And perhaps he had risen earlier than I and stepped out into the cool morning air to clear his head, and he would be returning any moment. Or maybe he had forgotten his request that I walk with him and was waiting for me at the shed, wondering at my delay.

Or maybe, a frightened inner voice suggested, he was lying somewhere with a bolt through his chest, his lifeblood long since seeped into the ground beneath him.

I gave my head an angry shake to dismiss that last grue-some thought. "Don't be foolish . . . He's here somewhere," I muttered, my clipped words drawing an answering snore from the sleeping hound.

At least I need have no worries on Pio's account. Vittorio would stop by to make certain that he had food and water, after which he'd allow the hound out to lift his leg upon the nearby wall before following the apprentices to their work site. And, soon enough, I told myself, I would be listening to my father laughing softly as I confessed my moment of folly in thinking him vanished like a mist.

Assuming an air of confidence I did not truly feel, I closed the door behind me and set off across the quadrangle in search of my father.

9

Excess of wind puts out flame, moderate wind nourishes it.

—Leonardo da Vinci, *Codex Atlanticus*

After a thorough search of seemingly every place but Il Moro's own bedchamber, I came to the alarming conclusion that Angelo della Fazia was missing from the castle grounds.

My first stop had been the shed where the half-built flying machine was stored like a prize bull. The hasp and lock that held the oversized doors shut still were secure, so I could not guess if anything was amiss. And as those twin doors were the sole entry, the only way my father could have been within was if someone had locked him inside the shed.

Feeling foolish, I called his name through a gap in the sturdy planks. I heard no reply, nor, when I put my eye to that same crack, could I see anything other than shadows, for the lanterns that had brightened the place the day before were unlit.

Afterward, I'd tried the kitchen, and the privies, and

even climbed the wall of the ill-fated garden to see if perhaps he'd had some excuse to return there. He'd been in none of those places nor any other in which I had looked. And when I'd questioned a few passing servants regarding his whereabouts—my father was a recognizable figure, thanks to his association with Leonardo—none recalled seeing him this particular morning.

Wild explanations for his absence began to tumble through my mind, and it was all I could do to make it back to the workshop without giving way to panic. I imagined my father lying in a far corner of the castle ground—ill, or perhaps injured—and unable to call for help. I pictured him encountering a crossbow-wielding assailant and chasing him past the castle gates, to lose him in the maze of streets and canals that was the city of Milan. Or, worse, I saw him catching up to the assassin in some shady back lane, with no witnesses to what happened next!

I gave my head a rough shake to clear it of such frightening visions. The simplest reason for my father's disappearance was that he had purposely departed the castle grounds, perhaps intent on purchasing some new tool for his project. Maybe he had left behind a note of explanation for me, which I had overlooked in my haste. Certainly, that made more sense than any other scenario my frantic mind had conjured.

But how to explain why he would have left the door to Leonardo's quarters open for anyone to walk inside?

If the Master were here, he would know what to do, I thought in despair. But he was riding about the duchy—who knew exactly where?—and might not be back for days. Worse, I was beginning to suspect that my father's disappearance must somehow be tied to Leonardo's absence.

I had retraced my footsteps to Leonardo's private quarters, the door of which still was securely latched. I peered past the

single window and saw that Pio no longer lounged upon the
bed, meaning that Vittorio must have already collected him.
I turned to head back to the main workshop, intent on seeing
if any of the other apprentices was still there, when for the
second time in as many days, I all but tripped over Tito.

"There you are!" I cried in mingled surprise and relief,
having all but forgotten him in my worry. At least he also
had not vanished strangely in the night.

Then I frowned.

"Why are you here?" I demanded, suspicion sweeping me
as I took in his startled expression. "Shouldn't you be at the
shed awaiting my father?"

Just as quickly, it occurred to me that perhaps Tito had
been to the shed and had concluded that Master Angelo had
gone missing. Perhaps he, like I, was searching fruitlessly for
him. Before I could say more, however, the youth's surprised
expression transformed into a look of outright guilt that sent
renewed suspicion through me.

Eyes wide, I grabbed his arm and gave it a rough shake.
"Tell me what's going on, Tito. I can see by your face that you
know something!"

"It's not what you think," he protested as he pulled away,
his cheeks red and his gaze unable to meet mine.

When I made no reply to that, he took a deep breath and
rushed on. "Very well, I shall confess. The Master told me he did
not need me today, and that I should go help work on the fresco,
instead. But since Davide and the others didn't know I was supposed to be with them, I thought to sneak away and spend the
day wandering about the city. I just wanted a bit of fun."

He ran a thin brown hand through his unruly black hair
and slumped onto the bench perched beneath the workshop
window.

"It was a perfect day. The sun had risen, and the sky

looked like one of the Master's frescoes. But I barely made it past the castle gates when I started feeling ashamed at the way that I was trying to deceive the Master. So I came back as fast as I could."

He paused and raised miserable dark eyes to mine. "Truly, Dino, I was on my way to the duke's quarters to join the others. I beg you, don't tell anyone about my transgression."

He must have mistaken my moment of stunned silence for censure, for he dropped his gaze again. But what had stopped me was not his attempt at deceit but his claim that the Master had instructed him not to join my father this day.

How could that be, when Leonardo had left Milan the afternoon before?

"And what of my father?" I demanded, trying to keep my voice from trembling while I waded through the youth's story. "Did he agree that you were not needed this day?"

Tito shrugged. "I assumed that the Master told him."

Then he frowned and looked back up at me again, a hint of resentment coloring his expression. "Why are you asking me all these questions? I already told you that I was in the wrong and that I'm sorry. What's this about?"

I struggled to find some clever way to phrase what I must say next, hoping to trick the youth into an admission . . . if, indeed, he were guilty of something more than shirking his labors. But in the end, I simply blurted, "Tito, he's gone. He's vanished from the castle!"

"What?"

Tito blinked a moment in confusion before breaking into a smile. "Dino, why do you fret? The Master has a habit of leaving when it suits him. Perhaps he went to the city to the workshop he shares with another master. I'm sure he will be back soon, and—"

"No, not Leonardo," I cut him short. "He was already

gone and will be absent for several days. It's my father who is missing!"

"Master Angelo?" Tito's smile vanished like a dove taking flight. "You're certain of this?"

"Of course! Do you think I would make up such a tale for your amusement? Tell me, when did you see him last?"

"Yesterday, before I joined you at the evening meal. Master Angelo and I finished our work for the day and locked the shed, and then we walked back to the workshop together. That was when we parted ways . . . he, to the Master's quarters, and I, to eat."

Hands on hips, I shot him a suspicious look.

"And I saw him later that night, while the rest of you were playing dice," I retorted. "That was when my father told me that Leonardo had left Milan for a few days, and that he'd agreed I should help once more with the flying machine. I was to meet my father here at the Master's workshop. But he was gone when I arrived, and the door was partly open. I've looked all over the castle grounds for him, but no one has seen him."

Those last words trembled suspiciously upon a sob, which I struggled to swallow back. Tito did not notice this slip in my boyish facade, however, for he had leaped from the bench and was peering in the workshop window as if to confirm that what I said was the truth. Then he swung about, jutting his face angrily toward mine.

"You said the Master was gone. What did you mean by that?" he demanded, his pockmarked face flushing darker still.

I hesitated, recalling that my father had sworn me to secrecy regarding Leonardo's abrupt departure. But surely under these circumstances, it could do no harm to reveal to Tito what little I knew.

"He's ridden off to find Il Moro and tell him that Constantin died trying to prevent a plot against all of Milan," I cried most dramatically. "And what of you? You said the Master told you last night that you would not be needed this day . . . and yet how can that be, when the Master had already left the castle when you claimed he spoke to you?"

The question hung between us for a few tense moments before something shifted in Tito's expression. I realized that alarm and not anger now suffused his features.

"It—it wasn't the Master who told me," he admitted in a tight little voice. "It was one of the castle pages who said he had a message for me from Master Leonardo."

I swallowed back the cold bile of fear that rose in my throat at his words.

"That makes no sense, Tito. Why would the Master go to the castle in the middle of the night to rouse a page when he could have wakened you himself? Quickly, tell me all that happened and spare no detail, for it might have some bearing on my father's fate."

He resumed his seat upon the bench, his feet shuffling at the sandy ground beneath them. "It was just after midnight when someone woke me up. At first, I thought it was the Master—you know his habit of summoning us in the night—but it was one of the castle pages. He bade me be silent and follow him outside. He said he had an urgent message from Master Leonardo."

His tone took on a sound of desperation as he went on. "It sounds foolish, in the light of day, but I was still half asleep and I didn't think to question why the Master did not come to me himself. And so I went with the boy."

"What happened afterward?" I prompted him when he hesitated once more.

Tito dropped his face into his hands, so that his words were muffled as he continued. "The page said that Leonardo had told him that some important men—diplomats, perhaps—were to examine the flying machine, but that it must be done under cover of darkness. Since I had one of the keys, I was to meet them there and unlock the door. The page said that the Master would join them later and would relock the shed when they were finished. He also said he was to tell me that Leonardo would not require my assistance the next day."

I stifled a groan at this confession. "Was my father at the shed, or the Master?"

"No, but I did see three men there. They must have been the diplomats."

"These men . . . did you see their faces?"

"Not their faces," he replied in a sorrowful tone, "for they were wrapped in fine cloaks and kept carefully to the shadows. They said nothing, but they gestured me away once I'd unfastened the lock. I—I was a bit nervous by then, so I hurried back to the workshop and took to my bed again."

He lapsed into silence while I took a moment to consider his words. I was certain that these three mysterious men were no more diplomats than were Tito and I. But could one of them be the mysterious robed figure that had spied upon me, or even be the man who had cruelly murdered Constantin? And if none was guilty of those crimes, who had sent them here? And did my father's disappearance have something to do with their arrival?

The cold knot in my stomach tightened as the questions flooded my brain, and I was certain that Constantin's death and my father's disappearance were connected.

"The shed was locked when I tried the door earlier," I recalled, "and I saw nothing amiss, so those three shadow men were careful to leave no sign they'd been there. Had I not gone there searching for my father, I would have had no cause to set foot near the place, at all."

I paused and frowned. "And with the Master gone—and you, Tito, sent to work once more with the other apprentices—it might have been days before anyone looked in the shed again."

The import of what I'd said struck me at the very instant that Tito leaped from the bench again, eyes wide.

"The shed!" he cried. "Quickly, we must check it!"

I made no reply but joined his frantic race across the quadrangle. I dared not give voice to what I dreaded to find behind its locked doors, lest speaking the words make it so.

And yet that was the most logical explanation for my father's strange absence. Perhaps he had awakened in the middle of the night with an idea for the flying machine, and so had gone to the shed to take measurements or carve a bit of wood. And perhaps he had arrived there to find these three mysterious men examining the craft and had confronted them, only to be overcome by their greater number.

I choked on a sob of denial at that last thought, even though I had to admit that this was the most likely scenario. Having overpowered him, it made sense that the men would have left him locked in the shed so that he would not be found for some time, rather than leave him somewhere on the grounds to be discovered at dawn.

The question was, had they abandoned him injured and unconscious, or had he suffered Constantin's same brutal fate?

With a shudder, I quickened my steps in hopes of outrunning the gruesome images that filled my mind. Thus, though Tito's legs were longer than mine, I readily kept apace of him as we neared the secluded spot behind the stables where the shed lay.

We both were gasping for breath by the time we reached the splintered shed and its barred doors.

The heavy lock that dangled from its hasp, once merely

a bit of metal, now represented an ominous portent of the secrets that might well be contained within. Tito fumbled in the pouch at his belt to find the key, to my anxious mind taking far too long to extract it from the small bag. But when he finally reached the key toward the lock, I impulsively stayed his hand.

His black eyes met mine in understanding. So long as the doors to the shed remained locked, we could pretend that whatever might lie behind them had not yet come to pass.

"Don't worry, Dino," he softly assured me. "I'm certain that Master Angelo has come to no harm."

I bit my lip, praying he was right and wondering how I could ever bring such grievous tidings to my mother if he were not. Reminding myself that no amount of wishing could change the outcome, I brusquely nodded.

"Open it, Tito."

He hurried to fit the key and in a single swift move twisted it so that the lock fell open. Removing the lock from the hasp, he pulled open one door, and the other, until they were spread wide enough so that he and I could walk abreast as we stepped inside the dark structure.

For the first few moments, the contrast between the sunlight and shadow was such that the shed appeared to be but a yawning black mouth. I squinted into the darkness, not daring to call out my father's name while I anxiously scanned the shadows for a huddled shape . . . a sprawled form.

And as our eyes adjusted to the dimness, we saw what it was that those doors had been hiding.

"The flying machine," Tito cried. "It's gone!"

10

Danger gives even the smallest bird swift wings.

—Leonardo da Vinci, *The Notebooks of Delfina della Fazia*

Tito's shout echoing in my ears, I rushed to the spot where I had seen the half-built craft but the day before. Now nothing but the wooden supports remained. The body of the flying machine, as well as the skeletal framework of wings, had vanished. The only sign that the craft had ever been there was the ring of wood shavings that had surrounded it. The once-neat circle had been scattered by booted feet, however, and was bisected by what appeared to be wagon wheel tracks.

Nor was my father anywhere within the small building. Relief swept me as I finally could admit to my worst fear, that he had fallen victim to some villain as Constantin had. But despair returned with equal swiftness. If not here, where was he? And, almost as important, who had taken Leonardo's glorious invention?

Regrettably, the how of it was all too apparent.

I could see the look of anguish on Tito's face as he realized that he had been deceived into allowing some unknown men to carry away what could have become Milan's most powerful weapon . . . a weapon that now might be used against her. Though, of course, how could anyone without the proper drawings and knowledge hope to complete such a sophisticated piece of machinery? Unless—

"They must have taken my father, along with the flying machine," I gasped out.

"Tito, don't you see? A half-built craft would be no good on its own. Whoever took it would need someone who could finish building it, who could explain how to fly it . . . and who could make more like it! They must have planned to kidnap the Master but took my father instead. For how could they have known that Leonardo had left upon a secret mission, when not even you were aware of it?"

"Dino, your words make great sense," Tito declared, though his expression remained doleful. "Master Angelo resembles Master Leonardo, and he was staying in his quarters. If these villains had but a general description of the man they were to kidnap, it would be an easy mistake for them to make."

"But who has him? Where have they taken my father?"

With that cry, I snatched off my wool cap and wrung it between my hands. Much as I wished to berate Tito for his terrible folly, I knew giving way to anger would do nothing to help us find either my father or Leonardo's invention. What we needed were cool minds and logical reasoning of the sort that the Master always employed.

But Tito was already ahead of me. His expression one of grim resolve, he rushed to the doors and pulled them open as far as they would go. Now enough sunlight spilled in to brighten all but the farthest corners of the shed. He returned and, sidestepping what appeared to be a fresh pile of horse droppings, knelt beside the disheveled wood shavings.

"Look," he exclaimed, pointing to the same tracks I had earlier noticed. "These wheel marks were not here yesterday. And see how far apart they're spaced? Of course, those men would have required something much larger than a cart to carry off the flying machine.

"And here."

While I was busy stepping off the distance between the two marks, Tito had risen to indicate a portion of the floor just inside the doors. "Look at the way the smooth dirt has been chopped up, as if by hooves. Surely there were two horses here, if not more."

Spotting yet another fragrant pile of manure, I had to agree with that last. Though I was impressed by his skill at deduction—indeed, his reasoning was worthy of the Master—my anger did not allow for anything more than a grudging nod of approval.

"But that tells us nothing other than that we are looking for a large wagon pulled by at least a pair of horses."

With a snort of disgust to hide the trembling of my lips, I once more donned my battered cap and marched over to where Tito stood. "We can learn nothing more from this empty shed," I decreed. "What is important is discovering the identities of those three men. Once we know that, we can better guess at their direction. Surely that page who summoned your last night would be of some help. Tell me, what did he look like? Would you recognize him if you saw him again?"

Tito's look of misery returned. "I—I'm not sure. It was dark. He was a page."

"Then we shall search out all the pages until we find the right one," I shot back and grabbed him by the elbow. "Hurry, and be sure to lock the shed behind us."

To my relief, he sighed and nodded.

"You must hate me, Dino, and I cannot blame you," he said as he pulled the doors closed again. "All that has happened is my fault. But I swear I will do everything in my power to help find your father."

I heard the grim purpose in those humble words, and my anger eased enough for me to give him an encouraging nod in return. "Surely you will remember something of significance. But let's take another look at the Master's quarters first, lest I overlooked a clue there."

"And we must ask the guards at the gates if a wagon tried to leave in the dark of last night," he suggested as we started at an urgent pace across the quadrangle once more.

Tito had claimed he'd never seen the faces of the three men; still, I was careful to scan the faces of every man I passed, lest one appear out of place. So intent was I on my task, however, that I did not see the familiar bulky figure of one particular female until it was too late.

Broad brown skirts and cape billowing, Rebecca the washerwoman swooped upon us like a ragged hen as we approached the workshop.

"Aha," she proclaimed in satisfaction. "I have found some errant mice, out playing in the field while the cat is napping."

Before we could protest, she had wrapped a beefy arm around both of our necks and was hugging us to her ample breast. "Does your master know that you are wandering about the castle grounds instead of laboring with your fellows?" she demanded, her cheeky grin belying her severe tone.

Tito was the first to extricate himself from her formidable grasp. With an offended air, he tugged at his tunic hem to straighten that garment again and slapped a quick hand to his chest—checking, I was sure, to make certain that his knife had not been dislodged by this assault.

"We are on Master Leonardo's business," he retorted, drawing himself up so that he towered over her by almost half a head. "Pray, step aside and let us pass by."

"Here, what sort of attitude is that for a young man to take with a lady?" the washerwoman shot back, her dark brows knitting in displeasure. Then, her pique vanishing as quickly as it had come, she added with a return of her grin, "You should take lessons from your young friend Dino. He knows how to speak like a gentleman, do you not, my boy?"

I had succeeded in escaping the older woman's genial embrace and was busy straightening my disheveled cap. Another time, I would have been pleased to engage her in banter; today, however, the seriousness of our current situation left me with nothing but blunt words.

"Good day, signora," I replied with a quick nod. "I fear that Tito is right. We are on a mission for the Master and cannot tarry. Please excuse us."

"And I am here to gather Master Leonardo's laundry . . . and perhaps have a few words with young Dino's handsome father," she added with a broad wink in Tito's direction.

Surveying the youth up and down, she added, "Course, I wouldn't say no to a bit of fun with a younger man, either."

While Tito blushed in equal parts anger and embarrassment at this ribald remark—for, admittedly, he was a comely enough youth if one overlooked his unfortunate complexion—I was eying Rebecca for quite different reasons.

The soft brown wool cloak she wore was far finer than the rest of her clothing, which was as rough-spun as she. Its fabric had been cut from a smoothly woven bolt, its edges hemmed in flamboyant blue thread in a distinctive stitch. But most important was the fact that I had seen this particular garment enough times to be certain of its true owner, no matter whose back it covered.

"That's my father's cloak you are wearing," I cried, clenching my fingers into fists lest I forget myself and snatch it off her where she stood. "My mother made it for him; I would recognize her work anywhere. Quickly, where did you find it?"

"What, this rag?" came the washerwoman's coy response as she preened a little, stroking its smooth lines. Then, seeing the determination in my face, she shrugged.

"Oh, very well, I found it upon the road as I was heading into the city at daybreak. But you know what they say. Something lost belongs to the finder, and bad fortune to the loser. Besides, how was I to guess it belonged to Signor Angelo? If I left it there in the road, someone else would have snatched it up."

"What road?" Tito broke in, his words as urgent as mine.

She gestured vaguely. "Toward the south, near the stream outside town where all the women do their washing. But what does it matter?" she added with a sigh. "I'll find another old rag to wrap myself in. Here, take it back."

Her expression one of martyrdom, she unfastened the cloak and tossed it to me. I hugged the garment tightly, breathing in my father's familiar scent, overlaid by the faint if persistent tang of onions that always accompanied Rebecca. Tears having nothing to do with onions pooled in my eyes, and I rubbed a brusque hand across my face to dash them away lest she notice. Unfortunately, I was not swift enough, for she peered at me with keen interest.

"Here, is something wrong?" The black brows dipped ominously, almost touching the bridge of her crooked nose. "Has something happened to Signor Angelo?"

Tito and I exchanged quick glances, and he nodded. I knew what he was thinking, that Rebecca might well be our best source of information. A woman of her station came and went as she pleased, so there was little of what happened at the castle that missed her. Already, she had unintentionally uncovered what could be a clue to my father's fate. Perhaps she also had seen something that would help identify the men responsible.

"Quickly, come into the Master's quarters so that no one overhears," I replied, "and we shall tell you all."

Still clutching my father's cloak, I unfastened the door and ushered the pair inside. For a foolish instant, I was prepared to see my father sitting at the table where I had last seen him. But, of course, the room was as I had left it, save that Pio no longer slept upon the bed.

While I fastened the door shut behind us, Rebecca took the opportunity to wander the small room, staring with avid interest at the Master's belongings crowded onto the wall shelves and strewn across the worktable. At my stern look, she put down the tiny clay horse that she'd pick up off the shelf. One of the remaining models for the immense, and as-yet-to-be-cast tribute to Il Moro's late father, it had languished there for more than half a year waiting for Leonardo to resume work on the project.

I gestured her to the bench. "What Tito and I are going to tell you must be kept secret," I began. "And so, before we say anything more, you must first swear an oath to God that you will not repeat it to anyone else."

I watched as various emotions flickered across her broad face, and despite the grave situation, I could not help a small inner smile. Her desire to learn one of Leonardo's secrets was surely battling with the keen knowledge that she would not be able to repeat that same tale to all and sundry. For I knew she was a pious woman who would not break such an oath should she make it; thus, her quandary.

Finally, she sighed and nodded. "Very well, I swear on the blood of our Lord that I will not repeat what you tell me," she agreed, crossing herself for good measure.

Satisfied, I nodded in return. "Very well, to start, have you heard rumors about Signor Leonardo's flying machine?"

"You mean Signor Leonardo's folly," she replied, her frown returning. "No man can fly like a bird, unless he has the devil's help."

"Perhaps," I replied, "but enough people believe in his invention that already one life has been forfeit over it."

I hastily revealed all we knew thus far about Constantin's murder. From there, I explained what had happened from the time I discovered my father missing to the point where Tito and I had learned that the Master's half-built flying machine had been stolen. I told her, as well, our theory that my father had been kidnapped in error, likely mistaken for Leonardo in the Master's absence. Tito interrupted a time or two to correct me or add a few details. By the time I finished, Rebecca's mouth hung open, and her face was as white as her wimple.

"But you have given us a fine clue," I added, "for you have found my father's cloak. It must have fallen from the wagon as he was driven that way . . . or perhaps he deliberately dropped it for someone to discover."

"And if you can take us back to that spot," Tito eagerly added, "perhaps someone nearby saw the wagon pass and can point us in the right direction."

The washerwoman clamped her mouth shut again, her dark brows once more diving down toward her nose. "I can take you there," she agreed, "but I can tell you already that the road runs but two ways . . . back here to Milan, or else south toward the province of Pontalba."

Pontalba? The word rang vaguely familiar in my mind, but for a moment I could not recall its significance. Finally, with a cry of surprise, I remembered how I knew the name.

"It was the Duke of Pontalba who agreed to marry Il Moro's cousin and ward, the Contessa Caterina. And when

she died"—I stumbled a little over that word—"he was satisfied to wed another of Ludovico's cousins to keep the peace
between the two provinces. Surely he could not be plotting
against Ludovico, when they are related by marriage and
bound by truce."

Or could he?

I frowned. Less than a year ago, Nicodemo lo Bianco,
the Duke of Pontalba, had been a sworn enemy of Ludovico
Sforza. Of course, I knew nothing else of the man, save what
I had seen of him that fateful night of the masquerade when
both a new peace treaty and Caterina's betrothal were to have
been announced.

The theme of the festivities had been the card game of
Tarocchi, with each guest dressed to represent one of the
individual cards in the playing deck. Nicodemo—tall, thin,
with a sunken chest and merciless twist to his narrow lips—
had chosen the Devil as his costume. I had always thought
his choice grimly appropriate for the role he had played that
night in damning Caterina to her fate, by circumstances if
not by deliberate intent.

Tito, meanwhile, was rubbing his chin in fair imitation of
the Master in deep thought.

"Are you quite sure that is the only direction the road
takes?" he asked Rebecca.

Not waiting for an answer, he turned back to me and went
on. "It is more likely the men were sent by the pope or even
by the French king. Think how clever such a plot would be.
While Il Moro is secretly meeting with the French king's
representatives, the king's other men are sent to kidnap the
duke's master engineer and steal his invention."

I considered his words a moment and then shook my
head.

"But would that not be Il Moro's first assumption? No, I

think it must be the Duke of Pontalba behind this treachery. Besides," I added with a bitter twist of my lips, "I suspect he is the sort of man who would not care if one of his villainous minions shot an unarmed youth in the back."

Tito looked for a moment as if he would have argued the point, but instead he simply shrugged. "Then let us set off for Pontalba. But it is two or more days' walk from here, and I fear they have many hours' start on us."

"Perhaps not so many hours," I countered, allowing myself a bit of hope. "After all, they could not sneak past the castle walls in the middle of the night with a large wagon without Il Moro's guard stopping them. Remember all the horse droppings in the shed? They must have kept the wagon there all night and left once the gates opened at dawn."

Before Tito could reply, Rebecca snorted and hefted herself to her feet.

"This is a pack of foolishness," she proclaimed. "You boys can't be running around the countryside chasing after murderers and thieves. Why not tell the captain of the guard what has happened and let him send his men in search of Signor Angelo and this folly of a flying machine?"

"Because the flying machine is a secret," Tito and I promptly chorused, earning yet another snort from the woman.

I planted my fists on my hips and met her disapproving frown with an equally dark look of my own.

"Rebecca, not only is my father's life in peril," I choked out, "but Signor Leonardo's safety is at risk, as well. Don't you understand? What you call a folly is in truth a dangerous weapon, one that would have allowed the Duke of Milan to reign supreme over all the provinces. Bad enough for it to be in his hands, but who can guess what will happen should the Duke of Pontalba gain control of it?"

I turned to Tito for support, and he gave a stern nod of

agreement. "Our advantage is that few in the court truly believe that the flying machine exists, save in the Master's imagination," he told her. "We must get it back . . . and in the meantime, no one must guess that it has been stolen, least of all Il Moro. For if he learns that the Duke of Pontalba has made a fool of him, he likely will cast the Master into prison for his carelessness."

"And don't forget my father," I broke in again. "He will remain a prisoner of Pontalba until he is no longer of use to the duke. And after that . . ."

I trailed off on those last words, unwilling to speak aloud what both Tito and I knew was the likely outcome should we fail. But as I was struggling to maintain my composure, the washerwoman clapped her chapped hands together and gave them a brisk rub.

"So that's the way of it," she proclaimed. "Very well, let's not waste more time. Tighten the belts on your tunics, boys, for we're off to visit the Duke of Pontalba."

11

In truth, whoever has control over such irresistible forces will be lord over all nations . . .

—Leonardo da Vinci, *Folio B*

"What do you mean, *we?*" Tito cried, his expression of astonishment at the washerwoman's words likely mirroring my own. "You're not coming with us."

"You cannot come," I echoed, "for our mission will be dangerous and requires great stealth."

"Stealth? Bah!"

Rebecca dismissed the word with the sweep of a broad hand.

"Stealth is the last thing you need. Surely you don't expect to sneak into the duke's castle like you're spies sent from the pope. You boys will be lucky to make your way past the main gates before the duke's guards catch you and string you up by your heels."

"And you think *you* can get past them without being

noticed?" Tito demanded, his expression growing more mutinous with her every word.

The washerwoman shrugged. "Oh, we'll be noticed, all
right. But my way, no one will pay us heed. Besides, I can
see to it that we drive a wagon in fine style just like the duke
himself, instead of walking like peasants."

"If we ride, we can save a good day's travel," I exclaimed.
"But how will you find us a wagon?"

For such conveyances were the purview of titled gentlemen or else those of the better classes who could afford the
luxury of a horse or two. How the washerwoman might put
her chapped hands on such a prize, I could not guess.

By way of answer, Rebecca gave her ample skirts a coy
swish. "Let's just say that I take care of the stable master's
laundry, and he lends me a cart and pony when I need it."

She followed those words with a broad smile and a wink.
I blushed as I realized that the man's clothing was likely not
all she attended to in return for such bounty. My reaction
drew a ribald laugh, and she gave me an amiable pat upon
the shoulder.

"Don't worry, little Dino. When you get older, maybe I'll
do your laundry for you, too."

While my blush burned brighter still at that last, she
straightened her skirts and then assumed a businesslike mien.
"You two boys find supplies, enough to last us a couple of
days. And blankets, too, as we'll be sleeping under the stars
for a night or two. I'll go get our wagon and meet you back
here in a short while."

She trudged out the door at a brisk pace, leaving Tito and
me to gape at each other for a moment. Finally, he managed
an indignant snort.

"Pah, what is she thinking, this washerwoman?" he
demanded with a scornful air. "We do not want her company.

Come; let us be off before she returns. This is man's work, and she will only hinder us with her female foolishness."

"What do you mean, female foolishness?" I countered, doing my best to hide my indignation. "So far, her plan seems better than any you have suggested. Where do you think you can find a wagon for us to travel in, and how do you think to storm the duke's castle? I say we travel with her. Surely we will draw fewer comments riding with her than wandering the road to Pontalba on our own."

Tito opened his mouth as if to protest further but then clamped his lips shut again and shook his head.

"Very well, Dino, I shall go along with you, but don't say I did not warn you. I can think of no greater disaster than having a woman thinking she is in charge of such a mission."

He patted the chest of his tunic under which his knife was hidden. "As for supplies, I have all that I need here," he declared with an important nod. Then, when I frowned, he was quick to add, "But I'll find blankets and water, if you will take care of the food."

"I'll get what I can from the kitchens. But I must also tell Davide that we shall be gone for a few days, lest he worry unduly."

"Just tell him that we're with your father and the Master conducting experiments out in the countryside," Tito said with a careless shrug before heading out the door, as well.

It was only after he left that it occurred to me to wonder what Leonardo would think should he return while we were gone and discover the flying machine's theft. Would he believe the worst . . . that Tito and my father and I had absconded with his great invention? Or would he realize that someone else, perhaps the person who had murdered Constantin, was behind the flying machine's disappearance.

Besides, unlike Tito, I was not naive enough to believe that we could rescue my father and recover the flying machine on our own. Even with Rebecca's dubious assistance, such a feat would surely require the Master's help . . . and, despite our earlier protests, that of Il Moro's army. Worse, what if Rebecca's dire prediction came true? If the Duke of Pontalba's men captured Tito and me before we could determine my father's fate, Leonardo might never know the truth of what had happened in his absence.

I grabbed up a scrap of paper and composed a long note, which I left upon his table, weighed down by the clay horse that Rebecca had admired. Then, fastening my father's cloak around my neck, I hurried out the door.

I stopped by the main workshop long enough to gather a few supplies of my own before going to the chapel to make our excuses to Davide. The senior apprentice asked no questions of me, for the rule was that we always had leave to follow the Master's orders, strange as they might sometimes be. And I'd not yet heard of any apprentice being caught in a lie, for no one wished to risk his hard-won post for nothing more than a day of freedom from work.

Obtaining the food had proved more difficult. Marcella—the brash young woman who had long ago taken a fancy to "Dino"—no longer worked in the kitchens, having secured a better position attending one of Il Moro's mistresses. With her gone, I was forced to find someone else who might be sympathetic to a young man's plight. I'd finally bargained with one of the newer girls, who agreed to my promise to sketch her portrait in exchange for some bread and cheese.

A short while later, I was standing at the Master's door, impatiently wondering what had become of my companions. Tito appeared a few moments later, arms laden with blankets and a few stoppered jugs of water. He gave my bundles an approving nod and glanced about.

"What has become of the washerwoman? See, I told you it was a mistake in judgment to trust her."

"You're wrong, Tito," I hurried to assure him. "Rebecca may not speak with honeyed words, nor is she a likely candidate for a priory, but I am certain her loyalty is above question."

"Perhaps," he replied with a dark look, "but it seems odd that she, of all people, discovered your father's lost cloak and then happened to be wearing it just as we were lamenting his disappearance. Besides, why would a washerwoman want to help us find the flying machine?"

I had no answers for his questions. And, though I had instinctively trusted the brash woman, I was dismayed to realize that Tito's words now put a small arrow of doubt into my heart. For surely someone of Rebecca's humble position could easily be seduced by coin. Did she know more than she was saying about this unsettling situation . . . and was she even now prepared to lead us into a trap?

Even as I considered this possibility, a harsh shout and a snap of reins cut short these bleak thoughts. I looked up to see a battered if serviceable two-wheeled cart hauling a pair of baskets, each large enough to hold Tito or me. The cart was pulled by a sturdy brown mare whose graying muzzle betrayed her age, though her shiny coat bespoke years of fond care.

Rebecca perched proudly upon the splintered bench that served as a seat. Her wimple had begun to unwind, the white length of cloth that wrapped her hair and swaddled her throat flapping with her every movement like a small flag of surrender. But there was nothing of defeat in her expression as she pulled the cart to a halt and gestured us over.

"Load up, boys," she commanded. "Put your supplies under the seat. Dino, you are smaller, so you can sit beside me. Tito, you can sit behind us."

We made haste to stow our gear and then clambered into our assigned spots. "What are the baskets for?" Tito wanted to know as he maneuvered his long legs around them.

The washerwoman grinned.

"Laundry," was her succinct reply. She gave the reins a snap, and we started off through the quadrangle toward the castle gates.

We made our way past the guards with little fanfare, save for a ribald dialogue between Rebecca and the blond-mustachioed captain, who had strolled over at her approach. The burly captain's heavy accent made most of his coarse if genial comments unintelligible to me, though Rebecca seemed to have no trouble understanding him.

While the pair bantered, I wrapped my father's cloak more closely about me and slumped in my seat lest the soldier recognize me. For it had been this same mercenary who, at Leonardo's direction, had carried my limp form from the castle to the sanctuary of Signor Luigi's tailor shop the night of that terrible fire. I deemed it unlikely that he would recall me—I had been costumed in a page's finery, my face blackened from smoke and soot—but I could not take that risk.

Reflexively, I reached a hand for my pouch, where I usually kept my notebook. But I had deliberately left the half-filled volume behind in my trunk, lest our mission end with Tito and me being tossed into the duke's dungeon or worse. I dared not risk losing the sketches into which I'd poured my grief and pain, for they were the tangible memories of my lost love. As with the other two volumes whose pages already overflowed with notes and drawings, that small book held a piece of my heart.

Rebecca's exchange with the captain, however, proved mercifully brief. A few moments later, our cart was through the gates and rolling into the city of Milan. I gazed about the familiar narrow lanes, the tall buildings on either side so close together that the street below was in perpetual shadow, save for when the sun hung directly above. Lines of gaily colored laundry were strung like rakish flags from one balcony to that of its neighbor across the way, adding splashes of color to the pale stone.

We rumbled over a small bridge, which arched atop one of the city's many canals, and I wrinkled my nose at the stench that drifted up to us. I had seen sketches of the Master's grand design for modernizing the city, a plan he had conceived in his role as master engineer to the duke. Such changes included a more efficient system of canals and sewers, which would render Milan more pleasing to the senses. Moreover, he claimed, new plumbing would reduce the incidences of deadly pestilence, which periodically swept Milan and its neighboring cities.

Unfortunately for the local populace, Il Moro was more concerned with Leonardo the artist completing the equine monument to his father than he was with seeing the master engineer bring greater efficiency to flushing away their collective waste.

By now, we were well into the city, and Rebecca was keeping us to well-traveled streets. One particular lane was more than familiar to me, for it was along this way that Signor Luigi had his shop. Indeed, the corpulent tailor had just emptied his piss pot in the gutter when our cart rolled past. Knowing he could not help but see me, I gave him an enthusiastic wave.

"Good day, signore."

His bushy brows flew up beneath his greasy fringe of black hair as he stared at me in surprise. He opened his mouth as if to shout something after us, no doubt wondering what two of Leonardo's apprentices were doing riding about Milan with a woman of questionable repute. Apparently thinking the better of it, he clamped his plump red lips shut and merely shook his head in exaggerated resignation.

The momentary encounter cheered me. The tailor had proved a valued friend, and I had missed his company these past months. Besides, if nothing else, Luigi could bear witness to our departure, should something untoward occur on our journey to Castle Pontalba.

Rebecca turned the wagon down a side street, and before long we were out of the city. The dirt road was relatively smooth; still, we bounced about every bit as much as we had through the rough stone streets of the city. I was reminded again why even the nobles preferred to travel by horseback or on foot rather than by wagon, for I had to keep my teeth clamped firmly together lest I bite my tongue at each bump.

She pulled the wagon to a halt beside the stream where she and several other washerwomen spent a good portion of their day scrubbing laundry in the chilly waters. Half a dozen of them labored there now, skirts hiked high and arms bared as they sloshed linens about in the basinlike shallows that served as their tubs. Like Rebecca, these women were sturdy and as muscular as many men, for the constant hauling about of wet clothing required a fair amount of strength. I wondered again how Rebecca's daughter, the fragile-looking Novella, managed such labors.

"Why are we stopping?" Tito wanted to know.

The washerwoman turned in her seat to address him. "I was late gathering my laundry this morning, so the other women were here at the river before me. They might have seen something I didn't. Not that it was my fault for lagging behind," she added with a sly smile. "I had a gentleman who wanted to show me the state of his linens before he would let me take them away to wash. I could hardly tell him no, could I?"

By now, I was becoming accustomed to the washerwoman's bawdy manner, so I merely shrugged. As for Tito, he looked faintly horrified but managed to choke out something unintelligible that I assumed was agreement.

But with her usual swift change of humors, Rebecca had already assumed a businesslike manner. She gave a brisk order that Tito and I should remain in the wagon and then tossed me the reins and clambered down from her seat.

We watched as she made her way toward two women who had hauled their baskets from the water to a sunny spot of grass along the bank and now were carefully spreading the clean clothes to dry beneath the late-morning sun. Tito, meanwhile, defied her command and jumped from the cart.

"It is just as I feared," he protested in an offended tone as he stretched his legs. "Not only has she taken over our mission, but now the washerwoman is giving us men orders."

"Would you rather walk to Pontalba?" I reminded him, refraining with an effort from recounting the numerous instances in history when a female had led the troops. "Besides, we are only guessing that my father and the flying machine have been taken to Pontalba. Be patient, and let us see if she learns anything of value from the other women."

Tito muttered a few uncomplimentary things beneath his breath, but I knew he could not disagree with my words. Despite my advice to him, however, I waited with barely restrained impatience of my own while the washerwoman chatted with her friends. Finally, Rebecca bade them farewell and started back to the wagon. As for Tito, for all his posturing, he quickly resumed his place among the baskets well before she reached us.

"What did they tell you?" came my anxious query as soon as the woman was in earshot.

Rebecca waited until she had climbed back onto the seat and settled heavily beside me before she replied. "We're in luck, boys. They say a large wagon did pass this way soon after dawn. It carried something large, but it was covered by canvas. And there was at least three men that they saw."

"I don't suppose that the wagon was flying the Duke of Pontalba's standard?" I asked with a sigh, knowing full well that was unlikely. "But could they tell that's where the wagon was headed?"

"It was that direction, and they was traveling like bandits was after them. So unless the pope has set up housekeeping someplace besides Rome, the Duke of Pontalba is our man."

"But how can we know that is the right wagon?" Tito protested. "If it is not, then we have lost many days going in the wrong direction."

Though his concern was a valid one, I clung to my resolve. "There cannot be many large wagons journeying between here and Pontalba," I pointed out, smoothing the edges of my father's cloak. "I recall the Master once saying that Il Moro had made a poor choice of allies, because there was nothing to be found in that province save sour bread and sour men. Why, Pontalba doesn't even have a grand city like Milan, just a crumbling castle on a hillside."

"Well, they've got a cabinetmaker and a flying machine now," Tito muttered, and then gave me an apologetic nod as he realized the carelessness of his speech.

Rebecca, meanwhile, favored us both with a dark look. "It's not too late to change your minds, boys," she told us. "We can still head back to the castle and tell my friend Fritz—he's the captain of the guard—what happened. He'll send his men out, if I ask him nice."

I gave my head a stubborn shake. "We already told you, Rebecca, no one else must know what has happened . . . not unless the Master himself approves it. We'll go on to Pontalba, with or without you, and find out the fate of my father and the flying machine. Tito and I are not afraid, are we?"

That last was directed at my fellow apprentice. Tito met my questioning gaze with a sharp shake of his head and a telling pat of his chest.

"We're not afraid," he boldly echoed. "You can go back to your laundry, washerwoman, if you're frightened. We don't need you. No matter what, Dino and I are traveling to Pontalba."

"Pah, you need me if you don't want to wear out your shoe leather," she said with a snort. "Now, hold tight. We've got a lot of miles to go before the sun sets on us tonight."

Taking the reins from me, she gave them a snap. The brown mare rolled an annoyed eye but obediently took off at a smart clip, heading south toward the province of white hills, where I prayed that my father would be found.

12

The air moves like a river and carries the clouds with it . . .

—Leonardo da Vinci, *Manuscript G*

The brown mare kept up a swift pace, hauling the three of us with ease along the road south to Pontalba. The road became progressively rougher, however, as we put distance between us and Milan.

At times, what had been a smooth highway dwindled to nothing but ruts running parallel to one another. Along those primitive stretches, the center strip of dirt and rough grass was seeded with rocks large enough to break an axle, so that Rebecca was forced to slow the mare to a careful walk. Despite the slow pace, we still bounced against the wooden seat with force enough to leave one's hindquarters bruised. But we were fortunate in clear weather and the beauty of the surrounding countryside that was liberally strewn with delicate new buds and leaves in celebration of spring.

For the most part, we had the road to ourselves. We

passed but one other small cart, and only a handful of travelers making their way on foot, all of which had come from the direction of Pontalba. None, when queried, however, recalled seeing a large wagon pass them by.

After hearing that same response each time, it was all I could do not to give way to discouragement. More than once I heard Tito mutter, "I told you we were going the wrong way," making me wonder if he were right, after all. But Rebecca did not yield her course, the loose edge of her wimple flapping triumphantly as she drove the wagon with skill.

"Doesn't mean nothing," she shouted in my ear after one such negative response to my questioning. "They coulda joined the road after the wagon passed by . . . or maybe they was told not to say they saw it." Her logic comforted me somewhat; still, I said an extra prayer that we had not gambled wrongly in our choice of destinations.

We had covered a respectable distance by the time a pale sun tucked itself behind the darkening hills. Rebecca insisted that we stop before every bit of light had faded, so that she could safely guide the mare and wagon a short distance from the road to a spot among some hillocks.

"Bandits," the washerwoman explained when we questioned her, that answer drawing grave nods from both Tito and me.

She needed no further justification. While I'd never actually seen a bandit, I'd heard tales of them since childhood, and how they were the plague of honest travelers everywhere. The fact that we carried nothing of value meant little. Many of these lawless men reputedly terrorized and killed simply for enjoyment, with profit but a secondary motive. Such an assault had been my father's greatest fear for me in journeying by foot from our home village to Milan.

Find a large group of pilgrims and stay closely among them, he'd instructed. I had been careful to heed his advice and so had managed my journey in safety. But I knew that others were not always so lucky. In fact, it was the regularity of attacks along the byways of Lombardy that explained why no one had questioned the Master's claim that Constantin had been struck down by such outlaws.

Thus, we took pains to settle the wagon in a low spot a good distance from the main track and tied the mare out of sight. Rebecca allowed us a small fire. We let it smolder long enough to heat several flat rocks that we would later tuck beneath our blankets and so ward off the worst of the night's chill. While the flames did their work, we ate our simple meal of bread and cheese. I surprised my companions with dried figs that the kitchen maid had added to my sack at the last minute, earning a grin from Tito, who had a fondness for sweets.

Once we finished our repast, I brought up the subject that had been uppermost in my thoughts . . . namely, how to gain access to Castle Pontalba and determine if my father and the flying machine were being held there. Tito's primary concern, however, was the advantage in time the kidnappers had on us.

"If we *are* going the right way, the duke's men will have plenty of opportunity to hide the flying machine—and your father, as well—before we get there," was his doleful prediction. "Even if we can make our way inside the castle, I fear we won't find them."

"They can't be very far ahead of us," I countered with more confidence than I felt. "And now that they are far from Milan, they won't have cause to suspect that anyone is in pursuit of them. To my mind, they will have done as we did and made camp at dusk, for surely they would not risk both the wagon and the flying machine on these roads in the dark."

"Dino's right," Rebecca spoke up. She paused to belch and pick a bit of fig from between her teeth.

"Traveling these roads after dark means inviting a broken axle or a lame horse," she went on with a wise nod. "They've found a spot and settled in, just like we did. They'll be up at first light and reach the castle before midday. If you boys don't tarry when the cock crows in the morning, we'll be at Pontalba by midafternoon. That'll give us time enough to poke around before nightfall."

"And we will need to gain the trust of the servants there," I continued. "The arrival of a strange covered wagon will not go unnoticed. Surely a maid or a page will see something and will be glad to gossip."

My enthusiasm faded a bit, however, as I finished, "But first, we'll need to figure out how to make our way into the castle itself."

"We can hide in Rebecca's laundry baskets and let her drive us inside," Tito suggested with a snort, pulling his knees to his chest and hunching his shoulders in fair imitation of someone confined to such a space.

I shot him a stern look, but Rebecca merely grinned. I recalled her comment when he'd questioned her about the baskets, and I wondered if she already *had* formulated a plan that involved laundry. For my own part, I'd had some vague idea that Tito and I might find entry by professing to be itinerant artists. The problem with that disguise was that we had no paints or brushes or panels with us to prove such a claim.

After a few moments' more discussion, we all agreed that it made no sense to speculate further until we saw what we would face at the castle. We banked our small flame, and the three of us settled beneath the wagon, wrapped in cloaks and blankets and with hot stones at our feet. I had feared that I would spend the entire night staring at the wagon bed above us and counting the wooden pegs in every slat while I worried over my father's fate. But the day's events had taken their toll on me so that, despite my concerns, I fell into a fast and dreamless sleep.

I woke at dawn with, not Rebecca's rooster, but a lark trilling in my ear. Unfortunately, that dulcet greeting to the day was drowned out by Tito's groans as he dragged himself out from beneath the wagon bed.

"Ah, by the saints, I can barely move! All that bouncing about in the wagon has bruised me like a marketplace pear."

My snicker at his discomfort promptly turned into a matching groan of my own as I crawled out of my blankets to find my own joints stiff. Indeed, my body ached as if the brown mare had spent all night stomping me with her sturdy hooves. Rebecca appeared impervious to the previous day's abuses . . . doubtless because of her ample natural padding. She had already crawled out from her blankets and was leading the mare back from the tree where she'd been tied overnight.

Furtively rubbing my sore nether regions, I limped my way over to the privacy of a nearby shrub to empty my bladder. For once, I wished my sensible trunk hose were of the foolishly exaggerated style lately favored by many of the nobles. The horsehair filling that gave the trunk hose that rounded shape, as if the wearer had small kegs tied to either hip, would surely have made the previous day's ride more comfortable.

We quickly broke our fast and climbed atop the wagon. This time, both Tito and I prudently folded our cloaks into seat cushions to make the next leg of our journey less painful. But our precautions proved unnecessary. As the sun rose higher, so did the road begin to improve. While we previously had traversed hilly plains, the byway had dipped into broad forests and stretched into a smooth ribbon of hard-packed dirt.

Thus we were able to travel without jostling the very teeth from our jaws, making greater speed than we had the previous day. Even so, we exchanged but a few words among us, each of us lost in our own thoughts as the morning progressed.

It was not long after the sun had passed its midpoint when I spotted our objective.

"There, between those two trees," I softly called and pointed. "That must be it . . . the Duke of Pontalba's castle."

Through gaps in the just-budding trees, I could see glimpses of gray stone towers thrusting against a cloudless blue sky. Rebecca slowed the wagon, both to give the brown mare a well-deserved rest and to allow us to take in our destination before we were on top of it.

"The trees, they should be clearing soon," she said in a low tone. And, indeed, we could see not far ahead of us that the forest did end abruptly.

The change in terrain was deliberate, I knew. Just as the dukes before Il Moro's time had commanded a wide swath of forest to be cut down around Castle Sforza, so would the past dukes of Pontalba have done the same here. A broad field of green encircling the castle would force any advancing army into the open long before they reached the castle wall, making a surprise attack upon the castle difficult. Moreover, the bare terrain allowed the defenders to more easily repulse their aggressors. With no cover to be found in that span between the forest and the castle, the approaching soldiers would be easy targets for Pontalba's archers.

Of course, the open field also meant that the castle's sentries would see our approach well in advance of our arrival at the castle gates.

The washerwoman halted the cart before we reached the

final row of trees. She hopped down from her seat and signaled us to join her.

"Act like you're checking out the mare and cart, in case
they can see us from here," she instructed in a soft voice as she
made a show of inspecting the harnesses.

I nodded and bent to examine one of the cart wheels, well
impressed with her tactical knowledge. Emulating her low
tone—I knew from working with the Master the strange
ways that voices sometimes traveled—I asked, "Do we wait
for nightfall and try to scale the walls?"

"What, and risk falling in the dark?"

This came from Tito, who was scrutinizing the mare's
hooves. He straightened and shook his head. "Besides, it
would be hard enough to find your way around the place in
the daytime. At night, knowing nothing of the castle's floor
plan, it will be nigh impossible."

"Tito's right," the washerwoman replied. "That's why we're
going to ride right up to the gate and ask to be let in."

"But how will we convince the guards to open the gate?"
I wanted to know.

Rebecca jerked a beefy thumb toward the baskets in the
bed of the cart. "We'll offer to do their laundry, that's how."

"You mean, wash clothes?"

The choked question came from Tito, a look of horror settling on his face at the prospect. Rebecca shook her head and
gave him a gentle smile, though the gaze she fixed upon him
held more than a hint of steel.

"Don't worry, my young apprentice, such work is far too
undignified for a fine gentleman like you. No, I'll tell them
you two are my sons and that I need you to gather up the
linens and load them in the wagon for me. I'll do all the
washing."

"But what about my father?" I broke in. "When will we search for him?"

"Oh, that's easy," she said with a careless wave of one chapped hand. "While we're gathering up the laundry, we'll grab a tunic for you from one of the pages. Put it on, and you can wander about the castle with no questions asked."

"What about me? Do I get a tunic?" Tito wanted to know.

The washerwoman shook her head. "I'll need you to help sort the clothes. Besides, it's Dino's father we're searching for, so his son should do the looking."

The familiar mutinous look flashed over Tito's face. Then he seemingly thought the better of whatever protests he had and simply nodded. "You're right; it should be Dino. And I can cause a distraction if someone takes note of him."

The washerwoman's expression was approving as she gave him a nod. Shrugging, she added, "But it's a big castle. You'd best let me nose around first and see if anyone knows anything."

At that, she gestured us back onto the wagon and urged the mare forward.

"How do you know so much about strategy?" I wondered in a respectful voice as we began rolling toward the clearing.

Rebecca flashed her bawdy grin at me. "Comes of bedding lots of soldiers, I guess."

I heard Tito's snicker behind me, but I contented myself with an absent nod. We had reached the clearing, and Castle Pontalba was coming into full view, distracting me from any further ribaldry.

My first thought was to acknowledge where the name of the small province must have originated. Ahead of us rose a broad hillock strewn with tiny white flowers, so that it appeared at first glance to be dusted with a light snowfall.

Though surely this was a phenomenon that occurred only in the spring months, the periodic sight would capture the fancy of all but the most hardened of men. Whether or not the remainder of the Pontalba lands possessed such charm, I could not guess, but the parcel upon which the stronghold was built deserved its evocative name.

Less charming was the castle itself, which crouched like a malevolent toad atop that scenic rise.

Squat and gray, it rose gracelessly from the blanket of white flowers, commanding in its breadth if not its height. I guessed its age to be far older than the starkly elegant castle at Milan. Even at a distance, I could see that part of the outer wall was crumbling, and at least one tower was in sore need of repair.

I suppressed a reflexive shiver. Once, this castle might have been a proud fortress, but that would have been several generations ago. Each subsequent duke doubtless had modified the original symmetrical design to his own liking, adding a turret here and another storehouse or barracks there. The result was an untidy sprawl that bulged at the seams of the surrounding wall and gave the appearance of a round of bread dough that had slipped to one side of the cooking stone.

Still, nothing of this scenario should have been threatening. I would have shrugged aside my sense of disquiet, had I not known why we were searching out the Duke of Pontalba. The man was guilty of theft and kidnapping and—at least, indirectly—murder. I did not think myself too fanciful to believe that the brazenly careless neglect of the castle reflected the similar shortcoming in the soul of the castle's owner, as well.

By now, we had reached the foot of the long rocky slope that led to drawbridge and twin gatehouses. Once past that point, and with the bridge raised for the night, we would be trapped within those rugged walls. Thus, any rescue and escape would have to occur in the bold light of day.

I dared not guess how we might accomplish such a thing. Instead, I wondered how my father had felt as he'd been driven up this ramp and into the castle. Surely, he'd been bound— perhaps blindfolded and gagged—and doubtless hidden beneath the same canvas as the flying machine. Did he know where he was? And did his captors yet realize that he was not Leonardo the Florentine . . . or did he have them convinced he was the same genius who had invented that craft?

I could only pray that he had; otherwise, his life might well be forfeit.

Two craggy-faced guards started toward us, staves at the ready and their attitude one of distrust. "Keep still, boys," Rebecca muttered, putting a hand on my knee as I gave a reflexive shudder. "And don't worry. If I can't get us past these fine-looking fellows with a few sweet words, I'll let you strap me to Signor Leonardo's flying machine and send me sailing off the top of this here castle!"

13

A bird in the air makes itself heavy or light whenever it pleases...

—Leonardo da Vinci, *Manuscript E*

Once again, Rebecca proved that a glib tongue and bawdy manner were as effective as a pretty face in winning over certain of the male species. Within a few minutes, she had determined that the castle's occupants were in need of a washerwoman's services. Not only had the guards agreed that she might solicit business, but they had turned over their own extra tunics to be laundered.

"I'll get them so clean you won't recognize them," she gleefully assured them before whipping up the mare again.

She had been pleased to learn from the guards that a laundry shed with immense kettles for boiling and rinsing clothing was already set up on the grounds. This meant we would not have to haul all the clothing outside the castle walls and find a stream where she could do the washing, and then carry it back again when we were finished. More important, it gave us an excuse to remain upon the castle grounds for several hours without being questioned.

"But if we start doing laundry, we'll be stuck here at the castle for the whole of the night," she warned us. "We won't be able to leave the job half-finished, not without stirring up suspicion. And they'll raise the drawbridge come dusk, so we can't sneak out in the middle of the night. That means that even if we find Signor Angelo, we won't be able do anything about it until morning."

When we nodded our solemn understanding, she added, "Of course, I'll have to bargain with the kitchen master for the water and the fuel for the fire. If he's like the rest of them, he'll want a few soldi for that privilege."

The laundry shed—a simple structure open on three sides and built atop a stone floor—was to be found not far from the kitchens. Rebecca hopped down from her seat to negotiate with the kitchen master, leaving Tito and me behind to watch the mare and cart. Although my eagerness to begin my search threatened to burst from me like a flushed quail from the grass, I schooled myself to patience and took stock of my surroundings.

My first thought was that the castle grounds bustled with surprising activity, for all that the walled fortress had appeared from the outside to be but a remnant of some past provincial glory. Indeed, the castle appeared well staffed with servants and artisans, a few of whom nodded our way as they trudged past. Most of these folk would live in the small wooden houses inside the main walls; others likely resided in the scattering of humble dirt and stone structures at the foot of the castle's outer walls. Of nobles and merchants, however, I saw none.

Satisfied, I turned my attention to the physical layout of the grounds. Here within the walls of Castle Pontalba, the haphazard layout was even more apparent. My artist's eye wept over the visual discord, one part of me yearning to sketch the fortress as it should have appeared: proud, unyielding, and—most important—symmetrical. But, sadly, no artist had lent a hand to the castle's ultimate blueprint.

Outbuildings were scattered with no obvious design. Several appeared long abandoned, their wooden roofs caved in and walls little more than stacks of rubble. As for the main structure of the castle, I could see that it had once been U-shaped. But another wing constructed of a paler and more smoothly textured stone—another barracks, I judged from its construction—had been added to the castle's far side in obvious afterthought. Towers lodged at each of the castle's four corners, though the one closest to us had partially collapsed into itself. The resulting effect called to mind a finger that had made unfortunate acquaintance with an axe.

Adding to the disharmony, even the surrounding grounds reflected a careless lack of design. Unlike Castle Sforza, with its manicured quadrangle and symmetrical walks, this castle boasted no expanse of green lawn; neither did it lay claim to any carefully tended gardens or shaded porticos. A few patches of green, no doubt growing simply by mistake, were the only flora to relieve the starkness of the hard-packed earth.

But architecture was not my main concern. I craned my neck for a better look at the walls. High above, a few of the duke's soldiers patrolled the maze of battlemented walks. They would pay those already within the walls little mind, I was certain, for their concern was with what occurred beyond the castle. Thus, our risk of discovery would be here on the ground.

Even so, I was not as nervous as I might have been at the prospect. In previously assisting the Master with solving other heinous crimes, I'd wandered Il Moro's castle with impunity while disguised as one or another of the household staff. I'd thus come to realize that if one were dressed as a servant and kept a properly humble attitude, very few people would question one's comings and goings.

What unsettled me was the fact that, given the untidy sprawl that was Castle Pontalba, my father and the flying machine could be hidden anywhere. And I had to suppose that the inner chambers would be as tangled a skein as the castle's outer plan. Not knowing my way about, once I began my search, I could readily become lost within the fortress's belly.

I thought to share my worries with Tito, but he looked more absorbed by the pair of comely kitchen maids who were struggling their way past with a bulging sack of grain. They could see little of him, however, for he had pulled his cap low on his forehead and pulled his cloak high enough so that it swaddled his chin.

"My disguise," he had whispered by way of explanation while Rebecca had gossiped with the guards. "Those three men who took the flying machine got a good look at me that night. If they recognize me here, they'll know we're after them."

I'd not considered that possibility and was grateful that he'd had the foresight to take precautions. But now, I needed his counsel. Only when I gave him a swat with my cap, however, did he tear his attention from the girls to me.

"Tito, where should I start looking for my father?" I softly asked. "Look at this place. He could be anywhere."

"Or he could be nowhere," Tito replied, what little I could see of his expression gloomy again, now that he no longer had the girls to ogle. "Remember, we don't even know if those men brought him and the wagon here."

"But we must go on that assumption. Besides, Rebecca will find out something. You saw how easily she handled the guards at the gate."

"Pah, I could have gotten us past them," Tito replied.

Then, with a shrug, he added, "Don't forget that the Master had the flying machine stored in an old shed. That's where I'd look first, anyhow."

I did not get a chance to reply, for Rebecca reappeared, a broad smile upon her face. She gestured us to jump down from the cart and join her.

"Good news, boys," she softly declared as she hooked an arm around either of our necks, drawing us to her in the now-familiar embrace. "I cut a deal with the kitchen master. He'll let us use the laundry shed and as much wood as we need for the fires. All he wants is a quarter of our profits, in return."

"That sounds like a lot," Tito protested as he tried to extricate himself.

Releasing her grip, the washerwoman shook her head. "He wanted half at first, but I made him see reason. So, boys, help me fill the pots and get the fires going, and then we'll collect our laundry."

"But what about the wagon?" I asked, my tone anxious. "Did you learn anything about it?"

"By Saint Jerome's lion, you are an impatient one," she replied with a shake of her head. "We'll find that out as we gather the clothes. First things first."

Retrieving the empty baskets, she sent Tito off to the stables with the mare and wagon. She and I began readying the kettles, each large enough to easily hold Tito and me both. There was water for boiling to be had from the cistern on the roof, so that filling the four vats—two for washing and two for rinsing—was an easy matter. By the time Tito rejoined us, we had fine blazes burning beneath each pot.

"With that much water, it'll take some time to boil," Rebecca reminded us. "Come on; let's get some laundry."

Carrying a basket between us—we would return for the

second one once this one was full—we followed the washer-woman as she began her rounds. As before, Tito and I let Rebecca do all of the talking while he and I gathered the filthy bed linens and stained tunics. Her casual question as she bandied with each potential customer was the same: had they seen a large covered wagon carrying perhaps three men arrive at the castle earlier that morning?

"They about run me and my boys off the road, they was going so fast," Rebecca would indignantly explain. "If they're here, I want a word with them about frightening good people because they're in a hurry. By the Virgin, we've got the same right to the road as them!"

At first, no one admitted to seeing any such men or wagon, and my spirits became as gloomy as Tito's. For surely so large a conveyance would not pass unnoticed by the entire castle. But then, one of the pages—a smooth-cheeked boy in a pale blue tunic who was struggling beneath a small mountain of clothing collected from his fellows—nodded at her query.

"I saw a big wagon come into the castle this morning," he agreed with a self-important air. "I couldn't tell what they were hauling, though, because there was a cloth covering it."

Then his eyes widened, and he stared at Rebecca in unfeigned alarm. "Pray, don't say anything to them! It was the duke's men driving the wagon. If you're lucky, they'll simply laugh at you. But if you make them angry, they could do worse! And if they find out I was the one who told you . . ."

He trailed off in misery, his fear of the soldiers obvious. I wondered in sudden anger of my own what cruel punishment these men had inflicted upon the servants of Castle Pontalba in the past. Then a shiver of trepidation swept me. If a mere page might suffer retaliation for so a minor a transgression, what might my father be enduring at their hands?

The washerwoman, meanwhile, gave the boy a reassuring

pat on the shoulder. "I won't say anything, child. And, besides, maybe it wasn't even the same wagon as tried to run us down. Do you know where they took it, so I can have a look?"

The page bit his lip, his round face pale, and I feared for a moment he would refuse to answer. Then, reluctantly, he jerked his head in the direction of the barracks.

"They drove it back there," he whispered. "And a while later, they took the wagon back to the stables. But it was empty by then."

Tossing the remaining tunics in my direction, he turned on his heel and scampered back to the main building from which he'd come. While I gathered up the garments from the dirt, Rebecca tapped a thick finger to her lips in thought.

"Let's get these clothes boiling," she said with a kick of the basket, "and then we'll visit the stables and the barracks."

We made our swift way back to the shed, where she sorted the linens and tossed half into the first vat. While Tito used a large paddle to stir, Rebecca added to the boiling water a ladle of brown soap from the covered bucket she'd brought with her on the journey.

"A fine soup," she said with a grin as the stained clothing swirled about in the pot. "We'll let it simmer for a time while we tend to our other business."

The empty basket between us, Tito and I followed the washerwoman to the stables. While she bartered with the stable master for the mare's care and the cart's storage overnight, the two of us slipped away for a look inside the stalls. Tito took one side of the long stone building and I, the other.

My search was the first to bear fruit.

"Here," I softly called, peering excitedly over a low wall. Behind the stalls I'd discovered an open shed where half a dozen or more carts and wagons of various sizes were stored.

One of them, in particular, had caught my eye. Not only was it far larger than the other conveyances, but a folded length of rough canvas had been left in its bed.

Tito rushed over to join me, his gaze following my pointing finger. He frowned and then shrugged.

"Come on; let's take a closer look," I urged and scrambled over the wall. Tito followed more slowly, so that I had already climbed into its bed by the time he reached the wagon.

"What do you think you are doing?" he demanded in a soft undertone. "The stable master might step in at any minute."

"Then you must keep an eye out and warn me, for I am looking for clues."

Though what clues there might be, I could not guess; still, I began scanning the wagon for something that might indicate that my father or Leonardo's invention had been transported upon it. My diligence was rewarded when I spied a few familiar brown threads caught on the splintered bed. Plucking them carefully from the wood, I held them up to my own brown tunic.

"They're the same," I said in an excited whisper. "Look, Tito. Ever since he joined up with the Master, my father has been wearing the same work tunic as we apprentices wear. He must have lain on the wagon beneath the canvas with the flying machine and snagged his clothes on a splinter."

"Let me see." Tito drew closer and viewed my find with a skeptical look. "I'm not so sure," he repeated. "Brown cloth is common enough, you know."

"Perhaps. But what of this?"

Nimbly, I hopped from the wagon bed and stepped off the distance between the two rear wheels.

"—Seven, eight. There, that matches the spacing of the wheel marks we found in the Master's shed. Add that to the canvas that could have been used to cover the wagon, and the brown threads that match our tunics, and surely we can be certain that this is the wagon in question."

"Dino, you sound almost like Master Leonardo," he said in an admiring tone. "Very well, you have convinced me. But now that we know where the wagon is, we must find out where its cargo has gone. Quickly, before we are spotted."

We hurried to rejoin Rebecca, who was keeping the stable master entertained with her ribald jests.

"Ah, there are my fine young sons," she declared, pausing to give us fond maternal smiles. "Handsome fellows, ain't they?" she said to the stable master, adding with a wink, "Course, they look like their sires and not me."

While the man left to gather his linens, I gave Rebecca a quick, whispered account of what I'd seen.

"Seems likely," she agreed when I'd finished. "Let's see what the barracks have to offer."

A few minutes later, we were carrying a basket of linen redolent of the stables. Our destination was the oddly out-of-place structure I'd noted earlier. Hunkered up against the main wall, it bore a resemblance to the barracks of Il Moro's men with its series of alcove entries.

I frowned. Perhaps there was room enough within one of those chambers to store the flying machine while still in pieces. Fully assembled, however, its wingspan would surely be too broad to be contained within those walls. And even if it could fit, none of the doors was wide enough to accommodate it being rolled out again.

Discouraged, I said as much to Tito and Rebecca. Tito merely shrugged, while the washerwoman tapped her lips with her blunt finger once more.

"But this is where the page said he saw the wagon halt,"

she said in a considering tone. "Maybe they unloaded here and then carried the pieces wherever they needed to go."

"But why do that? If they were trying to be inconspicuous, surely it would have made more sense to drive the wagon to the exact spot. Unless . . ."

I paused and eyed the nearby tower as an idea took form. From what the Master had told us of his design, the finished machine would have to be launched from a spot where it could catch the wind and gain height. Save for the slight rise on which the castle sat, the surrounding countryside in Pontalba was relatively flat. The only spot to offer any altitude was—

"The roof," I softly cried. "See how it has many slopes and flat areas all along the top of the castle? They must have carried all the pieces of the flying machine up the tower steps and to a flat section somewhere behind the battlements where they could be put together."

Tito nodded vigorously at first, but then his expression fell. "Wait, Dino. I've been in towers like that before, and the stairways all twist like corkscrews. The pieces of the flying machine are too long to ever wrap around those curves. How could they carry them up there?"

At his words, my own enthusiasm promptly faltered. I'd also been inside such towers before, and I feared that Tito was right. Some of those structures were built with but a narrow spiral of iron steps in their centers, with the opening at the landing above barely large enough for a man to pass through. Others had staircases of stone that wrapped along the inner walls, but the narrow steps did not easily accommodate more than one man abreast. Either way, it *would* be almost impossible to carry the flying machine up beyond the battlements.

Rebecca, however, was not prepared to concede defeat. Frowning, she studied the upper reaches of the castle with a scholar's intent look. A moment later, a smile spread across her round face.

"Maybe they didn't have to carry the pieces to get them up on the roof," she declared and pointed.

We followed her gaze upward until we saw what she had seen . . . a pair of ropes dangling from the battlements directly above us. With a few men above and a few below, it would be relatively simple to use the ropes to haul the body and wings of the flying machine straight up!

"I must get up there," I said with a determined jerk of my chin. "If the flying machine is on the roof, then surely my father must be somewhere near the craft. Perhaps even now he is working on it."

"Not so fast, my boy," the washerwoman protested, gripping my arm in one beefy hand lest I suddenly flee. "Remember what we said about finding you a tunic? Come."

She gestured us toward the heavy basket and then started at a brisk pace back toward the shed. Tito made a rude sound of protest, and I was hard-pressed not to follow suit. By this point, I was beginning to feel like Rebecca's brown mare, with all the hauling back and forth of baskets. But our masquerade had thus far yielded promising results, so I bit back any complaint and swiftly shouldered my portion of the burden.

Rebecca was already sorting through the remaining pile of tunics by the time we had reached the laundry shed. Plucking forth one with the fewest stains upon it, she tossed it in my direction. "This should fit. Quickly, put it on."

Removing my belt, I pulled the pale blue tunic over my own brown garb and then retied the strip of leather about my waist. Wrinkling my nose at the smell of someone else's sweat, I turned in a circle to model my disguise.

"Very good," the washerwoman approved. Then she frowned. "I don't mind saying, I'm a bit nervous letting you wander a strange castle by yourself. If you're found out, and someone suspects what we're about, it could go bad for all of us . . . Signor Angelo, included."

"The duke might toss us all into his dungeon," Tito darkly predicted. "Maybe I should go in your stead. I'm older, and—"

"No! Signor Angelo is my father, and I shall discover where they are hiding him. Besides"—I hesitated, glancing from one to the other of them—"if you or Rebecca found him first, he might refuse to go with you. He might fear that you are in league with the duke and that it is a trick."

Tito assumed a faintly offended expression at this last, but Rebecca pursed her lips and nodded.

"That is true. It is not impossible that the Duke of Pontalba has spies at Castle Sforza. There was the boy who tricked Tito and the figure that you, Dino, say you saw more than once. There might be others, as well."

Then she straightened the tunic on my shoulders and gave me a maternal pat. "Your sire would be proud of your bravery. Go, but be careful. And if you're caught, pretend to be simple and tell them that your mother sent you looking for more laundry, and you got lost."

"Ha, that should be an easy role for Dino," Tito muttered, but his amiable smirk took the sting from his words. Then, after reaching behind one of the pots, he plucked my cap from my head and plopped another one in its place.

"Here. I grabbed this off that page's head while he was busy sniveling about the duke's men."

Though a bit surprised at his callous attitude toward the frightened boy, I was pleased by his foresight in completing my disguise. Surely no one would have cause to question me should they see me wandering about the castle.

"I'll be back soon," I promised as I straightened the cap. "And I vow I will have news of both my father and the flying machine by the time I return."

14

Where the descent is easier there the ascent is more difficult.

—Leonardo da Vinci, *Codex Arundel*

Another bit of wisdom I had learned while conducting similar clandestine activities for the Master was that, if one carried some mundane object and walked with brisk purpose, one was seldom stopped or questioned by those in charge. Thus, I slipped into the main castle wearing my borrowed tunic and cap and bearing a small armful of folded table linens.

Had I been staring down from the vantage point of the clouds, I would have seen myself standing within the bottom portion of the U that formed the castle's main structure. I had entered the great hall, which stretched before me . . . dark and bleak and redolent with the smell of sweat and burned meat and woodsmoke. What little natural light there was came from the archer's windows along the front wall. Their purpose defensive rather than ornamental, those wedge-shaped windows narrowed from a recess large enough for a man to stand within to a mere sliver of an opening. The few stripes of sunlight they allowed in were mirrored by the remains of the previous night's blaze smoldering in the immense fireplace along the distant rear wall. Not surprisingly, the hall was empty, given that it would be several hours before the evening meal was served.

My footsteps rang loud upon the stone floor as I ventured a bit farther in, for only a scattering of reeds and no fine carpets had been put down to dampen the sound. A substantial trestle table lay directly before the broad stone hearth. A single matching chair, intricately carved and large enough for two men, was positioned behind it. I had no doubt this seat belonged to Nicodemo. Other tables and benches were arranged so as to leave a wide aisle from that main table, giving the duke a clear line of sight to the door.

Glancing to either side, I saw several threadbare tapestries hanging from the walls on ornate iron rods. Each woven work depicted gruesome scenes of hunted beasts, and none of them added any real cheer. Alternating with the tapestries on one wall was a series of alcoves. These presumably led to a single hallway that ran parallel to that wall, and where the servants might discreetly enter and exit . . . perhaps where a musician might be hidden away.

My tentative steps caused the large black hound sprawled upon a pile of dried reeds in the corner to lift its nose from its paws. From the aggressive tilt of its broad head, it appeared to be debating between the pleasure of confronting an intruder and the comfort of remaining snugly in its nest. The latter choice won out, for the hound contented itself with a half-hearted woof before sighing back into canine slumber.

Relieved, I started toward the adjoining chamber. My goal for the moment was to make my way up to the battlements above the barracks and discover if the flying machine was there upon the roof. I dared not try to reach the top by means of the tower that was part of the soldiers' quarters, lest I encounter the duke's men. But if I could find another way to access the roof, I could surely reach that particular spot, for all the upper walkways would be interconnected.

I passed several servants as I traversed the lower level, but none questioned me or paid me more than a glance. Keeping a keen eye out for a passage leading to a stairway, I decided to follow one of the older pages who was wandering a bit apace of me. He disappeared into an alcove, which turned out to conceal the hoped-for course . . . a narrow stone staircase. I waited at its foot long enough to be sure I would not stumble across him at the landing above before making my way up.

The staircase led to an open chamber that appeared to be the dividing point between two separate wings. I knew that I was unlikely to stumble across the duke here, for I had learned from Rebecca's conversation with his servants that his personal chambers lay in the right arm of the U. I assumed that, as with Il Moro's private residence within Castle Sforza, the Duke of Pontalba's rooms were secured from the rest, allowing him greater refuge should the castle ever be successfully stormed.

Tucking my linens beneath my arm, I went to the nearest window and leaned out to get my bearings. This high up, the windows were broader than those at ground level, so that I could comfortably sit upon the sill. But they did not overlook the outer wall and give a view of the open field beyond the main gate and guard towers. Rather, their view was that of into the inner castle grounds, and of the smaller towers and turrets not visible from the front.

Clutching the stone edges to stave off the sudden dizziness that threatened, I gingerly leaned out a bit farther. I could glimpse to my left a curl of smoke and the corner of the shed where Rebecca and Tito were doing the laundry. The barracks lay on the opposite side of the castle, the same side where the duke was housed. That was where I needed to be.

Aware that time was passing, I turned to the south wing, slipping past the first door. The next series of rooms were far smaller than those on the floor below, consisting of salons and apartments reserved for guests. Some opened into one another; others were connected by short halls. As with much of the rest of the castle, several of the rooms appeared to have been added as afterthoughts, portioned out of larger chambers.

Midway through, I startled a young porter and serving girl who were attempting a hasty coupling in one of the toilets. An odorous alcove set into the outer wall, it boasted nothing more than a slit of a window for ventilation and an open stone seat built over the cesspit far below. It was hardly a spot conducive to romance, though it likely afforded more privacy than the pair would know in their own quarters.

Muttering a hasty apology, I ducked out of that niche as quickly as I had entered and, their curses ringing in my ears, continued with my search.

Another alcove led to yet another staircase, this one consisting of rough stone steps that led upward in a spiral to a broad wooden hatch set into in the ceiling. My excitement grew, along with my trepidation. Surely I was getting closer to my goal.

Leaving the linens behind, I started up the first step, trying to ignore the sudden light-headedness that threatened. While I had never cared much for heights, my fearful adventures within the towers of Castle Sforza a few months earlier had intensified that dislike. Thus, the open design of this crude stairway was sufficient to set my heart beating far faster than its usual rhythm. Telling myself not to look down, I clutched at the wall for support and grimly continued my climb.

Sweat beaded my upper lip by the time I reached the top.

With an effort, I schooled my uneven breath and gave an experimental push upon the hatch, noting as I did so the heavy iron loops set into both that wood and the stone around it. A pair of iron bars could easily be slipped through those circles, making the hatch almost impossible to open from above should an enemy threaten. But for now, it swung upward with but a small squeal and landed with a muffled thud.

Aware that I had announced my presence should anyone be up there, I hesitated a long moment before taking the final steps to the level above.

To my relief, none of Nicodemo's men came bearing down upon me, swords drawn and ready for capture. Instead, I found myself alone at what was best described as a crossroads between two open doorways. Those doorways were situated at right angles, with each leading to a narrow passage.

The stone walls directly behind me were part of the outer fortifications, for they were notched with the familiar archer's windows. I squinted through one and glimpsed a bit of the forest through which we had driven earlier this day. I could see little more than chiseled rock by looking up, but I judged that I was right below the battlements. Heading to my right would put me above the barracks.

Still, I remained where I was for a moment, studying that passage in question. Opposite each window was an arched doorway, the wood fortified by iron strips and solid save for a gap at eye level that would allow someone to peer inside. On closer look, I saw that heavy locks hung from each latch.

At the realization, my heart began pounding as fiercely as if I were balanced on that open stairway again. I took a deep breath, seeking calm. Perhaps those doors merely led to a series of storage rooms secured by a jealous lord against possible theft, I told myself.

Or perhaps one of those doors concealed something else that the Duke of Pontalba did not want discovered . . . such as the kidnapped man whom he believed to be his ally's master engineer, Leonardo the Florentine.

Moving as silently as Pio the hound, I eased my way to the first door and peered through the slot. Another archer's window within allowed sufficient light into the small chamber for me to make out wooden boxes and barrels piled high. Arms, perhaps? Or grain and other supplies stockpiled in case of an attack? No matter; so many varied containers filled the room that no space remained for a prisoner.

With the same soft steps, I made my way to the next chamber and gazed through the slot. Similar to the first room, this one held rows of crates and piles of bulging cloth sacks. The next room contained much the same, as did the two after. Discouraged, I was prepared to give the final room but a cursory glance.

And then I saw that, unlike the rest, this chamber was empty save for a crude bed that had been placed beneath the archer's window.

Hardly daring to breathe, I squinted against the mixture of sunlight and shadows that filled the small space. Was that a figure wrapped in the tangle of blankets that covered this cot? I waited a seeming eternity for some sign of movement; then, deciding I must risk a sound lest by waiting I be discovered, I softly called, "Father?"

The blankets stirred, and it was all I could do not to dance in place as I waited in anticipation for a glimpse of my sire's face. "Father," I whispered again, impatience overriding prudence. "Father, is that you?"

The blanketed figure rolled from the cot and lurched to a standing position, wavering there a moment before staggering toward me. My moment of relief promptly transformed into a jolt of alarm. Was he ill . . . or perhaps injured? For any number of hardships might have befallen him in the short time that he'd been in the soldiers' custody.

As the figure drew closer, I frowned. My father was taller and broader than the swathed person standing beyond the door. Did the Duke of Pontalba perhaps have yet another prisoner under his control? But before I could question this unknown person further, small hands reached up to tug aside the blanket, revealing the face beneath.

I blinked. This certainly was not my father; moreover, this was no man locked within the chamber. Rather, the pale, pinched features and dull brown eyes belonged to a young woman!

"Who are you?" she asked, her voice so thin that I had to strain to hear. "Has the duke repented of his cruelty so that I might be released?"

The blanket had slipped to her shoulders, and I glimpsed a flash of fine silk gown in the deepest of blues. Her outer sleeves were fashionably slit so that her white chemise should have puffed with artful flair between those ribbons of azure fabric. But even in the dim light, I could see that the chemise was gray with dirt and the buoyant puffs flaccid. Her black hair—which must have once been braided with ribbons and twisted into a sleek, elaborate crown—hung untidily down her back.

She was no servant girl, I realized in surprise; moreover, she looked vaguely familiar. With a gasp, I cried, "Are you the Duke of Milan's cousin, the one sent to Pontalba as a bride?"

She stared uncomprehendingly for a moment before managing a small nod. "I am Marianna, Duchess of Pontalba . . . much to my eternal grief."

A tear trickled down one slack cheek, leaving behind a shiny trail, but otherwise she displayed no emotion. For myself, I could do nothing but gape in disbelief.

Though I had never spoken to her, I had encountered this one of Ludovico Sforza's many young relatives while in my guise as the Contessa Caterina's maidservant. A cousin to Caterina, as well, the plump Marianna had appeared a flighty girl prone to petulance; still, I had heard that she treated her servants with kindness. Following Caterina's tragic death, Il Moro had chosen her as a substitute wife to seal his alliance with his new ally, Nicodemo lo Bianco, the Duke of Pontalba. Whether or not Marianna had welcomed that honor, I did not know.

But seeing the girl's treatment at the duke's hands, I was abruptly grateful that the delicate and lovely Caterina had not lived to be the bride of that brutal man.

Though knowing the futility of the gesture, I still gave the lock on her door several frantic tugs. The heavy metal mechanism did not budge. Had Leonardo been there, he might have cleverly used a bit of wire to serve as a substitute key. Lacking both the Master's skill and a piece of wire, I could only rattle the lock in frustration.

"Your Eminence," I started to address her, to have her cut me short with a wave of one pale hand.

"Pray, do not address me as such, for I would take nothing of his, especially not his titles. I am Marianna."

"Very well, M-Marianna," I began again, stumbling a little at the informality of that address. "The lock holds tightly, I fear. I will have to find a key."

"The guards have the keys. Have you come to free me?" she asked, though with no note of hope in her voice. "Who are you?"

"My name is Delfina," I replied, deliberately using my true

name as I knew she could see nothing of me but my face. In her distraught state, chances were she would be more likely to trust another female than she would a boy.

"I'm a friend to the great master Leonardo at the court of the Duke of Milan," I went on. "Once, I was a servant to the Contessa Caterina. I am searching for my father, whom I fear is imprisoned by the duke, as well."

"Milan?"

That single word seemed to penetrate her hazy mind, and she stared at me, eyes widening. "Please, you must take word of my plight to my cousin Ludovico, so that he can rescue me!"

"Do not despair, Marianna," I replied, careful to keep my tone optimistic despite the anger that filled my breast at the thought of what she had suffered. "I vow upon the saints that Il Moro shall know what has happened. Take comfort, for you soon shall be released."

I prayed I was not giving her false hope. The matter of the flying machine's theft aside, surely Il Moro would not let his cousin be imprisoned in such a fashion! As soon as we returned to Milan, I would make certain that the Master knew of Marianna's cruel fate, so that he could advise his patron. And if Ludovico did not act, I had little doubt that Leonardo would find some way to gain her freedom.

"But what did you do? Why did the duke imprison you?" I wanted to know.

The girl blinked, and another tear slid unheeded down her cheek. "I did nothing save try to flee his cruelty."

I thought for a moment that she would say nothing more, and I wondered at the wisdom of pressing her. But after a few moments, she appeared to rally her wits about her. Her voice stronger, she went on. "I did my duty as my cousin Ludovico commanded. I tried to forget that the duke—my husband—was not young and handsome. But it did not matter. He cared naught for me from the start.

"Indeed, he wished to have me in his bed only so that he could get me with child. I could have borne that, had he left me in peace the rest of the time. But I had barely unpacked my things when he took from me my pens and my books. By that time, he had already dismissed my servants that had come with me from Milan, so that I was all alone."

She paused, and the first flash of emotion I'd seen from her—a combination of hatred and fear—now animated her face.

"When several months passed and I still did not carry his heir," she went on, "he accused me of taking potions so that I would remain barren. He said if I did not give birth within a year, he would have me stripped naked before the entire castle and stoned as a sorceress. That was when I knew I could stay here no longer."

I stifled a small cry at her words, unable to believe that sort of barbarity still existed in such enlightened times. "But how could you flee?" I asked. "Surely he kept you guarded."

She nodded. "I was not allowed to leave the castle grounds, but I was free to leave my quarters. I had made friends among some of the servants . . . in particular, a washerwoman from Milan who came on occasion to take my linens. I told her of my plight, and she agreed to help."

"A washerwoman?" I echoed in surprise, earning her nod.

Her tone stronger, she went on. "She agreed to hide me in one of her baskets and drive me out of Pontalba by wagon to take me back to Milan. She was taking a great risk—we both knew that if the duke learned that she had helped me, he would have her hanged—but she insisted. And, of course, I promised that my cousin Ludovico would pay her a great reward for her services. And so, a fortnight ago, we proceeded with our plan."

I could guess what must have happened next. Even so, I asked, "What then?"

"It was easy," she replied with a shrug, the gesture sending her gown sliding off her once-plump shoulder. "Her wagon was waiting at the laundry shed. I met her there under pretense of bringing her linens to wash. She put me in the empty basket and covered me with those linens, and then drove off. We made it past the guards, but she refused to let me climb from my hiding place lest someone traveling on the road take notice of me."

The tears began to fall more swiftly, and these she brushed away with an impatient hand. I could only listen in dread as she went on. "I don't know what went wrong. Someone must have seen me climb into the basket; that, or they discovered me missing and knew that no other carts save hers had left that morning.

"The duke's men found us before we had been gone an hour. I tried to protect her. I said she didn't know I was hiding in the basket, but they did not believe me. They returned us to the castle, and my husband had me locked away here."

She paused and gave a harsh little laugh. "He told me that, despite what I'd done, he would still honor our agreement. And so, he visits me every few days. I vow I would rather suffer the stoning if it meant he would never touch me again."

By this time, uncertainty was nibbling at a corner of my brain. Though Marianna's story rang with stark truth, the manner of her escape made me uneasy. Carefully, I asked, "What of the washerwoman? What became of her?"

"My husband took great pleasure in telling me she had been beaten and hanged for her offense. And so, my torment here is worse for knowing that an innocent soul died on my behalf." She sighed and shook her head. "Ah, my poor Rebecca, so plain of face but so good of heart. I pray each night to Saint Barbara that her suffering was brief and that she found her reward in heaven."

15

As the bat should not fly in the day, neither should the bird take wing after dark.

—Leonardo da Vinci, *The Notebooks of Delfina della Fazia*

*R*ebecca?

I frowned uncertainly. It was a strange coincidence that the washerwoman who'd helped the young duchess had the same name as the washerwoman I knew. Odder still, from the girl's vague description, that both were plain-faced women from Milan. But they had to be two different women, for Marianna's Rebecca had been hanged by a vindictive duke less than a fortnight earlier. My Rebecca was quite alive and doing laundry while I was skulking about Nicodemo's castle.

Unless the two Rebeccas were both the same woman.

Unless Marianna's washerwoman had never been hanged, but had instead pretended friendship as she betrayed the young girl to her husband the duke.

The unbidden thought came from nowhere. I shook my head

to banish the disloyal notion, but it refused to be dismissed. And, looking back on all that had happened thus far, it occurred to me now that the greater part of our adventure had fallen into place with suspicious ease. From stumbling across Rebecca wearing my father's cloak, to getting past the Duke of Pontalba's guards with nary a look, our path had been gently paved. I recalled, as well, that Tito had questioned why a washerwoman would risk helping us on so dangerous a mission.

Why, indeed?

And had it not been Rebecca who had hinted that spies might be conducting their furtive business in the shadows of Castle Sforza? Could it be that she was so certain about such clandestine activities because she herself was a spy for the Duke of Pontalba?

I shook my head again and took a deep breath. I would have to consider this later. For the moment, my task was to locate my father . . . assuming that Tito had not been right all along, and our quest was but a chase for wild birds. I had lingered here far too long with the young duchess. At any moment, the duke's men—perhaps Nicodemo himself!— might find me here whispering with their prisoner. I must learn quickly if she knew anything of my father so I could continue my search.

Though she still stood just inside the door, she had sagged back into her earlier listless state. Softly, I called, "I shall help you, Marianna, but you must first help me. Do you know if the duke's men brought another prisoner here today? He would be a tall man, pleasant of face, wearing a brown tunic, and with dark hair and beard."

I feared for a moment that she no longer heard me, until she managed a slow nod.

"I heard something . . . Perhaps it was today; perhaps it was yesterday. I did not bother to look. Several of them came through the passage. They spoke in rough voices and laughed cruelly, so I guessed that they had another unfortunate like me. Then they were gone, and I heard no more."

I swallowed back my disappointment at so vague a reply and gave her an encouraging smile. "Perhaps it was he. I shall search further."

"Wait!"

The cry was sharp, anguished. She had pressed her face to the gap in the door, so that I could see nothing but a pair of haunted brown eyes, the delicate flesh below them so dark it appeared bruised. "You must swear you will come back for me, Delfina. Swear it!"

"I swear upon my father's life that I shall see you rescued," I replied, crossing myself for emphasis. "Now, I must go find my father, so we can end this ugly business and send your cousin Ludovico to free you."

My words seemed to reassure her, for the tormented eyes vanished from the slot. Sighing, I turned toward the final door, which lay at the end of the hallway. *This must be the way to the roof,* I told myself as I started in that direction. By this time, however, I feared that my father and the flying machine were both lost to me . . . perhaps had never been in Pontalba, at all. Even so, I would first search the battlements for any clue before giving up and returning to rejoin Tito and Rebecca.

Barely had I put a hand to the latch on that door, however, when a thin voice drifted to me from Marianna's tiny cell.

"Leonardo. That's what I heard the soldiers call him . . . Leonardo."

"I found it. As we hoped, the flying machine is hidden up behind the battlements."

My eager words as I returned to the laundry shed drew cries of relief from both Rebecca and Tito. The latter dropped the paddle he was using to stir one pot of laundry and leaped lightly from the wooden step on which he'd been balanced to stand before me.

"Is it damaged?" he eagerly demanded. "Have they assembled it yet, or is it still in sections?"

"It is in sections, just as we last saw it," I told him as I stripped off my borrowed page's tunic and retied my belt over my own brown garment. Swapping out the pilfered cap for my own, I recounted how I had made my way from the great hall to a narrow spiral stairway at the top of the castle, which led up to the battlements.

I kept to myself, however, the way my heart had pounded as I'd climbed those final iron steps—each little better than a rung—all the way up to a small hatch that opened onto the sky. The dizzy sensation had intensified there, making me feel as if I might tumble from the parapets at any instant, no matter that I made no move. Steadying myself against a short chimney, I had swallowed back my nausea and taken stock of the situation.

As I'd hoped, the walks from one tower to another were all connected; moreover, several portions of the main roof were relatively flat and quite sturdy enough for a man to walk across. I had hoped to find the flying machine lying directly behind the battlements above the barracks, but the walks there were too narrow to accommodate its breadth. I would have to search out the craft, which meant avoiding discovery by Nicodemo's guard.

Fighting dizziness, I had lurched from battlement to wall to tower, keeping low as I clung with sweaty desperation to whatever sturdy bit of masonry was in my path. I had feared for a moment that my search had almost ended before it began when, but a few moments into my search, I heard the thud of heavy footsteps that announced the approach of a guard. Swiftly folding myself into a gap between two chimneys, I prayed the soldier would walk past without seeing me . . . and that I would be able to extricate myself again once he'd gone!

I soon resumed my search, losing but a bit of skin on one elbow as I wriggled free. It seemed as if I had been balancing upon the rooftop for hours, and sweat had soaked through both tunics I wore. In truth, however, it had been but a few minutes later when I discovered what it was that I sought.

Leonardo's flying machine—or, rather, the various sections of it—lay on a wide section of walk, looking as if it had been deposited in careless afterthought by some giant hand from above. The Master would have been outraged to see his grand invention so treated. Still, from what I could see, it appeared undamaged by the wagon ride and subsequent handling.

I'd not spotted the craft from below when I'd first entered the great hall; thus, I was confident that I, too, was hidden from all save someone watching from one of the towers. Looking down, I had an unobstructed view of the gatehouse and outer wall, as well as the open field beyond. If not for my fear of heights—that, and the fact that but a few feet from me the roof dropped at an alarming pitch—I might have enjoyed the hawk's-eye view of the world.

As I finished my account, Rebecca set aside her own paddle with which she was stirring a vat filled with clothes already boiled and scrubbed, and needing only to be rinsed. Climbing off the step, she wiped the sweat from her brow with the edge of her wimple and asked, "What about Signor Angelo?"

"I fear he was not on the roof with the flying machine, nor did I find him locked in any cell," I replied with a grim shake of my head.

Perhaps his kidnappers had not yet taken him from whatever cell in which they were keeping him, I had told myself. Or maybe, believing him to be Leonardo the Florentine, they had brought him for an audience with the Duke of Pontalba himself. But my fear for him eased somewhat as I realized that, at least until the flying machine was completed, he surely would be kept in good health to work on it.

"No, I did not find him," I repeated, "but I found someone who says she heard the duke's soldiers escorting someone they called Leonardo. So if the flying machine is here, my father must be here, as well."

I had debated whether or not to tell Rebecca and Tito about the Duchess of Pontalba. Finally, I decided to keep my peace, at least for the time being. If the Rebecca standing before me was the same one who had helped Marianna, I dared not let her know I had discovered her secret before I learned if the washerwoman intended to betray me, as well. As for Tito, he was too prone to quick emotion and might well blurt out some ill-thought comment in her company and thus reveal the secret.

Instead, I asked, "Shall we return to Milan? Surely Master Leonardo will have traveled back from his mission by the time we arrive and will know what to do next."

"We cannot leave until tomorrow," Rebecca sternly reminded me. "There's wash to be done, and we must do it."

And so the three of us continued the work she and Tito had begun. It was no job for the faint of heart or weak of body. This I quickly discovered as I used the paddle to lift the soaked clothing and linens—weighing far more wet than they did dry—from the pot. Letting them cool sufficiently so that I did not burn myself on the scalding water, I wrung the soapy water from them before transferring them to the rinse pot. There, after a bit of boiling and stirring, the process would be repeated, with the clean clothes piled in a basket again while waiting to dry.

"Hang the wash from those pegs," Rebecca advised Tito, pointing to the numerous wooden hooks that were built into the posts of the shed's three open sides. "There's a good breeze and a decent bit of sun left, so they should dry by morning."

Soon, the laundry shed more closely resembled a festival tent, swathed as it was in all sizes and colors of fabric. As for me, I was soaked in wash water and sweat, my hands and arms aching with my efforts. With Tito's help, I was able to keep apace of Rebecca, who did the preliminary scrubbing . . . far harder work than what I was doing.

When the final tunic was hung and the pots empty of all save filthy water, I sank onto the wet stone floor with a groan. "Saints' blood, I cannot imagine doing this every day," I gasped out. "How ever do you manage it, Rebecca?"

"It's easy enough once you've done it as long as me. Why, my little Novella can hoist a basket of wet laundry that would take you and your friend both to carry," she said with a proud grin. "And it's not a bad living. I work as I please and answer to no man."

Tito gave a puzzled frown. "But doesn't it bother you that people look down on you for what you do?"

"Pah, there's no shame in honest hard work," she retorted. "That's something you'd do well to remember, my fine young apprentice. Those that do scorn me, they can think what they want, so long as they keep paying me. Besides, I sleep easy at night, which is more than I can say for most nobles."

"I know I shall sleep easy tonight," I interjected with another groan. "I'm so tired, I could sleep right here among the laundry."

"We'll have a nice soft bed of straw in the stable," Rebecca replied with a return of her grin. "Come; it's time for the evening meal, and the kitchen master said he'd save us a bit of stew."

The stew proved surprisingly tasty, and I felt much restored by the time I had scraped clean the bottom of my borrowed bowl. As we ate among the other servants, I kept a keen eye and ear open for any gossip about either my father or the duchess. But it seemed that the servants of Castle Pontalba were not prone to undue chatter, for the conversation about us was cautious. I wondered if it was because we were strangers among them or if the talk was always tempered. Knowing what little that I did of Nicodemo, I suspected the latter.

I did, however, venture to question Rebecca on one matter. Keeping my tone casual, I asked her, "Do you know another washerwoman of Milan by your same name?"

She frowned, but I saw nothing of guilt in her expression as she replied, "By the Virgin, I cannot think that I do . . . but why do you ask?"

"It is nothing," I said with a dismissive wave. "But while we were gathering linens earlier, I thought I overheard one of the pages mentioning a washerwoman named Rebecca and thought it a curious coincidence."

Darkness had fallen by the time we made our way back toward the stable, which would be our room for the night. We deliberately took the long way about so that we passed by the barracks and the great hall, which had been empty earlier in the day. Now, however, soldiers whose dress marked them of rank joined men who appeared to be minor nobles as all filed toward that gathering spot. The aroma of seared lamb and baked fowl drifted to us, evidence that a grand meal was being prepared.

I gave a thoughtful frown. While the duke and his men were thus occupied later in the evening, I would slip back into the castle and visit the duchess in her cell. Perhaps she would have some idea where else in the castle her husband might hold his prisoner, so that I could continue my search. Failing that, I could at least offer her company and consolation.

But when I shared my plan with my companions—leaving out the visit to the duchess—both protested mightily.

"We'll be safely out of here in the morning," Tito countered. "Why risk being caught as a spy, when there is naught you could do, even if you found your father?"

"I agree with Tito," the washerwoman declared. "Besides, we have a long journey before us tomorrow . . . and we must fold and deliver all the laundry before we leave! Better you get a fair night's rest, instead. Now that we know the Duke of Pontalba is responsible for these crimes, we can leave the rescue to Signor Leonardo and his good patron."

"Perhaps you are right."

I gave a grudging nod, which seemed to satisfy them. Of course, this was not the end of it. I intended to wait until the pair was asleep and steal away as I originally planned. Risk or not, I could not leave the castle without making a final attempt to find my father.

Our makeshift bed was in the stall beside the brown mare. The wagon was parked here, as well, and Tito graciously offered it for Rebecca's bed, assuring her that he and I would sleep quite comfortably in the straw beneath it. I made no protest, for the sacrifice suited me quite well. Rising from a straw pallet would allow a far quieter exit than trying to clamber unnoticed out of the wagon.

I hid my impatience as well as I could while Tito and Rebecca amused themselves by swapping crude tales, their laughter causing the brown mare to snort her disapproval each time. The afternoon's toils apparently had changed the apprentice's opinion of our traveling companion, I decided, for he now seemed quite comfortable in her company. Finally, the pair exhausted their store of bawdy jests and agreed to call it a night.

"Remember, boys, we shall be up with the cock," came Rebecca's parting words as she climbed into the wagon. At Tito's snicker, she added in a mock-lofty tone, "And I mean the bird, you insolent young man."

I lay down on my makeshift pallet and feigned quick sleep, listening as my companions settled themselves. Finally, when their snores joined the mare's gentle nickering, I sat up. I waited a few moments longer; then, when their rhythmic breathing did not change, I eased into a standing position. Mindful of the crackling straw, I slipped out into the night.

I stopped by the laundry shed and snagged one of the freshly washed tunics. It still held a hint of dampness, but I knew the warmth of my body would soon dry it. Pulling it on over my head, I again traded my cap for that of the young page and made my silent way toward the great hall.

A blaze of light accompanied by hearty laughter spilled from the open doorway. Straightening my tunic, I slipped inside and grabbed up a discarded tray. So equipped, I boldly joined the other pages who were assisting at the meal.

My first observation was that, unlike the court at Milan, this one was noticeably absent of females, save for a handful who appeared from their scandalous dress and manner to be prostitutes. The place alongside the Duke of Pontalba was empty, and I wondered if Marianna had ever sat at his hand.

I noted, as well, that the men here were well armed . . . again, differing with Il Moro's court, where the gentlemen put aside their more blatant weaponry at mealtime. Including the duke, there were perhaps two score men, all of whom appeared already well into their cups.

I busied myself rearranging a few platters upon one of the

trestle tables and managed a good look at the Duke of Pontalba. I recalled him but vaguely from that ill-fated masquerade, but what I saw rang true to my memory.

Tall and slightly hunched, he had a craggy face whose thin lips twisted with cruel amusement. I judged from the droop of his eyes and pouchy flesh beneath his chin that he was quite a bit older than my father. But it was not until I saw him casually slap one of the pages who'd not been swift enough to refill his wine that I shuddered. I could understand why Marianna claimed to prefer death to his touch. In her slippers, I might well feel the same.

I had seen all I needed to see, I told myself. Only the first course had been served, so I was confident that the merriment would continue for some time. Thus, bearing my empty trenchers, I slipped into the nearest alcove. Handing off the tray to a surprised youth younger than me, I made my way down the hallway and turned off in the direction I'd taken earlier that day.

Retracing my steps was less easy than I'd hoped, for it appeared that Nicodemo was stingy with his candles and torches. Thus, the rooms that had been dim before were bathed in thick shadows relieved by the occasional flame in a recess in the wall. I gave myself a moment to let my eyes adjust to the low light and continued my careful way.

It took me longer than I expected to find the stone stairwell that led to the hall where the locked cells were. I paused before making that climb to pluck from my belt pouch the stub of candle I'd had the foresight to bring. Lighting it from a guttering oil lamp, I shielded the tiny flame with one hand and made my cautious way up the steps. The trapdoor above me opened easily as before and, taking care not to splash candle wax about, I climbed through it.

The archer's windows provided scant light, but enough

that I saw an oil pot in the recess nearest the hatch. I prudently lit it lest I make a misstep and tumble back through that hole in the floor, putting a gruesome end to my escapade. But the added illumination did not add much in the way of comfort. My shadow before me wavered wildly, a diabolical image that set my artist's imagination to work. Before, the maze of halls and odd-shaped rooms had seemed cold and unwelcoming. Now, draped in darkness, they hinted at phantoms and spirits that might well walk the place.

Shaking my head to rid myself of such fanciful notions, I made my cautious way down the hallway. I paused at the final cell and, lifting my candle, peered through the slot in the door. With an effort, I made out the swaddled figure lying on the cot, so silent and still that it might have been one of the Master's clay casts.

"Marianna," I softly called. "Marianna, are you awake? It is I, Delfina."

I heard the rustle of blankets, and a shadowy figure rose from the bed. I raised the candle high again, so that my face could be clearly seen. I prayed that she recalled my earlier visit, and that she had not attributed my presence to some fevered dream brought on by the strain of her captivity.

"Delfina?" a voice from within the cell echoed . . . a voice not Marianna's, and yet that was known to me. "Delfina, can that be you?"

The figure rushed toward the cell door, while I gaped in disbelief. But it was not until I saw the familiar face peering back through the slot that I was able to choke out in joyous relief the single heartfelt word, "Father!"

16

. . . the stronger wind will be the victor . . .

—Leonardo da Vinci, *Codex Atlanticus*

"Father, what are you doing here? This is Marianna's—the Duchess of Pontalba's—cell."

"I know of no duchess," Angelo della Fazia replied, "but the better question is, what are you doing here, my daughter?"

"Why, I have come to rescue you!"

Choking back a sob, I reached my hand through the slot in the door. My father caught my fingers in his, and I was relieved to find that his hand, while chilled from the dank cell, was as strong as ever.

"You've suffered no harm, Father?"

"I'm as well as can be for having spent two days tied in a wagon and a few hours more in the good duke's dungeon," was his wry reply.

He released my hand and peered through the slot, his kind brown eyes suspiciously damp as he surveyed me. "How did you find me, child? Have you brought Signor Leonardo with you?"

"I fear not. He had not yet returned from his mission to find the duke when we left, so there is but Tito and Rebecca the washerwoman and I."

I told him of the past days' events, explaining what had brought the three of us together, while he alternately nodded and shook his head at my tale. I recounted, as well, the clues that had led us to Pontalba, along with our theory that the duke's men must have seized him in error, having mistaken him for Leonardo.

"They took me without explanation," he confirmed with a nod. "It was well past midnight when I answered a knock at the door, thinking it might be you. Instead, it was three men in dark robes. They overpowered me, and before I knew it, they had bound me, hand and foot. Then they carried me to the shed where the flying machine was stored."

He paused and shrugged.

"They must have had little to go on to find their quarry save a description that fits me as well as it does your master. And as I was the only one in Signor Leonardo's quarters, their mistake was understandable. I could not protest that they had the wrong man, for they had gagged me when they tied me.

"But as I lay in the wagon while they waited for dawn to leave Milan—you and young Tito were right in your guess that we did not depart until morning—I overhead them speaking about me. Or, rather, the person they assumed me to be. Since I had seen their faces and knew something of their plan, I thought it the better part of wisdom to let them keep on thinking that I was Leonardo," he finished.

A frustrated tear slipped from my eye as I once again tugged at the lock. "And so you must keep pretending," I told him, "until we can rescue you from this foul place."

If I could manage to free him, we could sneak my father from the castle in Rebecca's wagon and let Il Moro worry about recovering the flying machine. I would have to find some way to steal the keys from the guards or else find a tool that would break the lock apart.

Then I froze, hand on lock, as it occurred to me that such a plan might prove to be but a retelling of Marianna's tale. I could not risk his life on Rebecca's loyalty, not until I was certain where it lay. For if she were but a tool of the Duke of Pontalba, our escape surely would be cut short, and all of us—my father and Tito and me—would be returned to a cell in Castle Pontalba.

"Oh, Father, what shall I do?" I softly cried. "I fear I must leave you here, after all. I do not know if Rebecca is to be trusted, and I cannot spirit you from Pontalba by myself."

"Fear not, my child," he assured me with a gentle smile. "I would not have you risk your life for mine. It is more than enough that you made this dangerous journey. You and your friends must return to Milan and seek counsel from Leonardo. As far as rescuing me, you need not worry . . . for I intend to liberate myself!"

"I—I don't understand."

"It is quite simple. Remember, Delfina, the ancient tale of the great craftsman Daedalus? He and his son lost the favor of the cruel king Minos and so were locked in the Labyrinth. Since the grounds and the seas around the kingdom were guarded, Daedalus determined that their one means of escape from that maze was by air. He built them both sets of wings, and thus they flew to freedom. And that is what I intend to do."

I stared at him in amazement. "Do you mean that you will escape Pontalba by flying Master Leonardo's invention?"

He nodded.

"It was I who suggested that we do the building upon the roof of the castle, though I claimed simply I needed the breezes to help test certain mechanisms. My plan is to modify Leonardo's design by adding wheels to the craft, so that I can roll it to the top of the roof and launch it by myself. The pitch of the roof should allow me to gain sufficient speed so that I will be safely airborne by the time I reach the drop-off point."

"But, Father, that is far too dangerous," I protested. "The Master said that craft should be launched over a pond or lake, so that if something goes wrong, the water will cushion the landing."

"I have no choice, child."

His expression grim, he went on. "I have heard the duke's plans for this machine. He wishes to have dozens of them at his disposal so that he can conquer the surrounding provinces . . . perhaps Rome herself. We cannot risk allowing such a dangerous weapon to fall into his hands. And so you can see that I must attempt this escape not simply to preserve my life but to stop the deaths of hundreds more."

"But, Father, the design is untested," I reminded him in a small voice. "If something goes wrong . . ."

I trailed off, unable to give voice to my worst fear, but he merely smiled.

"You should have greater faith in your master. If Signor Leonardo's design is true, and the winds and my strength hold, I shall fly the craft all the way back to Milan. If not, I will fly as far as I can."

Remembering that Daedalus's tale did not end happily—as best I recalled, his son Icarus lost his wings and plummeted to the earth—I could only shake my head at this dangerous plan. Still, there was sense in what he said. For even if Il Moro's men attacked the castle in an attempt to recover both him and the flying machine, there was little assurance that my father would walk free in the end. As vindictive a man as the duke gave all appearance of being, he might well kill the man he thought to be Leonardo rather than return him safely to Ludovico.

"Very well, Father, I shall trust your judgment," I reluctantly agreed. "We shall leave here in the morning, and as soon as we arrive back in Milan, I shall tell the Master all, so that he may explain the situation to Il Moro."

"Ah, you are a dutiful daughter," he replied with a smile. "Do not worry on my account, but keep yourself safe. Now, you should go, lest the guards come back and find you here."

I leaned up on tiptoe to kiss his cheek through the gap in the door; then, swiping away tears, I said, "Be careful. And know that if anything happens, I shall make certain that Mother learns the truth."

"Ah, your mother," he said with a wry smile. "There is something I should tell you about my journey to Milan that concerns her."

What that something was, I did not learn, for the sound of a slamming door below abruptly dimmed his smile. "Quickly, go," he urged. "All shall be well."

With a final nod, I pinched out my candle and hurried back to the hatch where I'd entered. The glow from the oil lamp in the wall was faint enough that I did not think it could be seen; still, I snuffed that light, as well, and waited silently to discover if anyone was coming my way. By then, my eyes were well-adjusted to the darkness, so I was able manage the stairs, though I clung to the rough-hewn wall for safety. I was breathing heavily by the time I made my way down the second staircase to the ground floor. The sounds of merriment still poured from the great hall, and a look up at the stars assured me that I had not been gone for all that long a time.

And so, I was taken by surprise when I reached the stables again, and Tito jumped from the shadows to confront me. His face dark with anger, he demanded, "Dino, where have you been? I woke up and found you gone."

"Tito, you squawk like an old woman," I replied, managing a light tone. "I stepped out to take a piss."

"Pah, you could not piss that long, no matter if you drank the entire vat of wash water. You have been gone for at least an hour."

Then his expression darkened further as he gestured at me and added, "And why do you need to wear a page's tunic to go empty your bladder?"

I gave a guilty start, remembering too late that I had not stripped off the borrowed tunic and returned it to the laundry shed. I hesitated; then, reassured by the sound of Rebecca's snores coming from the wagon, I lowered my voice further.

"Very well, I went back to the castle," I told him, "and this time, I found my father. If you swear that you can keep silent and say nothing, not even to Rebecca, I will tell you all I know."

After gaining his oath, I explained how I'd earlier discovered the duchess in her meager cell and told him of the odd coincidence of two washerwomen named Rebecca. I explained, as well, that I had returned in hopes of learning more from her, to discover Marianna gone from the cell and my father imprisoned there in her place.

"And he wishes us to return to Milan," I finished. "He will remain here at the castle. Once he finishes building the craft, he will make good his escape by flying it from Pontalba to freedom. By then, Il Moro will have been warned of what has happened and can pursue retribution against the Duke of Pontalba for his crimes."

Tito shook his head in amazement as he finished listening to my dramatic tale.

"This is serious business, Dino. I agree with your father. We must return to Milan as soon as possible and leave the rest up to Master Leonardo."

"Then let us get some rest. And remember, not a word of this to Rebecca. She may well be an innocent in all of this, but if she is not, we must watch her carefully lest she betray us, as well."

We arose to the cock's crow and made swift work of the now-dry laundry. By the time we had returned the linens to their owners, the pouch at Rebecca's waist jingled tellingly. She pulled out a handful of coins, which she split between Tito and me.

"Your share for your efforts. How does it feel to earn a few soldi for your hard work, my fine young gentleman?" she asked, her grin directed at Tito.

Tito eyed his share with suspicion. "I do not think this is one-third."

"And who said we would split the money evenly?" she countered, her black brows drawing down to her nose. "Besides, all earned was not profit. The kitchen master had to be paid."

"You are very generous, Rebecca," I interjected, giving Tito a not-so-subtle elbow to the ribs. "Shall I bring the mare and wagon, so we can be off?"

Not many minutes later, we had passed through the gates of Castle Pontalba and were driving at a quick pace toward the forest. It was not until we reached the trees, however, that I released the breath that I felt I had been holding ever since our arrival there the day before. Still, I could not help but glance over my shoulder several times lest the duke's men come in pursuit. Tito must have feared the same thing, for his gaze was fixed on the road behind us.

Sparing a glance at Rebecca, I wondered at her thoughts. I could read nothing in her expression, however, save an air of determination as she drove the mare with swiftness toward home.

As with the outward journey, we passed but a few people in either direction, so that the road belonged mostly to us. The washerwoman kept us going well past dusk, far later than she'd let us travel before. Still, I had to stop myself from protesting when we finally stopped for the night.

Though a chill hung in the air, we did not bother with a fire but wrapped ourselves tightly in our cloaks. We made a meager meal of bread and cheese, Tito having finished off the remaining figs the day before. By unspoken agreement, we limited our conversation to the latest gossip of Castle Sforza, but our talk had an air of forced joviality that fooled none of us. With the same silent accord we retired to our blankets soon after eating. Still, from the paucity of snores that followed, I suspected that I was not the only one having a hard time falling asleep.

Indeed, it seemed I had just dropped off into slumber when Rebecca was shaking me awake. The mare was soon hitched to the wagon, and we set off again as first light was breaking over the horizon. We were back among rolling hills interspersed with small groves, so that our travel took on a slower pace as compared to the day before. Heavy shrubs and sturdy pines flanked this portion of the road, which wound like a serpent's trail. We would reach Milan, I judged, at about the same time that the sun reached its zenith. From there, who knew what would be the next step . . . full-scale war, perhaps, or maybe stern diplomacy?

So caught up was I in such thoughts that, as we rounded the next curve, I took a moment to register what the appearance of a fallen pine tree across the road and a single man ahead meant.

Tito had no such moment of confusion. "Bandits!" he cried. "Bandits are awaiting us!"

More correctly, there appeared to be but a single lone bandit, stocky of build if stooped in posture. He stood a short distance before a thick tree trunk, which had been positioned most effectively to block the trail. But though he was alone, he was armed with an old-fashioned crossbow almost as large as he, which lethal-looking weapon he held aimed in our direction. He was helmed so that his face was mostly covered, and he wore a heavy brown jerkin over a black tunic and black trunk hose. Likely, he'd been a legitimate man in some noble's private force before turning to a life of unsanctioned thievery and murder.

Rebecca had pulled the mare to a swift halt, so that there were a dozen or so wagon lengths between us and the brigand. Despite my quite reasonable terror, I had to concede that his choice of ambush was clever. Even if we did not have his weapon to fear, we still could not drive around his roadblock for the trees on either side of us. Neither was there room to turn the wagon and flee in the other direction. The choices were surrender . . . or confrontation.

"Let go the reins and climb down," the man shouted, his guttural voice hinting at a Germanic accent.

I clutched at Rebecca's arm, which felt like warm steel beneath my hand. All the tales I'd heard of bandits robbing their victims ended with the bandits murdering those poor unfortunates. I doubted this man would be more merciful than his fellows in his treatment of us. If we did not take some action to evade him and his crossbow, the three of us would be found lying by the roadside, stripped of pouches and tunics and anything else that could be of value.

Thus confronted, my mind had gone swiftly blank when it came to clever plans. Praying the others had better kept their wits, I frantically murmured, "What shall we do?"

"If we climb down from the wagon, we are dead," Rebecca softly replied, echoing my unspoken fear. "But we have a small advantage in that he can kill but one of us with his crossbow. In the time it would take him to fletch it once more, the remaining two of us could be upon him. Tito must make ready his knife—yes, I know about it!—and I shall charge this brigand with our wagon."

She flicked a look at Tito.

"You and Dino, both of you shield yourselves as best you can until he has fired his weapon," she instructed in the same quiet voice. "With luck, we'll take him by surprise, and his aim will be off. My plan is to run him into the earth. Otherwise, if you and Dino can wrestle him down, I will put your blade into his black heart."

Though once I might have balked at so casual a plan of murder, I was no longer a sheltered girl with no knowledge of the cruel world. I had seen examples enough of man's depravity these past months to know that righteous self-preservation was the logical response to such a crisis. And so I gave a swift nod, while Tito murmured his assent.

But even this brief delay appeared to have enraged our assailant. He was moving toward us at a quick pace, his blond mustachioed lips—all that we could see of his face—twisted into a sneer as he shouted, "Get down, now!"

"Pray, do not harm us!" Rebecca cried in a high voice unlike her usual hoarse tones. "I am but a poor washer-woman. My boys and I have nothing of value. By the saints, let us pass in peace!"

"You have horse and wagon," he retorted, waving his crossbow in a threatening manner.

Then the man's sneer softened into what I assumed he intended to be a magnanimous smile. Lowering the weapon so that it pointed to the ground, he grandly added, "Don't be afraid, lady. You give me horse and wagon, I let you go."

"Don't believe him," Tito hissed, clutching the seat back and peering between us at the bandit. "He'll make us lie in the dirt, and keep the others at bay with his crossbow as he kills us one by one with his knife."

"I know," Rebecca murmured, and then called out, "May the saints bless you, sir. You may have our horse and cart, and welcome to it. *Yah!*"

With that harsh cry, she whipped up the brown mare. The horse gave an angry snort and leaped into motion, jerking the wagon forward. I made equal haste to slide down onto the boards at our feet, allowing Rebecca room to crouch low as she flailed the reins and drove straight toward the bandit.

In the instant before I shut my eyes and commenced praying, I saw his jaw drop in shock. Then, his lips twisting in outrage, he whipped his crossbow to his shoulder again and fired straight at us.

I heard the distinctive thwang as bolt left bow, and I flattened myself as best I could against the splintered boards. A heartbeat later, I simultaneously heard a sharp cry— Rebecca's or Tito's, I was not certain—and the crack of splintering wood as the bolt passed through the wagon.

And then I heard the most gruesome sound of all . . . a harsh scream and a series of soft thuds before Rebecca jerked the mare to a halt a few mere inches from the fallen tree.

17

A bird as it rises always sets its wings above the wind . . .

—Leonardo da Vinci, *Manuscript Sul Volo*

Quiet reigned for but an instant, broken by the mare's angry whinny and Rebecca's gasp of pain. I unfolded myself from my safe spot at her feet to see her grasping the upper portion of her left arm.

"Bastard nicked me with his arrow," she cried in surprise, while I sagged in relief to see that she'd not been pierced in a more vital spot. The splintering sound of wood I'd heard had been the bolt lodging itself in the wagon's sturdy rear panel. Tito was staring at the lethal projectile with wide eyes, and I guessed it had come flying within inches of where he'd lain.

"No, pay me no mind," she protested as I would have examined her wound. "We must be sure the scoundrel is dead."

Tito needed no further urging to action. With a warrior's cry, he plucked his knife from his tunic and, brandishing the blade most threateningly, leaped from the back of the wagon.

I clambered from my own seat and followed after him, wishing in desperation I had a weapon of my own to wave about.

I soon found, however, that I did not need any arms. The bandit lay crumpled on the road a couple of wagon lengths behind us, his spent crossbow dangling from his hand. Knife held high, Tito approached the injured man, halting a few feet from him.

It was apparent that the bandit's wounds from where he'd been trampled by horse and wagon were mortal. His lower body twisted at an unnatural angle from the rest of his torso, while bright blood frothed from between his lips. The impact had knocked the helmet from his head, finally revealing his face.

Unexpected sadness swept me as I saw he was not the older warrior that I had pictured from his weapon and posture. Rather, he was a man just past the flush of youth. What evil within had driven him to his murderous life, I could not guess, though I wondered if he regretted his choices in the face of imminent damnation.

Tito appeared to feel no such comparable sorrow. "Ha, you fiend, you got what you deserved," he cried, grabbing the crossbow from the man's slack fingers. "I shall finish you off, so that you do not prey upon honest citizens ever again."

"Then I . . . bless you . . . as savior," the bandit sputtered, teeth bared in a bloody red grin as he raised a weak gloved hand in parody of a consecration.

Shaken by that response, Tito lowered his knife and glanced at me uncertainly.

"Don't you see?" I murmured, clutching his arm. "In his condition, a swift death would be a blessing. It would be far crueler to leave him suffering here, easy prey for the carrion eaters and whatever other beasts wander these woods."

"Better we leave him, instead," Tito replied, though now his bravado rang false. "He would have let us suffer."

"But we are not like him."

"Fine, you kill him," Tito cried, face darkening as he pressed his blade into my hand.

My fingers closed reflexively around the fancy hilt, but my stomach lurched as I stared down upon the dying man. Though I had been involved in more bloody conflicts than any other young woman of my station could possibly imagine, I had wielded a weapon only in my own or the Master's defense. And never had I inflicted a killing blow upon anyone. But when simple humanity decreed that a merciful blade was the kindest action, I stood frozen in indecision.

Strong fingers abruptly pried the knife from my grasp.

"This is not the work for innocents," Rebecca decreed. "You boys are too young to suffer such a stain upon your souls, no matter that it is to bring release to one who does not deserve it."

I saw in some shock that she had stripped off her wimple to bandage her injured arm. Thus uncovered, she revealed for the first time a glorious crown of red hair—a stark contrast to her black brows—elaborately braided and wrapped about her head. As she knelt awkwardly beside the bandit, sunlight gleamed upon those fiery locks. The reflected light bathed her plump face in an almost saintly glow, which lent her a certain beauty I might not otherwise have seen.

"Quickly, make your last prayers and repentances," she commanded with stern calm, cutting the man's jerkin laces to bare his breast and pressing the blade tip to his heart.

She placed a beefy hand across his eyes and added, "You will be free of your suffering in but a moment, and perhaps God shall show greater mercy to you than you did to others."

"No," he gasped and reached up to pull her hand from his face. "I am . . . soldier. I see . . . death come."

"As you wish."

Not being a soldier myself, I could not bear to watch what followed but shut my eyes to block the sight. Still, I could not help but hear Rebecca's soft grunt as she shoved the blade home, nor could I block out the sound of the bandit's last groan. I waited until the shuffling noise that accompanied his body's struggle with death had ceased before I dared look again.

By that time, the bandit lay still, and Rebecca was cleaning the knife blade in the dirt. She crossed herself; then, rising with an old woman's awkward moves, she heaved a weary sigh and handed the knife to Tito.

"We've no time to give him a decent burial. Carry him away into the trees, and hurry back. We must move the log blocking the road before we can continue our journey."

Between us, Tito and I handled the grim task of dragging the dead bandit into the dark glade. When I went to cover him with a few fallen branches, however, Tito gestured me to stop.

"Wait; we'll need this," he declared.

Heedless of the blood and urine that stained the dead man's clothes, he tugged at the man's belt until he'd freed the large pouch which had hung from it. I saw that the bag contained several fresh bolts, crudely carved but lethal, nonetheless. I nodded at the prudence of this move—had we not just witnessed a most frightening demonstration of why one should travel armed?—and waited while he did a swift search of the bandit's jerkin for any other weapons.

Finding none, he gave me a quick nod and headed back toward the road. I spared a few more moments to toss the branches atop the still form; then, offering up a fleeting prayer for the repose of the bandit's cruel soul, I hurried after Tito.

By the time I reached him, the apprentice had already retrieved the crossbow from the road where he'd left it and had hooked the pulling mechanism to his belt. Stepping foot into the stirrup mounted on the weapon's stock, he managed with an effort to fletch another bolt. He left the armed crossbow in the wagon bed, and he and I joined Rebecca where she stood staring at the fallen tree.

"It can't be that heavy, not for one man to move it about by himself. See how the large end is propped on a stump?"

She pointed to the half-circular swath in front of the log, which gave the appearance that something had scraped across that portion of the road multiple times. "He would have dragged the tree trunk by the smaller end."

We found that the log did move easily, almost as if poised upon a pivot. A few moments later, we had cleared the path and were prepared to board the wagon again.

"Here," Rebecca said with a sigh and tossed the reins to Tito. "My arm is paining me too much to drive."

While Tito checked over the doughty mare to make certain she'd suffered no harm in the trampling, I helped settle Rebecca upon the blankets we'd brought. I was relieved to see that her injured arm no longer appeared to be bleeding, while the wimple she'd used as a bandage was tied as neatly as any wrapped by a surgeon. But I knew that putrefaction remained a real danger. As soon as we returned from Milan, I would ask Signor Luigi for the same healing salve that, once before, the tailor had used upon me.

"Drive quickly, Tito," I told him, "but be mindful of Rebecca's injury."

He started off at a brisk pace, handling mare and wagon with surprising skill. I did what I could to shield the washerwoman from the worst of the bumps, but I could see her biting back moans of pain each time he rumbled across a particularly rough patch. Seeking to distract her, I spent some minutes describing to her the latest fresco we'd been helping the Master to paint.

"All in all, the images are quite glorious," I finished, "though some are unaccountably strange. Still, if our Lord did walk upon the water, could it not be possible that he might also have floated above the ground?"

Then I sighed. "It is sometimes difficult to reconcile all I have been taught with what I have learned from the Master. Indeed, sometimes I do not know if Signor Leonardo is merely mocking God, or if his vision is genuine and he sees more than the rest of us."

"Pah, do not worry, child," the washerwoman wheezed with a small grin. "I have found in my time that those who protest the loudest against God are those who mostly desperately wish to believe in his existence. Learn what you can from your master, but never fear to stand up for your beliefs."

"Rebecca, how did you become so wise?" I impulsively asked. "You know so much of the world, and yet you are just a—"

I broke off abruptly and blushed, realizing the affront couched in my intended praise. Yet, rather than take offense, Rebecca merely chuckled.

"Just a washerwoman," she finished for me. "You may say the word, my boy . . . It is no insult, despite what some might think. And surely you must see that my job is far more than washing clothes."

When I looked at her quizzically, she went on. "Why, I am more a confessor to my customers than any priest. By looking at a man's soiled linens, I can tell if he is a glutton or a drunkard . . . if he is celibate or licentious, or if he beds women other than his wife. And yet my lips are sealed, safe as if he had gone to a confessional. But unlike many priests, I keep all my secrets to the grave."

I gave this revelation careful measure before regarding her in good-natured dismay. "I had never considered such a thing," I said with a shake of my head. "But you may be assured that in the future, I shall treat my linens as the open book they are!"

She grinned again and settled back down to rest. For myself, I took the time that followed to reflect upon the recent suspicions I'd had regarding her loyalty. It had taken more than a bit of bravery to face down the armed bandit, and as much courage to dispatch him, rather than leave him to die an agonizing death. And all through this journey, she seemingly had devoted herself to keeping Tito and me from harm.

Could the same woman who had acted with such valor also have betrayed a frightened young duchess, surrendering her to certain death?

I told myself, no. Too much about her words and deeds marked her as one to be trusted . . . but then, it was the cleverest of fiends who often appeared the most kind. *If only I could read people with the same ease Rebecca claimed to read bed linens,* I thought with a sigh.

The remainder of the journey passed in relative silence, for Rebecca had passed from sleep to deeper stupor. I noted in some alarm that her face had gone pale while her cheeks burned brightly. I used what remained of our water to bathe her brow and moisten her dry lips, while I urged Tito to greater haste.

It was with a heavy sigh of relief that, near noontide, I finally spied the spires and buildings of Milan in the distance.

Giving Tito direction, our first stop once we rumbled into the city was at Signor Luigi's tailor shop.

"What grave mischief are you at now, my, er, boy?" he demanded of me, his bushy brows shooting upward at the sight of the unconscious woman lying in the wagon bed.

Not waiting for a reply—after all this time, Luigi was far too familiar with my often dangerous exploits to be surprised by much—he summoned his two apprentices. Between the four of us youths, we managed to carry Rebecca inside and settle her upon a bench. Then, shooing away the other two boys, the tailor swiftly unwrapped the makeshift bandage and examined her wound.

"Was this done by an arrow . . . or perhaps a bolt?"

"She was shot with a crossbow defending us most bravely," I told him. "More than that, I cannot say for the moment . . . but I beg that you help her."

"Pah, why am I always the first you come to, and yet the last you confide in?" he protested, but without any true rancor.

Disappearing behind the curtain that separated the shop from his personal quarters, he reappeared a moment later carrying a basin of water and two jars. Opening one, he poured a measured amount of a white powder into the water and used the concoction to bathe the wound. Though the bleeding was long stanched, I saw that the gash was swollen and alarmingly red.

As he worked, Rebecca began to stir, staring with bleary eyes about her. "Where am I?" she protested and tried to stand.

Luigi put a firm hand on her shoulder to hold her still. "You are in my tailor shop, my good woman, brought here by these two boys who decided your well-being was more important than my business. If you will sit quietly, I will tend to your injury and gladly send you all on your way."

With the wound cleaned of dirt and splinters, he opened the second jar. While Tito and I wrinkled our noses in protest, he slathered the familiar foul-smelling ointment with a heavy hand before tying a clean cloth about the injured arm. Afterward, he shoved the jar into my hands.

"Make certain someone applies the salve no less than twice a day, and give her herbed wine for the fever. And now, I have done all I can do."

I tucked the jar into my tunic and gave the tailor a quick hug. "Many thanks, signore. We shall take her to her daughter, who will care for her. And when all is done, I promise I shall give you an account of all that led to this."

"Pah, I shall believe that when your master pays his latest bill," he retorted, though his black eyes gleamed with keen humor. Giving the washerwoman an exaggerated bow, he added, "It was a pleasure, my good woman . . . and I strongly advise that you stay clear of young Dino in the future, lest you find yourself in far worse straits the next time."

With that caustic dismissal, he opened the door and gestured us out into the street. Tito and I settled Rebecca into the wagon again and started at a quick pace through the city toward the castle. Now I had time again to worry about my father and the duchess. Surely Leonardo must have returned from his mission and read the missive I'd left behind for him. Perhaps he'd already concocted a plan. If not, we would be able to do naught but wait for his arrival, knowing in the meantime that my father's safety hung in the balance.

Fortunately, Rebecca's captain was not on duty at the gates, so that we made it past Ludovico's guards avoiding any awkward questions. My heart thumping loudly in my chest, I focused my attention on the Master's quarters, half hoping that, by sheer force of will, I could make him be there, though he was not. Tito glanced back at me once and shook his head.

"Calm yourself, Dino. You bounce about like Pio the hound. We shall be at the Master's quarters momentarily."

I managed with an effort to heed his words, though the final few minutes of our journey seemed the longest, yet!

Tito had barely halted the cart before Leonardo's step when I leaped out and began a frantic knock upon the door.

"Master, it is Dino! Tito and I have returned with news!"

When the door did not immediately open, I could feel my stomach plunge as it had when I'd first stood atop the roof of Castle Pontalba. Tito shook his head and jerked a thumb in the direction of the main workshop. "Perhaps he is there, instead."

I did not bother climbing back aboard the cart again but sprinted around the corner. The first thing that I saw was four large wagons waiting outside the workshop door. The door itself was propped open, and the apprentices, who should have been busy at work upon the fresco, were running back and forth between wagons and workshop with solemn purpose.

"Dino!" I heard my name called.

I looked over to see Vittorio beside one of the wagons. He gave an awkward wave as he used the other to balance a board upon one shoulder. "Finally, you have returned!" he cried, his expression one of relief. "Quickly, the Master awaits you."

I needed no further urging but rushed inside to find the workshop awash with frantic activity unlike any I'd ever seen. Davide was standing atop one table and directing the other apprentices with shouts and gestures. Some were cutting lengths of wood, while others were splashing paint upon large sections of canvas, which had been stretched on head-high frames. Davide spotted me but had no time for a greeting. Instead, he simply pointed in the direction of the fireplace along the far wall.

While normally it burned with a cheery flame, the hearth now raged like hell's own furnace, spewing a blast of heat and a blaze of light that momentarily stopped me in my tracks. Throwing up a hand to shield my face, I saw that an anvil had been set atop the hearth, and that a lone figure stood before it, wielding a hammer, which sparked against an immense blade glowing red with heat. With a final crash of the hammer, he set aside the blade and turned in my direction.

My first thought was that the fire god Vulcan had taken up residence in our workshop, for the man before me looked hardly human. He wore nothing save black trunk hose girded by a large leather belt, and his bare torso and arms gleamed with sweat. Where his face should have been, I saw but a black, masklike countenance, around which russet brown hair—appearing almost ablaze itself in the flickering light—spilled like a halo. He was an awesome and glorious figure, and I could do nothing for a moment but simply stare.

Then the fire god plucked aside his mask, and I saw in relief that beneath the emotionless facade lay Leonardo's familiar face.

18

Fame should be represented in the shape of a bird . . .

—Leonardo da Vinci, *Manuscript B*

"**M**aster!" I joyfully cried and rushed toward him, only to halt in confusion as he held out a warning hand.

"Not so fast, my young apprentice," Leonardo declared, a hint of a smile warming the look of weary determination on his face. "Come too close, and you may be burned like a moth rushing into a flame. I cannot afford to have you combust in such an undignified manner until you have explained all that has happened these past days. As you might guess, it was your dramatic missive to me that has put all of this"—he waved the hammer to encompass the bustling workshop— "into motion."

Setting aside mask and hammer, he grabbed up his tunic and pulled it on; then, taking me by the arm, he led me through the whirl of apprentices back outside the door. By now, Tito had moved the wagon, and Vittorio had joined him in checking on a surly if now fully conscious Rebecca.

Confusion reigned for a few minutes as Leonardo took swift stock of the situation. Under his direction, Rebecca was installed with much protest in Leonardo's own bed, with Vittorio dispatched to bring back Novella to care for her injured mother. Tito, meanwhile, was charged with returning the valiant mare and the wagon to the stable, leaving me alone to explain the past days' events to the Master.

"Now, tell me all," he commanded, gesturing me to the bench outside his quarters. "Have you and Tito discovered the fate of the good Signor Angelo and my flying machine at Pontalba? Speak quickly, for time is short, but leave nothing out."

I obediently launched upon a detailed account of all that had happened since the morning, seemingly a lifetime ago, when I had discovered my father missing along with the Master's invention. Leonardo listened with keen attention, occasionally nodding or inserting a sharp question to keep me on track. He appeared saddened but none too surprised to learn of the Duke of Pontalba's traitorous treatment of his young bride. Neither was he taken aback to know that Nicodemo had perpetrated the kidnapping and theft against his supposed ally.

"There was little to trust about the man," was his grim reply, "though I suspect Ludovico will be less surprised by his perfidy than were we."

I went on to explain my father's bold plan to rescue both himself and the flying machine from Nicodemo's clutches. "The duke intends for him to build a flock of such crafts, which he will use to terrorize the surrounding provinces. My father said that the duke must be stopped . . . and he would sacrifice himself, if need be, to accomplish that."

I choked a little over those last words, but Leonardo

merely nodded. "Signor Angelo did well to keep his masquerade, pretending to be Leonardo the Florentine. Otherwise, we
would be praying over his corpse right now. But I fear that he
may not be the man to fly my craft from Pontalba."

"What can you mean?" I countered, instinctively jumping
to my parent's defense. "He is skilled enough to complete the
design and clever enough to understand its workings."

Leonardo smiled a bit at that last. "Ah, see how the cub
bares valiant claws to protect its father, who in truth needs
no such defense."

Then he sobered. "I agree, my boy, that your father is a
man of many talents. But it is the fact that I designed my
craft for a man of my height and weight. Signor Angelo is
somewhat shorter and stouter than I. The difference may
matter little . . . or it could prove of great significance."

Chastened and more than a bit unnerved by this last, I
finished with the account of our ambush on the road back
to Milan. Rebecca's role in this, as well as our adventures in
Pontalba, brought sincere praise from the Master.

"A valiant woman, indeed, for all her other shortcom-
ings. I know of few females—and almost as few men—who
would display such courage." Then he added with a thoughtful frown, "For the moment, we shall assume that the matter of two washerwomen with the same names is an odd
coincidence and nothing more. But recall that one must be
careful of dismissing a truth out of hand before all facts are
known."

I nodded my somber agreement.

"So much has happened," I declared, "and yet much
remains concealed in secret. I still have no notion who dealt
our dear Constantin his fatal blow, nor can I guess where else
to look for an answer."

"I suspect that all shall come clear once we have put the

rest to right," was his cryptic response. "Recall that we have
yet to identify the young page who rousted Tito from sleep
and set this all into motion. And there is the matter of this
strange robed figure—whether man or woman—that you
claim to have seen watching since your father's arrival."

I dropped my head into my hands and groaned. "Saints'
blood, it is a tangled web. What if we never learn the truth?"

"The truth has many versions . . . and often much time
must pass before we know which version we should have
believed."

He stood abruptly and flicked his long fingers in the
familiar gesture of impatience. "But you have told your tale
well, my boy. And now, surely you must be curious to see
what your earlier words have wrought."

We returned to the main workshop, and I saw now that a
group of apprentices was loading one wagon with what I realized were some of Leonardo's war machines. I had thought
them but Leonardo's private notations, alive on paper but never
destined to see the light of day . . . and yet here they were. A
small catapult had already been neatly stowed, and now the
youths were carting a trio of portable cannons, the gun of each
designed to be taken apart from the body and wheels. What
appeared to be a combination rolling barricade and ladder,
large enough to shield five or six men, also sat to one side.

I stared for a puzzled moment, surveying this strange collection, before the obvious answer came to me. "Master," I
cried in surprise, "can we be going off to war?"

"In a manner of speaking, yes."

Gesturing me back into the workshop, he went on. "As
soon as I read your letter, I spoke with the captain of Il Moro's
guard, who claimed that his wrists were bound. It mattered
not even if we knew with certainty that the Duke of Pontalba
had broken the treaty and was behind the theft of the fly-

ing machine. The captain cannot send his men into Pontalba unless Ludovico himself first declares Milan to be at war. And so I decided that if I could not have Ludovico's soldiers at my disposal, I would create an army of my own."

He indicated the canvas-covered frames I had seen earlier. Paolo and Tommaso were at diligent work upon a pair of them, and I realized they were painting life-sized figures of men-at-arms.

"They've finished a small force already," he said, pointing to stack of similar canvases drying nearby.

"And, see, I have raided my stage sets that I use for the various pageantries," he added, nodding toward the collection of flat props, which included trees and bushes and carts. "In another hour or so, we shall be finished loading the wagons and be ready to set off."

"We're going to attack Castle Pontalba with painted soldiers?" I asked in no little confusion.

He shook his head.

"I seek only to give the appearance of siege. From a distance, it will appear as if we have all of Milan's army ready for attack. My intent is to approach the castle in parlay, representing myself as Ludovico's captain of the guard, and negotiate the return of Milan's master engineer."

"But, Master, can this work?"

"Perhaps. I have already dispatched an urgent message to Il Moro explaining what has occurred and asking that he agree to send his troops against Pontalba. But since the duke may prove fickle—or his army be tardy—I will not wait for his response. As for my plan, Nicodemo will know that Ludovico's force is greater, and with luck he shall see the virtue of cooperating without bloodshed. If not, then we shall serve as distraction for as long as possible, until reinforcements arrive . . . or until our deception is discovered."

He stopped short of saying what might happen should the Duke of Pontalba learn that he had been duped by an artist and a group of apprentices. Still, I was able to guess at a plausible ending myself, and that bleak outcome dampened my initial enthusiasm over the Master's plan. But inaction could prove equally dangerous, not only for my father and the duchess, but for the entire province.

And so I put myself to work loading our supplies. Tito had also joined our ranks, a large bundle balanced on his back as he scaled one of the wagons. Once the last prop had been securely packed, once the buckets of water and bags of food were loaded alongside the weaponry, we tied concealing cloths across the wagon beds and then assembled back in the workshop.

Leonardo entered a moment later, dressed now in black and red parti-colored trunk hose and a white tunic, over which he'd laced a heavy black leather jerkin. A sword dangled from one hip, and a long knife from the other, while a helmet was tucked beneath one arm. Looking less the great artist now and more the hardened soldier, he gestured us to gather closer.

"We are about to embark upon a mission of great importance in the name of the Duke of Milan," he intoned with the gravity of a bishop. "Already, all here have given me their vows of secrecy as we made our preparations. Your job going forward will be to provide distraction by appearing to be part of an armed force poised to attack Castle Pontalba . . . and so I shall ask for another vow, one of loyalty."

He paused and raised a hand to silence a sudden eager stirring among the youths.

"First, however, I will have you recall that what is to come will be but a masquerade," he went on. "You will be performing as if in a pageant. You will not fight or otherwise bear arms but simply add an air of veracity to the role that I shall play. That does not mean, however, that your part is unimportant . . . nor does it guarantee that you will not face true danger at some point."

The murmurs, which had earlier settled down, resumed again at this disquieting possibility. A few of the boys glanced uncertainly among themselves, the cheeks of more than one youth growing pale. Leonardo allowed this interlude to continue for a few moments and then raised his hand again for order.

"I will assure you once more that your participation in this mission is strictly voluntary," he continued. "You are apprentices and not soldiers; thus, I cannot force you to join me. Neither will I think the less of you if you choose to remain behind. And the only reward for those who take part is the knowledge that they will have helped preserve Milan and rescued two of our citizens cruelly held captive in Pontalba as we speak. So make your decision carefully but quickly . . . and all who wish to join me, step to my right hand."

He flourished the hand in question most dramatically, and for an instant all was still. Then, with nary a murmur, every apprentice—myself, included—marched over to his dexter side. Leonardo waited until we were settled in place and then surveyed us with a look of pride.

"Very well, then lift your own hand, and vow that you shall follow my orders these next few days with the same obedience that a soldier pays to his captain."

The flurry of hands and eager cries of agreement brought a proud tear to my eye. Surely with so valiant a band, my father would soon be rescued, and the duchess and the flying machine both restored to their proper places.

"And now," Leonardo continued, pointing to a pair of large barrels beside him, "if you are to play the part of soldiers, you must look the role. I have assembled a fine collection of tunics and jerkins, as well as mail, which should serve our purpose. Each of you choose a proper uniform for yourself and then gather in the empty wagon outside the workshop."

The next few minutes took on the element of a mock battle as we apprentices scrambled to find white tunics and dark blue cloth jerkins that fit from the one barrel, and appropriate bits of armor and mail from the other. The swiftest among us claimed breastplates and helmets, while the others had to be satisfied with mail headpieces and gloves.

Once I had my own gear in hand, I slipped away to the Master's makeshift forge. A few moments' foraging among the leftover bits of iron and other metals yielded success. Concealing the objects that I'd sought inside my belt pouch, I brushed the soot from my hands and rejoined my fellows.

Soon enough, it was a respectable-looking contingent that clambered into the fourth wagon reserved for the "troops." Tommaso, Paolo, and Tito each took the reins of one supply wagon, while Davide prepared to drive the one that would carry the remainder of us apprentices. All four conveyances were, in turn, harnessed to matched steeds that must have come from Il Moro's own stables. I wondered how the Master had managed so bold a feat and then shrugged. Leonardo had his own way of laying hands on whatever he needed, be it horses or tunics.

Eying my borrowed helmet with its flamboyant black plume in satisfaction, I balanced it upon my knee as Davide whipped up our team and drove our wagon into the main quadrangle. The other three wagons followed in precise formation after us, making a grand sight as we slowly rolled toward the main gate.

But where, I wondered, was the Master?

The sudden clash of hooves accompanied by what sounded

like a dozen swinging swords heralded his approach from behind us. As one, we turned and then gasped, our eyes wide with awe. For Leonardo, now wearing a warrior's gleaming breastplate and helmet, was driving what could only be but another of the fantastic war machines he had designed for Ludovico.

But while pulled by a pair of ordinary black stallions, this was no commonplace chariot. Each elaborately carved wheel was equipped with twin scythes mounted at its axle that spun as the vehicle moved forward. Evil-looking spikes studded the wheels' frames and provided additional defense should the spinning blades not suffice to stop a flank assault. Larger scythes were mounted on a shaft protruding behind the chariot and turned in concert with the wheels to protect against a rear attack. The largest blade of all was mounted on yet another shaft, which rose high above the driver's head, spinning like a silvery bird of prey.

Impressive as the sight was now, I could imagine how it would look in battle, the scythes enveloping the driver in a whirlwind of steel and singing a sure promise of destruction for any man or beast who drew too near the chariot. Never had any of us seen such a machine before . . . nor, I guessed somewhat smugly, would the Duke of Pontalba's men ever have been privy to such a sight.

We gave a fine cheer as Leonardo passed us by to lead our convoy toward the castle gates. Whatever agreement he had concocted with the captain of the guard must have been successful, for the heavy wood and iron grille was already raised, and the path before us was clear.

With a dramatic flick of a lever, the Master shut down his whirling blades, so we departed the castle with far less fanfare . . . and with far less likelihood of endangering any innocent passersby! He took a quicker route through the city than Rebecca had used, so that before long we were on the road and headed toward Pontalba.

"Wait! Signor Leonardo!"

We were but a short way down the road when several of us heard that faint salutation, repeated more than once over the rumble of wagon wheels. Curious, we all peered back, but the remaining wagons blocked our view of the way from which we'd come. It was not until we reached a small curve in the road that we could see past the last wagon again to discover the source of those frantic cries.

I was not sure whether to laugh or groan at the sight of a familiar cart bearing down with eager speed upon us. This time, the mare who pulled it was gray, and the driver was a beautiful young girl . . . but the sturdy figure doing the hailing was none other than the washerwoman Rebecca.

By the time we slowed for another curve, the nimble Novella had maneuvered the cart alongside us. Rebecca, arm bandaged and wimple restored, gave us all an offended look.

"You cannot be off without me!" she cried. "What if you need my help again?"

"Rebecca, you are injured," I countered in no little concern. "You should be resting and tending to your arm instead of driving about the countryside."

"I can rest later. Signor Leonardo needs my help now."

I glanced over at Novella in appeal, but she merely lifted a slim shoulder and kept driving. Doubtless the girl had long since learned that her mother was to be treated as a force of nature, something to be endured and not to be contained. As for Vittorio, he was grinning broadly. Gesturing the girl closer still, he stood and with a nimble hop went from our wagon to the cart.

"Do not worry," he declared as he took the reins from an admiring Novella and settled in. "I shall keep them apace of us, and when we stop to rest the horses, the Master will decide if they stay or go."

It was on the tip of my tongue to reflect that the Master might not have much choice in the matter. After all, it was a public road, and the washerwoman had as much right to it as he. The battle between Milan and Pontalba might not be the only fight we witnessed these next days, I wryly told myself. But I would not protest her coming with us, should I be queried on the matter. Indeed, I found myself unaccountably cheered by the washerwoman's doughty presence.

Settling more comfortably myself, I let my thoughts linger on my father's determined words he'd spoken the night I had left him. He had put aside his past doubts to envision himself soaring from the highest rooftops of Castle Pontalba and swooping like a hawk out of his enemy's reach. If my father dared to attempt so dangerous a feat on his own, then perhaps the Master's plan was not so impossible, after all.

Perhaps an army of untrained boys with no weapons but paint and their wits might find victory against an army when led by such inimitable generals as Leonardo the Florentine and Rebecca the washerwoman.

19

The flight of many birds is swifter than is the wind which drives them . . .

—Leonardo da Vinci, *Codex Atlanticus*

Led by Leonardo, our makeshift army traveled south at a swift pace toward the Duke of Pontalba's castle. As before, the road between both points was but lightly traveled, and even the Master's fantastical chariot drew but a few curious glances from the pilgrims that we passed.

The expected clash between Rebecca and the Master did not occur, after all. I guessed that he had anticipated this turn of events, for he'd been quite cordial to the two women. In a courtly gesture, he'd positioned their cart in the place of greatest safety between his chariot and our wagon. I was grateful for this action, for I could see that Rebecca was yet weak and feverish despite her protests of fine health.

And though all of us knew the import of our mission, it was to be expected that a band of young men could not remain somber for hours on end. Thus, we passed the time that first day with stories and riddles. We had but a few hours of sunlight to guide us, however, for our journey had begun well after noontide. We stopped when darkness made travel too difficult along the dark, rocky road.

As with my journey with Rebecca and Tito, we did not bother with a formal camp but sheltered beneath the wagons. We were fortunate this time in having Philippe take charge of our meals. One of the newer apprentices, he had spent time in the castle's kitchens before joining Leonardo's workshop. His stint there served us well, for he was as talented with a ladle as he was with a brush, conjuring tasty meals from the meanest of rations.

We resumed travel at dawn. That departure was accompanied by much lamentation from those youths unaccustomed to the wagon's constant jostle through the day, followed by a night's makeshift pallet upon the ground. As I had been one such youth but a few days earlier, I had taken pains to pad my chosen spot in the wagon with both cloak and jerkin. Thus, I was perhaps the only one of my fellows not nursing bruises upon his nether regions from the earlier ride.

Spirits lifted with the sun, however, and no one complained when the pace grew quicker. The one bad moment— at least, for some of us—came a few hours later when our convoy passed through the glade where Tito and Rebecca and I had confronted the bandit little more than a day before.

I turned in my seat to exchange wary glances with Tito in the wagon behind me. Although I had seen the rogue mercenary handily dispatched, I could not help but fear that another one might leap from the underbrush to take his place. From the look on Tito's face, I surmised that he felt much the same. Ideal a spot as it had proved for an ambush, surely some other murderous fiend would eventually happen upon it and set up his own deadly business, as had his predecessor.

Equally unsettling was the knowledge that what the scavengers would have left of the dead man's body still lay hidden but a short distance from us. Here in this place of murder, a chill seemed to hang over the road that had nothing to do with the canopy of trees blocking the noon sun. Indeed, I would not have been surprised to see the man's shade—or that of one of his victims—rise from the same spot where he'd breathed his last.

"Fah, it smells like something died," one of the other apprentices muttered.

That observation elicited much exaggerated pinching of nostrils and retching sounds from a few of his fellows. For myself, I swallowed back the bile that rose in my throat and gave thanks that Rebecca appeared to be sleeping and so not need be reminded of the cruel deed that had been forced upon her.

Despite my fears both rational and fanciful, we made our way unscathed through the glade and continued our journey. It was just before dusk when we reached the long band of forest that surrounded Castle Pontalba. At Leonardo's direction, we drove the wagons off the road and into the trees some distance, so that our caravan would not draw undue attention should some traveler pass us by. He instructed us to silence, as well.

"Hold to your words as a miser clutches his coins, and speak with gentle tones if you can communicate in no other fashion. For now, surprise is the very essence of our plan, so that an intemperate call could mean our failure."

By this time, my bones were weary with so much travel; still, I did not hesitate when the Master summoned Tito and me to follow after him. Moving upon feet silent as a wolf's paws, we made our way to the forest's edge for a closer look at the sprawling Castle Pontalba. At a signal from the Master, we halted at a spot behind where the tree line ended and dropped to our bellies, taking cover in the underbrush lest we be spotted.

"It appears that the Duke of Pontalba could use my architectural services," was Leonardo's first observation, the comment made in a wry undertone as he studied the fortress's muddled lines.

The sharp angle of the sun's dying light dealt harshly with the place, casting much of the castle and outbuildings into gloomy shadow well before the end of day. We were too far away to see if any guards manned the gatehouse, though the drawbridge still lay open in dubious welcome. I did spy what appeared to be at least two sentries patrolling the parapets. The Master glanced at his wrist clock, perhaps to coordinate the time of the patrols, before turning to me.

"Tell me all you recall about the castle's interior, and where within its walls that you found Signor Angelo and my flying machine."

I was quick to oblige. The flying machine was not to be seen from this angle, though I pointed out the spot on the slated roof where I'd found it. After another moment's thought, I was able to identify the tower I'd climbed to reach the upper level where the duchess—and, later, my father—had been imprisoned. I also described the great hall and the men I'd seen there.

Leonardo listened intently and waited for Tito to give a brief description of the fortress grounds. When we'd both finished, he gave an approving look that encompassed Tito, as well as me.

"You have managed some fine reconnoitering," he said, "and now we must put your intelligence to work. But first, we will set up camp and assemble our army."

With the same care, we slipped from our hiding places and retraced our steps back to the wagons. By that time, the other apprentices under Davide's direction had worked with silent efficiency to unload the wagons. Leonardo, appearing pleased at the progress, gathered his troops together for more instruction.

"We are fortunate," he said, "in that we will have half a moon to work beneath, for we cannot risk any other light . . . and yet the night will not be so bright that we might be spotted from the castle's parapets. So, let us divide into three teams so that I may make your assignments. As soon as darkness falls, we shall set a stage such as Pontalba has never before seen."

We used the short respite to make a quick meal. I checked on Rebecca, who had roused from her slumber and appeared somewhat restored as she softly bantered with Vittorio.

"Make certain she takes the herbed wine and allows you to put salve upon her arm," I reminded Novella in quiet tones. "And it is important that she rests tonight, lest we need to call upon her counsel tomorrow."

Once darkness had settled firmly upon the forest, we began our work. Under Leonardo's exacting direction, we moved with swift silence to set the canvases with their painted men-at-arms just behind the first line of trees at the forest's edge. Arranged into several small squadrons, their wood frames were camouflaged by those props depicting boulders and various bits of greenery. Interspersed among the false army were the actual weapons we'd brought with us, lacking only ammunition to make them deadly.

The work took several hours, so that our labors did not end until well past midnight. Huddling together beneath our blankets, for the night had grown quite chill, we prepared for a few hours of fretful sleep.

"Do you think we shall be killed?" I overheard young Bernardo ask Tito in quiet, quavering tones not long after we'd settled in.

I did not catch the words that Tito said in response, but they seemed to satisfy the younger boy. Whatever his answer, I prayed that Tito was right. Though the Master had claimed that our role would be little more than a masquerade, I feared that the cunning Nicodemo lo Bianco might prove a more formidable foe than Leonardo anticipated.

Dawn rose upon a substantial-looking army poised at the forest's edge . . . or, at least, that was how it was designed to appear from the vantage point of the duke's castle. Leonardo had cleverly added further verisimilitude to the scene with a score of campfires, which he'd had lit as the sun eased past the horizon. Tended by one of the younger apprentices, their curling plumes of smoke hinted at a greater force camped behind that false front line. The Duke of Milan's standard—a wily garden snake twisting across an azure field—was planted prominently beyond the last of the trees, proclaiming to all who might look which particular noble this army served.

But, clever as he was at pageantry, Leonardo knew that an unmoving illusion would soon be seen for what it was. Thus, the remainder of us apprentices had already donned our makeshift uniforms. Spreading ourselves wide among the painted forces, we milled about with purpose, adding needed motion to the static scene. And while we had been bidden to silence during the night, our conversation was now encouraged . . . taking care, as Leonardo reminded the younger ones of us, to keep our voices at a manly pitch.

It was not long after the first cock crowed that we heard a shout from atop the castle walls.

"Finally, they stir," Leonardo murmured in satisfaction. "Let us see if our opening performance is convincing enough to for them to request the next act."

From our concealment behind some of the painted back-drops, we watched as more soldiers gathered atop the battlemented walks, spreading themselves along that front. It was fully daylight, however, before we heard the familiar squeal and rumble that was the drawbridge dropping into place. A few minutes later, the immense wooden gate rose high enough to allow a small contingent of helmed and armed men on horseback to ride in tight formation from the castle.

"Aha, our subterfuge was convincing," the Master observed in satisfaction as the half-dozen riders halted halfway between the castle walls and the forest's edge. "It appears that they wish to parlay."

He had already donned his gleaming helmet and breastplate and strapped his sword to his hip, assuming the role of captain of Il Moro's guard. He started for the small clearing where Davide was harnessing the twin black steeds to the scythed chariot. Two of the draft horses had been pressed into service to play military mounts and waited, smartly blanketed and saddled, beside the chariot. Tommaso and Paolo had been similarly assigned martial roles and were dressed in matching helmets and breastplates slightly less ornate than those that Leonardo wore. They climbed atop their borrowed horses and, each balancing a tall staff that flew the Duke of Milan's familiar serpentine coat of arms, awaited orders.

"Master," I asked, barely able to hide the anxiety in my voice, "will you demand my father's release first thing?"

"I will not tip our hand immediately," he replied with a shake of his plumed head.

Frowning in the castle's direction, he went on. "I shall begin by appealing to the Duke of Pontalba as an ally of Milan and let him think we wish his help in tracking down those responsible for the crime. He will have but two choices at that point . . . either claim ignorance of the matter or admit his culpability and offer me terms for the return of your father and my craft. I suspect that he will not relinquish either without a fight, but I hope our show of force will at least make him consider that option."

"But what if that does not work?"

He glanced my way again and laid a comforting hand upon my shoulder. "Fear not, my boy. We shall retrieve your father, one way or the other."

He motioned the other apprentices closer.

"Should I be able to talk myself past the castle gates," he addressed us all, "I have instructed Davide how to maintain our illusion in my absence. Follow his orders as you would mine. You draftsmen are not to leave your posts unless Davide deems the situation too dangerous and calls a retreat. Most important, you are not to engage anyone from the castle unless on my express orders."

We murmured our assent and stepped back as the Master climbed into his war machine. Paolo and Tommaso each put a heel to flank, setting their steeds toward the forest's edge. Leonardo and his chariot followed after, the machine's deadly blades keeping to their sheathed position until the trio broke out into the open.

I could almost hear the gasp from the opposing forces as soon as the chariot with its singing blades came into view. The sun was high enough so that it reflected off those whirling scythes with blinding radiance, the sight calling to mind Ezekiel's fiery chariot. Had so small a force of men ever before stirred hearts to such awe? I wondered, eyes wide. Surely, in the face of Leonardo's grand invention, Nicodemo would see the prudence of negotiation rather than war.

After what appeared to be a deliberately circuitous route— doubtless meant to allow everyone from the castle who was watching a good look at the magnificent machine he was driving—Leonardo and his two men halted before the duke's contingent.

Of course, we could hear nothing from our vantage point at the forest's edge. Neither could we see much of what was happening beyond a few broad gestures exchanged between the Master and the man who appeared to be Nicodemo's spokesman. After but a few minutes' conversation, however, Paolo and Tommaso abruptly wheeled their horses about.

"Why are they leaving the Master alone with the duke's men?" Vittorio asked in some alarm as the pair began a brisk trot back toward us. "And, wait—he's being captured!"

"He's not captured," Bernardo protested, his voice quavering. "They're just taking him to the castle. Right, Dino?"

"No weapons are drawn," I assured him with more confidence than I felt, "so I'm sure that is the case. But let us watch to see what happens."

For, as we were speaking, we could see the soldiers splitting their ranks in two. Now three of the horses and riders made a wide circle around to the rear of the chariot. The other three soldiers remained in place and simply whirled their steeds about, leaving Leonardo and his scythed machine neatly positioned between the two groups of mounted men. At a signal from their leader, they began a measured trot back toward the castle . . . keeping, of course, a prudent distance between themselves and Leonardo's whirling blades.

Tommaso and Paolo had returned by this time. Quickly dismounting from their horses, they hurried over to where the rest of us stood. Paolo raised his hand to stave off the questions we fired at him; then, plucking off his helmet, he addressed Davide while making sure that the rest of us could hear him.

"The captain of the guard was quite bold," he explained. "He demanded to know why Milan's army was camped upon their doorstep, given that Milan and Pontalba are allies. The Master told him that it was a matter he could discuss only with the Duke of Pontalba himself. Of course, the captain protested that and, of course, the Master acted as if he would not give way. But finally, he told the captain that Il Moro's court engineer had mysteriously disappeared from Milan, along with one of his inventions . . . and that someone claimed spies from Pontalba were responsible for the crime."

"That was when the captain agreed that the Master might speak with the duke," Tommaso spoke up, continuing the tale. "The Master gave him two conditions. First, he wished the meeting to be private, so that his men—he meant me and Paolo—must be allowed to return to their fellows. Second, he said he must be free to depart the castle whenever he wishes . . . and if he has not rejoined his men by noontide, Milan's army will assume that Pontalba has broken their treaty and act accordingly against them."

"Look!" Vittorio interjected before Tommaso could say more. "They're closing the gate."

As the last rider cleared the entry, the heavy wooden grille began a slow descent, closing with a thud that we could hear from where we waited. The finality of the sound struck us all silent, as if we'd watched our beloved Master descend past hell's fiery gates.

Davide was first to break the silence. After glancing at the sun to judge its position, he turned to the rest of us.

"Why do you tarry? Master Leonardo left us with crucial tasks to perform in his absence. Lorenzo and Giovanni"—he gestured to the two youngest boys—"make sure you keep the campfires burning. You others, man your posts so that you can be seen."

Soldierlike, we jumped to attention, doing our best to make twenty youths appear as two hundred. The remaining horses had been relieved of wagon duty and stood blanketed and saddled. Our best equestrians mounted them and rode to the clearing, where they began imitating the same maneuvers that Constantin and I had watched Il Moro's men practice in the castle's quadrangle.

I joined the remaining apprentices in playing my part as a man-at-arms. Following the Master's earlier directive, we each stepped into view at one spot for a few moments. Then, slipping back into the trees, we quickly moved to another place, repeating the drill. A few times, I added a different color plume to my helmet or replaced my breastplate with a tunic of mail, so that I gave the appearance of a different person.

Had my father's life not been at risk—not to mention the lives of the Master and the duchess!—I might have found this masquerade most exciting. As it was, my somber expression surely mirrored the countenance of a man prepared for battle.

Sometime later, I took a respite from my role to retreat deeper into the forest and relieve my bladder. That business accomplished, I settled upon a fallen tree trunk and, pulling off my helmet, squinted up at the sun. Perhaps an hour had passed since the castle gate had closed upon Leonardo's retreating figure . . . perhaps two. All I knew with certainty was that his deadline of noontide was still some hours away. Wishing I had a wrist clock like the Master's to more accurately judge Time's passage, I sighed and reached again for my helmet.

"Dino!"

The soft voice calling my name belonged to Tito. He stepped out from behind a concealing tree, and I saw in consternation that he was dressed once again in his apprentice's tunic. Before I could question why he had abandoned his post, he started toward me. I saw to my surprise that he was accompanied by Rebecca.

Though her injured arm was still wrapped, Signor Luigi's

treatment must have been effective, for the washerwoman looked much restored. Even so, I viewed the pair with some suspicion.

"What are you doing?" I demanded in the same low tone. "The Master left us with orders to make it appear as we were Il Moro's army."

"His orders!" Tito gave his head a disgusted shake. "Bah, I fear Leonardo's orders may bring death to all of us."

So saying, he seated himself on one side of me, while Rebecca settled on the other edge of the tree trunk. Thus surrounded, I crossed my arms and shot him a sour look.

"What is this you say, Tito? The Master would do nothing to put us in danger. His plans never fail."

Though, of course, I promptly recalled that such was not always the case. How could I forget his elaborate scheme the night of the masquerade, the same night when we'd first laid eyes upon Nicodemo lo Bianco, dressed in a devil's finery? Two people had died most terribly as a result of Leonardo's well-intended machinations.

Pushing that memory firmly away, I moderated my tone and added, "Very well, tell me your thoughts . . . but do it quickly, for I must return to the front lines."

20

The winds blow in great change, and not always for the better.

—Leonardo da Vinci, *The Notebooks of Delfina della Fazia*

Tito glanced side to side, as if to reassure himself no one was listening. Lowering his voice further, he went on in an urgent tone. "I told you that my uncle was a soldier. I have learned much from him, and I fear this subterfuge will be found out. And if it is not, I am certain that the duke will not release the Master back to us, no matter that he thinks an army waits outside his walls."

"That may be," I agreed, "but if that happens, Il Moro's true army will eventually arrive to take our place."

Tito shook his head. "But don't you see? For all that the castle appears in disrepair, it has withstood many attacks before. They have a fine well and stores enough to last a long siege. Do you truly think Il Moro will want to spend weeks—or even months—waging war simply to rescue the Master and your father?"

"But the flying machine——"

"——is of no import," he exclaimed, cutting my argument short. "You and I could build another for Il Moro, and surely this thought will occur to the duke, as well. He will know that Leonardo's sketches with all his notes are still in his workshop, and he will know that we have worked upon the design long enough to have a fair understanding of its principles. Your father and the Master, and anyone else"—he paused to give me a significant look, and I knew that he meant by that last the Duchess Marianna—"they are dispensable. All that matters is the notes. We must act now or live with the consequences."

My stomach twisted into a hard fist of stone as I reluctantly considered the truth of Tito's words. No matter how brilliant an artist and inventor Leonardo was, he was no military general . . . nor had he ever been a soldier.

Moreover, I knew that Il Moro's affection for his master engineer was limited to his current usefulness. Doubtless many other artists and inventors were waiting for the opportunity for such a patron as he. Ludovico would go to war if it served his cunning purposes, and not out of loyalty or sentimentality.

I glanced at Rebecca to gauge her opinion on the matter. Her broad face was drawn in serious lines as she nodded.

"I fear Tito is right," she replied, no trace of banter in her tone. "That duke, he won't willingly free your father. And with Signor Leonardo, he's got another hostage to barter back to Il Moro. But I have an idea how to smuggle your father from the castle, if we can but gain entry."

In a basket of laundry, perhaps?

The question rose unbidden to my lips, but I bit it back. The Master must have been certain of the washerwoman's loyalty, for he had allowed her to accompany us this far.

And should the Duke of Pontalba learn that the man he thought was Leonardo the Florentine was instead Angelo the cabinetmaker, my father might never have the chance to put into effect his own plan of escape.

Taking a deep breath, I returned Rebecca's nod with one of my own. "Very well, I agree that we must do something. So what is our plan?"

Rebecca's broad face split into a wide grin. "Why, same as last time. We do some laundry."

A short time later, I was once again wearing my simple apprentice's tunic and seated beside Rebecca as she drove her cart toward the castle's gate. We'd told Lorenzo and Giovanni, the only ones of the apprentices who noticed us hitching up the cart, that we were acting under Davide's orders; thus, we had avoided any questions from the pair. For her part, Novella had agreed to distract Davide with claims of a twisted ankle long enough for us to be beyond call before he noticed our defection.

Unfortunately for our plan, the senior apprentice was not easily misled from his duty. Barely were we halfway across the cleared field when Tito grasped my arm and softly said, "Look, Davide has come after us."

I turned in my seat to see that the senior apprentice— dressed in helmet and breastplate, and mounted upon one of our makeshift war steeds—was indeed galloping in our direction. Wheeling most dramatically around us, he halted in our path and drew a flashing sword, so that Rebecca was forced to pull up her mare or run over him.

"What are you doing?" he asked in an outraged undertone as he pointed the weapon at us. "The Master gave strict orders that no one was supposed to approach the castle. Quickly, turn your cart around."

"We cannot do that," I softly countered. "My father's life is in danger, and the Master's plan is flawed. We must attempt to rescue him in another fashion, lest they both remain Pontalba's prisoners."

Davide's lips folded into stubborn lines, and his sword remained unyielding. "The Master gave us orders, and we must follow them."

Helpless, I exchanged glances with Rebecca. She gave me a small nod; then, her expression kindly, she addressed the youth.

"You did your duty fine. What's more important, you gave the soldiers on the parapets a good show," she told him. "Now, make us a bow so they can see all is well, and then you must let us pass."

"I cannot do that. The Master trusted me with this duty, and I will not let him down," Davide protested, though I saw an uncertain wobble to his sword. "Please, turn back."

"We won't turn back," Rebecca countered, her expression growing stern. "And the soldiers are going to get suspicious if we keep sitting here showing our gums to the breeze. Don't worry; I'll tell Signor Leonardo that you did your duty. And these boys"—she indicated Tito and me—"will take the punishment he deals them."

The sword wobbled a moment longer. Finally, with a great sigh and look of consternation, he sheathed his weapon and made us an exaggerated bow from his saddle.

"Very well, you may pass, but only because I cannot stop you short of using a blade," he retorted in a tone of disgust.

Shooting Tito and me a baleful glance, he added, "No matter what other punishment the Master deals out, know that you two draftsmen will have no other task for the next year but to boil the gesso every day to atone for your insubordination."

I gave Davide an apologetic look but made no reply. While boiling animal skins to make the gluelike substance needed for coating blank panels was a foul job, I would have taken on a litany of far more disgusting tasks if it meant saving my father's life. I saw a flicker of understanding in Davide's eyes, however, and knew that in his heart he did not fault us for what we did. With a final salute, he put a heel to his steed's flank and trotted back toward the forest.

"Well, that's done," Rebecca said with a sigh of her own as she whipped up the mare again. "Now, let's see how we fare with the soldiers at the gate."

We continued at a moderate pace toward the castle. The morning sun was warm upon our backs, and yet the sight of the brooding fortress was enough to make me wrap my father's cloak about me more tightly. The washerwoman's expression was neutral, but as close as we sat I could feel the tension in her beefy arms and knew she must be as nervous as I at what was to come. As for Tito . . .

I spared a glance behind me. Though he, too, kept a neutral countenance to his pockmarked face, his dark eyes burned with eagerness. Abruptly, I wondered if his insistence in launching this rescue mission came less from concern over my father and the Master and more from a feeling of high adventure. For surely in every young man lurked a secret dream of facing down an army single-handedly while defeating a cruel duke and rescuing a duchess.

I had no time to reflect further on this, however, for we had reached the portcullis. One of the guards, stave in hand, peered through the wood and iron grille at us. Recognizing Rebecca, he barked, "You, washerwoman, what is your business?"

"Foolish man, you know my business."

Grinning broadly, she tossed the reins to me and hopped

from the cart. "I've come to finish the laundry," she declared as she approached the gate. "My boys and me, we worked all day the last time we was here, but there was more laundry than we could do in a day. I promised the kitchen master I'd return today to finish the job."

The guard's frown deepened. "No one's allowed in or out, not without the captain's approval. Can't you see that Pontalba is under siege by Milan?"

"Under siege?"

Gasping, she clutched at her large bosom and whirled about with great drama to survey the clearing. Then, with a chuckle, she turned back to the guard.

"Pah, do you mean those poor excuses for soldiers that I saw lurking about in the forest? They did not look like men ready to fight."

A second guard had joined the first and was listening with some interest to Rebecca's report. He shoved a sharp elbow into his fellow soldier's ribs and grinned while Rebecca preened and smirked, swaying her broad skirts in a seductive manner.

"Pah, I think they're less than men, if you know what I mean. The ones I saw were too busy with dice or drink to notice a comely woman come across their path, let alone summon the energy to fight. Why, I was almost here to your gate before they noticed that I had passed by."

The first guard was grinning, as well, and he exchanged glances with his fellow. "Why don't we let the washerwoman in, and she can tell us about everything she saw in the forest."

"I'll tell you that gladly, and more," she replied with a bawdy wink, "but you must let my boys gather the laundry while we talk. A lady has to earn a few soldi, you know."

The guards stepped away from the gate to discuss the matter, surely a favorable sign. I pretended disinterest in the

entire process, though my heart pounded so wildly that I was
certain it must be noticeable even through the tightly laced
corset I wore beneath my tunic. After an interminable few
moments, they came to a decision.

"You can come in," the first guard declared, "but you cannot stay long. Let your boys gather the laundry, and you're
off. There's a stream not far from the castle where you can do
your washing, if you have no fear of Milan's soldiers."

"Pah, I know how to handle soldiers," she said with another
broad wink for the pair before she climbed back into the
wagon again. The rumble and squeak of chains followed as
the gate rolled up once more to let us inside the castle walls.

We rolled to a stop just inside the gate, and the second
guard took hold of the horse's bridle. Rebecca climbed down
once more, while Tito scrambled into her seat and took up
the reins. Her bawdy grin dropped for an instant, and I was
alarmed to see the look of exhausted pain in her face. In the
next moment, however, the grin was back as she made mock
shooing motions at us.

"Off with you, boys, and be quick. Gather the laundry
and put it in the baskets, and come back here. I'll be waiting
with these fine gentlemen," she declared, giving us a significant look as she hooked an arm through each of the soldiers'
elbows.

Tito nodded and lightly whipped up the mare.

"Can you believe our good fortune?" I murmured to him
as we headed toward the kitchens. "We can hide my father
and the duchess inside the baskets and smuggle them out
that way. The guards will not question us or look inside, for
they gave us leave to bring laundry back through the gates
again."

"Or perhaps it is another trick." He slanted me an unreadable look and added, "You should beware, Dino, lest you be

too readily fooled. The world is far more complicated than you might think."

Stung a bit by his dismissal of my enthusiasm, I made no reply as he pulled the cart to a halt alongside the kitchens. A few of the kitchen boys were milling about, but they spared us no more than a glance. I wondered if the rest of the castle realized that they were supposedly on the brink of siege. Surely everyone should be making preparations for a possible attack, I thought in some confusion.

I wondered, as well, what had happened to Leonardo's grand chariot. We had passed by the main doors leading to the great hall, and I'd not seen it there. It was far too unwieldy to store away in the stables along with the other carts and wagons.

I frowned as the most likely possibility came to me. Doubtless the Duke of Pontalba had seen the glorious invention and, as he had with the flying machine, decided to claim it for his own. Perhaps it sat in one of the inner courtyards awaiting Nicodemo's dubious pleasure.

Tito, meanwhile, was digging into the baskets. I had assumed them to be empty, but to my surprise he plucked a pair of familiar tunics from one.

"See, Rebecca saved these from last time we were here," Tito said as he tossed one to me and swiftly donned the other. "Now we may wander about in disguise."

I pulled my borrowed tunic over my own garb, sniffing at it in satisfaction. This one had been freshly laundered by the capable washerwoman, unlike the previous soiled garment I'd worn. Tying my belt over it, I gave Tito a nod.

"I shall go in search of my father. They must have him on the roof working on the flying machine, so that is where I shall begin my search. You go to the dungeons and look for the duchess. Perhaps that is where the duke has moved her."

"I shall look," he agreed, "but if I find her, how will I free her? I doubt that the guard will give me a key."

"Ah, but I shall."

I shot him a lofty look as I reached into my pouch. With a flourish, I plucked forth one of the heavy pieces of curved wire that I'd borrowed from Leonardo's forge before our expedition had set out.

"I've seen the Master open locks with such a wire before," I explained as he gave me a puzzled stare. "You simply fit it into the lock as you would a key, and twist it about until the lock yields. It did not appear to require much talent."

"I think I would do better to leap upon a guard from behind and steal his key, instead," the youth replied in a doubtful voice, though he dutifully tucked the wire into his own pouch. "We'd best hurry. And be sure you find a bit of laundry that we can use to cover the tops of the baskets."

We quickly parted, Tito toward the kitchens and I retracing my earlier steps toward the great hall. Slipping inside past the broad doors, I saw to my surprise—though perhaps I should have expected such a scene—that the great hall was again filled with men. Some soldiers, others minor nobles, all appeared in the midst of a minor uproar. Nicodemo lo Bianco, the Duke of Pontalba himself, presided over the chaos in his tall, carved chair.

This day, he was dressed in a long black tunic, over which was belted an ankle-length coat of gold and white brocade, heavily edged in black fur. A broad, puffed black velvet hat with a rolled brim of gold silk perched atop his balding head, adding further shadows to his craggy face. Rather than soften his features, the fineness of his garb emphasized the cruel slash of his lips and sagging flesh beneath his eyes and chin.

Or perhaps it was simply the contrast that made him

appear far more repulsive than he was. For, standing before Nicodemo was the man whom many claimed to be the most handsome in the entire court of Milan. Breastplate gleaming and flamboyant plumed helmet tucked beneath his arm, Leonardo was in the midst of making his case.

Moving from the duke's line of sight, I ducked into one of the alcoves. Here, I could see but not be seen for the shadows, or so I prayed. The Master was speaking, his tone measured; still, I could make out but a few words, for the duke's men were muttering among themselves, seeming unconvinced by the speech they were hearing.

Abruptly, Nicodemo raised his hand.

"Enough," he called, his harsh voice ringing through the hall. As silence fell, he addressed the Master.

"I have listened to your accusations, Captain. They are couched in flowery words in an attempt to deceive me into thinking you approach as an ally and not an enemy. But they are accusations, nonetheless."

He stood and thrust a beefy finger in Leonardo's direction. "You think yourself clever, but I am not Ludovico's fool! You have come to me with this false charge simply to pretend cause to violate our treaty." Apparently satisfied that he had made his point, he sat once more. "And so, I must make a decision," Nicodemo continued in a more deliberate tone. "I could allow you to return with your men to Milan, so that you might tell your duke that Pontalba has nothing of his . . . or I could hold you here until Ludovico comes and makes his apologies to me in person."

"My men are waiting for me, Excellency," Leonardo coolly countered. "If I am not returned to them hale and hearty by noontide, they will consider me a captive and your action one of aggression. As for my flowery accusations . . ."

He paused and shrugged. "Just as Pontalba has its spies in

Milan, so Milan has its spies in Pontalba. Let us agree to that much. And so, let me speak plainly."

"Do go on," the duke replied with an ironic nod.

Nodding in return, the Master continued. "We know that you hold as a captive Ludovico's court engineer, the great genius Leonardo, a man of unrivaled talents known to all the surrounding provinces. We also know that you have stolen his magnificent invention, the likes of which has never before been seen, and that you intend to use that invention for ill."

He paused again . . . solely for dramatic purposes, I was certain. Then, like a magician performing his final illusion, he gave a sweep of his hand.

"And so, I present the Duke of Milan's final offer. Return both man and machine without delay, and our great excellency will forget this vile breach of your alliance with him."

"And if I refuse?" Nicodemo countered with a feral grin.

Leonardo shrugged again. "If you refuse, you must prepare yourself for a siege that you shall not win."

The muttering recommenced, and far louder this time. I watched in alarm as the nobles and men-at-arms began putting their hands to their hips, fingers stroking sword hilts. The situation was fast growing dire, I realized. Moreover, I likely had but little time left to find my father and make our escape before the guards were ordered to seal the gate.

I was prepared to slip away as silently as I had entered, when I heard a stir at the rear of the hall. Two men-at-arms were striding down the broad aisle toward where the duke sat, a third man a prisoner in their grasp. Though I could not make out his face for the small crowd that had surged closer to the aisle for a better look, I recognized in dismay his mane of dark hair and his bearing.

Halting alongside the spot where Leonardo stood, the

soldiers released their prisoner and stepped back a few paces. The duke surveyed the two men, his feral grin returning.

"See, Captain, I am not an unreasonable man," he said with cool joviality. "I have complied with part of your demand. Here is your missing master engineer, Leonardo the Florentine."

21

*. . . the bird would follow other rules which will subsequently
be defined in due order.*

—Leonardo da Vinci, *Codex Arundel*

Leonardo spared the briefest of looks at my father before
giving the Duke of Pontalba a cool bow.

"My thanks, Excellency. You are a reasonable man and a
worthy ally of Milan. And now, perhaps we might discuss the
terms for returning the flying machine."

The duke chuckled.

I winced, for the sound uncannily resembled that of the
chain as it raised and lowered the castle's portcullis. To my
relief, his amusement was short-lived. The chuckling ceased,
and his features slipped back into their familiar lines of cold
deliberation.

"My good captain, you misunderstand me," he replied,
tapping his fingertips together. "I have no intention of giving

up the flying machine. Indeed, I wish to build many more like it. And so, upon further consideration, neither will I relinquish the man who designed it."

A ripple of laughter washed over the room. Nicodemo, looking pleased with himself, leaned back in his chair and awaited the reaction of the man he believed to be Ludovico's captain of the guard.

I could not see Leonardo's face, but I noted an almost imperceptible tightening of his bearing. His tone no longer conciliatory, he replied, "That is unacceptable, Excellency. Milan demands the return of both man and machine."

"Milan . . . demands!"

Nicodemo's roar filled the room as he leaped to his feet, all pretense of humor gone. I reflexively skittered back a few paces, for the force of his outrage was palpable. Some of his men shuffled a few prudent steps to the rear, as well, no doubt having seen previous examples of the duke's lapses into fury.

Leonardo, however, stood unmoving.

The duke strode around the broad table that separated him from the rest of the hall, the broad skirts of his surcoat twitching like a wild cat's tail with every livid step. Planting himself inches from where Leonardo stood, he raised his beefy forefinger again.

"How dare you think you can tell the Duke of Pontalba what he must do? I do not answer to you nor to Ludovico!"

Snapping a look at his nearest man-at-arms, he commanded, "Take this so-called captain and hang him from the gatehouse tower, so all his men can see what I think of Milan's demands!"

I slapped both hands over my mouth to stifle my horrified cry. But as the guards seized Leonardo from either side, I heard my father's voice ring out.

"Halt, lest you act with too much haste! If you hang him, you will have executed the very man you wish to keep alive . . . for he is Leonardo the Florentine, and not I."

"Listen to him not," the Master protested with equal vigor as a mutter of puzzled voices rose around them. "The man beside me is Leonardo. It is his life that you wish to preserve."

"He seeks but to spare me," my father called out. "I am Angelo della Fazia, a simple cabinetmaker. He is Leonardo."

The murmur of voices grew, while a flash of uncertainty washed over Nicodemo's craggy features. Signaling his soldiers to release their captive, he gazed from Leonardo to my father and back again, a dark frown furrowing his high brow as he took in the resemblance between the two.

"Pah, I could well believe that my foolish spies might kidnap the wrong man. And so it is possible that he"—the duke jerked a thumb at my father—"is an imposter, and you speak the truth. But, as they say, you may always know when a man from Milan is lying by the fact that his mouth is open."

Turning to his soldiers again, he commanded, "These two are of no import. The flying machine is all I want. Hang them both, and be done with it."

A roar of assent rose from the men within the hall, drowning out my cry of fear. Barely had the soldiers laid rough hands upon both their captives, when a familiar voice cried out over the chaos.

"Wait, Uncle! I can tell you which one of these men is Leonardo the Florentine."

The claim came from the dark-haired youth with a pockmarked face who was pushing his way through the milling men to where the Duke of Pontalba stood. Earlier, he'd been dressed in a plain brown tunic, but he no longer wore an apprentice's simple garb. Instead, he was clad in red and gold parti-colored trunk hose, over which he wore a blue silk tunic trimmed in gold, his white shirt puffed through the many slits in his sleeves. With a rolled brim hat of gold similar to his uncle's sitting rakishly atop his head, he was all but unrecognizable as my friend Tito.

"What have you done?" I softly cried, knowing full well that he could not hear me but unwilling to believe that the youth whom I had considered to be both a friend and ally was apparently neither.

And yet, as my thoughts tumbled back over the events of the past weeks, the revelation made an odd sort of sense.

Tito had claimed his uncle was a soldier, which was surely the truth, for the Duke of Pontalba was a military man. Too, he drove a team of horses with far greater skill than a humble apprentice would possess. And, more than once, had I not heard him dismiss those of lesser ranks with a callousness that did not befit an apprentice's station? As for the knife I'd seen him brandish, I had known at a glance that it was far too fine a weapon for a youth such as he to possess.

But why would a young man of his background buy an apprenticeship to a master painter?

The soldiers, meanwhile, had halted at Tito's words and gazed uncertainly at the duke for direction. Shaking his head in disgust, Nicodemo gestured them to bring their prisoners forward once again.

"Very well," he agreed, his sour tone matching his expression as he spared a glance for the youth beside him. "Stay a moment, and let us pause to hear what my worthless nephew has to say about this."

A blush darkened Tito's face, but his expression was defiant as he pointed at the Master.

"This man is Leonardo the Florentine, inventor of the flying machine. The other man is who he claims to be, nothing but a cabinetmaker who was staying with Leonardo. I gave your spies a fine description of the person they wanted. It is not my fault that they took the wrong man."

Nicodemus raised a sparse brow. "Are you saying, boy, that you've known from the start that the man we were holding was not Ludovico's master engineer?"

The duke's tone was mild enough, but something in his expression made Tito sputter as he answered, "I knew . . . That is, I came back to the castle to tell you . . . but I—"

Swift as a knife strike, Nicodemo slapped his nephew. The sound of flesh against flesh was loud enough for me to hear where I stood. Tito staggered from the impact, clutching at his jaw. To his credit, however, he promptly straightened and, heedless of his now-bleeding lip, met his uncle's cold gaze.

"That is for allowing me to look like a fool before my men," the duke remarked, though with far less vitriol than I might have expected.

His fury apparently spent for the moment, he strode back around the table and again seated himself in his carved chair. Turning an ironic look on Tito, he waved a careless hand.

"My apologies, Nephew," he said with mock graciousness. "In all the excitement, I forgot to welcome you home to Pontalba again. And now, since you were supposed to be my eyes and ears in Milan, perhaps you will enlighten me with any other information that you have neglected to provide."

Dabbing the back of his hand to his lip, Tito nodded.

"Very well, Uncle. The Duke of Milan's army is not waiting in the forest preparing to lay siege. In fact, Il Moro is meeting secretly with the French king's representatives and is unaware of what is happening here in Pontalba. He knows nothing of the missing flying machine or the supposed kidnapping of his master engineer."

"But the men in the forest—"

"—are but an illusion concocted by Leonardo," Tito cut his uncle short with a small smirk of satisfaction. "The so-called army is but twenty of his apprentices, and many painted canvases cleverly arranged to look like rows of fighting men."

"You are certain of this?" the duke demanded, his expression one of genuine surprise.

Tito shrugged. "I was there, and I helped arrange the props myself."

Nicodemo sat silent for a moment, tapping his fingertips together as he considered the situation. Finally, he replied, "This is, indeed, a bird of a different feather. Twenty boys, you say?"

At Tito's nod, the duke shot Leonardo another feral smile.

"You are quite clever, Florentine, and another time your plan might have borne fruit. This time, however, I fear your cleverness will be your undoing . . . but, for the moment, I have decided to keep you and the cabinetmaker alive."

Turning to his captain of the guard, he commanded, "Remove these two to the dungeons, and have your men mount up. I want you to scour the forest and bring me those boys. Those who resist, run them through with your swords where they stand. The others, bring to the castle and toss them into the dungeon with their master and the cabinetmaker."

To Leonardo, he said in satisfaction, "We shall see if Ludovico chooses to bring his true army to Pontalba once he learns of your fate. If he does, those boys of yours will make a fine greeting for him, hanging from my parapets. And, if he does not, I'm sure they will prove able workers in my quarry cutting stone to rebuild my castle."

Whether or not Leonardo made a reply to that last, I did not wait to hear. I was already hurrying through the narrow passage, a plan half-formed in my mind as I retraced my steps through the castle. For the moment, I could do nothing for my father and the Master, but perhaps I could save my fellow apprentices from a cruel fate!

My breath was coming in panicked gasps by the time I reached the flimsy iron staircase that spiraled up to the roof. Knees shaking, I managed the steps as swiftly as I could, all the while knowing that time had me trapped on either side. It would not take the duke's men long to assemble and ride out, meaning that I had to finish my preparations before they spilled past the castle gate. Neither could I forget that Tito knew I was here in the castle with him. Sooner or later, he would come looking for me . . . and if he discovered me too soon, all would truly be lost.

I eased open the door to the roof, mindful of the soldiers that I had earlier seen lining the parapets. I had to assume they were still there, keeping watch over Leonardo's illusion of an army. Given that I wore my borrowed page's tunic, I could claim to be delivering a message from one of Nicodemo's other men should I be seen and questioned. But, for the moment, this portion of the walk appeared deserted.

As before, that first step out onto the roof sent me swaying. Taking a steadying breath, I started along the walkway in the direction where I had last seen the flying machine. Only then did it occur to me that perhaps the craft still lay in pieces. It had been but a handful of days since my father had vowed to finish building it so that he could make his escape by air and fly it away to Milan. If he had not yet completed his work, my plan was for naught, and I might as well surrender myself to the duke, then and there.

A heavy hand abruptly closed over my arm and cut short my musings, while the suddenness of the assault caused me to stumble alarmingly close to the parapets. The same hand jerked me upright again, and an angry red face pressed close to mine.

"What are you doing up here, boy?" the guard demanded, his breath faintly redolent of the cesspit. "Quick, speak, or I'll toss you off the roof."

"Please, I was sent with a message," I cried in unfeigned fear as I struggled to regain my wits. When his grip on me loosened, I managed, "His Excellency has discovered that there is no army in the forest, only boys playing at being soldiers. The other men-at-arms are being sent on horseback to round them up. You—you are to go with them."

I tossed out that last with the fervent prayer that such an order was breaking no soldier's protocol. By this time, a second guard had been attracted by the commotion and joined his fellow in time to hear my last words.

My stomach lurched as the pair exchanged cruel grins, but to my relief their amusement was not directed at me.

"Pah, I thought there was something odd about it all," the second man declared as his companion released my arm. "As for the other, it sounds like fine sport."

"Why should the others have all the fun?" the first guard agreed with a laugh.

Leaving me to my own devices, the pair moved with eager purpose in the same direction from which I'd come. I waited a few moments longer lest any other guards appear; then, emboldened by this small success, I continued on my way.

A few moments later, I found the flying machine in the same place that I'd left it . . . and I gave a soft cry of relief to realize that my father had not been idle in his captivity. For no longer was Leonardo's grand design but hewn lengths of wood and frames of stretched cloth. Instead, the craft now appeared as some fantastic, gossamer-like creature—not quite bird and not quite insect—which had landed by some providential accident upon this slate roof.

Knowing that my life depended upon it, I swiftly went

over every one of its lines to assure myself that the flying machine was a finished work. Both cloth-covered wings had been affixed to the sleek body, their total span almost four times my height. Lengths of braided cord and leather served as its sinews, connected at various points on both wings and body, and attached to a series of foot pedals and hand levers, which the pilot would control.

I gave each an experimental push and was gratified to see the wings sweep up and down in measured response. The rudderlike tail had been completed, and a simple knob pulled up and pushed down made that nether limb of the craft rise and fall accordingly.

And no longer did the flying machine hunker on its bladderlike underbelly much as a sickly goose. Instead, four large wheels had been added to either corner of the supporting frame, raising the body sufficiently so that the entire craft could roll about with ease on a flat surface.

I spotted a rope looped through a stirrup mounted beneath the craft's nose, and I let my gaze follow that cord's length to its starting point. Someone, no doubt my father, had tied the other end to a short chimney at the top of a slanted section of roof behind the flying machine. Tracing a path back down from the chimney and past the craft again, I saw that it led to a spot where a section of the parapets had long since been broken away from the roof's edge, leaving a sheer drop to the ground.

Recalling my father's plan, I guessed that it would be but a simple matter for a single person to use that rope and stirrup like a pulley to drag the craft back toward the chimney and tie it off. Once the pilot was settled in the craft, he—or she—could release the rope and allow the flying machine to roll down that incline again. The path was both long enough and steep enough so that, by the time the craft reached the roof's edge, it should have gained sufficient momentum to fly like a captive hawk abruptly freed of its jesses.

But what would happen if my father had misjudged the angle and speed?

The fleeting image of a hawk tangled in her hunting laces and plummeting to the earth flashed through my mind. At that thought, fear gripped me with so cold an embrace that I dropped to my knees and squeezed my eyes shut.

Folly, my inner voice cried. To attempt such a flight was to court certain death! The Master had said that the craft should be tested over water at first, lest a failure cause it to drop from the sky. What madness had led me to think that I, Delfina della Fazia, could accomplish a feat that had been the sole purview of birds and angels, up until now?

The sound of shouting men and stamping horses from the main courtyard below pierced the veil of fear that wrapped me. I eased over to the parapets, peered down, and caught back a gasp. Two score or more mounted men, and at least twice that number on foot, were gathering below me.

I saw no archers, and I reasoned that the duke would not want to waste good arrows on such a sparsely numbered opponent. But the other weapons I saw were equally deadly. Some of the soldiers brandished swords; others wielded crossbows or pikes. And all were readying themselves and their steeds to hunt down fewer than twenty young men, unarmed save for what sticks or stones they might snatch up in defense!

Tears welled in my eyes as I heard the soldiers' cruel laughter and jokes ring loud above the sound of hooves and steel. The Duke of Pontalba had given his men leave to slaughter those apprentices who resisted them. Taken unawares as they surely would be, the youths would have no time to flee but would be forced into either submission or battle.

Davide would fight back, I told myself . . . and Paolo, and Tommaso, and Vittorio. Would the others stand their ground as their friends fell around them? Or would they realize the futility of resistance and give their surrender, to find death later once the duke deemed them of no further use as hostages?

But if the soldiers could be distracted long enough as they poured out from the castle, the apprentices might yet make their escape. With eight horses among them, they need not flee on foot but could abandon wagons and gear, and gallop off toward safety. Even riding two up, they would have a small advantage of speed over their pursuers' more heavily laden steeds. How long and how far Nicodemo's men would follow after them, I could not guess. But at least they would have a chance at escape, a chance they would not have if I chose the coward's path now and stood aside to watch the coming debacle.

Thus resolved, I scrambled to my feet. The sound of the soldiers below echoing in my ears, I rushed back to the flying machine to make final preparations for victory . . . or, failing that, provision for a quick and glorious death.

22

*. . . the famous bird will take its flight, which will fill the world
with its great renown.*

—Leonardo da Vinci, *Manuscript Sul Volo*

I had several minutes to prepare for my bold flight, I was
certain, for it took time to ready so many soldiers all at
once. And Nicodemo's men would surely feel no great haste,
knowing now the nature of their opponents.

Rope in hand, I began dragging the flying machine
upward toward the chimney. The task proved harder than it
looked, for the incline was steep, but soon enough I had tied
the craft off so that its nose pointed down the slope.

Next came the task of strapping myself onto its frame . . .
and, once again, I felt my courage quail as I contemplated
that step. Large as the craft was, there still was little there to
support me, so that it would be like climbing onto the back
of an immense bird and clinging to its feathers for dear life.
How could I consider trusting so fragile-looking a frame?

"Father would do it," I sternly told myself. "And the Master would not be afraid."

Besides, my inner voice reminded me, what was there to lose? If I did not make this attempt but simply waited for my own capture, I likely would end up dead alongside my fellows.

"Far better to die like a hawk than as a mouse," I softly proclaimed and settled myself facedown upon the framework.

My last task would be to strap myself in. First, however, I spared a moment to test each pedal and lever, amazed that my lightest touch moved the great wings with ease. I had feared that I might not be able to reach those controls, designed as they'd been for a man of the Master's height. Fortunately, they were positioned in such a way that they could be reached from various angles. All I would have to remember was the proper sequence of pedaling and flapping to keep the craft aloft once it was airborne.

All I would have to remember, indeed!

The commotion from the courtyard was growing louder. I knew, however, that I must take my cue from the now-familiar squeal and rattle of heavy chain that would signal the portcullis being raised. For the soldiers would not pour from the gate like ants stirred from a hill; rather, they would ride out and arrange themselves into formation first, before charging toward the tree line beyond. It would be at the moment when they began the assault that I would let loose the rope and sail the flying machine from the castle roof.

I managed a weak smile at the thought of the chaos I would cause. The sight of me gliding hawklike above the field would cause no end of consternation among the soldiers, while striking terror among the horses. Surely many a frightened steed would unseat his rider . . . and surely many a superstitious man would drop to his knees in the belief that he was about to be visited with divine retribution.

Once aloft, I would remain airborne for as long as I could, giving my fellows the time to make their escape while the duke's men were thus distracted. And afterward, if my strength and the winds allowed it, like Daedelus, I would pilot the craft on to safety, perhaps as far as Milan.

But, if my fate instead mirrored that of the luckless Icarus, at least my spectacular demise when I hurtled to the ground should prove an equal distraction.

Knowing I could not put it off any longer, I reached for the first strap, which would go around my torso and fasten beneath me. My nerves were stretched as taut as the canvas on my craft's wings, while sweat had begun to trickle from my brow. And still, the gate had not risen. Saints' blood, how long did it take to gather arms and saddle horses and be off?

I paused in fastening the belt and sat back upon my heels, craning my neck in hopes of a better look. From the angle where the craft was poised, however, it was impossible to see the activity below. Still, the hum of preparation continued, and I lent my ear to that activity as I once more settled upon the frame and reached for the harness. Indeed, so carefully did I focus my attention on those sounds that the soft scrape of footsteps was almost upon me before I realized I was no longer alone on my rooftop perch.

I turned to gaze with dismay but not much surprise at the richly dressed youth standing before me. Knowing what I now did, I could see some small resemblance between him and his uncle that proved the relationship. Perhaps it was the hint of fleshiness beneath his eyes and chin that hinted at a different profile to come as he aged, or perchance the similar watchful look in his dark eyes. Or maybe it was that look of disdain as he surveyed me, for all purposes helpless before him as I lay sprawled atop the flying machine's frame.

Almost without meaning to, I glanced at the knife that

hung from his belt . . . the same knife he'd hidden under his tunic before. Dressed as a young nobleman, he could carry the weapon as it was meant to be displayed. He caught the direction of my gaze, and a smile flitted across his lips as he lightly touched the knife's hilt. I shivered, all too aware that I was stretched before him like a lamb ready for sacrifice. With a swift thrust of that blade, he could dispatch me before I had time to drop the harness's loose end and scramble to my feet.

Barely had that thought crossed my mind when he dropped to one knee beside me. But rather than slip his knife between my ribs, he grabbed me by both shoulders and unceremoniously yanked me from my spot atop the craft, tumbling me in a heap upon the slate roof. While I dragged myself back up to a kneeling position, he demanded in a petulant voice, "What are you doing with my flying machine?"

"Your flying machine?"

Surprise made me forget my momentary fear. "This is the Master's flying machine," I protested in no little indignation and scrambled to my feet. "He and my father built it, and you have no claim to it."

"But it is here in Pontalba now, and so it belongs to us."

Recalling his uncle's treatment of him, I wondered at the fact that he claimed loyalty to the duke. Was that blood tie tighter than the bonds of apprenticeship he shared with me? I feared so, for his features had tightened into the same stubborn expression that Davide had worn earlier that morning as he tried to stop us midway to the castle.

But as Davide had wavered when faced with compelling logic, perhaps Tito might also be made to see reason. Or, if I could but give him the means to deflect any guilt from himself, perhaps I might yet retain him as an ally.

"Surely you had no hand in this unsavory plan," I insisted

in as calm a voice as I could muster. "Recall the page, who summoned you in the middle of the night? And what of the three mysterious men you told me about, the ones who held my father tied in a wagon all night while they waited for dawn to smuggle him and the flying machine past the castle guards? Surely these crimes were their fault, and not yours."

The offer made, I waited to hear him agree that it had all been a terrible mistake . . . waited to hear him confess that he had somehow been duped by his uncle. That hope, however, was extinguished with his next words.

"There was no page," he replied and gave a snort that mocked my gullibility. "I told you that, so you wouldn't question why I believed I'd had a message from Leonardo. And the men were three of my uncle's soldiers, who came to the castle that day disguised as laborers.

"I even vouched for them," he added with a grin at his own cleverness. "I told your captain of the guard that they had been hired to assist Leonardo, so that they never questioned the wagon coming in and out."

Then his grin faded.

"It should have been a perfect plan. How was I to know that Leonardo had chosen that day to leave Milan without telling anyone but your father? I instructed the guards where to find him, told them what he looked like. Fools that they were, they never asked your father's name but decided he matched the description that I'd given them and took him away."

Shrugging, he added, "Of course, the kidnapping was but a last-minute solution. We didn't really need him, not the way I'd planned it. I could have finished building the flying machine myself, if I'd still had all of Leonardo's notes."

Leonardo's notes.

Full realization came to me, so terrible that it stopped the

very breath in my lungs. And yet, how could it be? He had
been one of us for many months, sharing the same work and
the same meals, sleeping but an arm's length from his fellows. We had given him our trust and our friendship. How
could he have forgotten that sort of comradeship, no matter
that he was nephew to a duke?

And how could he have betrayed us all by callously murdering the most worthy one of our number?

"It was you," I managed when I could draw breath again.
"You killed Constantin . . . shot him as he was rushing to
warn the Master that you had stolen his notes on the flying
machine!"

"No! Constantin was the thief!"

Tito's indignant response was all the more unsettling
for its genuine note of dismay. Giving his head a violent
shake, he went on. "He thought he was so clever, the way
he watched me when he thought I was not looking . . . the
times he followed after me and pretended it was but chance
that we ended up in the same place. I warned him to leave
well enough alone, but he would not. And then I found him
snooping about in my trunk."

He referred, of course, to the wooden casket stowed
beneath his cot, which was large enough to hold his extra
garb and other personal belongings. Each apprentice was
assigned one. Though none could be locked, it was a matter
of honor that no boy disturbed another trunk without first
gaining permission from its owner. The senior apprentice's
suspicions must have been well-founded for him to have broken that unspoken rule.

"That's when Constantin found the pages you'd cut from
the Master's notebook," I guessed, earning a careless nod in
reply.

"I didn't bother to deny it, for what good would it have

done? Instead, I told Constantin who my uncle was and said that if he forgot all he'd seen and heard, I would make certain that he was well paid for his silence. He pretended to agree, but instead of giving the pages back, he ran off with them. I had to stop him. I—I couldn't let him ruin my plan."

He hesitated, as if regretting he'd confessed this much, before he went on. "My uncle had given me a crossbow, as well as the knife. It was lying at the very bottom of my trunk, wrapped in a cloak. I'd almost forgotten I had it, until that moment. I grabbed it up . . . and I went after Constantin."

Abruptly, as if his legs could no longer hold him, he slumped from his proud stance into a sitting position on the roof beside the craft.

"I didn't mean for it to happen," he said in the pat tones of one who was repeating an oft-told tale. "All I wanted was for Constantin to give the pages back, to pretend that he knew nothing. But he ran off to the garden, where I knew the Master was working. I watched him try the gate. When it turned out to be locked, I thought I was saved. But then he started climbing the wall."

A tear rolled down one cheek as he spoke, and he swiped it away with an angry hand.

"I was too far away to stop him any other way. I—I don't think I meant to shoot him, not really, but somehow I pulled the trigger. I saw the bolt hit him in the back, and I saw him fall. I waited for someone to come after me, but they didn't. And so I knew he must have died before he could tell the Master what I'd done. But the worst part was that I no longer had Leonardo's notes, and so I had to come up with another plan. And that was when I decided to kidnap Leonardo, as well."

"But why, Tito?" I demanded, unable to hold back my own anger. "Why did you do your uncle's bidding, when you knew it was wrong? You could have told the Master what the duke was planning, and he would have seen to it that you stayed safely in Milan and never had to return home to Pontalba again. What could your uncle have promised you in return, that you would resort to kidnapping and murder?"

At my mention of his uncle, Tito touched a reflexive hand to his bruised mouth, and his expression tightened. I recalled that his father had died when he was but a boy, so it must have been the Duke of Pontalba who had served in that role for him ever since. Unwilling sympathy momentarily cooled my heated emotions. What must it have been like for him as a child, being left with a brutal uncle whose approval he surely must have craved, while he feared the man himself?

Tito's gaze met mine again, and he smiled a little.

"You don't understand. Finally, I had the chance to make my uncle proud of me. He always thought me a fool and a weakling because I loved to paint. The only way he would let me join Leonardo's workshop was if I pretended to be but a common youth so that I could act as his spy at Castle Sforza. It was my own idea to steal the flying machine and bring it back to Pontalba. When I told him my plan, my uncle promised that if I could accomplish that, I would be the first one to pilot it. And he said that once we built a whole fleet of flying machines for Pontalba, I would be captain over all of them!"

My first instinctive thought was that the duke would never have handed over such responsibility to his nephew; still, from the note of pride I heard in Tito's voice, I knew that he had believed his uncle's promise. Taking on such a glorious post would surely have seemed a vindication of all he might have endured at his uncle's hands to that point.

The moment of satisfaction faded, and he turned an angry look on me.

"Most of what happened is your fault, you know . . . yours, and your father's," he cried in an accusatory tone. "If Signor Angelo had told my uncle's men that he wasn't Leonardo, or if you hadn't listened to Rebecca and insisted on coming here to Pontalba, nobody else would have had to die. But because of your interference, my uncle will have you and all the rest of them—your father, Leonardo, all the other apprentices—slain or thrown into the dungeon, just because it pleases him."

Even as he'd made that cruel accusation, I heard the sudden familiar sound of the portcullis opening. The shouts of the soldiers drifted up to us as they put heel to flank and began moving toward the gate. Soon, the duke's men would be riding down the ramp to the open field. They would assemble into formation there, I knew, before beginning their assault upon the handful of boys hiding in the woods.

I had to act as they began that march but before they reached the trees.

"Tito," I pleaded, kneeling beside him and grabbing his hand. "There is still a chance for you to make amends. Let me take the flying machine as I planned. If I can keep it airborne, I will use it to distract your uncle's men while the other apprentices make their escape. I can do nothing for my father or the Master, but perhaps I can save some of them."

"Pah, why do you care what happens to a handful of common apprentices?"

"They are my friends, Tito . . . just as they were yours."

Not waiting for an answer, I released my grip on him and hurriedly lay atop the craft again, tightening the belt with shaking hands. Tito remained where he sat beside the craft, watching me with an unreadable expression. The strap fastened, I reached a hand for the end of the rope that held the flying machine tied in place. A single jerk would pull the knot free, and the rope would slip back through the ring as the craft made its descent down the roof.

I shot another anxious look at Tito. Slowly, he stood, and for a frantic moment I feared he would somehow try to stop me. But instead he said, "If I let you do this, you must swear if they capture you that you never saw me here, that I came too late to stop you."

"I swear by all the saints," I softly cried as I heard a shout from the duke's captain of the guard and the answering rhythmic clop of hooves drift up from below. They were moving down the ramp and would momentarily be in formation. "Let me do what I can to save them . . . please, for Constantin's sake."

By way of answer, he stepped back from the craft. I gave him a grateful nod and made another hurried check of the pedals and levers. Lightly, I began to flap the wings, feeling with that tentative movement a slight lift of the craft's frame. The momentum coming down the slanted roofline would be sufficient to keep me going as I reached its end, but I would swiftly plummet back to earth if I did not pedal fast enough to keep the wings moving at a quick pace. Yet if I flapped too hard as I cleared the roofline, I risked catching the wingtips upon the slate, causing me to lose control.

The rumble of hooves upon the ramp had ceased. I knew they were spreading their mounts into formation, with the foot soldiers taking up their positions to the rear. In another moment, the captain would give the signal to surge forward . . . and that would be my signal to take flight.

Any fear that I had earlier felt was gone, replaced by an oddly calm sense of purpose. No longer was I concerned with what might happen if I fell from the sky. All that mattered was staying aloft long enough to disrupt the ranks and give my friends time enough to flee. I barely had time for a half-murmured prayer to whatever saints might be listening to keep me strong, when another shout drifted up from below.

Taking a deep breath, I yanked the rope.

For an interminable moment, the craft remained motionless, so that I feared the rope had become tangled in its frame. But an instant later, and with swiftness far greater than I could imagine, it began rolling forward.

Though my descent down the ramplike roof must have taken but a few seconds, time slowed to the point that I took in every instant with an almost languorous clarity. I began to pedal, inwardly counting off each stroke, *one, two, one, two.* The canvas-covered wings rose and fell with the graceful precision of a dove taking flight, while their soft whoosh reminded me of a night owl's hushed pursuit of its prey. My confidence grew, for surely this design so closely mimicked a bird's anatomy that it lacked only feathers!

But as a thrill of triumph shot through me, I heard an anguished shout. I glanced back long enough to see Tito running after me, arms outstretched and face twisted in anger as he cried, "No! Stop! It's mine!"

Stay back, I tried to shout, but the words lodged in my throat. All I could do was pray that he would come to his senses, though I knew with sudden certainty how this must end.

For I was moving too fast for him to catch me; moreover, the break in the parapets was but a few lengths ahead of me. In the space of a few more seconds, the flying machine would be airborne. And still I heard the cries as Tito continued his pursuit, seemingly heedless of what lay ahead beyond the castle's edge.

Yet I could not worry about him anymore. All I could

do was keep pedaling while praying that Leonardo's grand design would prove to be no folly but a triumph of genius. Ahead of me was nothing other than sky, cloudless and far bluer than any I could ever recall seeing.

And then, abruptly, the ground dropped out from beneath me.

23

It shall seem to men that they see new destructions in the sky . . .

—Leonardo da Vinci, *Codex Atlanticus*

I screamed . . . not so much in terror as in sheer exhilaration. For, after that first petrifying lurch as the wheels slipped off the castle's edge, the craft swooped upward. I was flying! The Master's invention worked!

One corner of my mind registered an echoing shriek of terror from somewhere behind me, the doleful cry cut short a heartbeat later. I dared not look back, but I knew to my great sorrow what that sound meant.

Tito.

Blinded by the thought of losing what he'd shed both blood and soul to gain, he had forgotten that the roofline ended. Or perhaps he hadn't. Either way, he had followed after me and plunged to what most certainly would have been his death.

I prayed that his uncle the duke would treat him far more kindly as a corpse than he had treated his nephew in life.

As for me, I had loved Tito as a friend. Despite the evil he had done, I could not help but mourn the youth that I had thought him to be. Later—if there was a later for me—I would ponder whether or not justice had been served in the end. For the moment, however, my concern was focused on keeping control of my craft.

I felt as if I were cradled upon some invisible cloud, so gently did the craft hover. Each movement of my feet made the great wings rise and dip down again in a rowing motion, so that the craft glided atop the breeze like a ship rolling upon the waves. Yet, press one pedal too hard, and the craft wobbled. Press it too softly, and the machine tilted at an alarming angle. I found, as well, that the hand controls allowed but the subtlest change in altitude or movement. In order to make a circle, I needed to adjust the splayed tail that served as rudder, using yet another control.

I clung with grim purpose to the hand levers, concentrating on keeping the flying machine level while I studied the formation of soldiers below me. From my vantage point, they looked like chess pieces neatly spread across a dark green board. I stared in fascination, feeling almost as if I could reach down and pluck them up, one by one, and move them where I chose. Already, they were almost halfway across the field, their armor and weapons glinting beneath the late-morning sun. Recalling myself to my purpose, I shook free of my fancies and cautiously guided the flying machine above the soldiers' path.

The craft's shadow spilled over the field like that of some giant mythical bird, throwing a dark stain over men and beasts. Had any of the soldiers noticed this anomaly, they likely dismissed it as a wayward cloud crossing the sun's face. The horses, however, realized something was amiss . . .

perhaps instinctively recalling an ancient time when predators swooped down upon their ancestors from out of the sky.

As my shadow touched them, the armored beasts shied and whinnied in fright, breaking formation as they sought escape from their perceived attacker. This was what I'd hoped to accomplish, I thought with a small surge of triumph. More confident in my abilities, I adjusted the craft's rudderlike tail and circled over the troops again.

Fear exploded into panic as one terrified steed after another thrashed and bucked, trying to unseat their riders. The foot soldiers following behind broke ranks, as well, scrambling out of range of flailing hooves. Faced with this abrupt dissolution of his forces, the captain, struggling with his own frightened mount, raised an arm and with a shout called a halt to the charge.

It was at that moment that one of the mounted men, who had been unceremoniously thrown by his horse, stared up and saw the flying machine.

His cries and frantic gestures caught the attention of his fellow soldiers, who followed his gaze upward. A chorus of shouts punctuated with pointing fingers arose from the disarrayed troops. Some must have known of the flying machine's existence, for I heard faint cries of, *Leonardo, Leonardo.* Others, perhaps more superstitious than the rest, must have attributed the sight to divine intervention, for they fell to their knees and raised their arms in supplication.

For myself, any fear I'd previously felt was gone, replaced by an intoxicating sense of supremacy as I saw the power that I wielded. Indeed, I laughed. What would these battle-hardened soldiers say, I wondered, if they ever learned that a mere woman had disrupted their well-armed forces? Feeling quite invincible now, I wheeled the flying machine about and, with a slight dip of my wings, abruptly swooped low like a hawk rushing to strike.

And that was when I saw one foot soldier raise his bulky crossbow and fire it directly at me.

I pulled up abruptly. The bolt whizzed past me, its power far greater than I could have imagined at this distance, so that I surely would have been impaled had I not taken such evasive maneuvers. But a glance at my left wing showed me that the craft had not escaped unscathed. I could see daylight through the tear in the canvas through which the bulky arrow had passed.

A solid thud to the framework beneath me shook the craft. Someone else had fired off another bolt, this one lodging firmly in wood. Fighting back panic, I pedaled faster, trying to take the flying machine out of range. Yet a third bolt tore past, this one thankfully missing both me and the craft.

With a few more flaps of my wings, I was out of range, or so I prayed. But the soldiers' attention was focused on me, and I knew I would face an onslaught of bolts and spears should I venture back too close again. More to the point was the fact that my limbs were rapidly tiring from the effort of pedaling to keep the craft aloft. My soft life as an apprentice had done me no favors in this particular instance!

Frantic, I weighed my options. My diversion had worked; of that, there was no doubt. But if I gave up my assault, the soldiers would return to their original mission of tracking down the apprentices. Though I'd bought them a few precious minutes' head start in their retreat, it was not enough time to assure my friends sufficient lead on their pursuers to make good an escape. I would have to continue my tactics in order to gain them more time.

Feeling quite vulnerable now, I grimly turned the flying machine about for another pass over the soldiers. And that was when I heard the unmistakable sound of canvas ripping.

The source of that chilling noise was immediately apparent. With each flap of my wings, wind had caught at the fabric damaged by the wayward bolt and further weakened it at that spot. Finally, the canvas had given way, resulting in a tear that stretched between two of the wing's largest ribs. Air poured through the gap while the craft, unbalanced, began to waver, so that it took all my efforts to hold it steady.

And, once again, I was drawing within range of the crossbows. Another tear in that wing could send the craft spiraling out of control. A direct hit on its body might splinter a support or cut through a cable, resulting in the same outcome. And if the bolt hit me . . . Saints' blood, that did not bear thinking about! But what other choice did I have?

Though my legs had begun to burn with the effort, I redoubled my pedaling in hopes of increasing my speed and gaining some altitude. I could see a group of the soldiers preparing for my return, crossbows raised as they stood in tight formation. The horsemen, meanwhile, had dismounted and wrapped cloaks over their steeds' eyes to settle them, so that they would remain quiet during the attack. The remaining foot soldiers stood at the ready, doubtless charged with effecting my capture should the others bring down the flying machine.

I had no illusion that I would make it through unscathed in what likely would be my final pass. My only hope was that most of the bolts would miss their targets, and that any hits did but minor damage . . . to me or to the craft! Unless the flying machine proved too crippled in that aftermath, my plan was to continue flying north for as long as my aching legs would endure. When I could go no farther, I would attempt a landing and—should I crawl from the wreckage in one piece—make my way on foot back to Milan.

I could think ahead no further than that.

A barrage erupted below me, perhaps a dozen bolts releasing

skyward. Tied as I was to the craft's frame, I could do nothing but hunker in place and squeeze my eyes shut as the deadly arrows chased after me. In quick succession, I heard three, then four, then five of them pierce the frame, the sharp crack of wood like small explosions in my ears. A second volley followed the first, these bolts slicing through the wings. And then a flare of pain burned through my thigh, as if someone had slapped a glowing poker from the Master's forge upon my flesh.

I screamed in equal parts agony and fright, and the craft gave a sickening lurch. For a moment I feared I might faint, but my head cleared enough for me to pull the flying machine level again. I glanced back to see how badly I was injured, almost swooning again at the sight of the heavy bolt that had ripped through the wooden frame and pierced my leg.

No, not pierced it, I amended with a relieved gasp . . . merely grazed the flesh. Though the bolt had torn through my trunk hose to hold me skewered like a bird on a spit, I found that I could still move my leg. Still, the bloody stain that was rapidly widening along that leg was alarming, as was the searing pain. But I was still in one piece and able to keep flying . . . That was, assuming that the craft remained intact.

More canvas abruptly rent, and the flying machine dipped and turned back in the direction from which I'd come. I gave the rudder a frantic pull, but the lever broke loose in my hand, the tail drooping like that of a defeated cockerel. I was headed down, and I would crash there amid the soldiers. My best hope was that I manage to take a few of those brutal men with me as I splintered apart.

My vanity made me pray that my corpse survived the impact in one neat piece.

As when I'd taken off, time slowed so that I was privy to

every detail. From the distance, I heard the blare of trumpets sounding a charge . . . odd, because they seemed to echo from the forest and not the castle. Then, in a flash of silver, I saw bursting from the castle gates a magnificent chariot pulled by two black horses and carrying two dark-haired men, while whirling blades around them sang of victory and death. And, most strangely of all, the scores of painted soldiers that we'd set up among the trees the night before came abruptly to life, pouring onto the field on foot and on horses, their numbers far superior to the Duke of Pontalba's men.

I smiled, the pain of my injured leg forgotten and any fear of death left behind. Certainly, this must be but a final trick of my now-fevered mind, I told myself as I calmly watched the ground rushing up to meet me. Still, I would die happily, knowing that, at least in my imagination, Leonardo had won the day and my father was free.

And afterward, when I moved from darkness back into light, surely Constantin would be waiting to greet me, his smile proud as he stood alongside his father and welcomed me home.

24

Science is the captain, practice the soldiers.

—Leonardo da Vinci, *Manuscript I*

Much to my surprise, I did not die, after all.

Instead, I awakened sometime later to find myself lying upon a soft pallet in one of our wagons, wrapped once again in my father's cloak. His expression anxious, my friend Vittorio hovered over me.

From the canopy of trees above him, I guessed that we were back in the makeshift camp where we apprentices had gathered the night before. No longer did I hear the sounds of shouting men and clashing arms and frightened horses. Now the whisper of breeze was broken by a lark's cheery song and the occasional call of one apprentice to another as they gathered up pieces of the Master's stage setting.

"You're alive," Vittorio exclaimed in satisfaction, adding with greater relief, "and none too soon for me. I have needed to piss for a good hour, but the Master charged me with keeping watch over you until you woke up, lest you sink away altogether and breathe your last!"

I was not sure if that final observation was meant to spur me to health or simply to warn me that my prospects were dire. Assuming the former, I shot him a wry look and managed to reply, "Fear not; you don't have to stitch my shroud just yet. And I will do my best to keep breathing, so take yourself off to piss with my blessing."

While Vittorio rushed off to find an accommodating tree, I gingerly took stock of my physical state. Despite my assertions to the contrary, breathing proved more difficult than I expected, for my ribs ached with every inhalation. I put an experimental hand to my throbbing head to find it bandaged, with the cloth over my forehead sticky with drying blood. But my greatest alarm came when I realized someone had cut away one leg of my trunk hose in order to bind up the gash on my thigh.

By now Vittorio, still adjusting his tunic, had returned to my side. I gestured him nearer and indicated my bandaged leg.

"Who—who did this?" I asked in no little trepidation, all too aware that the required surgery upon my garb might have revealed a certain lack of my supposed anatomy to anyone observing the procedure.

Vittorio snickered. "Don't worry; no one save your father saw what dangles between your legs, for he insisted on bandaging you himself. Novella gave him some of the same salve that Signor Luigi prescribed for Rebecca, but he made her look away lest you be embarrassed later."

He snorted at my sigh of relief, unaware that it was the preservation of my disguise and not my modesty that comforted me. Then, at my request, he told me all he knew of what had happened while I lay unconscious after my dramatic landing in the midst of what was briefly to become a battlefield.

I had not imagined the glorious sight of Leonardo and his chariot charging out onto the field of fire, my father at his side. The pair had escaped Nicodemo's dungeon with relative ease, given that Leonardo had had the foresight to hide in his tunic a ring of keys, each being the master to a different style of lock. As for the painted army come to life, the truth had been equally prosaic if no less a marvel.

For the soldiers I'd seen rushing from the forest in great numbers to clash with the Duke of Pontalba's men had not sprung from our canvases; rather they had been Ludovico's own army. Leonardo's message to the duke had met him but a day out from Milan. How he might have worded his entreaty, no one save he and the duke knew, but apparently the note was sufficient to spur Il Moro into dispatching his troops posthaste. Thus, the army had been almost on our heels as we traveled to Pontalba.

It had been my father, Vittorio explained, who had braved the battle around me to rush to my side and carefully extricate me from the flying machine's wreckage. With equal valor, he had dodged flailing swords and thrusting spears from both sides to carry me to the safety of the trees, not knowing at that point if I still lived or not.

The fighting, meanwhile, had continued, but not for long. During the initial clash, a group of Ludovico's men had gained control of the castle's gate before the unsuspecting guards could lower the portcullis and raise the drawbridge. The remainder of the duke's army had quickly subdued Nicodemo's smaller force and commenced an orderly invasion of the castle.

As for the remaining apprentices, they were all safe. They had taken cover beneath the wagons and watched the action on the field with the same enthusiasm as if it had been a feast day pageant. Though my dramatic diversion had ultimately proved unnecessary, Vittorio staunchly reassured me that it would have gained them much crucial time had not the soldiers from Castle Sforza fortuitously arrived.

"You know how Davide is," he reminded me with a grin. "He worries like an old woman. He saw the flying machine atop the castle and feared the Master's plan had gone wrong. He had already given the order to mount the horses by the time the gate opened. Had Il Moro's men not appeared to protect us, we would have ridden off. We would have been far ahead of the duke's soldiers by the time they finally tired of watching you flap about the skies like an old hen."

Of course, they had all thought me dead when they saw the flying machine gracelessly tumble to the ground. I was gratified to learn that my presumed demise had quite dampened their earlier enthusiasm for battle, and that spontaneous cheers had arisen once they saw that I remained among the living. Later, after the fighting had ended, the Master had examined his battered craft. He had opined that it had been the leather bladder, intended to facilitate a landing upon the water, which had ultimately cushioned the impact enough for me to survive with but minor injuries.

The gash on my leg, though painful, had already stopped bleeding by the time my father rescued me. More troubling, Vittorio explained, was the blow to my head that I'd suffered. After evaluating the damage to his invention, the Master had checked on the welfare of its luckless pilot. He had taken one look at my unconscious form and instructed that I was to remain unmoving for the remainder of the day and through the night, lest I do further damage to my battered head. Assured that I likely would survive, he and my father had returned to the castle where the captain of Il Moro's guard was busy interrogating the Duke of Pontalba.

Wisely, Nicodemo had not mounted any further defense once it was apparent that his men were outnumbered. Instead, he had played the role of aggrieved noble, protesting that he had been duped by Leonardo into believing that Milan was prepared to lay siege to Pontalba. With the same vigor, he had claimed that he'd only just learned about the kidnapping of my father and theft of the flying machine. That plan, he assured the true captain of Ludovico's guard, had been solely the idea of his nephew, who had acted on his own and apparently had fled the castle in all the commotion.

It was not until much later that someone had noticed Tito's broken body lying at the castle's foot, hidden in the grass.

Vittorio's words confirmed what I'd already guessed, but to hear Tito's fate pronounced with such finality dimmed the small triumph I had felt at realizing that the duke had not prevailed. There was more, of course. By now, word had spread among the apprentices that Tito had been no common youth, like themselves, but the Duke of Pontalba's nephew. They knew, as well, that his true purpose in Milan had not been to serve in Leonardo's workshop but to act as his uncle's spy.

His expression uncertain, Vittorio paused in his account. "Is what they said about him true, Dino? Did Tito steal the flying machine? Because, if he did, I fear that he also must have murdered Constantin."

I wondered if Vittorio had somehow suspected his friend of that crime, all along, for him to have so swiftly come to that conclusion. But along with condemnation, I heard the note of hope in his voice that begged me to dispel the tales. For a heartbeat, I was tempted to oblige him. After all, what good would it serve to point further fingers of guilt at Tito, when both he and Constantin were already dead?

With my first burst of energy depleted, I had but strength

to nod once and reply, "He confessed all to me, in the end. It was he who stole the Master's flying machine and kidnapped my father . . . and it was he who brutally shot down Constantin lest he reveal Tito's plans."

Vittorio's face momentarily crumpled, and I saw the sheen of tears in his eyes. In a rough voice he demanded, "How could he do such a thing? We were his friends, all of us . . . and Constantin, more than the rest."

"His need to find favor with his uncle became more important than any of our friendships," I explained, my own voice shaky. "But, in the end, he realized the evil he'd done and sought to make amends. He could have stopped me there on the roof if he'd truly wished, before I took the flying machine. Instead, he let me try to save the rest of you."

What I didn't tell Vittorio was what happened in those last seconds, how Tito had cried out in anger and come running after me. But I was certain he had never meant to catch me, certain that he had deliberately kept running even as he'd reached the castle's edge.

Neither did I admit to Vittorio what had occurred as I lay in the wreckage of the flying machine, drifting in a painless sea of black.

How long I drifted there, I did not know. After a time, however, the darkness had begun to lift, banished by a light blazing upon some distant horizon. I had been surprised but not truly frightened to find my inner being rising and moving toward it, leaving behind my body still sprawled upon the field.

The light had grown brighter as I neared it, and yet I felt no need to shield my eyes. Vaguely, I realized that I had come upon a place that was welcoming but at the same time forbidden to me beyond a certain point. And so I halted and waited for what might come next.

I had sensed more than seen another figure pass me by, continuing toward that light until it held him fully in its embrace. It was then that I recognized the figure as Tito! He stood silently facing that brilliance, and I sensed an air of expectancy about him that puzzled me. But soon enough the same feeling of anticipation gripped me, as well, though I had no idea for what—or for whom—we waited.

A moment later another figure had appeared, this one stepping out from the very heart of the light to face Tito. *Constantin,* I had gasped, and I took a reflexive step forward.

Constantin had glanced my way, as if hearing me calling his name. And then he smiled. While he had not lost his familiar expression of kindness, I sensed about his being something richer, deeper . . . almost as if the pettiest of life's emotions had been stripped from his being and been replaced with some higher wisdom. While he was still the friend that I had loved, I realized that he was no longer quite who he had been.

He gently shook his head, and I knew he meant that I could move no closer, not even to make my final good-byes. My heart had twisted a little, but I made no protest. Turning from me, he reached out a hand to Tito, who clasped it gladly.

In that moment, I had sensed a change sweep over Tito, as well. It was as if his old cares and emotions suddenly had been burned away by the light, leaving behind the very finest essence of him. He, too, had glanced back in my direction and offered the same wise smile as Constantin had bestowed on me. And then, side by side, the pair had walked off together into the light.

Vittorio's concerned voice roused me from my thoughts.

"Dino, what is wrong? You're crying," he declared, conveniently forgetting that his own eyes held suspicious dampness. "Is the pain growing worse? The Master said I might give you a sip of the herbed wine to help ease it."

"No, I am better," I replied with some truth and managed a small smile. The smile twisted into a grimace, however, as I added, "But I probably should take a bit of that wine and rest for a while. I fear that when I finally face my father and the Master to confess my sins, I will need all my strength."

"Ha, what you will need is swift feet," he cheerfully corrected me as he produced the wine jug in question and poured a few sips' worth into a wooden cup.

"I have never seen the Master so angry before," he went on. "It is lucky for you that you were already struck senseless when he first saw you. Once he knew you were in no great danger of dying, he threatened all manner of dire things to punish you for disobeying his orders."

Though somewhat daunted by his words, I pushed aside that particular worry long enough to swallow the wine. By the time the cup was empty, however, another concern had occurred to me. "What of Rebecca? She was at the gatehouse when I left her. Has she returned here?"

Vittorio shook his head, his moment of amusement fading. "Novella went in search of her, and I have not seen either of them since," he replied, worry evident in his tone. "But surely they must return soon."

I prayed that he was right, but I feared he might not be. Though Rebecca had proved herself a valiant companion in this adventure, I still found my trust hampered by questions about her that I could not yet answer. At least one of those the Duchess of Pontalba could address, assuming that the cruel Nicodemo had not already carried through with his threats against her.

I meant to ask Vittorio if the Master had confronted the

duke regarding his ill-treated wife. Before I could pursue that thought, however, the wine and my protesting body finally took charge, and I drifted into sleep once more.

My resulting dreams were not easy, for in them I was once again piloting the flying machine. But rather than plummeting to the earth, I instead found myself unable to land, doomed to hover in the skies above Castle Pontalba like a sailor cast adrift at sea. It was with relief that I struggled awake sometime later to find that the pain in my head and leg had begun to subside. But more reassuring was the sight of my sire's familiar face—looking far more stern and worn than usual—gazing down upon me.

"Father," I cried and reached out a hand to him. "I feared I might never see you again."

"As did I," he replied, his tone severe though he cradled my fingers gently in his. "Were you one of your brothers, I would find a stick and beat a measure of sense into you, despite your injuries."

Then his grip on me tightened, and I saw remembered fear flash over his features.

"Child, what possessed you to attempt to fly Signor Leonardo's invention like that?" he demanded. "You could have had no way of knowing if I had finished connecting every line and securing every joint. And no one, not even your master, could have said with any certainty if the craft could remain aloft. Had not every saint in heaven been watching over you, you surely should have died this day."

"I checked each line and joint," I hastened to assure him. "And don't forget that you had already told me you intended to use the flying machine to make your escape. If you were not afraid, how could I be?"

He sighed and shook his head. "I do not doubt your bravery, for few men would have dared such a feat. But why did you disobey Signor Leonardo's orders and make your way into the castle, in the first place?"

"Tito convinced me that the Master's plan was flawed, and that your life and his were in danger," I confessed, realizing once more how well the youth had drawn me into his net of lies. Or had it been Rebecca who had convinced me of the particular plan? Now I was not so sure.

More shaken than I cared to admit by this uncertainty, I explained to my father how I'd secretly witnessed Leonardo's audience with the Duke of Pontalba . . . including Nicodemo's threats to hang both him and the Master, along with the other apprentices. I told him, too, of my final encounter with Tito on the roof, and how he had confessed to Constantin's murder. My father's frown deepened, and I knew he had been as stung as we apprentices by the betrayal of the young man he had taken under his wing.

When I finished my account, I asked, "But what of the treaty between Milan and Pontalba? Will there be war?"

"I suspect not . . . at least, not for the moment. It appears that both sides have agreed to pretend that this encounter never happened, so long as the Duke of Pontalba relinquishes both his wife and the dowry she brought with her. As for the treaty, it likely will not hold any longer than it takes Il Moro's army to return to Milan."

"Pah, I would have preferred to see Nicodemo hanging from his own parapets, as he threatened to do with us," I muttered with no little heat.

Though gladdened to know that the duchess would gain her freedom once more, I could not repress the bitterness that swept me. The duke would suffer no punishment for his evil deeds, no matter that he was responsible for the deaths of two young men and would have commanded many more to be killed had Il Moro's army not arrived in time to halt that

heinous crime. Instead, he would continue to feast with his
men, perhaps find another young wife to torment, all the
while making war on his neighbors and callously murdering
anyone who proved inconvenient.

And none of this was fair.

Once, I would have been swift to make this protest aloud
rather than simply harboring the thought. But over the past
few months, I had come to accept the Master's oft-made
assertion that life was not fair and never had been. With that
acceptance, however, had also come the certainty that the
actions of a single person could sometimes tilt those scales
back in the opposite direction, so that right could be made
to outweigh wrong, and justice could be made to conquer
chaos.

Regrettably, I suspected that I was not that person . . . at
least, not this particular time.

My father, meanwhile, was nodding his agreement. "I
understand little of politics and less of warfare, but I can recognize a scoundrel when he crosses my path, no matter that
he be draped in velvets and silks. The Duke of Pontalba is
a villain, and your Duke of Milan is little better. They care
only to fatten their coffers and gain glory for themselves. By
Saint Joseph, I will be glad when we return home again."

So saying, he released my hand and smiled. "You must
rest, while I help your fellows finish loading the wagons for
our journey tomorrow. The afternoon grows late enough that
we will remain camped here with Ludovico's army tonight
and take our leave at first light with them."

It was not until after he left me alone did I have the chance
to consider his declaration that *we* were to return home. Surely
my father had not meant that he expected me to accompany
him, I thought in dismay. With those words echoing in my
ears, I began to prepare my arguments, more than willing to

protest any such attempt to roust me from Milan . . . until a far more alarming possibility occurred to me.

What if the Master truly were as angry as Vittorio claimed? No matter that my motives had been pure, I had flouted his orders and managed to destroy his grand invention before he'd ever had the chance to test it himself. He might decide that I was no longer worthy of my post and dismiss me as his apprentice. Thus disgraced, I would have no choice but to return home with my father, after all.

And if that happened, my long-held dream of becoming a master painter would end as abruptly as had my ride upon Leonardo's flying machine.

25

Even the swiftest bird cannot always escape the cage.

—Leonardo da Vinci, *The Notebooks of Delfina della Fazia*

We departed Castle Pontalba at dawn the next day, our small band bordered, front and rear, by the Duke of Milan's army. Davide again drove the wagon that carried us apprentices. Behind us, my father had taken the reins of the wagon that Tito had driven, while Paolo and Tommaso were once more in charge of the others. With the soldiers setting our pace, we traveled more swiftly than we had even under Leonardo's command.

The whirling blades of his chariot safely folded down, the Master took his place near the front of the mounted troops behind the captain of the guard and his highest-ranking men. The army's supply wagons and a company of foot soldiers came next, followed by our wagons. The remaining foot soldiers and a contingent of mounted men brought up the rear, providing more than sufficient defense should the Duke of

Pontalba break the treaty before we'd left his small province and send his soldiers after us.

Il Moro's young cousin Marianna—the former Duchess of Pontalba—perched upon a small white steed among the mounted soldiers before us. Dressed in the same now-ragged finery that she'd worn while in her cell, she was flanked by what appeared to be the two largest of the men-at-arms.

Though their armored chargers were almost twice the size of her dainty beast, I suspected that the soldiers were there not so much to provide protection as they were to catch her should she lose her grip and tumble from her mount. Such was not an unlikely possibility, for she appeared more alarmingly fragile now than she had in her cell. But Marianna had proved herself worthy of her Sforza ancestors, despite her weakened state.

While I lay recuperating upon my pallet the night before, my father had related more of that day's events. The liberation of the duchess had proved almost as dramatic as the clash between Milan and Pontalba. She had refused the captain of the guard's suggestion that she be taken from the castle in one of the wagons. Instead, upon learning that she had been freed from the duke's clutches, she insisted she would ride her own horse through the gate and all the way back to Milan.

"I shall not give him the satisfaction of seeing me carried from this place," she had declared, her scornful tone leaving no doubt as to her opinion of her husband.

Impressed by her strength of mind, the captain ordered his men to retrieve her mount from the stables and had helped settle her upon the small steed himself. Then, flags flying and trumpets blasting, his soldiers had made a great show of escorting her with every ceremony from the castle grounds.

Listening to my father's account, I had felt a swell of

admiration for the young woman. And if the saints continued to watch over her, perhaps Marianna's story would end
far more happily than had that of the tragic contessa she had
replaced.

But as our journey continued, I concentrated my thoughts
on my own situation. I had the advantage of my soft pallet at
the front of the wagon bed where I could stretch out to rest.
The remaining apprentices sat shoulder to shoulder in far less
comfort than I, though none seemed inclined to complain.
The stories and riddles that had passed the time for us before
were not to be heard on this journey, however, for each youth
was caught up in his thoughts.

Once, and to no one in particular, Bernardo sat up straight
and declared, "I hate Tito! I shall never forgive him."

The words spoken, he slumped so that his chin rested on
his knees. His eyes gleamed with unshed tears as he glared
about him, as if daring someone to contradict that pronounce-
ment. The rest of us turned sympathetic looks on him, for
we knew that Bernardo had particularly admired the older
youth. And all of us felt, to some degree or another, the same
sense of angry betrayal over what had happened.

But Tito was not the sole object of our thoughts. Though
I was supposed to be convalescing, I found myself leaning
up from time to time to see if Rebecca and her daughter had
come into view behind us in their borrowed cart to join our
march. Vittorio, too, appeared to be watching for them, for
his gaze remained fixed on the dwindling landscape behind
us. I knew he was concerned about Novella, and I regretted
that he'd been forced to watch over me the day before instead
of joining the girl in her search for her mother.

The two women still had not made an appearance as morning slipped into afternoon. By that time, I was sitting up
along with the other apprentices, for I was feeling much more

restored by an earlier dose of the herbed wine and a few more hours of sleep. Vittorio's earlier look of concern had faded to weary resignation, and I guessed from his glum expression that he feared he might never see Novella again. Seeking to offer a bit of reassurance, I changed spots with Bernardo so that I was sitting beside him.

"I'm sure that Novella and her mother are well ahead of us on the road," I murmured. "Rebecca likely slipped past the gates with her cart when the fighting started, and she took Novella away to keep her safe. Chances are they are almost to Milan, and you'll find Novella waiting there at the castle gates for you."

"I pray you are right," he muttered back, his expression growing bleaker still. "I don't know what I would do if I lost her for good."

I realized any further attempts at comfort would likely ring hollow. I left him with his thoughts and lapsed into sympathetic silence, for I had other worries of my own beyond the washerwoman.

I had waited all of the previous evening for the Master to check on me as I languished upon my makeshift bed in the wagon. Racked by guilt over the destruction of his flying machine, I longed to make my apologies and beg his forgiveness. But while my father stayed close by, and the other apprentices visited with me, in turn, Leonardo did not make an appearance. When I'd finally voiced my concerns to my father, he had attempted to set my mind at rest.

"Signor Leonardo made certain to inquire after your health when I saw him at the meal," he assured me. "But he is busy with other matters and likely wishes you to have your rest. You will see him again, soon enough."

The other matters he'd mentioned proved unsettlingly apparent. From where our wagons were arranged, I had a

view of the inner encampment where the captain of the guard
and his men had built a series of fires for heat and cooking.
They had also erected a small tent for Marianna's use. I had
seen Leonardo there with her, bending over her in a solicitous
manner as she spoke to him. What she might have been saying, I could not guess, but an unworthy blade of jealously had
pierced my heart at the sight . . . the emotion all the worse
for the fact that I held them both in high esteem.

I had seen the Master again in the morning, not long
before we began our exodus from the strip of forest bordering
Castle Pontalba. Again, I had no chance to speak with him.
While the troops and wagons began moving into formation,
Leonardo had returned alone to the wreckage of the flying
machine. From a short distance, the fallen craft resembled
nothing so much as a mighty hawk knocked from the sky
by a well-placed arrow. Wings crumpled and body broken
in half, it lay in the same spot where I had made my fateful
landing the day before.

Leonardo had carried with him a lit torch he'd fashioned
from a rag-wrapped tree branch that had been dipped in oil.
While we apprentices watched in respectful silence from the
nearby trees, he touched the torch to each canvas-covered wing,
in turn. The cloth had caught fire almost immediately, burning
long enough so that the framework beneath ignited, as well.
He put the torch to the body, waiting until the entire craft was
burning brightly before tossing the torch onto the makeshift
pyre. Not many minutes later, the once-glorious craft had been
reduced to an unrecognizable pile of smoldering sticks.

Feeling rather as if I had just witnessed a funeral, I had
limped back to the wagon alongside my fellows, who main-
tained a similar sober silence. By this time, the soldiers with
their horses and equipment had taken their places on the
trail leading back through the woods. Our gear was already

packed, so we had but to settle ourselves in our assigned places and be off.

"It could have been repaired," Tommaso had observed as we reached the wagon. Then, giving voice to the question uppermost in all our minds, he'd added, "I wonder why the Master did it?"

I wondered again at that same question as the captain of the guard called a halt to our journey just before dusk. Though my injured state excused me from any labors, I still insisted upon helping my fellows with a few light tasks as we settled ourselves for the night. The Master came by our small band's site once to speak privately with Davide. Had he glanced in my direction, I might have rushed to his side and begged a word with him. But he left us again for the company of Il Moro's men without ever having looked my way.

Later, after another of Philippe's tasty meals, I wrapped my father's cloak about me and set off to find my parent, feeling in need of his counsel. He sat apart from us, leaning against the wheel of the wagon he'd been driving and idly carving a small figure from a bit of wood. This time, he was far more direct in his response to my complaints.

"Cease your lamentation, for this situation is of your own making," he reminded me in a stern tone that made me blush in shame. "Had your master been anyone other than Signor Leonardo, you would have been beaten for your actions, no matter that you were injured. As for making your apologies, you would have had no opportunity to beg mercy, for you would have long since been dismissed from your post and forced to find your way back to Milan on your own. Consider yourself fortunate that he has said nothing to you as of yet."

As I sat in contrite silence at his knee, he assumed a kinder tone.

"Surely you understand by now, child, that Leonardo is different from all other men. And I speak not only of his genius but in the way that he approaches life. One thing that sets him apart is that he does not view his apprentices as but hapless servants to be commanded. Instead, he sees them as young men he can mold into a semblance of his own greatness, if they will but heed his teachings. And no matter what anyone else might whisper, he loves them as his own sons. Thus he feels a father's disappointment when they stray . . . and a father's pain when they are taken from him in death."

"I know, and that is why I long to make amends," I replied, feeling myself dangerously close to tears. "But I cannot do so if he acts as if I am not there."

My father smiled just a little at that.

"Just because he is a man of genius does not mean he cannot sometimes succumb to unworthy emotions," he assured me. "I suspect that you offended him by doubting his plan, and you stole his glory by flying his grand invention before he had a chance to do so first. Give him more time, and I am sure he will be amenable to your apology."

"But what of you, Father?" I ventured, realizing that what he'd said about disappointment and pain applied to him, as well. "Have you forgiven me . . . and will you force me to return home with you once we are back in Milan?"

"Of course, I have forgiven you," he said and laid a light hand upon my bandaged head. "As for the rest, were it my choice . . . yes, I would bring you back home again, so that I could keep you safe, just as I did when you were a girl. Moreover, now that I see how you live and work among so many young men, I cannot continue to give my blessing to your masquerade."

When I made a soft sound of protest, he added, "But I have seen you exhibit bravery and honor, as well as dedication to your craft. And so, since you are a grown woman, I will not put out a hand to stop you, should you wish to continue in your role. I suspect, however, that the choice is neither yours nor mine, any longer. Signor Leonardo will make that decision for you."

We spoke a bit longer of less consequential matters. Then, with a fond kiss upon my cheek, he pressed the wooden figure he'd carved into my hand and sent me back to my own wagon.

The other apprentices were already settling in for the night, for we would rise before the sun to begin the final leg of our journey. I paused before climbing into the wagon to take a look at the gift my father had given me.

It was a hawk, wings tucked as if prepared to dive. Though tiny enough to nestle with ease in my palm, it was carved with painstaking detail down to the talons spread wide to snatch up its prey. I closed my hand over it again, wondering if his choice of figure had been deliberate, or if the past days' events had caused his idle fingers to reflexively give life to the imagery of flight.

Climbing into the wagon with somewhat greater ease than the day before, I made myself comfortable on my pallet. I ignored the temptation to gaze over at the soldiers' camp and see if the Master sat again with Marianna, or if he simply wandered about chatting with the captain of the guard and his men. My father was right, I told myself, and I should wait to speak my piece until Leonardo made known his interest in conversing with me.

After applying Luigi's salve to my healing leg, I took a larger dose than necessary of the herbed wine, so that I fell into quick and dreamless sleep. The call to rise arrived long before I was ready for it, and we were well on our way by the time the sun crawled from its own warm bed to light the horizon.

Though dreading how my situation might end, I was as anxious as the rest of them to return home to Milan. I barely blinked as we passed the spot where Tito and Rebecca and I had been ambushed, for the odor of death had once more been replaced by the scent of warm earth and new leaves. The apprentices had shaken off the previous day's reserve and again chatted idly among themselves. Only Vittorio held back from conversation, his look of misery more telling than any words to explain his concern over Novella.

But he joined in the small cheer when, by midday, we could see the towers of Milan's cathedrals in the distance. Soon enough, we were through the castle gates and milling about the quadrangle.

While most of Il Moro's men split off to return horses and arms to the stables and armory, the captain of the guard and a few of his men paused for a moment to regroup. Then, arranging themselves in formation around Marianna, they started toward the Duke of Milan's private quarters.

The small contingent passed by our wagon, and Marianna glanced our way. While the other apprentices ducked their heads in a show of respect, my gaze abruptly met hers. She blinked, and I saw her pale lips form the startled word, *Delfina?* before the soldiers following after blocked her from my view.

Once we pulled up our wagons before the workshop, Davide began directing the unpacking. The work progressed swiftly, for all of us were anxious to return to our mundane tasks after the excitement of the past several days. Before long, the last of the painted canvases had been put away in a far corner of the workshop, and the canons and catapult returned to the nearby shed where they had been stored. Finally, with a collective sigh, we regrouped around our familiar hearth and waited for the Master's return.

He and my father arrived back at the workshop a short while later. We all rose to greet him, though I took care to stay to the rear of the group, half-hidden by Tommaso, who was far bulkier than I. The Master received our welcome with obvious gratification before gesturing us to silence.

"First, let me say that I am proud of your bravery in the face of the danger that we found in Pontalba. While we were unable to preserve the flying machine"—a few looks and murmurs turned my way at that—"we recovered our good Master Angelo and rescued the Duchess of Pontalba from the cruel treatment she had endured at the duke's hands. I shall make certain that Il Moro is told the vital part that all of you played in this drama."

He allowed us a moment for a small cheer, and again raised a hand for quiet.

"And now we must face the truth that one of our own was the one who betrayed us and cruelly murdered Constantin," he went on, his expression sober. "While I cannot excuse the evil that Tito did, I must remind you that one can never truly know what is in another man's heart and mind. And so I tell you that while we mourn Constantin, we should also grieve for the Tito who was our friend, rather than curse the traitorous murderer that he became."

I saw a few heads nod in understanding, though most of the other apprentices stood in stony silence. I understood their anger and mourned Constantin as a brother, but I knew that Leonardo was right. Any hate for Tito that we clung to would diminish our love for Constantin. Besides, there was no vengeance to be had in this world and—assuming that my strange vision had been true—all already had been sorted out in the world after. And so, as with the destroyed flying machine, we would do best to walk away from the wreckage of our trust and simply rebuild it from scratch again.

What further words of comfort the Master might have given us, I could not say. Before he could speak again, the workshop door flew open with a crash.

Framed by the sunlight pouring in from the doorway was the same robed and hooded figure that had shadowed me since my father's arrival in Milan. Barely did I have time for a gasp, when the figure stepped forward and shoved back its concealing hood, revealing an all-too-familiar face.

Now my gasp became a moan of disbelief. I could but stare in return, praying with fervor that I was still befuddled by the herbed wine and that this was but a terrible dream.

My prayers, however, went unheard. I stood helplessly by as, with lifted hand pointing dramatically in my direction, the figure cried out, "This is an outrage! Signor Leonardo, I demand that you return my daughter, Delfina, to me at once!"

26

When many winds strive together, then the waves of the sea have not a free course . . .

—Leonardo da Vinci, *Codex Atlanticus*

At her cry, the other apprentices stepped away from me, so that I was left standing in the center of the ring that they formed. Miserably, I glanced from face to face. Some stared back at me with wary expressions; others wore looks of outraged disbelief. Vittorio was gaping in openmouthed astonishment, while Davide merely gave his head a gentle shake, his expression one of private vindication.

Bernardo was the first to speak up.

"You mean that Dino is truly a girl?" he squeaked, curls bobbing and cheeks flushing as he pointed at me. "But it can't be. A girl cannot paint!"

By way of response, my mother tossed aside her cloak and shoved through the ring of stunned young men. Her dark blue skirts swishing like an angry feline's lashing tail, she advanced on me and seized me by the arm.

"Yes, Delfina is a girl," she declared in outrage, "though one would hardly know it, to look at her. Of course, this is all her father's fault, allowing her to run away from a perfectly fine marriage."

Her fiery gaze promptly landed upon my father.

"You thought you could fool me, Angelo, pretending you had no idea where our daughter had gone," she cried as he gazed miserably down at his feet. "I found the missives she sent you, and I guessed that you had a particular reason for accepting a commission in Milan. That is why I followed you here, to see if my suspicions were correct. But I never expected this!"

Taking in my disheveled appearance from head to foot, she went on in a heated tone. "I could not believe my eyes, at first, that one of those boys was in truth my own daughter. And before I could confront her, you and she disappeared. I had no choice but to pay for a squalid room in town and wait until the guard I bribed brought me word that you had returned.

"I don't know what the greater scandal is," she went on, barely pausing to draw breath, "the clothes she is wearing or the fact all of you were too blind to see the truth. And what is this?" she demanded and gestured at my bandages. "Have you injured yourself?"

"It is of no account," I replied, pulling my arm from her grasp and drawing myself up with as much dignity as I could muster. "I was shot with a crossbow and hurt my head when I crashed the Master's flying machine. And do not blame my fellows for my deception, for I took every care to keep them from learning the truth."

"Pah, and what of Signor Leonardo?" she countered with

a derisive gesture in his direction, more concerned with that question than my litany of wounds. "Surely a man who has spent years painting both men and women must know a female when he sees one."

I had opened my mouth to defend Leonardo, when his gaze abruptly met mine. Instead of surprise, I saw in his dark eyes a glimmer of wry knowledge. Stunned, I clamped my lips shut again and felt the blood drain from my face.

It cannot be, I thought, sending him a pleading look in return. But rather than deny the accusation, he gave me the faintest of nods. I felt my insides plummet, as they had when the flying machine had first leaped into nothingness.

Saints' blood, he knows . . . likely has always known!

I shut my eyes against the sudden tears that threatened. I had been the blind one, not he. All these many months I had thought myself so clever, so careful, and yet in the end I had not deceived him. But knowing the truth, why had he allowed my dangerous masquerade, when its discovery would have brought equal censure down upon him?

Swept up as I was in my own misery, I barely heard him snap a command to my fellows.

"Draftsmen, take the canvases you just stacked, and carry them back outside. Use your blades to scrape every bit of paint from them, so that they look new again. And when they look new, scrape them yet again."

His expression far sterner than I'd ever seen it, he added, "And before you go, I will have the vow of each one of you that no whisper of what you have witnessed will go beyond the workshop doors."

"I swear I shall say nothing, Master," Davide promptly spoke up, hand on his heart as he gave me an encouraging nod. The other apprentices made their promises, as well . . . some grudging, and others rueful, but all were in accord.

The Master acknowledged their words with a satisfied nod. "Very well, be off. But keep in mind that your vow is to bind you for all time. Any transgressor will be found out and dismissed from his apprenticeship, and every master in the province warned that he is not to be trusted."

The severity of his threat was sufficient to gain their silence, had any of them been inclined to gossip. Spurred on by Davide, they grabbed up their knives and canvases and filed out of the workshop. At that, Leonardo turned to me.

"Your parents and I have much to discuss," he said, his tone surprisingly mild, given all that had happened. "Perhaps you will be good enough to retrieve Pio from the stable-boy and bring him back to my quarters."

Before I could reply, my mother shot him a baleful look.

"How dare you order my daughter about, Signor Leonardo! You are fortunate that I do not demand an audience with the duke himself to reveal the nature of your perfidy. In fact, I have a mind to—"

"Silence!"

The outraged command that cut her off came not from Leonardo but from my father. His mild features suffused with anger, he strode to where my mother and I stood.

"You forget that Delfina is my daughter, and that her welfare is my responsibility," he clipped out, wagging a finger in her face. "Signor Leonardo and I have a few matters to discuss concerning her. You may remain here and listen to what is said, on the condition that you conduct yourself as an obedient wife and hold your peace. Delfina shall go after the dog, as her master ordered."

For a moment, I thought my mother would rail back at him. To my surprise, however, she gave a grudging nod.

"Very well, Angelo, I shall leave the matter to you. But

perhaps you will have her put on my cloak so that she is not parading about the grounds half-naked."

I looked to my father, who nodded that I should comply. Grateful for his intercession, I made no protest but grabbed up the cloak and flung it about my shoulders before limping off toward the stables.

What was said between the Master and my father, I never knew for certain. I had no doubt, however, that the days of my apprenticeship were at an end. Even if my father had agreed that I might remain behind at Castle Sforza, I knew the Master would not allow it. With the truth about me revealed to the entire workshop, the likelihood of discovery by the duke was far too great, so that neither Leonardo nor I could take that risk.

By the time I had shed a few hot tears over my plight and returned from the stables with the boisterous Pio in my arms, my parents were waiting for me outside the Master's quarters. I gave the small hound a final kiss and opened the door, smiling mistily as I watched him trot over to Leonardo's bed. With his usual long-legged grace, he leaped atop it and curled upon the pillow, settling in with a pink-tongued yawn for canine dreams. Gently closing the door after him, I turned to my father.

"Will I be allowed to retrieve my things and make my good-byes to my friends?"

"Certainly," he said with a kind nod. "We shall return on the morrow, and you will have a chance to bid them farewell."

"And Master Leonardo, may I see him once more? I—I still owe him an apology."

I heard my mother's genteel snort, but my father gave me a small smile. "Of course, you shall see him tomorrow, as well. He is anxious to speak with you a final time."

Unlike me, my mother had not traveled to Milan on foot; instead, she had made her journey in a small cart she had borrowed from one of my father's friends. The cart awaited us outside the workshop. A small mercy, I told myself, for my leg still ached from the bolt's angry blades. My father helped us into it, and we drove in silence toward the castle's main gate.

The sight of the clock tower there and its immense flanking turrets almost undid me, bringing a flood of memories both bitter and sweet of my time at Castle Sforza. While I had once been loath to gaze upon those towers, I all but wept at the knowledge that I would never see them again. My apprenticeship in Milan had been so short, and yet I had lived and loved and faced death more than enough for many lifetimes.

How could I return home to my small village, with no future before me but a single bleak room in my father or my brother's house . . . or perhaps a loveless marriage, with never another chance to paint grand masterpieces as I'd always dreamed?

But, stubbornly, I managed to hold back my tears. Too soon, we arrived at the small but clean room that had been my mother's abode for the past few days. I allowed myself a bit of grudging admiration for her, for she had made her way alone to Milan and without the protection of a boy's disguise. Perhaps she and I were more alike than either of us had realized.

At my mother's insistence, my first act was to strip off my boy's garb and put on one of her gowns. My fingers fumbled a bit over the feminine ties and laces that I'd last grappled with several months earlier when I'd been disguised as Caterina's maidservant. My mother welcomed the change with a tight smile, though she shook her head in despair over my cropped hair.

"Pah, we shall have to make do until it grows out again," she exclaimed. "Ah, well, I shall simply tell our neighbors that you suffered a fever while you were traveling that required it be cut off."

Later that night, after a meal far better than any I'd had for some time, I settled on a pallet in the corner of the room. It was strange, not hearing the snores of my fellow apprentices around, but my parents' soft breathing. I waited until I was certain they were both asleep. Only then did I release the storm of tears that had built inside of me . . . tears for Constantin, and Tito, and myself. The pillow in which I buried my face muffled my sobs, so that no one else heard them, but my swollen eyes come morning could not be disguised.

Surprisingly, my mother made no comment. Instead, she had helped me dress my wounded leg and, once I was dressed, put her hand to restoring my cropped locks.

"Ah, such beautiful hair," she murmured as she ran a comb through it as she had when I was a small girl. "Mine was never so thick and shiny. How you could have borne to cut it, I cannot understand, but we shall fix it."

When she had finished, my mother handed me a small mirror to survey her handiwork. I saw with a bit of pleasure that, despite my red eyes, I looked quite presentable. She had braided the short length with several ribbons and draped a small veil above the nape of my neck. While the lower portion of the veil fluttered loose, she'd tied the other two points beneath the small cap I wore so it appeared that the cloth covered a neatly coiled braid.

"Signor Luigi would be proud," I muttered as I put the

mirror aside, recalling the tailor's painstaking restoration of my hair with borrowed locks that he had braided into my own as he'd created my maidservant disguise.

By that time, my father had returned from whatever errand he'd taken himself upon while my mother labored over me. His eyes brightened as he saw us standing side by side.

"Ah, Delfina, you look almost as beautiful as your mother," he exclaimed, drawing a reluctant smile from his wife. Sobering, he asked, "Are you ready to return to the castle?"

Thankfully, my father insisted that my mother stay behind. "Let the girl make her farewells in peace," he declared in the same stern voice he'd used on her in the workshop.

Throwing up her hands, Carmela had made no further protests, though from the stubborn set of her mouth, I feared my father might hear about this later.

We spoke little on the way . . . my father, likely because he did not know what to say, and I, because I feared another cloudburst of tears like the storm that had soaked my pillow the night before. In my lap, I held my apprentice's brown tunic, neatly folded. Somehow, the thought of giving it up seemed the hardest task yet to come, and I clutched the familiar rough cloth as a child hugged a favored toy for comfort.

Our journey back to the castle was unbearably long and yet far too swift. When we finally reached the workshop, I found myself frozen to my seat. Seeing my hesitation, my father gave my hand a squeeze.

"I realize it will be difficult, facing your friends this way, but you will regret it if you do not see them one last time," he urged in a kind voice. "And those that are your true friends will not care if you are a youth or a maid."

Biting my lip, I nodded and let him help me from the cart. The workshop door was ajar to let in the warm breeze, and I could hear the apprentices' familiar voices as they went about their tasks. Lightly, I stepped past the threshold and, still clutching my tunic, gazed at them fondly one final time.

Paolo was the first to notice my presence. The others quickly followed his gaze, and all chatter ceased as they stared in my direction, seeing me for the first time as I truly was. I stared back and in a small panic realized I could find no words, either. Indeed, I was prepared to turn and flee when Davide stepped forward, a smile upon his face.

"There you are, at last, and far prettier than I could have imagined," he said with a gallant bow. "I am very pleased to meet you, signorina, but I confess that I shall miss our young friend Dino, whose place that you took."

"I shall miss him, too," I admitted, swiping away a tear. "And I shall miss all of you, as well. Pray tell me that you do not hate me for my deception. I wanted the chance to study with the Master, and I could not do so in my true guise."

"There is nothing to forgive," he declared, his tone gracious as always. "You simply have proven that you will let nothing stop you from pursuing your life's passion. It should not matter if you are Dino or Delfina, so long as you are talented with a brush. The other apprentices would do well to imitate you."

"Wait; does that mean I have to dress as a girl?" Vittorio cried in mock alarm, rising from his seat at the workbench. "If so, I fear I will never be a great artist, after all."

His jest drew laughter from the rest of them, dispelling the uncertain silence that had held them. One by one, they came to join Davide, until I was surrounded by a score of cheerful youths all speaking at once.

"You played your role well," Tommaso exclaimed in admiration, drawing nods from Paolo and most of the others. "I confess I had no idea you were not a boy, no matter that your cot was next to mine."

"Bah, I could have told you she was a girl," Bernardo declared, gazing about with an important air.

Philippe promptly nudged him in the ribs. "Then why didn't you?" he demanded with a grin as the others genially jeered.

The youth shot him a dark look. "Because no one ever asked, that's why," he replied and crossed his arms over his chest to emphasize his words.

While the others laughed, Vittorio stepped forward and gave me a shy smile. "I confess I did not guess, either, but I hope we can still be friends, no matter that you are a girl."

"Of course, we can," I replied, not caring that the tears were running freely down my cheeks. "And you may still call me Dino, if you wish."

He grinned, but before he could answer, a hush fell over the workshop. As always, such a respectful silence meant that Leonardo had stepped into the room.

Slowly, I turned to meet his warm gaze, feeling suddenly shy to be standing before him as my true self. He gave me an approving smile before turning his attention to the apprentices.

"It is good to hear all of you laughing again, after the sorrow that has held us the past days. But now, I fear there is work still to be done on the duke's fresco, so you must make your farewells to your dear friend and be off."

"Do you have to go?" Bernardo asked in a plaintive voice, his lower lip quivering as he rushed over to me. "Truly, I don't care if you're a girl, after all."

"I fear I must," I replied, aware that my own lips were trembling. "And the Master is right. We must not linger any longer but must say our farewells."

The next few moments were a blur of tears and hugs and smiles as I said good-bye to each youth in turn. Vittorio was last to step forward, and for a moment we could do nothing but stare at each other.

With a choked little cry, I hugged him and whispered, "Vittorio, you were always a true friend. I shall never forget you. Take good care of Pio for me."

"I shall," he said, trying manfully not to weep but in the end not succeeding. "And perhaps you can come back to Milan one day to visit us."

"Perhaps," I agreed with a hopeful smile. "After all, my father has begun to take on many important commissions, and he will need someone to assist him in his travels. And surely he will find another patron here in Milan."

Vittorio nodded vigorously. Then, with another quick embrace, he turned and vanished through the workshop door, leaving me alone with my father and Leonardo.

The two men exchanged glances, and my father gave me a nod. "Why don't you let me pack up your belongings, while you take a walk with your master in the quadrangle."

A few minutes later, Leonardo and I were sitting upon the familiar bench in one of the greens where we had plotted and planned many a time before. Wordlessly, he handed me a fine scrap of embroidered linen, and I wept into it quite copiously for several moments. When I was finally able to speak past the tears, I managed the question that was uppermost in my mind.

"How—how long did you know that I was not a boy?"

"Almost from the start, when you first came to my door showing me your coin and asking to pay for an apprenticeship," he replied, gazing across the grounds toward the clock tower.

With a small smile, he turned his gaze on me. "Your mother was correct, though I know you are loath to hear that said. I've sketched and painted countless men and women over the years, and in my notebooks I have catalogued the many differences between the male and female form. I would be remiss as an artist, had you not raised my suspicions."

"But why did you allow me to become your apprentice, if you knew I was not what I claimed to be?" I asked in confusion.

He shrugged. "Your eagerness pleased me, and your talent with the brush was far greater than most of the boys I'd taken on. It did not seem fair that you should be denied the training you sought, simply because you were the wrong sex. And so I decided that if you did not tell, I would not ask."

"Signor Luigi guessed quickly enough," I told him with a rueful shake of my head, "and he did not hesitate to accuse me. But he found the deception amusing, or so he claimed, and so he helped me when he could to keep my secret safe."

Another thought occurred to me, and I sat up straighter, staring at him with no little alarm. "Did anyone else suspect the truth . . . any of the apprentices?"

"Constantin had his suspicions, but we had an unspoken agreement similar to the one I had with myself. And so he took care to make sure that you were never put into a situation where your modesty would be compromised or where someone else might guess the truth."

I dabbed at my eyes again with the soaked bit of linen. "Constantin was a true friend," I said in a small voice. "I miss him terribly."

Recalling the main reason I had wished to speak with him, I blurted, "I am sorry about the flying machine, Master. I accept that you are angry with me, and I would not blame you if you never forgave me for what I did. But you must believe that I would never have touched it, save that I knew the duke was prepared to send his men to slaughter the apprentices. I—I thought if I could but fly it long enough to distract the soldiers, they might make their escape."

I had hoped to make a far more eloquent apology than that, but the words had tumbled out almost before I realized it. With nothing more to say, I stared down miserably at the brown tunic I held in my lap and waited for whatever words of censure might come. Instead, and to my surprise, I heard him softly sigh.

"My dear Delfina, I was never angry at you," he replied. "My condemnation was for myself. The craft was untested, and for all my fine theories and boasting to your father, I had no proof that it would fly. I had already lost Constantin and Tito. Had you died, as well, I would never have forgiven myself."

He sighed again, the soft sound full of harsh regret. "But even when I knew you were safe, I was too proud to show my fear before you and the others. Instead, I preferred to let you think that I was angry. And so you can see that it is I who should beg your forgiveness."

His words made my heart rise with the same exhilaration I'd felt as I swooped about the sky. Eagerly, I shook my head.

"There is nothing to forgive, Master," I cried. "But tell me, why did you burn the flying machine, instead of carrying the pieces back to the castle with us and repairing it? For it did fly, after all, just as you said it would!"

"And that is the reason I had to destroy it."

The finality in his words took me by surprise, but before I could protest, he went on. "What I've seen these past days confirms my greatest fear, that mankind is not yet ready for such power. We are not civilized enough to control the earth, let alone have dominion over the skies. Two young men died most cruelly—and many others could have easily joined them—and all for a frivolous theory of mine that I foolishly allowed to rise from the pages of my notebook."

"But what will you tell Il Moro?" I asked with no little concern. "I thought he expected a demonstration of the flying machine. Surely you will not be able to deny him, now that his soldiers have seen it."

"I will tell him that the craft has a fatal flaw, and that my theories were wrong. And, as a small consolation, I shall give him the bladed chariot."

I nodded, not quite as hopeful as he that Ludovico Sforza would be content with what he would deem a far inferior prize. Then, recalling the tunic, I bundled it into a smaller package and held the well-loved garment out to him.

"I fear I must return this, so that you may give it to whichever young man takes my place."

"Ah, but not quite yet."

He shook his head and gazed down upon me with the familiar smile that I realized was not that of a father or a lover, but instead of a faithful friend. Rising from the bench, he offered me his hand.

"For, my dear Delfina, I have a small surprise for you," he declared, his warm fingers gripping mine as he lightly pulled me up to stand before him. "Signor Angelo has convinced his good wife that you should remain in Milan for another day or two to gain back your strength, before you undertake the journey back to your home. And so, with his permission, there remains one small task I must ask of Dino before he leaves us for good."

"A task?" I echoed uncertainly, my grip on the tunic tightening. "But what would you have me do?"

"You shall see on the morrow. Return to your bed to rest,

and I will meet you outside the duke's private chapel in the morning . . . let us say by the time the clock tower strikes the hour of eight.

"And do not forget, young Dino," he added with a smile, "to bring along your tunic."

27

There is in man who desires to sustain himself amid the air by the beating of wings . . .

—Leonardo da Vinci, *Codex Atlanticus*

I met Leonardo the next morning at the appointed hour outside the iron gates leading to Il Moro's private quarters. Uncertain what to expect, I had dressed in the simplest of my mother's gowns and carried my apprentice's tunic draped over one arm. The Master noted this last with an approving nod as he greeted me.

"You appear much restored," he observed, taking me in with a quick glance from head to foot. "Is Signor Luigi's salve performing its usual miracle upon your wound?"

"I am almost healed," I assured him . . . and, quite surprisingly, I realized I spoke of my heart and not simply of my flesh.

For, sometime in the night, as I tossed restlessly upon my pallet, I had found within myself an acceptance of my fate.

Though I might shed more tears in the days to come, regretting all I had lost, I would also rejoice in what I had found in the Master's workshop. While I had known fear and sorrow and pain, I had also found adventure and love and true friendship. None of this would have been mine had I not ventured from my room and set off on my grand journey so many months ago.

Leonardo seemed to understand what I had meant, for I saw answering warmth in his gaze. With a gallant gesture, he escorted me past Il Moro's guard and led me down a familiar passage to the duke's private chapel. I made my genuflections and then gazed about me with a sigh.

Not many days ago, that same chapel had been little more than four walls covered in flaking plaster, cobwebs and grime clinging to its corners. Constantin had still been alive, and Tito had yet to succumb to treachery and murder . . . and I was still the boy apprentice Dino. But now, new layers of plaster had been smoothed over the walls and long since dried; the background for the various scenes had been stenciled on in black dust and drawn over in red ink; and perhaps half of the fresco had already been finished, the soft colors of the tempera glowing beneath a row of oil lamps hanging from the beam above.

And now it was I—Delfina, and not Dino—who stood here alongside Leonardo, with Tito and Constantin only memories.

The Master gave me no time to linger on those doleful thoughts, however, for he began an eager explanation of the work that had already been done. I listened intently, aware this might be the last of his lectures I ever heard. Much of the background work, I knew, had been completed by Paolo and Davide, who could cleverly match the Master's style and so had been charged with the fresco's lesser details. The main figures had been painted by Leonardo, though I wondered in some amazement when he'd found the time. And then, with an inner smile, I guessed that he had likely stayed up all the previous night, gripped by one of those furies of creativity that so often held him captive for hours at a time.

I recognized the scene directly before us, for it was the one that I had found faintly shocking when I'd first perused the Master's sketches. But, seeing the idea brought almost fully to life, I began to understand Leonardo's intent.

This particular scene from the missing years of Christ's young adulthood was, as Leonardo envisioned it, a time of great learning. Surely he had been a voracious scholar, familiarizing himself with the teachings of many lands and many cultures. And thus it was one of these exotic lands that the Master depicted.

Just as in the sketch I'd seen, the painting's background illustrated a land of blazing sun and bright colors. The buildings and temples were portrayed with exotic detail, from the rows of jewellike tiles painted around every window and door, to the golden domes atop many of the taller edifices.

With a smile, I noted that among the flurry of palm trees and grasses that dotted the landscape, tigers lurked and monkeys scampered. Parrots adorned in feathers of green and red dangled from a dozen tree branches, their curved beaks opened to emit what would have been a deafening chorus had they been real and not plaster. I even spotted a thick serpent curled upon a rock, its upper body stretching almost as tall as the humans nearby who appeared not to notice its menacing presence.

But, delightful as the scene was at first glance, it had far deeper purpose.

I had studied with the Master long enough to understand his theories of composition. I knew he aligned every painted boulder, every tree, every minor figure, so that the arrangement formed lines that drew the viewer's eye inexorably to the painting's central subject. But had he simply scattered the rocks and parrots and temples heedlessly about this particular scene, every eye still would have been drawn to the painted figure that sat in silent contemplation, unaware of the splendid distractions about him.

The traditional golden nimbus about his bowed head identified the figure as that of the Christ. But this version of our Lord was far different from any I'd ever seen. While not as young as the boy who had astounded his elders in the temple, neither was he the Christ of middling years already embarked upon his glorious mission of salvation. Instead, the dark-haired youth appeared little older than I, his handsome face with a hint of a beard retaining traces of the soft roundness of boyhood.

He wore but a snowy loincloth, revealing the tanned limbs and broad chest of a young man who engaged in physical work . . . as a carpenter, perhaps.

But most compelling was his pose. Legs crossed as if seated upon the ground, he instead appeared to float several feet above it, eyes shut and head bent in prayerful attitude.

Not surprisingly, a crowd had gathered around him to observe this miracle. Men and women, boy and girls, dark-skinned and light, they appeared to have come from many lands. Some knelt, and others stood . . . while a few had prostrated themselves, hands over their heads lest their unworthy eyes glimpse such glory. All were united, however, in the looks of joyful awe upon their faces as they bore witness to this marvelous sight.

"It is beautiful," I breathed, swept by awe of my own as I took in every detail.

Appearing gratified by my compliments, the Master

smiled. "It is a minor piece," he said with a casual wave of his hand, "though I am pleased with it, nonetheless. But I did not bring you here to admire what I have done. Rather, I intend to put my apprentice Dino to work."

When I gave him a puzzled look, he pointed to a section of blank plaster not far from the painted image of the young Christ. Perhaps half the size of a *giornata*—the traditional amount of wall space that could be painted in a single day before the fresh plaster dried—the empty space was strangely out of place amid this finished work. Even the plaster appeared recently applied . . . as I suspected that it had been, from the telltale flecks of white I noticed on the Master's left sleeve.

"You will recall that, before all this sad business happened, I told you it was time for you to put aside the plaster blade and pick up a brush. And so, I have saved this spot for you," he said, pointing to the unblemished square.

I was aware that my mouth had dropped open in a most unseemly manner. "You—you wish me to finish a portion of your fresco?" I finally managed, hardly daring to believe this could be so. When he nodded, I could only shake my head in return.

"But what shall I paint?"

"Whatever you wish. The spot is yours to do with as you will. Everything you need is already here."

He gestured to a small table, upon which had been laid out jars of finely ground pigment, along with a jug of water and a bowl of fresh egg yolks. Combined, those simple ingredients would make the soft shades of tempera that would seep into the plaster and bring it to life. A row of shells, shallow with pearllike inner bellies, waited to be used as dishes for each color. Beside them, a short vase held brushes of all sizes.

"Do not tarry," he went on, idly picking up a jar of pigment and then putting it aside. You have but a few hours before the plaster dries." Before I could make a reply to that, he turned and strode out the chapel door, leaving me alone with the fresco.

I stood transfixed for several long moments, staring at the blank plaster and wondering again how I could possibly fill it. But as I gnawed at my lip in frustration, fearful lest I disappoint the Master in this final task, a familiar voice seemed to speak in my head.

It's easy, Dino, I heard Constantin's soothing words, sounding as real as if he were standing beside me. *Just paint what you know . . . Paint from your heart.*

And suddenly I knew what I was meant to depict upon that pristine square of plaster. Smiling, I pulled my tunic over my gown and reached for the bowl of egg yolks. Piercing each yellow globe, I poured their contents into the various shells. Carefully, I added water and pigment, until each new mixture of tempera was the shade and consistency that I sought. Then, taking up a soft brush, I began to paint.

It was well into the afternoon when I put down the brush a final time. Stripping off my tunic, I stepped back to survey my work. Though my hands and arms ached with the hours of effort, and my injured leg throbbed from standing upon the cold stone floor, I felt a swell of excited satisfaction. Surely the Master would be pleased, I told myself . . . but if not, somehow it mattered little. I had accomplished what I had set out to do, and I could point with no little pride to this small bit of fresco as being my finest work.

Still, I spared a final critical eye for my painting. I had taken care to blend my background to the surrounding fresco, so that it joined seamlessly with the rest of the scene. Each color had been applied with care, layered one atop another with painstaking precision. But most important was the trio of male figures I had painted within that small landscape. They had sprung from my brushes with a skill I'd not realized I possessed, glowing with life upon what had once been but a blank square of plaster.

Blinking back sudden tears, I studied the image of a young man—thin but wiry and possessed of a calm smile—who sat upon a grassy knoll. His hands casually wrapped around one knee, he watched with happy amazement the miraculous scene before him. Behind the youth stood a man old enough to be his father. Though his hair was gray and his features and body thicker, he bore a striking resemblance to the young man upon whose shoulder his strong hand rested. His air was respectful, in keeping with the wonders nearby, but his look of paternal pride was reserved for his son.

A short distance behind the pair, a second young man was poised in mid-run, as if rushing to see the miracle before it was too late. Indeed, such was his hurry that his cap had tumbled from his tangled mane of black hair. He did not look back, however, but kept single-mindedly to his pace. A smile danced upon his pockmarked face, and his expression was that of a true believer whose faith had at last been confirmed.

I was still studying my work when the chapel door creaked open behind me. I sensed the Master's presence almost before I heard his soft footsteps upon the stone floor. Wordlessly, he paused beside me and for a long while studied the portion of fresco into which I had poured my heart. At last, he turned back to me.

"Well-done, young apprentice," he said, the warmth of his smile soothing all of my aches. "I had expected much of you, and yet you surpassed those expectations. This is a work worthy of a master."

Before I could reply, his smile broadened into a grin. "And I see you have taken a master's liberty by putting yourself into the scene, as well, if perhaps symbolically."

He pointed to the painted image of a hawk perched upon a tree behind the figures of Constantin and his father. Dark of feather and green of eye, the small raptor lifted a single wing, as if about to take flight.

I felt myself blush as I returned his grin. "I could not help myself . . . though, of course, I would never have dared to paint my face among the worshippers."

"Ah, but that is half the fun," the Master countered, his grin taking on a sly edge. "Surely you saw that I did not hesitate to give myself a most prominent role in the scene."

Staring at the fresco, I frowned for a moment as I tried to pick him out from the painted crowd. It was then that I noticed what I had missed before, that the Christ figure bore more than a passing resemblance to the Master as he must have looked a decade earlier.

"But what if the duke notices?" I gasped out, torn between being scandalized and amused by this subtle bit of blasphemy.

Leonardo merely shrugged. "I suspect he will be more likely to believe that the resemblance is to himself, if he notices anything at all."

The soft chime that was his wrist clock sounding the hour put a halt to that moment of amusement.

"It is finished," he softly said, a shadow stealing over his handsome features. "You have done what you were meant to do here, and it is time for you to leave us. Your father is waiting outside the chapel gates to take you back to the city, so that you can start for your home on the morrow. And so, I fear that nothing more remains than to say good-bye to my dearest Dino."

You cannot say good-bye, I wanted to cry out, *for I cannot bear to leave the castle, to leave you!* But a painful lump had lodged in my throat so that the words remained unspoken.

Swiping away a few errant tears that had slipped down my cheeks, I took a steadying breath and asked instead, "Will you make my farewells to Signor Luigi? He was a true friend to me, and I shall miss him despite his sharp tongue."

"I will tell him," he agreed with a hint of a smile, "no matter that the good tailor will be loud in his protests before he ever admits his fondness for you."

"And Vittorio, do not let him pine too long for Novella," I rushed on. "He thinks himself in love with her, you know."

"I know, and I shall counsel him to patience, for I suspect the washerwoman and her daughter may one day return."

"And don't forget Pio. He must have his game of wrestling with a bit of blanket each day."

"The hound will have his amusements, I assure you."

Unable to think of any further excuses for delay, I lapsed into silent misery. I knew I should flee before I made a fool of myself, and yet I yearned to draw out this last moment for as long as I could. I cared not that each passing second deepened the wound in my heart, if it meant I could spend a few heartbeats longer in his presence.

Leonardo met my anguished gaze with a look of regret and spread his hands in a helpless gesture. "Delfina," he said softly, "you must leave now, no matter that it breaks my heart to see you go."

"It breaks my heart, too," I whispered so quietly that I wondered if he heard the words.

And then, choking back a sob, I fled the tiny chapel as if the devil himself were at my heels.

EPILOGUE

For once you have tasted flight you will walk the earth with your eyes turned skywards, for there you have been and there you will long to return.

—Delfina della Fazia, *The Notebooks of Delfina della Fazia*

It was several days after I had returned to our small town that I found the courage to unpack the bag containing the apprentice Dino's worldly possessions. The rough sack held far more upon its return journey than it had when I had started out . . . just as I had brought back with me far more knowledge of the world than had been mine when I left. And so, gently, I poured the bag's contents out onto my bed.

To be sure, one part of me had been tempted to consign it all to the fire, to put that small portion of my life behind me, but in the end I could not. For among the items were the three notebooks that I had kept in emulation of Leonardo.

More than books of sketches, the tiny volumes had become a chronicle of my life during those months when I had lived at Castle Sforza. The memories they held burned with both passion and pain . . . memories far too raw, most of them, to be held up for examination in the light of day. But one day, I would want to relive those moments of love and fear and laughter.

Just not yet.

Two of my three notebooks I had already tied shut, for the secrets they held had threatened to spill from them in careless disregard for my own feelings. I found another piece of cord and secured the third book, as well. Many of its pages were still blank, but that was as it should be. Should I ever be tempted to keep such a notebook again, I would find a fresh new volume in which to begin.

For good measure, I wrapped all three volumes together in a heavy silk veil and tied it into a neat bundle. That bundle, in turn, I carefully hid atop my wardrobe, out of sight of anyone else but where I could retrieve it whenever I wished. That accomplished, I began sorting the rest of Dino's possessions.

My bowl and spoon were there, as was much of the coin that my father had given me to pay for my apprenticeship, and which I had hidden in the toe of my spare boots. A change of linen and a cloth with which to scrub my teeth added to the pile. I'd also accumulated a few small trinkets from the occasional market day. The tunics and trunk hose in which I'd first disguised myself had belonged to my younger brothers, but they had long since outgrown those clothes. I shook that boyish garb free of its wrinkles and folded it into a neat pile. While I no longer had a use for the clothing, I was loath simply to toss it away.

Along with that simple garb, I found that my father had also packed away the page's outfit that Luigi the tailor had made for me at Leonardo's request. I felt a twinge of guilt at seeing it there, for it was far more costly than any clothing I had ever owned. Had I packed my own bag, I would have left it behind so that another youth might wear it should Leonardo find himself in need of an apprentice disguised as a servant.

With the same care I might have used with a fragile bit of old lace, I folded the silk and velvet garb into a second pile upon my bed and then eyed both stacks of male clothing. Sooner or later, my mother would guess that I'd fled the house in my brothers' borrowed garb, and so would come looking for it. No doubt she would burn the offending garments if she found them, seeing them as flagrant reminders of my transgressions. But the page's costume, she would have no cause to know ever existed.

I grabbed up those clothes and, wrapping them in another veil, carefully hid them atop the wardrobe alongside my notebooks. Then, not allowing myself to examine my motives for that impulsive act, I looked to see what remained.

I had sorted through everything, and yet here was something that I did not recognize . . . That was, not entirely. For whatever the flat, rectangular object was, it was secured in what appeared to be the same scrap of green silk that Leonardo had used to conceal his model of the flying machine. Curious, I untied the cord that held it.

The silk slipped from a small wooden panel perhaps half the size of those that my fellow apprentices and I spent hours sanding for the Master's use when a commissioned portrait came his way. And, indeed, it was a portrait that I held, the soft oils glowing as if lit by a candle, though my room was dim. I immediately recognized it as Leonardo's work, for his gifted hand was evident in every delicate brushstroke.

But what took my breath from me was the subject of the painting itself.

It was an unusual composition, to say the least . . . the head and shoulders of a dark-haired youth, cloth cap upon his head and garbed in a simple brown tunic. I could not see his face, for he was turned away, his gaze fixed upon a large mirror whose silvered surface he'd reached out a hand to touch. Reflected back at him was not his youthful face, however; rather, it was that of a young woman with green eyes and a luxuriant braid of dark hair.

Her be-ringed hand stretched out in mirror image of his, so that their fingers seemed to touch despite the glass that separated them. But the woman in the mirror was not looking at the youth whose reflection she was. Instead, she gazed out with just a hint of a smile past his shoulder, her attention fixed on the world beyond.

I stared a long while at the painting, torn between laughter and tears at this amusing yet poignant image of me that Leonardo, in his brilliance, had somehow captured. When he had painted it, I could not guess, for I had never sat for this likeness. The oils were long dry, however, so he must have finished it before the truth of my identity had been revealed.

Had he thought the completed portrait but a witty trick of his brush that I would appreciate, or had he poured his heart into it in the same way I had poured mine into my fresco?

I sighed a little and shook my head, for I knew Leonardo da Vinci well enough by now to guess at that answer.

Still, I would cherish the painting always, though I would never dare hang it for all to see. Instead, with a final admiring look, I wrapped the portrait of Dino reflected as Delfina in the green silk once more and retied the cord. I left my room a few moments later, carrying the rest of Dino's worldly goods to give to my mother, to do with as she would.

As for the portrait, by then it was safely hidden atop my wardrobe along with my page's outfit and my notebooks, waiting for the day when I would have cause to look upon it again.

AUTHOR'S NOTE

More than 400 years before the brothers Wilbur and Orville made history at Kitty Hawk, a man named Leonardo da Vinci was busy documenting the anatomy of birds and the vagaries of the wind. His ultimate goal: to build a craft that would allow a man to fly like his feathered brethren. This was no passing fancy on the part of Leonardo. Over a period of years, he dissected, observed, and sketched every movement of a bird's flight so that he might understand what allowed them to gain the clouds, while Man was relegated to the earth. His writings culminated in the detailed *Treatise on the Flight of Birds* compiled sometime around 1505.

As for his drawings, they progressed over the years from scholarly studies of birds and their wings to fledgling designs that resemble today's parachute and helicopter. He went on to sketch numerous detailed variations on winged crafts that incorporated the principles he had documented in his writings. Some, like a pair of immense wings strapped to a man's back, were admittedly fanciful; others were amazingly reminiscent of modern gliders. History does not record

Leonardo ever making a successful flight in one of these contraptions . . . but then, I suspect that history did not record quite a bit of the Master's more outrageous doings.

Further notes. For those who have been following the action with a historical atlas in hand, you've likely noticed that the tiny province of Pontalba is not to be found within the Duchy of Milan . . . or anywhere else, for that matter. Both it and the unpleasant Nicodemo, Duke of Pontalba, are my own creations. As for the spunky Marianna, she is one of several fictional relatives that, purely for story purposes, I've given Il Moro in the course of this and past books.

Finally, the quote in the epilogue attributed to Delfina della Fazia is actually a well-known citation that has long been credited to Leonardo da Vinci . . . though likely it was never written or said by him at all. But while no Leonardo expert has discovered those words among the Master's volumes of work, neither has anyone yet identified the actual writer of this lofty sentiment. And so, with greatest apologies to that unknown author, I've taken the liberty of putting those words into Delfina's mouth. For I have no doubt that, following her dramatic flight around Castle Pontalba, she must have recorded a similarly memorable affirmation in her own notebook!